The Darkest Oath

A GOTHIC ROMANCE OF FORBIDDEN LOVE, IMMORTALITY, AND REVOLUTION

LAUREN LEE MEREWETHER

Published by LLMBooks Publishing, Fort Worth

While the author has taken great lengths to ensure sensitive subject matters are dealt with compassionately and respectfully, some readers may find this book troubling. It contains violence and dark adult themes. Depictions of abuse and violence are never romanticized.

For permissions and to visit the author's website, see:
www.laurenleemerewether.com
Cover Design by Artscandare Book Cover Design

Library of Congress Control Number: 2025909930
Paperback ISBN: 978-1-961759-27-5
Hardcover ISBN: 978-1-961759-28-2
eBook ISBN: 978-1-961759-26-8

Contents

PART THREE

Part One

CHAPTER 1

The Chains of Vengeance

SIEGE OF DAMASCUS, LEVANT, 1148

"DO YOU WISH TO LIVE, ROLLANT?" An ethereal whisper wove through the din of battle, cutting through the clash of steel and the cries of the dying.

The whisper tickled Rollant's ears like a wisp of wind carrying words not meant for the living. Rollant moaned through strained breaths and shattered lungs.

"Angel of death, take your enemy," he rasped with unfocused eyes, searching the skies for God's messenger. He assumed the origin of the whisper was divine—a sign from the heavens. But only fallen bodies strewn across the blood-soaked ground were in sight.

His gaze, blurred by the edge of death, drifted to the silhouette of Arnoul, his brother-in-arms, looming over him. The cries of the Saracen enemies echoed in the distance but faded to the slowing heartbeat in his ears. Rollant grasped at the fragments of the past moments, trying to piece together the fatal betrayal and pleading with God on why He let him fall to Arnoul's blade. Arnoul, the man who had shared his food, his cot, his horse—the long years spent training, fighting, and saving each other—*he* was the one who struck him down?

Rollant's mail-clad fingers, clumsy and weak, drifted toward the wound on his neck. Blood poured warm against his chainmail coif. Breath and blood warred within him—both desperate to escape his broken body.

"Forgive me, old friend," Arnoul muttered softly, though too soft for the weight of his sin. He wiped his blade clean with Rollant's surcoat, the sacred white stained red. "But your lands, your title—they were ever meant to be mine."

Rollant wanted to scream, but his voice failed him. Life fled from him as the sun perched as a bloodied halo above the walls of Damascus. The ruddy sunlight cascaded onto the once-proud Crusader banners, now torn, ragged, and scorched by fire. The frayed threads fluttered in the smoky air as a last stand for God and the Holy Lands.

Memories of his beloved wife and precious daughter flashed before his eyes. Amée's gentle touch warmed his cheek, and her laughter echoed in their home tucked away in the Chartreuse mountains outside of Lyon, France. Cateline's tiny hand reached for his to walk by his side in their garden. Dread far deeper than the pain in his flesh pierced his heart at the thought of leaving them with traitors such as Arnoul.

"Do you wish to live?" The whisper came again, clearer this time—a woman's voice, cold and thin. Not a messenger of God.

Rollant pushed through the blurry vision and focused on Arnoul's voice that planted him in the brutal present.

"Do you wonder why I have cut you down?" Arnoul shook his head and gritted his teeth.

Rollant gasped for air but narrowed his eyes in hatred.

Arnoul nodded. "A knight as brave as you deserves an answer." He leaned upon his heavy, engraved sword. "Our noble King Louis the Young sees you alone in all things. He has refused to favor the rest of us. Too much glory upon your head. Too much favor from the king." Arnoul's words wavered as though he struggled with what he'd done, but his eyes remained steady. He lifted his boot from Rollant's crushed hand, the bones broken and useless from Rollant's last desperate attempt to defend himself.

"God have mercy on my soul; His will be done," Arnoul murmured. "But life shall be better without you to claim all the King's favor. For now, I may have a chance to cause the King's eyes to shine. For now, the King may greet me with a smile and remember my name."

Rollant stared in disgust at the man who had once been like a brother to him.

Arnoul kneeled and placed a heavy hand alongside Rollant's cheek—a cruel reminder of their false friendship and loyalty once shared on the battlefield. "Sorrow fills me, my friend. Be with our Lord, Rollant. I shall see that your wife and daughter be properly cared for, as is right."

A spew of venom desired to leap from Rollant's tongue into the cursed man's face. His lips twitched with words unsaid. How dare Arnoul, a traitor, a betrayer, speak of honor and care? The twisted sense of righteousness showcased Arnoul's greed and decay. How had Rollant not seen through to the envy beneath his mask? A choked, blood-filled gasp flew over Rollant's lips.

Amée's face, flawless in its memory, appeared before him. Pearl-white skin, her almond eyes gazing at him as they always had—full of love. He could almost hear her voice and feel the warmth of her hand in his. Cateline, too. She would grow into a woman without him. She would never again feel his arms around her in protection or love.

If a Saracen had struck him down, he would have surrendered his soul to the Lord, finding peace in the knowledge his death was in God's honor. But not like this—betrayed by a selfish, greedy act. He was a righteous warrior for the crown of France, and he deserved an honorable death! Arnoul mocked him and stole it all.

Something feral surged in Rollant's chest with a last, wretched pulse of life. With what strength remained, Rollant swung his fist upward, connecting with Arnoul's throat.

The betrayer slumped back, clutching his neck, and coughed with a violent rasp. He snarled as he regained his breath. He twisted his head to sort out the pain.

"Still so much fight in you, even at the end," Arnoul said through coughs and a broken voice. "Our battle shall be worse with your absence."

Darkness clawed at Rollant's vision. His breath came in shallow gasps. His strength faded. No words could be spoken. He wished a weapon had been blessed to his hand, so to drive it through Arnoul's chest. But both hands lay limp and powerless in the dirt—unable to move anymore. Yet he clung to life in actionless rage. It piled up in his heart and weighed heavy on his back teeth.

The world around him grew eerily silent, as if the dark tendrils of death reached for him. A cold stillness replaced the action of battle. Arnoul's footsteps sounded distant and hollow as he moved away.

Amée's face was the last vision he held, but it warped into a bright light.

The whisper came a third time in an alluring croon. "Do you wish to live, Rollant?"

Rollant's heart stilled. His mind, once consumed with thoughts of vengeance, filled with the faces of his wife and daughter. The thought of leaving them vulnerable made his soul cry out in despair. He would do anything—*anything*—to stay with them.

A dark figure loomed over him with celestial hair floating like sunrays behind her head. Her eyes shimmered like distant stars. The coldness came with her presence and lay heavy on Rollant's body. "A knight so brave and just should not endure such treachery. A blameless one the King needs. I am his sorceress, a guardian for his lineage, and I choose you."

She presented an offer of salvation laced with cruelty: "I shall give you eternal life if you give your years in service of the French crown."

The weight of the offer pressed down on him. Eternal life was meant for the righteous with the Lord in Heaven, not in this world.

Her wintry fingers wrapped around his heart and squeezed, cutting his debate short.

"Do you desire life?" she asked, softer but more insistent. It came from a place beyond death, beyond the light of God. It wasn't natural. It wasn't right. Eternal life came from God, not from dark forces. Whether his acceptance of the sorceress' offer would sever him from his creator forever stilled his soul.

But knowing Arnoul would take his precious Amée and raise Cateline sat raw in his belly. If he accepted the offer, he would live and ensure Amée and Cateline were protected and loved, but after their passing, he would never see them again. But if Arnoul, who succumbed to Lucifer's temptations, took care of them, their souls might be lost, having been led by Arnoul's ill-fated guidance.

Icy tendrils crept down his spine, and the light faded the more he thought. The enigma pressed against his chest, tightening it and taking away his breath. The sorceress would only present this offer once. He had one choice: natural or unnatural, right or wrong, survival or surrender. Questions plagued him: How long was eternity? How long until he went mad after Amée and Cateline were stolen by time? Would he age but never die? The consequences of eternity could not be weighed. If it could not be weighed, then his answer should be no. But yet, she dangled his family before him like a golden dream. Who would care for Amée and Cateline? Him or Arnoul?

"Make your choice or death it shall be, and with your wife, Arnoul shall replace thee," she crooned in a sultry whisper. Her form held him, frozen, suspended between life and death.

There would be no peace, no reunion in Heaven, only endless years trapped in a body that refused to die. And yet, it was the sacrifice he was willing to make for his family.

"Yes," he said with closed eyes without further thought of the consequences that would surely come. The moment the word slipped from his tongue, the release of death was snatched away. His chest seized, filling with a breath not his own. Its piercing freeze burned its way down his throat.

The sorceress' celestial hair faded and transformed as the world twisted and sharpened in focus. Her presence faded into the folds of darkness with a simple whisper, "It is done, Chevalier Rollant de Montvieux."

Time had passed. Bright stars littered the night sky. God's creations glared at him with cruel disgust. Blood cried up from the trembling ground. Agony seared his limbs as the bones in his hand snapped back together with a sickening crunch. His body contorted and spasmed as life sprang to his limbs. Blood reversed its flow and returned to his neck in an even stream, choking him, drowning him, until he breathed with clarity and ease. Every breath, though, was frigid and foreign. Heavy and oppressive, the night pressed in on him as though the stars and the earth had recoiled from his return.

Spent, his body collapsed atop the dirt. Tears filled his eyes. At least he could still serve God by protecting the crown. The thought was hollow and did nothing to soothe his fractured soul. He did not feel complete; he did not feel whole. He had fallen from God. Maybe he did not have a soul anymore, just the spirit given not by the creator but by a sorceress. Perhaps that was why each breath was foreign and bitter.

"What have I done?" he whispered, fearing a colder, darker, and far more painful life of no escape. He had stood for honor, for loyalty to God and the king. Yet he lay there with the steel of his brother's sword still warm with his blood. He had trusted Arnoul and believed in the righteousness of their cause. Every day, he had trained to be a warrior to protect holiness. Every night, he prayed for strength to remain blameless and to keep a repentant heart. Now, all he saw was the empty shell of that honor, that lifelong purpose, crumbling away under the weight of betrayal and immortality. Where was the justice?

Arnoul walked away free to live, free to die, free to take his land and wife. Rage burned in his chest. Arnoul had forced his hand in accepting the sorceress' deal. If that traitor had not cut him down, he would not have had to give up death to save his wife and daughter from that miserable knightly imposter. He was condemned to wretchedness because of Arnoul's treachery, Arnoul's wrong. It was Arnoul's doing. Arnoul deserved punishment. Arnoul had stolen his honor, his peace, his hope of a life with God. Arnoul deserved pain. Arnoul deserved to die.

"I shall him slay." The words escaped through clenched teeth, his voice hoarse. His body trembled from the rising fury that spread through him like fire, hotter than the stars. The pain that had once gripped him was gone, replaced by a fierce clarity. The thought of God's will lingered in the corners of his consciousness, but his mind was consumed by one thought —Arnoul.

Pushing himself up from the dirt, his limbs ached, but strength had not left them. The world around him seemed to narrow, the stars above shrinking into insignificance. His fingers curled into fists, the knuckles white against the night.

Rollant would serve justice. He would make Arnoul live the same agony he felt when he was struck down by a man he had once called brother.

He crossed the bloodstained expanse of the Crusaders' encampment with swift strides. His unwavering resolve propelled him forward and muted the laments of the injured and dying. He glided like a phantom as if enveloped in darkness by the sorceress herself, causing his surroundings to fade into a black blur.

The man who betrayed him lay asleep, exposed and unsuspecting, beneath the tattered remains of a Crusader banner. His sword was still close at hand, with Rollant's ale and salted meat bag thrown by his side. The thief!

Arnoul stirred gently, mumbling in his sleep, "Forgive me."

The moonlight illuminated his contorted lips and furrowed brow in nightmarish slumber, as Rollant drew Arnoul's sword into his hand.

Slay him. Cut him down as he has done to me. The thought blazed in his mind, filling him with the cold burn of hate. Arnoul deserved to die. He had taken everything—honor, trust, and life itself. Rollant had followed the code of knights, fought for God and country and king, and now it all lay in ruins at Arnoul's feet. He was cursed to life forever and never be one with God.

"End it," he muttered as his knuckles grew white around the hilt of Arnoul's sword. It would be a cowardly murder. An unarmed, sleeping man would be no threat. Yet the stale, foreign air passing over his lips, not full in life but neither in death, ground to silence every code and honorable virtue to which he had pledged his life.

His hand wavered. The blade trembled. A strange chill crept into his chest and stayed. The sound of an indecipherable whisper echoed in his skull. Doubt gnawed him. He blinked. His vision blurred. He could feel her presence—the sorceress. If he were condemned to live forever, then Arnoul would be condemned to die for his betrayal. If the sorceress granted Arnoul immortality, too, then Rollant would be a thorn in Arnoul's side for all eternity.

He raised the blade high. The steel glinted in the moonlight. His vision tunneled, focused on Arnoul, who was unaware that the Angel of Death waited for him. Oh, how it must have been when Arnoul took the blade to Rollant's throat mere hours before. The treacherous thought sealed Arnoul's fate.

In a swift arc, Rollant wrenched the blade back and brought it down, cutting Arnoul deep in the throat, severing the voice before a single scream could escape and wake the soldiers who slept nearby. Arnoul's gurgling filled the space between the dying and the immortal. Arnoul's eyes beheld Rollant and grew wide beneath the moon. The color drained from his face as if he'd seen a ghost.

"This is no dream, old friend," Rollant whispered.

Arnoul's hands scrabbled at his neck, and blood spurted from his lips. Rollant spat on Arnoul's surcoat and watched as the light faded in Arnoul's eyes.

Rollant's heartbeat thundered in his ears, drowning out all other sounds. The rush of satisfaction he had expected, the moment of triumph —none of it came. He had expected to feel free—freed from the betrayal, from the pain, but there was no glory there, only emptiness.

A hollow victory.

Arnoul, once his brother-in-arms, was now nothing more than a body like all the rest.

"Reap what you sow," he said to Arnoul's spirit. "He deserved to die," he whispered in an attempt to ease the vengeful monster back into the black pit of his belly. The urge to vomit remained in the monster's descending path. His breaths were ragged—colder than the breaths before.

His fingers still gripped the sword hilt, but its weight felt wrong, as though it no longer belonged in his grasp. He threw it down by the traitor's feet. He shivered, now able to feel the icy winds of the night. His breath turned to fog before his face.

The whisper returned—so faint he almost missed it. But it wasn't coming from the wind or the battlefield—it came from deep inside himself. The familiar voice, thin and cold, curled the edges of his mind. His heart faltered as her power sent him to his knees. His hands caught his body from the drop. Arnoul's dark blood coated his fingers. He had killed a man in a coward's act of revenge. It was not justice. It was not honor. It was not pure.

It was savage.

He lifted his quivering fingers to his face. Arnoul's blood ran down his finger like a tendril of darkness racing toward his heart and chasing away the rage that had consumed it.

The sorceress's voice drifted through him, her tone no longer alluring but dripping with disappointment. "You have chosen a path darker than even death."

She appeared before him again, her form solidifying out of the shadows. Her celestial hair floated in the night, but her gaze did not evoke the warmth of starlight. Her lips curled into a smile, though it was far from kind. "You have taken more than his life, Chevalier. You have forsaken the honor that once defined you." Her eyes glowed faintly in the dark. "And so, your punishment will be as eternal as your immortality."

Rollant's breath stilled. "Punishment?" He gasped. Fear wrapped his legs. "But you gave me life."

She moved closer, her ethereal form swirling with a cold wind. "I gave you life, but your actions have bound you to something far worse than death. You were not just. You were not noble." Her gaze flicked to Arnoul's lifeless body. "And now, you are no different from the traitor who lies before you."

Rollant's heart sank as her words settled over him like a death shroud. "I have done right," he tried to argue, even against his own thoughts.

"You did what was easy. Gave way to fleshly vengeful desire." Her voice was cold, cutting through him like the sword he had thrown at Arnoul's feet. "You have not killed for justice," she said. "You killed for vengeance. And now, you shall suffer for it."

Rollant staggered back, crawling away from her. His eyes widened as her swirling form passed over Arnoul and came to him.

"What suffering shall I endure?" he asked, afraid of the answer.

The sorceress's expression grew more somber, her eyes narrowing as if she pitied him. "Your beloved wife and daughter, the two women you hold most dear."

"Please," he whispered and shook his head. His limbs went weak. His heart struck still at the mention of Amée and Cateline. His voice cracked, and tears welled in his eyes. "Anyone but them."

The sorceress swayed her head against the breeze, telling him it was what he feared. "They shall be taken from you the moment you cross the threshold of your home. Their lives, like your own, shall be forfeit because of your actions. But because I see your love for them, I shall give you an option. Therefore, you may never return home, and they shall enjoy long lives,"—her finger rose—"or you cross the threshold to see them one last time."

Rollant fell to his side. He had accepted the sorceress's deal to see, love, and care for his wife and child. Now, she was taking them away just like Arnoul had done. He snarled at her cruelty, a knife in his belly. "You cannot do such a thing!" he cried.

She stood as a silent sentinel; her gaze was past him as if it had already been decided.

His heart broke like his body and his mind.

"Please," he struggled to his knees and bowed his head before her. "Spare their lives. I will do anything. I beg you." His voice crumpled with a sob. The strong, resolute knight was reduced to nothing. "Please, I shall—"

The sorceress silenced him through an icy tendril to the heart. "It is done," she said, her words as dark as the blood staining Rollant's fingers. "And more shall be taken from you for begging when I have already extended grace. Know this, Chevalier Rollant de Montvieux: should you ever embrace anyone in love, they too will breathe their last. Your heart will be forever empty, your touch forever cursed."

"No . . ." The word tore from Rollant's throat, hoarse and raw. He scrambled to his feet, the weight of her curse crashing over him like a tidal wave. But she vanished like smoke, and he was left gasping into the night amid the murmurs of the king's camp. He turned toward his home across the sea, as though he could somehow outrun her words. Amée. Cateline. Their faces flashed before him. Tears ran down his cheeks. What had he done?

But the curse had been sealed. Her words were absolute. He had abused her gift of life. Rollant would live, but he would never truly be alive again. For as long as his body endured, he would walk the earth with the knowledge that his love, his embrace, would forever bring death to those he cared for.

Part Two

CHAPTER 2

The Shadow of Betrayal

PALACE OF VERSAILLES, JANUARY 1788

ROLLANT'S THUMB pressed against the top golden button of his blue-uniformed coat. Its engraved fleur-de-lis indented his flesh as if the royal symbol still branded him as its enduring servant to the king. He flicked it, but the metal bit back, mocking the vow made under duress.

He scoffed at his reflection in the long mirror.

The Justaucorps, the King's Bodyguard's uniform of loyalty, power, and prestige with its golden fringe, gleamed beneath the candlelight. Flawless as the day it was issued. A perfect soldier's attire. It would have inspired awe in most men. But he had worn the white and the blue for six hundred years. It was no longer a uniform. It was a cage.

He straightened the cuffs with rigid fingers.

The white waistcoat, the spotless culottes, the gleaming rapier hanging from his hip—all for show. Chainmail and a broadsword would've served better to protect the king.

They had taken his armor and given him embroidery.

He still bore the body of a twenty-six-year-old knight—vibrant, strong, and well-defined. But the eyes in the mirror belonged to a man who had lived too long—a man desperate to die.

On the chest of drawers lay a small glass coffin containing a delicate, dried rose Amée had given him before she willingly died in his arms. His fingers hovered over the glass top and studied the faded petals preserved in amber. Amée's memory had become just as fragile, but for a moment, the blurry image of her peaceful face in death etched into his mind.

He clenched his fist, hating he hadn't been able to see her face in the last few hundred years, at least not entirely. Maybe one day, she would only be a name, and if there was anything worse than condemning himself to this life, it was forgetting the face of his beloved wife.

As he did every morning, he took his small dagger and ran it across his hand to see if he could die that day. He winced at the cut, but the small wound healed after a short while. He wiped the blood away. Six centuries of trying all options, enduring the pain, and still, death refused him.

He returned the dagger to the open drawer, laying it to rest atop his knight's surcoat, having kept it. Once bright white, a symbol of his honor, duty, love and righteousness, the fabric had faded to a sullen, threadbare grey. Only duty remained, and no longer by choice. The red stain of betrayal on its hem had blackened over time like a wound that never healed.

He stared at the reminder of the price of greed and vengeance for a moment longer. His hand quivered with the condemnation it incurred all those years ago, then tapped the drawer shut. The soft clink of the wood meeting its frame echoed through the room like a barrier between him and the past he couldn't change.

He raked his lush brown curls back from his forehead before placing his powdered wig and a silver-trimmed *Bicorne* hat on his head. The hat's white cockade adorned the black wool as a symbol of loyalty to the crown.

He glanced around the modest, private apartment in the attic. It was close enough to the king for him to fulfill his duties, yet far enough away to keep his immortal secret from everyone else.

The scent of old wood and candle smoke lingered in the air. He had lived in the apartment since the Palace of Versailles was first built when the wood was new and smelled of the forest.

Faint laughter floated up from below, perhaps from a courtier's joke or some whispered scandal. Rollant stilled for a moment at the life in the palace and sighed. In another century, it wouldn't matter. They and the subjects of their gossip would all be dead.

He straightened his back to face the day ahead and noted the perfection in his uniform before quietly descending from his isolation in the attic. He passed through the upper levels, where minor courtiers, servants, and officials hurried, unaware of the centuries of history passing silently beside them. A few pretty girls flashed him their best smiles.

One called to him, "Monsieur de Montvieux." Another, "Votre Excellence. Captain of the King's Bodyguard."

He ignored them and the whispers that followed. What could he offer them but ruin? The thought of anyone being drawn into his cursed existence tightened the chains of his isolation. To their eyes, he might have been a mysterious officer with a sharp uniform and an enigmatic air who could indulge their whims, but he lacked any desire.

He was numb.

A hollow man could not return love, and love had become a poison he dared not taste again.

Entering the palace's first floor, ornate golden columns lined the wall of windows and mirrors. Sunlight flooded the hall, and the mirrors opposing them returned the volley of light. The crystal chandeliers guided his path from above in sparkling succession. The soft clack of Rollant's black leather boots on the marble floor added to the bustle of the courtiers and noblemen whisking to and fro. Heads turned to him, eyes lingered, but Rollant did not meet their gaze.

Chins dipped at the sight of his uniform or as a faint gesture of respect for a figure they knew only by reputation. He walked amid them, expressionless, eyes ahead. They all were nothing but fleeting shadows, alive one day and gone the next, just like those who had come before them. He was not of their world anymore; he was not of anyone's world.

The King's Apartment loomed ahead, filled with life of courtly affairs, but Rollant's path took him away from the crowds. He passed the royal bedchamber and the entertainment halls and entered through tall, carved doors into the King's Cabinet, the *Cabinet de Conseil*. Two royal guards flanked each side of the entrance, signifying His Majesty's presence within the King's Cabinet.

The heavy gazes of the five royal ministers stared at Rollant as he entered, but he paid them no attention. Instead, he took his silent, watchful position half in shadows behind the King—a well-fed man of thirty-three who fidgeted with a brass lock in his hand beneath the table. The guard Rollant replaced left without a word. The door softly clicked shut behind him.

Deep blues and gilded flourishes decorated the walls. A grand chandelier spilled dim, steady light over the silk-covered table and its ring of high-backed oak chairs. At the head of the table, nearest the intricately framed hearth, sat King Louis. It was the warmest place in the room, and the most embattled.

Portraits of the Bourbon kings lined the walls. Rollant had known each one personally from cradle to coffin. King Louis XVI would one day be just another portrait on the wall—the only question was *when*.

The King toyed with a lock in his hand, turning it again and again. Its repeating click echoed across the marble floors. His round face, flushed with the indulgence of court life, betrayed none of the poise expected of a monarch. Only his eyes, darting from minister to minister, revealed the fear creeping in from beyond the palace walls.

The king's boyish obsessions with lock-making and mechanical hobbies mocked his vast intellect. He was too bright to make a decision. He had been thrust beneath the royal spotlight late in life and had found himself ill-equipped for the throne. His obsession was not so much childish as an escape of a mind overwhelmed by the unfortunate affair and the inopportune time.

Étienne Charles de Loménie de Brienne, Minister of Finance, cleared his throat. "As I was saying, Your Majesty—the treasury is empty. Dismissing Calonne did not resolve the crisis. Nor did his publications help."

Louis clicked the lock again.

The Minister of the King's Household, Antoine-Jean Amelot de Chaillou, reached beneath the table, plucked the lock from Louis' hands, and shoved it into his belt pouch. "Perhaps, Sire, we begin with looking at fiscal options," Amelot said, patting his belt bag like a chastising father. "We cannot ignore the crisis."

Louis leaned back and pulled his hands to the top of the table. "Are you suggesting again that we raise taxes? I will not raise taxes. The people suffer enough."

Brienne nodded. "That or another war, but one that brings coin, not just glory. We've only just ended the war in the Americas." He sighed and shook his head. "I understand your willingness to help the colonies pursue liberty from the British, but its price did not benefit France—"

"It avenged our defeat against the British in the Seven Years' War," interrupted César-Henri de La Luzerne, Minister of the Navy. He turned his attention to Louis. "Your Majesty, you made a wise decision to help the Americans. The other great powers are compelled to respect us yet again. And by far, *nothing* brings me greater joy than to know the British are weakened by their loss overseas. I stand by the monarchy's decision to aid the colonies."

Brienne sneered. "Yes, yes, but your victory and your revenge cost us one hundred million *livres*!" He pounded both fists on the table at the sheer amount of funds spent on the conflict. "Your war debt crippled France!"

Armand-Marc comte de Montmorin, the Foreign Affairs Minister, waved him off. "Your view is too narrow, Minister Brienne."

Brienne sighed and settled his hands. "The people are starving. Food riots, bad harvests, bad winters," he paused and shook his head. "Our standing with other nations will not feed them."

Louis stayed silent and fidgeted with an imaginary lock in his fingers atop the table.

Rollant watched them grow silent. They squabbled over kindling while the house burned. Not that he cared. He'd seen it all before. Different king. Same nonsense.

"My King," Brienne began again. "Since His Majesty refuses to raise what taxes we do have, and the parlements refuse tax reform, we will no longer be able to borrow if we cannot pay our debts. France will collapse without drastic reform. This is a fact."

"And what of the parlements?" Louis glanced up with timid eyes. "The parlements, filled with nobles, guard their privileges under the guise of law. They will reject your reforms again, as they did Calonne's."

"If we do nothing, we risk rebellion. Call the Estates-General. Let the Third Estate vote on the reforms," Brienne said.

Chairs scraped as the other four ministers gasped and bristled.

"The reforms will pass with the Third Estate voting," Brienne finished with unwavering confidence in the working class voting to tax the nobility, the Second Estate, and the clergy, the First Estate.

The Minister of Justice and Keeper of the Seals, Chrétien François de Lamoignon, interjected in the succeeding silence.

"At this moment and onward, the King's authority is vulnerable. Calling the Estates-General will undermine the crown for all time. It hasn't been called since 1614, and nothing came of it but a decade of interference and revolt. Give the Third Estate a voice, and they'll demand more. Equality. Then power. You'll lose your throne."

Louis glanced toward Rollant. Their eyes met. Mortal burdens, but Minister Lamoignon was right.

"Don't mind him, Sire." Montmorin waved Rollant off. "He knows nothing of this."

Rollant stared at the intricate scrolling on the wall opposite him. The sad fact was that, at an immortal twenty-six years old, he knew more than humanly possible. He was both the youngest and the oldest man in the room. With an ageless face, he glanced at the portraits on the wall, masking the centuries he had witnessed.

Amelot leaned toward the king. "Calling the Estates-General will alienate the nobility."

"Minister Brienne," King Louis dipped his head, giving Brienne permission to speak freely against the violent opposition in the room. Amelot, Montmorin, La Luzerne, and Lamoignon leaned back and lifted their chins.

"I am grateful for the opportunity, Sire," Brienne said. "The people are restless. Restless people breed rebellion, and rebellion breeds revolution—just as it did in the colonies. The Estates-General will buy the crown time. Give them a voice; perhaps they will not yet demand blood."

Montmorin shook his head and interrupted. "What of the crown's reputation amongst the great powers we have fought to earn back?"

Lamoignon silenced him with a raised hand and rose, his face taut. "Once you give the Third Estate a taste of power, they will demand more. They will not stop at taxes. You will give up your power and your lineage of great kings. The Just, The Sun King, The Beloved; they shake their heads."

Louis leaned back, his face ashen beneath the chandelier's light. His hands, empty of his locks, clenched into fists and bounced on his thigh until, finally, he rose to his feet slowly with distant eyes. He folded his hands behind his back. "I will . . . consider the matter further."

Rollant followed Louis out of the Cabinet and down the hall filled with opulent mirrors. Louis let out a long, despair-filled breath. The quiet corridor was empty save for the two royal guards at the entrance to the King's Cabinet at the other end.

"Chevalier Rollant de Montvieux, you have been with the royal family for centuries," he said in hushed tones. "What path would you take?"

Rollant hated when the kings would ask him for advice. It was a sheer reminder of his eternal punishment of life.

"And be plain, Rollant," Louis said, his head drooping. They slowed their pace. "What should I do?"

Rollant suppressed a sigh. He had already told him what to do several times in the last few years, but the king never listened, or if he did, never acted. Rollant was tired of talking. "I am in no position to advise the king in this manner."

"For the sake of Heaven, out with it." His harsh whisper passed through clenched teeth.

Rollant sighed. "If I wore the crown, I would bypass the parlements and institute tax reform without calling an Estates-General, with military power if needed, forcing the nobility and the clergy to pay taxes and, even more, their fair share of taxes to alleviate the burden on the people and ensure their bellies are full without dividing your authority in the process. I would not delay as each passing day your power slips away."

Louis stopped with jaw agape. "And kill my people by using military force?"

"No." Rollant regained his patience. "You must wield power," he said, whispered, peering down at the king. "Absolute power as king while you still have it."

Louis shook his head and looked at the masterfully painted ceilings. "Lord God Almighty, my soul is yours. What do I do?"

Rollant nestled into his former sense of nonchalance. He hadn't uttered a prayer in a long time, yet his childhood in the age where God was everything hadn't left him either. He didn't dare say there was no God, though he had spat in the divine's face when he'd accepted the immortal deal.

The eerie echo from the Hall of Mirrors muted in his ears. He gave the King the correct answer again, but he doubted Louis XVI would do it, not with four of five ministers not worth the silk they wore. Lamoignon was the only one who spoke any sense.

"Rollant," the king interrupted his thoughts. Frustration stained his pale cheeks. "You side with Lamoignon then?"

"I side with what my eyes have seen come to pass. I side with history, *your* history, the lineage of your ancestors. Do as I told you in haste before matters decline further, and you'll keep your family crown."

Rollant shut his mouth, having already said too much and not in the proper tone.

Louis motioned for him to enter his empty bedchamber, a room adjoined to the ostentatious king's room where the Sun King had expired. Nether Louis nor his predecessor liked the big, open, cold room. They much preferred the smaller, warmer, adjacent room.

Rollant closed the doors behind them, and Louis sat on the bed's edge. Louis' trembling fingers pulled the wig from his head, revealing a matted mess of short brown hair.

"I cannot override the parlements," he muttered, sinking his face in his hands. "I want to be a king of the people. I want them to love me, unlike my grandfather, who abused the crown," he said.

His hands fisted, and he banged his forehead in gentle beats. "I cannot override the parlements *I reinstated* at my grandfather's passing to appease the nobles who are of the few who still support the monarchy."

Rollant stood at attention like a coat of armor lining the halls. He had seen kings rise and fall, domestic and abroad, King Louis XVI was no different. This king would doom himself and perhaps the crown with inaction or the wrong action. But Rollant didn't fear it. Someone somewhere would rise again, and he would still be stuck in this immortal condemnation of false living. At least, they could all enjoy the rest death had to offer, and if they trusted in the Lord, eternal rest in paradise. For Rollant, though, it didn't matter; it was all meaningless. He longed for something he could never have, so after centuries, he finally did not see the point in longing for it. Lucifer had won his soul. The deal had been made in a moment of rage and weakness, and he was forever enslaved to it.

Louis had fallen backward, sprawled out on his bed, mumbling incoherently, like he had done when he was a child. The poor man was overwhelmed, worried, and at a complete loss though the answer was right in front of him.

Rollant shifted his weight at the awkwardness but finally decided to comfort the man he had known for thirty-three years. Rollant sat beside the king.

Tears formed in Louis' eyes. "I . . . I never asked for this. To be king. I was never made for war, hunger . . . the burdens. The people are angry, but how do I make them understand that *I* am not their enemy? The nobility refuses to be taxed."

Rollant nodded. The nobles, if not suppressed, would end all things known. They had come close to abolishing the crown under Louis The Just nearly two hundred years prior. "The unfortunate matter is that your grandfather did not listen to me either and ran up the debt and spent more time with various women than he did attending to the state. They see you as king and, therefore, their enemy."

"Yet I am not him."

Rollant hoped he did not have to be evident to the point of condescension. It seemed the king was going to force him to be.

"How is that my responsibility to correct his errors?" Louis rasped.

"Because you wear the same crown." Rollant shot him a glare a father would a son.

Louis wiped his eyes and sat up, spine curved with his head between his knees. "I don't want this."

"And yet you have it." Rollant's voice held no warmth or reassurance. Louis was like his ancestors, and Rollant grew weary of watching weak men cling to crowns they did not deserve. The weight of centuries of service burdened his broad shoulders, built and defined through fifteen years of swinging a heavy steel sword. He stood up and rested his palm on the pommel of his rapier as a gesture of control.

Louis lifted his head and stood up hastily. He paced back and forth before his grand bed. Indecision snaked through his shoulder blades and held them tight enough to see through his coat. He stopped in front of Rollant and placed both hands on each of Rollant's shoulders.

"I trust you more than anyone for your sheer amount of experience." Louis' eyes flickered with a rare moment of resolve, though Rollant knew the king would not follow his advice.

"Go, Rollant. Go into the streets of Paris. See what is happening there beyond Versailles." He pressed his lips thin. "I cannot trust the whispers of nobles or the demands of ministers. Take a month if you must or more, but return with the truth of how the people feel and with answers." He patted Rollant's shoulder. "Do you need anything from me to do as I have requested of you?"

Rollant shook his head.

Louis' brow furrowed. "Not even a place to stay or commoner's garments?"

Rollant shook his head. "A king once gave me land outside of the city walls in Charonne. I have a house there. It has not been touched in a decade or more, I'm afraid, but I can make do."

Everything he had acquired over the centuries had been sold for gold and stored in the floorboards. It was more than he could ever need in several lifetimes. Squatters had probably broken in, given the tumultuous times. He figured it didn't matter because he had all eternity to buy and sell and kick people out of his home.

Louis withdrew his hands and placed them behind his back. "Go, then, Chevalier Rollant de Montvieux."

"As you command, Your Majesty," Rollant said with a bow. He left and made sure the two guards from the King's Cabinet had moved to the guard room of the bedchamber before following the King's command.

As Rollant moved between scurrying servants and courtiers, he knew only one of two outcomes would come to pass: the crown would be saved, or he would witness its end. Either way, France would change.

Soon after, he stepped from the gate at the Palace of Versailles dressed as a commoner with a bag of his clothes, coin, Amée's rose encased in glass, and his dagger.

He mounted his horse, which a servant had brought to him.

The soft gallop of hooves against the road stirred a memory of his days as a knight but without the heavy burden of his armor. He had forgotten how freeing it was to let God's breath rush past his face. A small flame warmed his heart in the peace it brought for the moment, giving him the falsest of hopes that perhaps the divine still loved him and wanted him in his Heavenly glory.

The sounds and luxury of Versailles faded to silence along the road until the clamor of unrest and tension in Paris spilled into the air like a tide that even an immortal man could not stop, nor did he care to. His heart turned still and cold once again as he neared his forgotten nobleman's estate on the very eastern outskirts of the city, in the quiet, calming village of Charonne.

It was a modest stone home amongst the mostly empty apartments he had built long ago. He hadn't collected rent in a long time and let the few residents live there for free. It looked like they returned his neglectful kindness by tending to his home, little garden, and double-stall stable. The old street was empty as he trotted to the stable behind the house. He put away his horse, giving her a carrot and patting her mane in appreciation for her journey to Paris before walking to the home's entrance on the street.

"Restless, rebellion, revolution," he muttered as the door to the home creaked open. The wintry winds blew the dust from the furniture. He would have to remember that saying for when the next king asked for his advice, that is, if there was a next king.

CHAPTER 3

Cries of the Forgotten

FAUBOURG SAINT-ANTOINE, PARIS, FEBRUARY 1788

THE AIR FILLED with smoke and dust on the corner of Rue du Faubourg Saint-Antoine and Rue de Charonne. Flour and soot marked the men and few women who had come to the community's bakery, *Au Pain Roux*. It was a place of sustenance filled with the hungry eyes of those unable to buy its limited reserves of bread. The sun lowered in the west, and the crowd pushed inside the cramped, weathered building.

Two men, Malo and Yves, closed the wooden shutters on the windows decorating the store's faded stone façade. An additional oil lamp was lit from within. The shadows gathered in the corners, and the glow of the wood-fired oven illuminated the rear of the bakery owned by the twenty-four-year-old Gabin Roux, who stood in front of the stove facing the crowd. His stretched, large shadow swept over the small mass of people.

Élise stood beside him with a tight jaw and downcast eyes. She adjusted her sleeves to hide the faint bruises Gabin had left her the week earlier. He had such a strong grip, and she had such a stubborn mouth.

Élise glanced at the long, worn wooden counter and the near-empty shelves behind it. Her mouth watered for warm, fresh bread, a delicacy she had only tasted a few times in her nineteen years of life when she had been especially good for Gabin. It sickened her that he made her beg, but she was grateful to him that she had a cot to sleep on and something to put in her belly most nights. It was better than with her father or her aunt. She had a good life with Gabin. She bobbed her head at the reassurance. Her thoughts were broken by Gabin's heavy hand on her bruised shoulder. He squeezed, and she winced.

"Now, my little dove," Gabin gritted. "You will only say what we have discussed, or we shall have another . . . talk." He swept his finger down the underside of her jaw at the veiled threat.

She nodded, but stiffened under his grip.

Freedom called her but the price of rebelling against him would cost her the only place she had to sleep and eat. His hold kept her prisoner. She envisioned taking his hand off of her shoulder in a defiant stance against his oppression. But she remained still, letting him squeeze the fresh bruise. He wanted her to whimper, but that she would not do. Her eyes hardened.

Freedom was a distant dream for herself, but soon, she hoped, freedom for others would come. No one would have to go hungry again. No one would be forced to live the life she lived as a child and now lived as a woman. It was her rallying cry. Her voice was the weapon she yielded, and her body marked the battle bruises of wielding it.

"My dear," Gabin said. "You are so lucky I keep you fed and warm. You remember that. So many times, I could have kicked you into the streets, but I didn't because I love you. Remember that, my dove."

"I will," Élise responded in trance. "I love you too, Gabin." Of course she loved Gabin, she told herself. He had rescued her from her father's drunken fists and her aunt's ring of child thieves, who punished her if she didn't meet the daily quota. At least Gabin's violence was tolerable, and he did share his food when he had it even if he did make her beg—it was more than what her father and aunt had done.

The corners of her lips turned up at her savior. Her shoulders softened and his grip solidified at the new slack in her body.

"That's my girl," Gabin said in a gruff whisper. The warmth from the brick oven dominating the back wall cast a soft glow on his handsome face, adorned with chiseled cheeks and jaw. His thick, auburn hair, reminiscent of his surname, reddened from the glow. He was the man every man wanted to be and every woman wanted to be with. If the women were pretty enough, he fulfilled their wants. But Élise was his woman, no one else dared to touch her. He pressed his lips to hers while his fingers held her chin in a firm grip. He bit her lower lip before pulling back. "Remember, say only what we have discussed if I let you speak."

"Yes, Gabin," she whispered.

He released her, and she scanned the room. A few eyes watched her, some envious, some in pity, and some indifferent. But they all shared one purpose: the need for bread.

Gabin spread his arms wide.

"Brothers!" His voice boomed, and the place quieted. "Thank you for coming to this week's meeting." He cleared his throat and flashed a smile at the women in attendance. "The price of bread and the gross taxes are what brings us here today. The reward of those who labor beneath the crown is that bread costs nearly a week's wage. Do I set the price? No. Ingredients are expensive, and I barely make anything, knowing I must feed my community. So, who is driving up the price of flour and oil? Not I, not you. It is the royals and the nobles and their wasteful spending, just as the former Minister Calonne said in his papers. Our grievances must reach the king's ears, and he'll see the injustices we face and remember that we are his people. We need to gather the courage to speak up and remind them that the common man matters and we are not backs of which the elite walk."

His words were rehearsed and repeated from the prior meeting. Gazes turned inward. Chins drooped. Long blinks became commonplace. Élise could feel the fleeing passion. She wanted change. She needed it, if not for herself, for her people. The only way to get what they wanted was to act. Gabin, for all his worth, was not an effective speaker to stir conviction, and she was. It was one of the reasons why he beat her to silence. He couldn't afford to have a woman be better at him than something. They all agreed with everything he said, but the call to speak up was not enough to ignite the spark or fan the flame of change. They were hollow words, not sincere words to rally action.

One of the men who closed the bakery's shutters, Malo, raised his hand and blurted out, "Speak up to who?"

Gabin scoffed at the disrespectful interruption of his speech, but before he could answer, a man named Yanis yelled out, "We should send someone to the king!"

"No, to the Parlements. Calonne said they rejected tax reform," a woman's voice echoed off the stone walls.

"The Parlements have no regard for us," Malo cried, just as Gabin said, "The king might hear us."

Soon, bickering ensued and Gabin lost control of the room. Élise stood silent, watching the division occur before her eyes. They would never accomplish anything if they were not united. She pushed her way to the corner and grabbed a wooden crate while forming the words she was going to say. She calmed her nerves and pushed Gabin's punishment from her mind. He had tried and failed. She would save the night, and he would not take kindly to her rescue.

Ignoring the pain in her shoulder and her back, she placed the crate upside down in the middle of the bakery and exhaled the knots in her belly before stepping up to speak.

"Calonne published papers indicating how the king's spending habits and stances on state affairs have left our children starving and the cost of bread soaring." Her voice deepened and garnered attention. She let rage and purpose fuel her words. Rage at the suffering and the purpose to end it. She spoke before Gabin could reach her and pull her down from the crate.

"We, the people, bear the brunt of the elite, as Gabin Roux said. The injustices of the monarchy and the privileges of the nobility hinder us from having full bellies at night. The parlements rejected Calonne's reforms, which would tax the nobility and the clergy, so they would pay their fair share in tax instead of overwhelming us to the point of starvation and depravity."

At the last words, Yanis cried, "Here. Here," signaling his agreement. Gazes were no longer inward. She had their attention; now, she needed to ignite the spark. She drew from her past to relate as Gabin simmered, unable to reach her through the crowd. At least he was not stupid to pull her down when the people listened.

"As a child, my father took nothing but rum and ale after my mother passed and beat me, his own child unconscious every night because I said I was hungry. He blamed me for his plight. Just as the king beats us to the brink of death, he blames us for the country's empty treasury. There is no more money, as Calonne stated, yet the elite looks to us to pay for it while they keep spending and spending and spending, not on us, not to feed us, but on their own luxurious and fanciful feasts and fine silks to wipe their dirty mouths after indulging in exotic meats and fresh vegetables and warm bread."

Heads nodded in agreement. Jaws grew taut, and brows grew heavy with the burdens they each faced.

"And why is this?" she cried. Glances were shared, but no one answered. "Why?" she asked again from the depths of her belly. "We were promised bread. We were promised safety and security. As an older child, my aunt saved me from my father but only to exploit me as a child thief, stealing from the poor to feed my aunt's family. My cousins and I stole; if we did not steal enough, we were left to sleep outside with nothing but our clothes and nothing to eat or drink except the water from the gutters. Her family ate while her kin lay in the dirt with grumbling stomachs! Is that not how the elite, the king, the nobility, and the clergy all eat while we, their countrymen and women, lie in the dirt, unable to make bread and eat the most basic food of all? They feast while we starve!" she yelled, pointing west toward the Palace of Versailles.

Fists raised with angry growls of agreement.

"So I ask you again. Why? Why do we stand here in the shadows, starving and poor, forgotten, while they hoard gold in their coffers and eat as to fatten a calf?"

Nostrils flared, and feet shifted.

"Is it that we are less than them?"

"No!" The response blasted her in the face.

"Is it that we are not worthy?"

"No!" The people yelled.

"You want to know why?"

"Yes!"

"Because we allowed it to happen!"

The people shut their mouths and looked upon her with wide eyes.

"Yes, that's right. We let them take our money and waste it. We let them take the fruits of our fields and squander them and hoard them for the wealthy and the powerful. We let them squeeze every drop of sweat and blood from our brows and veins. We were promised bread in return. What a weak deal we made. They kept it all for themselves. So what should we do?" She asked with a heartbeat in her ears. "What should we do?!"

"Take it back!" a man yelled.

"Take. It. Back!" she repeated and pointed at the man who answered correctly.

The people chanted. "Take it back. Take it back!"

Her cheeks flushed with triumph. Gabin's eyes found hers. He was not chanting. She couldn't hide her smile of victory. It was odd how Gabin claimed to fight for the same cause, yet he was no different than the elite. He used her in the same way. She assumed every person would use someone for their own gain. It was all she knew, but she hoped it might be better in another world than the current one. The only way to truly know was to fight for a better France, one with equality and justice, where suffering would be no more. It was her dream. It didn't matter how strong Gabin was or how hard his fists hit her body; it was worth it to have the people rally around *her* words, captivated by *her* message of unity and rebellion.

A tall stranger slipped into their meeting place—she alone saw as the others were engrossed in chanting, jumping up and down with fists in the air. Upon first glance, he seemed to be the same as the others—an ordinary man there to hear the words of the meeting. But the details slipped through her initial glance. Her focus faltered momentarily as her gaze returned to the stranger who came to lean upon the side wall with an unreadable expression. Though he wore the clothes of a commoner, his shirt was pressed cleanly and bright white beneath an untorn coat. He was well-fed, not with a round belly but with firm muscle beneath his breeches and poet blouse. No soot graced his face, and any sweat he might have had was dabbed away. Her first thought was a king's informant. There was an air of unforced confidence and authority around him, the way his eyes surveyed the place—measured and detached. He seemed unfazed by the dirt and desperation around him. There had been rumors that entire meeting places would go silent because the attendees were thrown into prison.

Her eyes narrowed slightly, but she ignored her growing unease and curiosity about the man's identity. She didn't know how to steer the people away from rebellion anyway, given that she had already fanned the flame with their chanting. Her natural ability to orate only went so far. Her gaze lingered on the stranger, and she could feel Gabin's hot stare burning the side of her face. It was too late, she reasoned, to save them from prison if the stranger indeed were there to silence them. The people needed to hear her last words, and she did not want to instill doubt.

"United!" she yelled, and they repeated.

"United, we shall be heard. United, we shall demand our needs. And united, we shall take back what is ours. Sleep well tonight, my fellow countrymen and women. Sleep well, for a time is coming when we shall be heard around the world."

The bakery and the people in the streets pressed in, erupting in cheers, applause, whoops, and hollers. She stepped down, and her shoulders, back, and hands attracted the happy pats of her peers. Gabin approached her. She ignored his heavy footsteps and, instead, made her way out of his path and toward the stranger in the back.

The stranger met her gaze, and his jaw fell slack at the sight of her. It was as if he had forgotten everyone else in the room. Something about his longing eyes drew her closer. His silent attention sent a familiar shiver through her legs. He stood like a sculptor's greatest masterpiece; his beauty needed no exaggerated gesture or show. His relaxed posture deceived his powerful build and surely hidden strength. Every detail seemed crafted with purpose, from the contours of his face to the shadow of stubble that softened his cut jawline. Gabin was handsome, but this man was striking. Gabin flaunted his beauty and bragged about his strength, but this man's allure lay in subtleness and mystery that boasted of both strength and restraint. Though his exterior called her to come hither, she shut her falling jaw and told herself he was probably like every other man she had ever met, and if not, he would surely throw her in prison for her words that evening.

CHAPTER 4

A Flicker in the Dark

FAUBOURG SAINT-ANTOINE, PARIS, FEBRUARY 1788

THE WOMAN who had been speaking approached him under the oil lamplight softly swaying above. Its warm rays cast a marble glow over her bare arms and blushed her cheeks, as if an angel had kissed them. And her eyes were as dark as the woman he had once married. Her eyes reminded him of the first life he'd once cherished.

"Amée?" he whispered. His voice broke from the weight of memory and fully lost in the past.

Her eyes hardened, and the warmth left her face. "My name is Élise. You'll do well to remember that, stranger." Her voice was not as soft or feathery as Amée's, yet it sounded wounded, holding a certain sultry, dangerous allure.

Rollant flinched, reality snapping in, and he wondered how long it had been since he had said Amée's name aloud. He swallowed the ghost of guilt. It had been at least a century.

"I will remember," he replied, tracing her face with his gaze. Her features were worn, too worn for her age. Yet she possessed a raw kind of beauty that defied expectation—a beauty forged from survival and determination to hope. Vitality lived in her expression. Her hair, as dark as ink, was loosely tied in a defiant red scarf, with falling strands that caught the light of the oil lamp. Her dress was plain but carefully mended. Each stitch was a testament that though she was not of wealth, she refused to fall and made each hardship polish her strength. She was indeed a flame in the dark. It was no wonder the people gave such a response to her fiery speech. It was no wonder he had to enter the bakery from the streets to see who spoke such empowered words.

Élise sized him up; her eyes scanned him from head to toe. "You're well-nourished, I might say," she said and poked him in the chest as she rounded him like prey. He stood still and let her measure him as he did her.

She squeezed his bicep, raising an eyebrow. "A former soldier, I presume?"

He chuckled and nodded. "I fought for the Americas and ended my service with His Majesty's Navy just this past month," he lied. The words slipped through his teeth with ease. Lies were almost second nature, unlike his time in the Second Crusade. He had been a man of honor, but after watching love die and trust shatter, he realized lies were necessary.

Élise crossed her arms. "Lots of men claim they were sailors." Skepticism curled her lips and set in her gaze.

He leaned in slightly, lowering his voice as though letting her in on a secret. "The sea's a cruel mistress. Only a few return to speak of her—those who survive have the scars to prove it. What would you like to know to prove the truth?"

She met his gaze, and he could see the doubt slipping away as curiosity took it's place.

"Anything," she said with a dismissive wave.

She was not hostile or friendly; her responses reflected someone who had learned to live between civility and suspicion.

"Well," he said and leaned back. "I was stationed aboard the *Vaisseau Ville de Paris*. We shipped out in '81 under the command of Admiral de Grasse, and fought the British Royal fleet in the campaign off of the Chesapeake Bay." He only needed to sound convincing to turn a lie into a believable truth.

"Hmm," she murmured, still with questions in her eyes.

He pressed on, seeing she was not yet satisfied. "We escorted supplies and troops for General Washington of the colonies and fought off the British frigates. I earned my salt with the *HMS Terrible*; a fierce battle, it was," he said, thankful he had paid attention to the Minister of the Navy's reports all those years ago. He gazed off with a pause, letting the weight of the false memory sink in. To bring an air of authenticity to his eyes, he thought of Arnoul putting a hole in his neck and he returning the same and forever changing his fate.

She glanced at the other men in the room. Their nods of approval told him she was leaning toward belief.

Rollant continued for their benefit and to seal his credibility, pushing Arnoul away from thought. His voice lowered again. "The sea teaches patience in a way I've never been taught before. To survive, you watch the horizon for threats." His gaze slid to her. "Much like you, watching for wolves in your den," he said, complimenting her.

She received it with a soft smile, and something flickered in her eyes for a temporary pause in time, something warm and uniquely hers.

He fought the pull of it and remembered the sailor character he was portraying.

"Is there anything else you'd like to know?" he asked with a charming, practiced smolder.

She scoffed but couldn't hide her curiosity. Glancing again at the men to his right, she straightened her back. With her gaze averted, he kept his eyes on her. He traced the curve of her high cheekbones and delicate nose above her full rosebud lips—carrying both the promise of a velvet touch and the risk of thorns. As soon as his gaze dropped, he saw a bruise peeking beneath the shoulder strap of her shirt. A bluish-purple stain marred her skin and told a story she wouldn't share.

As if sensing his gaze, her eyes snapped back to his, and she tugged the strap to cover the bruise. It was a telling indication that someone had made the bruise, not by accident.

He chewed his lip at the many women he had seen beat over the years and remembered how a fire of righteous anger burned in his chest at each injustice. But he forced himself to remain still before Élise by reminding himself he was only there for a month to answer the king's request, and he would not become entangled in these people's lives. There was a reason why he lived in the attic of the palace. It was easy up there to pass the days and no longer care.

She shifted uncomfortably under his silent stare with shoulders drooping. "So, who is this Amée woman you spoke of?" she asked, tilting her head back with shadowed eyes. Her voice hardened, likely to shield herself from anything he might say.

"Amée," he whispered. The name hit him hard out of his trance.

He wished Élise hadn't asked about his late wife. The name still tasted like ash on his tongue after centuries. The wound in his heart had never healed. Rollant blinked, forcing himself to look away from Élise. His heart clenched, not just from the memory but from the cruel realization that no matter how deeply he cared, he would always be alone.

"Someone I once loved and lost," he answered her. His tone gave away more depth than he intended.

Élise's face softened for a moment before she scoffed with a smirk. "You think me a fool? You are, but what? Twenty-five years at most? What loss could you possibly know?"

The corner of his mouth curled up in sorrow as he remembered his Amée and sweet Cateline. His gaze turned inward. "Yes, twenty-six, but it is still a time capable of great loss."

Élise shifted her weight again, regret flashing across her features. Her tongue swept across her plump bottom lip as if wishing to recall her words. She sighed and dropped her arms. "I am sorry, Monsieur. I didn't mean to offend."

"No apology is needed," he whispered. He had seen Amée and Cateline from afar, watched them grow, but never dared to hold them until Amée asked to die in his arms once she had fallen ill in her advanced age. It was then he knew the curse was real, watching Amée take her last breath in his embrace. They had lived long lives without him. The Black Death swept through a hundred years later and took all of his descendants with it. He buried them on his land, isolated and hidden in the Chartreuse mountains. Every time he returned to his first home, he brought bags of flowers to place over their graves and roses for Amée.

"You have tearful eyes at her memory," Élise whispered and took a small step closer. "It's best not to let the men here see them." She wrapped herself in her arms and loosened the shield she had put up. "I truly apologize for mocking your lost love," she spoke in a hushed tone. "Most men do not care about their women—not the sailors, anyway. It's always the next port, the next conquest."

Rollant blinked back the sting of pending tears. He had not felt the urge to cry in more years than he could count. He pushed those memories down where he kept them.

"You are too kind, Madame," he said, returning to the present, though a bitterness coated the edge of his expression. But his voice remained warm in the character of a common former naval soldier.

Her eyes turned down. "Mademoiselle," she whispered with a blush rising on her cheeks.

"Mademoiselle," he repeated, barely hearing her. She wasn't married.

They locked eyes briefly before Élise shifted, putting space between them as though remembering he was a stranger. He scanned the room, and a few men were looking his way and speaking behind cupped hands.

"Don't mind them. They are just wondering who you are. Never seen you before," she said.

"Well, to further ease their worry," Rollant said. "You can tell them I am from Nice," Rollant said. The truth sat easier on his lips. He was born in the post-Roman town when the homes were still made of stacked stone with pitch roofs. He came from a long line of knights and soldiers in medieval Provence. His family surname was reminiscent of the mountains where his family had forged deep roots: Montvieux, "old mountain."

Élise sighed again with a smile, releasing some tension between them. "You are very observant. We don't trust newcomers easily, but if you seek freedom, then you are one of us—until proven otherwise."

"I have craved freedom for a long time," he said, biting back the pain that rose inside of him as he thought of every painful death he had suffered and every rebirth. Freedom was a fleeting, unattainable dream.

"Happy to hear it," she said and fidgeted with the sleeves of her shirt. "What is your name, Monsieur, since you know mine?"

Rollant inclined his head as the heat of embarrassment kissed his cheeks. He had been rude and forgotten to introduce himself.

"Rollant Montvieux."

He dropped the "de" from his name to not signify his noble origins and draw suspicions.

Her eyebrow lifted. "Rollant, not Roland?" she asked with a coy smile. "Your parents must have had a fondness for Old France," she said.

"They passed when I was a boy, so I could not ask them."

Her smile softened, and a dark hue flashed in her eyes. "My mother also passed when I was young. My father did not want me, so I was sent to live with my aunt." She studied him as if she wanted him to speak, but he did not know what to say to her.

They stood in silence with the weight of shared loss hanging between them. Were they trading scars? Rollant straightened up. He knew not to trust these quiet moments—they led to attachment, to weakness, to pain.

"Do I pass your check?" he asked, a polite smile returning as if polishing armor.

Her eyes ran over his face and broad chest, and she returned his gaze with a small, lighthearted smile. "For now."

He thought her smile was meant to be playful, but there was a hidden warmth behind it, something genuine that stirred a place in him long frozen. It was nothing like the raw intensity he had felt for Amée, but there was a familiarity—a spark of life where there had been only emptiness for so long. It stirred his heart with a soft beat of light, a flicker in the darkness that had claimed him for centuries—a dangerous light.

He laughed in surprise at himself. Six hundred years, and he thought he had seen it all, felt it all. But she—Élise—was different. He had seen pretty girls before and even flirted once or twice, but it always ended the same. They aged. They died. And he remained ageless with empty arms, forever separated by the sorceress' curse. His laugh faded.

"What is so funny, Rollant?" Élise asked with eyes lit with the fire of the speech she had just given.

His smile didn't reach his eyes. "My apologies, Mademoiselle. You have taken my words from me," he said, wrestling with the smile that wanted to grow.

"When is your next meeting?" he asked, steadying himself.

"In a fortnight," she said. Her eyes dulled. It was most likely a lie.

"Here?" he asked.

She nodded.

"I'll see you then," he said with an even-tempered voice and backed away from her. Something tugged at his chest, urging him to stay, as he turned to go. But he reasoned with it and forced himself to the street.

She would age. She would die, just like everyone else. Her life would be like the morning dew in his, and he wouldn't be in the city long enough to care what happened to her with the bruise on her shoulder or what became of her speech.

He wouldn't let himself.

Yet, as he disappeared down the Rue de Charonne, the memory of Élise's smile lingered. He shook his head to clear his mind of whatever feelings had overcome him while inside.

"Of all people," he muttered. "Why her? Why now?"

He shut his eyes tight, wishing to banish the image of Élise's face, which he could see clearly, and replace it with Amée's since it had been reduced to a blurred outline. He swallowed the lump in his throat and wanted to feel nothing again.

He determined he would only be there as long as necessary to fulfill the King's command and nothing more. Élise was just another pretty face, and Amée was his love. The one he longed for. The one who loved him for all forty years after he returned home from the Second Crusade and deprived her of any semblance of a normal life.

He palmed his face, the temporary giddiness in his heart replaced with a solemn, bitter sense of duty.

"Forget Élise," he whispered. He shoved his hands in his coat pockets and headed to the inn up the street, chin down and walking with a forward lean, fighting against the harsh winter winds.

He cleared his mind and focused on the chanting and the people's response to the crisis. He had witnessed the French people were indeed restless, and only time would tell if they would act on rebellious words or seek revolution. He had a month to gain their trust and determine when the rumors would come to fruition.

CHAPTER 5
The Weight of Possibilities

FAUBOURG SAINT-ANTOINE, PARIS, FEBRUARY 1788

Élise watched Rollant exit the *Au Pain Roux* bakery. Gabin and Yves flanked her. She flinched at Gabin's heavy arm that fell across her shoulders. She thought he would pull her aside and up the stairs to his cramped living quarters, but instead, he shook her.

"What are your thoughts about the stranger, dove?" Gabin asked her out of the side of his mouth. He had seen her interaction with Rollant, and she hoped he did not have any suspicions of her attraction to the man.

Her nose turned up. "He has a kind heart; I'll give him that," she said with a brief pause. "But he is too well-dressed, and his lingering perfume . . ." She trailed off, reminding herself of its earthen aroma of old wood and candle smoke that had made her want to embrace him. A stab of guilt pressed on her heart as Gabin had cared for her the past few years. "Or perhaps it was just his musk. Either way, he said he had just returned from the Americas. A navy man. Maybe that is why his clothes are too neat." She added for effect, "Born in Nice."

Gabin's grip tightened, pressing harder into the bruises he had given her. She caged her whimper and looked him in the eyes.

Yves broke the unspoken jealousy in Gabin's gaze. "It's your call, Élise. You spoke to him the most."

The others who had not left yet gathered around her as she pondered her conversation with Rollant. They exchanged glances, and concern was etched on their faces. They feared he was also an informant.

Malo asked, "Do you want us to follow him?"

Élise shrugged and gestured to Gabin. "It is Gabin's call. He is our leader." She hoped it would buy at least a few fewer slaps that night.

Gabin barked. "Sylvian, Olivier, Yanis—see where he goes, see what he does."

Élise nodded them off as if begging them to follow orders.

But Olivier raised a finger and said, "If he is the king's informant, what do you want us to do?"

"Nothing," she said instinctively, feeling Gabin's nails dig into her flesh. She shouldn't have answered for him. "We will just make sure to speak lies when he is here," she offered.

Half the crowd scoffed. A boy named Mael laughed, "You don't want to kill 'em?"

She grabbed Mael's collar and pulled him close, mostly to rid herself of Gabin's grip. "Kill him? So the king has much more reason to take our heads? Right now, we only speak of freedom, but we will not spill blood in stupidity."

Heads nodded, and Gabin slapped Mael on the shoulder. "He's just a boy; he'll learn."

"A boy with a weapon is a man." She pointed a finger in Mael's face. "You remember that."

Mael's lips turned into a scowl. "I will," he huffed and yanked out of Élise's grip.

"Leave the boy alone," Gabin said and pushed Mael away. He turned and barked at the three he had ordered prior. "Go."

"We're off," Sylvian said, and the three tasked with trailing Rollant left.

Élise could feel the stares on her back and face, but she locked gazes with Gabin. He was the main attraction for the women there, but his anger was something to avoid. His eyes raged. He didn't like how she had handled the evening or her answer to the question meant for him.

She glanced around the room and answered the crowd first. "If the stranger ends up being an informant, I'll be the first to take a life, and it will be his. But at the right time, so we don't find ourselves in prison or with the guillotine."

Gabin laughed. "You, little dove? Take a life?" He walked up and grabbed her chin with an iron grip. "Next time, let the men talk." He shoved her away toward the stairs. "Now get upstairs and prepare for bed."

She regained her footing, and her eyes darted around the room. The women's heads were down, but the men's eyes slid between her and Gabin. They sensed Gabin's insecurity, it seemed. It was enough for her, and so she turned and ran up the stairs as fast as she could without another word.

"Little dove wants to be an eagle," Gabin laughed. His voice carried up the steps, and subsequent laughter chased it. She threw open the door to the cramped living quarters—a bed, a chair, table, wardrobe, and a basin. Rage built in her chest and spread to her quivering fingers. She hated him, but she loved him. She wanted to escape him, but she couldn't spit in his face by running away. He needed her just as much as she needed him. She stood in the middle of the one-room apartment, warmed by the baker's oven below. A shiver ran down her spine, remembering in stark contrast, the cold nights at her aunt's home and the blood her father drew. At least Gabin's hits always seemed to land where clothes could cover any lasting marks. Even if she wanted to get away, she had nowhere to go. Everyone in town loved Gabin. He was their leader. They would not take her in out of fear of disrespecting the community's only remaining honest baker—the man who had the connections for flour and oil. The man who fed them as cheap as he could, despite the prices.

She released the rage through long, deep breaths, knowing her punishment would be worse if she met or exceeded Gabin's anger when he arrived.

Her gaze drifted to the wardrobe with a broken door and the chipped basin. They seemed to bear the weight of her existence. The furniture felt heavy with the resignation of keeping her shackled there. Her balled fists slowly released her fingers until they fell limp by her sides. She lived life on her hands and knees, but at least it kept her breathing. As long as she had breath, she nurtured the spark within her, and it would take more than fists and the winter cold to put it out.

The sun had retreated and left the moon in its place. She had always been up before dawn since before she could remember. Her knees buckled from exhaustion, and she leaned into the bed before letting herself fall into her spot, stained from Gabin's other conquests. Her mind slipped unbidden to the stranger's face in the dim candlelight.

Rollant—she remembered his name with surprising ease and, more so, the way he had looked at her, not with possessiveness like Gabin, her aunt and father, but with a painful longing. He thought she was his former lover, but even still. How he must have loved Amée—she felt it in every word about her and his every unguarded glance.

Élise's chest tightened, and she closed her eyes, wishing, yearning to be looked at in the same way. Never had she seen such love in a single gaze that she thought, at first, it must have been false. Yet his eyes were piercing, his gaze unwavering as he spoke of Amée. He must have been a true man. He possessed a calmness and level-headedness she had never witnessed before. A man like that wouldn't raise his hand to anyone out of jealousy as Gabin did.

She shivered once more, sensing the phantom warmth of his steady gaze, and a peculiar sense of hope ignited inside her—a subtle, risky notion that perhaps, just perhaps, there were men who didn't feel the need to dominate others to feel powerful.

Élise laughed bitterly at her own foolishness. But the stranger was just that—a stranger, someone who might very well turn out to be a spy and put them all in prison. She had every reason to distrust him and question his intentions and sudden arrival. And yet, she could still feel the spark of that brief, silent connection they had shared. For the first time, someone had seen her, saw through her façade, and even though it left her exposed, she felt emboldened.

She rolled to the edge of the bed, her fingers tracing the rough fabric of her skirt, still lost in thought. Maybe Rollant was a passing shadow in her life, another illusion of hope she couldn't afford. Such genuineness he portrayed. Too good to be true, perhaps, but as she lay in the bed warmed by the ovens below, her thoughts strayed to the stranger with the deep voice and loving gaze.

"Let the fortnight pass quickly," she murmured, hoping the days were a blur before seeing him again. With Gabin's footsteps thudding up the steps, she wondered how the night would end if it were Rollant ascending the stairs.

The door flew open, shattering her thoughts. Her body flinched as it grappled to hold onto her mind's image of Rollant.

"Élise!" Gabin barked, his voice dragging her back to her cage.

She jolted up with open eyes and braced herself for the new bruises she would wear in the morning as he marched up and knocked her to the floor.

CHAPTER 6

Echo of the Past

LE MARAIS, PARIS, MARCH 1788

ROLLANT TRAVELED north to Le Marais after gaining information from the crowded streets of Bastille and Saint-Jacques-la-Boucherie. Faubourg Saint-Antoine had given him a clear sense of unrest. He moved deliberately between the neighboring districts, listening and observing craftsmen, merchants, and dockworkers along the Seine. Each person gave a new perspective, but the same complaints were on every tongue, and the same bitterness was etched on every face. Unfounded rumors were prevalent, such as hatred toward the Queen, who spent lavishly, though Rollant knew the opposite to be true. The king would hear it all from his lips.

Yet beneath his disciplined exterior, a quiet desire nagged at him. A fortnight was quickly expiring, and the residents of Faubourg Saint-Antoine would again meet at *Au Pain Roux*. He did not need to return, as he already knew the sentiments of the neighborhood, but thoroughness was his nature. His visit to *Au Pain Roux* had been his first day out of his Charonne home, and it was likely there were pieces he did not notice. He would need to scour the streets again and perhaps find Élise in the crowd.

No.

He would not search for Élise, though he would still greet her if he happened upon her. Otherwise, he would forget her.

But as he moved through the streets of Le Marais, her smile flickered in the corners of his mind. As bakers and merchants argued over the price of bread, her porcelain face and fiery eyes made his heart beat faster. Even the scent of fresh bread, warm and rich in the evening air, failed to drive her away.

"She is only an exceptional speaker," he muttered and tried to focus on the rose Amée had given him. He attempted to see his late wife's face, but it was only a blur. It seemed that the sorceress had stripped him of holding his love in his memories, or perhaps it was just a machination of time. No one had taken residence in his thoughts like Élise had since Amée and Cateline and the traitor Arnoul. He thought he had fortified his mind well enough, but it seemed the one conversation with Élise had fractured his fortress.

The streets began to crowd as the night took the sky. He passed by slowly, listening to each meeting place.

"There is no food! They hoard it at the palace!"

"The king squanders our taxes!"

"The Queen is the ruin of this country, and the King follows behind her like a dog!"

The same sentiments—he'd heard it all before. He studied the men and women in attendance—furrowed brows, bared teeth, scrawny appearances. Élise was right. He stood out as well-nourished. He shook his head.

"Stop thinking about Élise," he muttered.

The lamplighters walked the streets, lighting the oil lamp lights. Taxes paid for them. The Sun King made sure Paris would be a city of light, yet in all its glory, it sat on a foundation of decay and rot—where hunger eroded peace and rage simmered around every corner. The Sun King's city of light had become a city of shadows. Though he despised thinking of Élise another time, he knew she was right yet again. The people were all being primed for something greater than themselves. His eyes were unclouded as he stood in the street listening to the grievances. Usually, he would be numb to it all, but Élise stirred within him that which had long been dormant. His feet kept walking, one after another, as he pondered. It was more than just her resemblance to Amée, or least, what he remembered of Amée. Élise had said something unique in her speech at the bakery: "We let them."

Out of all the meetings and disgruntled people, no one had yet said anything about the people's responsibility. The finger had always been pointed toward the crown, but Élise pointed the finger to the people. It had given him pause then and every night since. She had the intelligence of a true advisor; too bad she would never see the King's Cabinet. Perhaps she could have stirred the king to action and guided him in his failings.

A screaming woman, mad at the injustice of her world, took his attention for a moment. He bit his lip in thought. Maybe the king was too detached, too far removed, for too long, to have any real connection to the people he governed. In the gap, rumors and falsehoods burgeoned from the dark soil of despair.

The sharp night winds lost the sun's warmth, and Rollant shoved his hands in his pockets as he returned to the inn, for which he paid for a room earlier in the day. The innkeeper was a royalist who was more than willing to offer a room for the king's secret guard. Three familiar men were down the street from the entrance to the inn. They had been following him ever since the night at *Au Pain Roux*. He wondered if Élise had sent them or if they had come of their own free will.

Regardless, he did not acknowledge them as he passed by and entered the inn, leaving him the upper hand should anything occur.

In the morning, he had planned to go to his Charonne home to collect his belongings and return to the king early with more information than needed. However, as he gazed out his tiny rented room's window at the oil lamp-lit streets, all he could think of was Élise walking toward him under the swaying warm light.

Finally, he said aloud, "I will go back to *Au Pain Roux* first and ensure I did not miss any vital information." He slumped on the uncomfortable bed and leaned back with his hands behind his head against the dumpy pillow.

"And seeing Élise one last time will assure me that I must walk away from her and put her out of my mind." He closed his eyes. "It will confirm that Élise is a temporary, fleeting distraction. I will reassure myself no true desire lingers, and if I can't put her out of my mind, then well, it's because of her speech, nothing more."

It had been a long fortnight, too much walking and insufficient food. He drifted off to sleep, murmuring, "And it is not like I could ever care for her or else condemn her to the fate of the sorceress' curse should I ever hold her."

No, he had an oath to uphold for all eternity, and there was no room for anyone except Amée to be his companion. Amée's memory was sacred. He would never betray her memory, though the burn of not clearly remembering her face stabbed his heart. She alone had earned the right to stay with him. Élise had not.

CHAPTER 7

The Path of Longing

FAUBOURG SAINT-ANTOINE, PARIS, MARCH 1788

THE WOODEN SIGN with *Au Pain Roux* burned into its worn surface swayed in the midday breeze. Rollant walked past the entrance while glancing inside. He saw men but no Élise, so he kept on walking. She could be anywhere in the district. Just because she had spoken in the bakery didn't mean she lived there.

But he wasn't there for Élise, he reminded himself. He adjusted his coat and pressed onward, taking the sharp corner onto Rue de Charonne, slowing his gait and taking in the townspeople. This part of the city needed a good cleaning. The dirt and grime on the streets had not been apparent at night, but the sunlight did not hide the stains on the stones. People hustled back and forth across the street. Heated haggling stung his eardrums. It was much different than the palace filled with whispers. He stood a head above others, or perhaps it was how he walked—fully upright. The others slumped over from burdens as if too tired or too weak, too thin, to afford the energy to pull back their shoulders in the hustle of life. These people were suffering, and he would make sure the king knew of it. Just as he resolved he had seen enough, a red scarf caught his eye.

Élise.

There she was, handing a small chunk of bread to a group of children. Their hands grabbed at her skirt and arms. One pulled her down by the hair to kiss her cheek. Her laugh echoed down the street as a hope-filled beacon in a sea of bitterness. A corner of Rollant's lips turned up at the sound of its crystal ring.

He trailed her for a while, observing her hand out chunks of bread to the elderly, the widowed, and, more assumedly, orphans. The small act of sharing food in the middle of a hunger crisis softened his hardened heart.

Most would hoard or price-gouge the poor. Generosity was usually the first casualty of scarcity. But perhaps there was some good left in the world. Or, he reconsidered his grand notions for Élise's motivations. These people could have paid for the bread in advance, and she was simply making deliveries. Maybe she worked at the bakery and sold small pieces of bread for an overpriced amount to those who could not go to the bakery. His lips thinned. It was most likely the latter. From his experiences over the centuries, selfishness won whenever people became hungry to the point of violence.

"Forget her," he told himself as he hurried past her. But she turned suddenly and bumped into him. She tripped. He caught her before she fell—one hand on her arm and the other steady at her lower back. They locked eyes, and he pulled her upright. The warmth in her closeness and her breath on his chest muted his tongue. His fingers lingered on the fabric of her dress before he forced them away from her. She had not died, so he did not love her—it was just infatuation. He could walk away from infatuation before it blossomed into something more, or at least he hoped.

"Rollant?" she asked in a whisper, quieting the chaos around him.

His eyes must have lit. She remembered him from fourteen days prior, not only him but also his name. After centuries in the king's courtrooms and dalliances across the country and the world in honor of the king, words were not foreign to him, yet with Élise, words were all but forgotten.

"It is good to see you again," she said with a smile, smoothing her apron.

He returned with a smile of his own that he forced himself to erase from his eyes.

"Where have you been?" she asked, putting her hand on her hip.

He fumbled with his words as they finally returned to him. "I've been traveling around the neighboring districts, trying to find a place I could call home." He looked past her with a faint smile. "No one's waiting for me where I come from."

Élise shifted her weight, clearly uncomfortable with his lonely answer. "Well, I don't know how much you have saved, but outside the city walls is probably your cheapest option."

He nodded, his gaze locking with her eyes. "I was afraid of that. But from what I can tell, you are right about the prices, Mademoiselle."

She adjusted the bread in its cloth wrap to ensure the heat didn't leave it. "I bet you don't remember my name, do you? It's why you haven't used my name yet." Her eyes narrowed as if she had already written him off. "I'm just a pretty face to you, aren't I?"

He chuckled at the direct questions that had accusatory implications for his nature. She had pegged him for a skirt-chaser.

A smug grin passed over her mouth. "Like all the rest, I see," she muttered.

He shook his head and held up his hands. "No, no. You see, you are incorrect, Élise."

Her grin fell flat at hearing her name, but her eyes grew wide in surprise.

"And you are not just a pretty face; though, you have a beautiful one," he said. A rosy flush grew on his cheeks. Had he just called her beautiful? Aloud? He had to stop and walk away forever. The test of his will had failed. He needed to bid adieu and return to the palace attic, where living in immortal punishment was easier.

She scoffed. "You may know my name, but you are a liar. No one has ever called me beautiful."

"Then everyone must be blind," he said without a second thought, desperately wishing to keep his mouth closed.

She stepped back and visibly swallowed. "I have to go," she stuttered, narrowing her eyes before spinning on her heels.

Against his better judgment, he followed and walked beside her. "Are you making deliveries? I could assist you."

"These aren't deliveries," she said quickly, eyes straight ahead.

"No?" His will shattered, thinking his latter judgment of her was incorrect and made her even more desirable. "Then what are they?"

She side-eyed him. "Nothing."

Rollant wanted to tell her he had seen her hand out bread to numerous people, but that would indicate he had followed her for quite some time. At her continued silence, he asked, "Would you like me to leave?"

"No, I mean, yes." She shook her head. "I . . ." She took a deep breath and stopped walking.

Rollant stepped to face her. Again, their gazes locked.

"If you ask me to leave, I'll never engage with you again if that is what you wish," he said, wishing she asked him to leave because he feared he was not strong enough to walk away as he had previously determined he would.

Her mouth opened, but no words came out. Her eyes searched his. "Gabin . . . I am with Gabin Roux," she said with a shallow breath as if he should know who that was. "I am his woman. Not married, but he saved me from my father and aunt, as I'm sure you heard me say in the bakery two weeks prior."

Rollant's lips pressed together as his chin ducked. He could walk away. She gave him an open door but did not tell him to leave. However, he needed to walk away from Faubourg Saint-Antoine to save himself from the heartache of watching her die either by time or in his arms. If he had loved her, she would have died when he caught her from falling. Something so simple could have ended her life, but there was a light in her eyes as if begging him to stay, as if she needed him for a small sanctuary in the hardship of life.

He felt pulled to Élise, and along with it, a pang of guilt surged in his belly. Yet, there he was, asking too many questions and entering the dangerous ground before the fall. Amée's memory warned him to stop. But the allure of human connection with a woman that intrigued him after centuries of solitude, distanced from all, kept him rooted to the present, cherishing each forbidden moment and feeding the craving his heart desired.

"Say something," she said in hushed tones. It was more of a question than a statement. "I apologize if I have misunderstood your compliments as interest in me or if I gave you an indication of interest. I only thought I should be upfront with you."

He shook his head. "No, you have not misunderstood," he said with a hesitant smile. "You have stolen my words yet again, Mademoiselle." The brisk spring winds whipped through them as if telling him to "Go, now." But he defied it, unable to draw himself away. "Do you need my assistance with your non-deliveries, or do you want me to leave you alone?"

He bit back his error. He should have left, but something within needed the absolute confirmation of her desire for him to leave.

"I want you to . . ." Her voice trailed off as she cradled the bread in her arm and again adjusted the flap. "I want . . . or rather . . . if you have the time . . . I request your assistance." She kept her eyes on the bread.

"I'm glad to," he said and stepped out of her way.

Her eyes snapped to his with a furrowed brow. "And you want nothing in return. I cannot pay you for your time."

"I want nothing but your company," he said and hated himself for it.

Both corners of her mouth lifted, and her eyes seemed to be at peace. It was enough for him to forgive himself.

"I think you might be getting the raw end of the deal," she chuckled.

"I doubt that," he said and gestured to hold the bread for her, to which she refused. He folded his hands behind his back as they walked. It was foolish to let his heart venture into this acquaintanceship. He had already vowed long ago when Amée passed in his arms never to let himself linger near love, for his sake and the one who held his heart. "I wanted to hear you speak again," he said. "Will you also be at *Au Pain Roux* tonight?"

She straightened up and turned her shoulders to him. "I must tell you why I acted the way I did the last time we spoke. I was not sure of your intentions at our meeting place. There are rumors to be wary of newcomers."

"And why is that?" he asked.

She spat the question. "Are you an informant, Rollant? Are you here to throw us in prison?"

His eyebrows lifted high. "You have a straightforward nature, Élise. It fits you well," he said with eyes that ran over her face. "And no, I shan't be doing anything of the sort."

Her head inclined, and he finally put two and two together: Au Pain Roux and Gabin Roux. His mind flashed seeing her two weeks prior and the hesitant glances she gave to the same few men, or had it been only to a single man?

Before she replied, he asked, "Does Gabin own the bakery?"

"Yes," she said, unsure where this line of inquiry would go.

"Do you live there with him?"

She swallowed the lump in her throat, and her cheeks turned red. "If you are of an old soul, you would not like the answer."

"I believe in God," he replied, "but I'm sure he has no use for me anymore."

She pulled the sleeve of her shirt down on her wrist, where he noticed a bruise.

"Why do you ask?" Her eyes were cast down, not on him.

"I couldn't help but notice the bruise you tried to hide on your shoulder the last I saw you and the bruise on your wrist today. The way you said Gabin Roux as if he was an important figure in the community and that you 'were his woman', instead of 'we are together.'"

"It's a hard life," she scoffed, eyes still averted. "You get hurt working. I'm sure you are no stranger to bruises during your service at sea."

He gently guided her cheek so that her eyes followed to align with his. Her irises betrayed her—the deep depths swirling in doubt and despair. "If Gabin is hurting you, I will not stand for it. If I see it or hear it, I will take action," he gritted. Many women were beaten by their husbands. He ignored it and sat in his attic apartment, letting the times change naturally, but it infuriated him that another man dared lay hands on the one before him. He had never beaten Amée. He loved her too much to treat her as property. It seemed his thinking was an out-of-place norm, but he never cared about social norms anyway.

"Don't worry, then." She snapped her face from his touch, and he replaced his hand behind his back. "You'll never see it, and you'll never be around to hear it," she replied, validating his assumption. "And if you did anything to Gabin, this whole community would hang you from the streetlamps."

He leaned in. "They could try," he said with a smirk.

She laughed with a jolt and wiped away a sudden, runaway tear. "You have a good heart, Rollant. " Her voice was thick. "I can tell already. Not too many men like you." She sniffed and hardened her stare. "But stay away from Gabin. Do not cross him. Not for my sake. The world needs good men. And this community needs Gabin. He feeds them for cheap. He isn't completely horrible."

"Are these then free meals from Gabin?" He gestured to the bread in her arms.

She chuckled and wiped away another tear. A row of teeth bit into her bottom lip as she shook her head. "This is my free meal from Gabin. My daily wage for working for him."

"You share your *earned* meal with others? I would argue it is not free." Rollant tilted his head in awe of such a woman—sharing when she had so little.

"He gives me three baguettes from the night before and shares his stew with me in the evenings if I did what he told me to do." She shrugged as they continued walking to her next stop.

"This Gabin withholds food from you as punishment?" Rollant shook his head, and the injustice tightened his shoulders.

"Of course."

"This is common, then?"

"My father did and my aunt did too. I assume I never knew any difference." She peered up at him. "How would you punish someone who disobeyed?"

"It would depend on what they did, I suppose. But even prisoners are fed," he said as a man bumped into his shoulder, running past them.

"Well, then, maybe I am Gabin's prisoner. You know I can never leave him. And I hope you aren't staying for a chance to . . ." She sighed. "I cannot leave him. He will hunt me down. I am his, and everyone knows it." Her voice lowered, and he could barely hear her over the bustling streets. Their moment of calm and peace had been overrun by reality.

They walked in silence until she said, "You can leave if that was your goal."

Rollant said nothing for a while. He didn't know what his goal was with Élise. He just wanted to know her. He was attracted to her. He hated this life for her. But their relationship could never be more than a modest friendship. He looked off at the merchants lining the street. He could leave; she told him to, in fact.

But again, he couldn't. He would help her through life as much as he could, which wouldn't be much. He had to return to the king soon, but he could still leave a friend behind in case he needed one later and give her an opportunity for a new life should she ever find herself able to leave Gabin.

He changed the subject and said, "If you could have anything to eat, what would it be?"

"What?" she asked with a chuckle. "I half expected you to continue down the street without another word."

He shrugged as a child ran past him, making him walk closer to Élise. He brushed her arm with his as he moved her out of an unfocused man's heavy gait down the street. "I need a friend or a familiar face in these parts," he said close to her ear. He pushed the desire to move the loose strands behind her headscarf out of mind. "Would that suffice as a reason to stay in your company?" he asked as the two moved back to a respectable distance.

"I suppose," she said, glancing at a woman who stared at her and Rollant. She turned her attention back to Rollant. "To answer your question: If I could have anything to eat, it would be a meal shared with a big family next to a warm hearth. We would all eat a roasted chicken, seasoned and cooked to perfection, fresh vegetables with a butter sauce, warm, fresh bread with an assortment of fancy cheeses . . . " She laughed. "My mouth is watering already."

"Maybe add a pastry or two," Rollant leaned in with a smile.

"Yes, and maybe a tart. Oh, and chocolate. That would be a luxurious meal fit for someone . . . who is not me." She wiped her mouth and wet her dry lips with her tongue. "Why would you ask me such a question, Rollant? Make me wonder what a different life would be like yet again."

"Again?" he asked.

A sheepish grin grew on her mouth. Her cheeks flushed red like wine spots. "Oh, I . . . It's nothing," she said and diverted from their path. "I will be right back," she said and hurried up to a door, handing a piece of her bread to the patron who answered her knock.

She dodged a horde and made it back to Rollant's side. "I have one more stop, and it was part of why I asked your assistance," she said. "This family is very ill. The father died, and the mother is sick and cannot work for food. The children work to pay the rent, but they have a horrible cough. They always need something done around their home, and I am so tired after I visit with them. I hope I have not misled you."

He smiled and thought it odd Gabin wasn't there to help her, or maybe not odd at all.

"You have not," he said. "As you told me, I am well-nourished and can lend my skills."

Her sheepish grin returned. "I appreciate your help, Monsieur, and I am amazed at your memory." She nodded to a side street situated next to a carpenter's store. "It is this way."

They walked side by side until the street narrowed, and she took the lead. The air was stale, and the spring breeze did not reach the corridor. They finally came to a small apartment complex, and Élise entered. The shared bathroom's pungent aroma filled the hallway. She went to a door down the hall and opened it.

"Greetings, Madame Marie," she whispered.

"In here," a woman rasped. Élise pulled a full baguette and a pouch from her bundle and placed them on the small table in the single-room apartment.

"Who's this?" Marie, curled up in bed, said and pointed a weak finger at Rollant.

"This is a new friend. I've asked him to help me with the chores you need."

"He'll come back and rob me or kill me or take my children. Why did you bring him here? Now he knows where I live? You've doomed us all."

Élise adjusted the woman's thin pillow and sat her up to allow her to drink some water. "I would never do such a thing if I did not think him a good man."

"Hmm. If you find me murdered, then my blood will be on your hands," Marie said with a cough.

Élise peered over her shoulder at Rollant. "Could you please stoke the fire and heat the water pan for her bed? Its grown cold."

He nodded and did what was asked of him without a word. His presence frightened the woman, and he didn't want to scare her further.

After spending some time there cleaning, washing, and cooking porridge, they left. Marie called out after Élise as they headed to the door, "Bring him back. He was good."

Élise smiled at Rollant before answering Marie. "I think today was just a one-time visit. I'll be back tomorrow."

"Have a good night, Élise. I wish a good life for you." Marie snuggled in her warm bed to wait for her children to return.

The door closed, and they walked back to the street.

Rollant noticed out of the three baguettes she had started the day with, she only had a third of one left. "Are you hungry, Rollant?" she asked, offering him the last of her bread.

Her hand grazed his, and he wanted to grasp it and kiss her fingers. His admiration of Élise's kindness mirrored that of Amée. He would not fall in love again, though. He couldn't, for Élise's sake, but Élise was making it hard not to be mesmerized by her.

"You earn three baguettes from the night prior and share almost of all of it with others? Including me, a man you've only known for a few hours?" He gave in to his desire and grasped her hand, holding the bread out to him, and pressed it back into her arm. "I cannot."

"I was hungry as a child when my aunt forced me to sleep outside with no food if I didn't bring in enough stolen coins." Her gaze turned inward. "A stranger gave me a piece of bread to eat. I never saw him again, nor would I remember his face if I did meet him, but it made me realize I might have died that night with nothing to eat. And that generous slice of bread saved my life. I vowed if I had ever had bread, I would share it."

Rollant asked, "Even if it is a risk that you may not get to eat?"

"In the end, it's all risk—surviving or not." She pressed the bread toward him.

He smiled in awe of her as he folded the bread cloth around it and put it back in her arms. "Do you need to be anywhere? I found a cafe in Bastille that would be out of Gabin's communal reach. I would assume you haven't eaten yet today. I, of course, would have you back to Gabin's bakery before sundown." He told himself to stop, and yet her act of genuine selflessness had stirred the selfishness within him. He did not intend to stay long enough to build a memorable friendship, and yet he was asking to take her to a cafe for the day.

"Oh, I cannot afford a cafe," she said, shrank back from him, and glanced around.

"It will be my way of saying thank you for your friendly company today," he said. "Come with me, or if not, I do not want to take your bread. I don't have a need for it. The navy paid well enough, and I've saved a little," he said with a chuckle.

"Well, you should save it more. Don't spend it on me."

"I insist. And we can get away from prying eyes and ears," he said, glancing at a few women whispering to each other but alternating glances at Rollant and Élise.

Élise sighed. "I am only afraid they will tell Gabin I was with you."

"Well, I will tell him that I took you to Bastille to help me, and if he wants to hit me, he can fight me like a man." He smirked and lied. "I was the best sprawler on the *Ville de Paris*."

Élise shook her head. "You?" She bit her smiling lip and tilted her head. "Well, just this once. I can plead with Gabin if he hears about it." She gave the rest of her bread to some children on their way to Bastille.

THE BASTILLE PRISON FORTRESS, a symbol of royal power, imposed upon the skyline. Wealthier homes intermingled with the working class, however, where weathered artisans and craftsmen shops lined the grimy streets of Faubourg Saint-Antoine, cafes and taverns lined the cleaner streets of Bastille. He led her to Le Lys Blanc, a small cafe near the northern border of the Bastille district, where the faint aroma of roasted coffee lured in patrons before they could see the sign above its worn wooden doors and stone façade.

He could afford the rare restaurant the nobility frequented and give Élise the meal she dreamed of. Still, he needed to blend in, so he brought her to the subtle sanctuary of Le Lys Blanc, with intimate two-person seating catered to the working class and hushed conversations about the future of France. He guided her to an open table by the fire and let her sit next to the warmth while his back faced the brisk spring air in the middle of the room.

She fidgeted with her apron and glanced around at the well-polished wooden panels and the few pastoral paintings decorating the minimalist walls. The room's warm, low light cast Élise in such a beautiful glow, especially with the hearth light shining behind her as if God was presenting her to him, a gift in his immortal plight. Thus, it would be a short-lived gift, for it wasn't the place or the time to grow attached.

"I've never set foot in a cafe before," she whispered just as a boy approached the table.

"Drinks, food?" the boy asked with a break in his voice. He slapped his dingy towel over his arm.

"A coffee, black, bread, cheese, and perhaps a stew and a pastry." He gestured to Élise. "For you?"

"The same," she said quickly, with a blush covering her cheeks.

"I'll be back," the boy said, running off to the wooden counter where the shop's owner fulfilled orders.

Rollant turned his attention back to Élise.

"That is so much. I cannot pay," she said in hushed tones. "I don't have any coin. None at all. Everything I earn is in food for barter."

He placed his hand atop hers. "I have coin. I told you I saved, and I insisted you come and intend to pay for your meal as a thank you."

"But it is too much," she said, placing her other hand atop his. The naturalness of his hand in hers captured his breath. Her eyes fell on their intertwined hands.

"It is not enough," he whispered. He would remember her touch as he remembered Amée's. He could feel himself falling quickly for this woman. It was just an infatuation, he told himself. He would return to Versailles in the morning, and she would be old or dead by the time he ventured this far out to the city again. He inched his hand away from hers to where their fingertips lay adjacent.

Her deep sigh and quivering fingers told him all he needed—she was falling fast for him as well. Her hands crept back into her lap. Her shoulders relaxed, and she nestled into her wooden chair with a reupholstered cushion. "Well, I thank you." She glanced at the window across the room.

"No one knows you're here, Élise. I made sure no one was following us," he said, remembering the three men from the bakery. He hadn't seen them since Le Marais.

He rubbed his lip as he watched her settle. Her eyes closed, and her chin dipped in slight reprieve. She leaned forward, elbows on the table, her hands covering her face.

"Tell me, Rollant," she whispered, folding her hands near his and settling her gaze squarely on him. "Why would a handsome man with coin and clean clothes want to spend his day with me?"

She lifted her chin. The slight twitch in her lip implied her cautious curiosity, either daring him to explain or silently urging him to lie due to their raw attraction and inopportune situation.

His instinct was to pull back from the answer, to let his heart return to its cold and indifferent state, yet the thought of leaving the following day without genuinely knowing her tugged him in the opposite direction. His voice softened, yielded like he was sharing a truth too weighty for her fragile frame.

"You intrigue me, Élise," he murmured with a heavy undertone.

A sigh of relief followed by a smile lit on her lips. "As you intrigue me," she whispered.

"You are an enigma that I haven't seen in centuries." He covered in his error. "I mean years that felt like centuries." His chest tightened. He was losing his armor, his guard, the character he'd built. "You have a fire and a mind I've never seen. If you advised the king, maybe the people would not be in such a situation," he said, the words coming unwelcome.

Her eyes lit at the vast compliment.

The young server returned and set down two steaming cups of coffee and a plate of bread and cheese. "Your pastries and stew are coming," he said. "Pay at the counter once you're done."

They both offered him a distracted nod.

"I am honored you think so highly of me." Élise tore off a piece of bread and dipped it into her coffee as though savoring even the most modest meal.

Rollant did not respond but studied her as she ate, her fingers lightly touching the bread and the quiet gratitude in her expression. There was a woman unaccustomed to indulgence who took pleasure in small things and hid a core of resilience. He wanted to ask her a hundred questions, all ones that could root him to this place and time—ones that could ultimately break his resolve to distance himself.

"Why do you stare at me?" she asked.

He lifted his handle-less cup of coffee to his lips and blew the steam from the top. "As I said, you intrigue me."

Her eyes prevented him from taking a sip. Their depths were dark, fathomless, and layered with untold stories, yet piercing and alive with a fire that had withstood storms and held him still. She studied him in return, trying to see the man beneath his polished armor.

She swallowed and dabbed her mouth. "You know of my drunken father and my child-exploiting aunt. You know of Gabin, but I know nothing of you, except you are a sailor who fought in the Americas and an orphan whose parents passed when you were young." Her eyebrow lifted. "But if you were assumedly raised as an orphan in the streets and spent recent years on a ship, how are you so cultured?"

"One could ask the same of you," he replied and finally took his sip. The bitter black slid down his throat with ease. The beans had been roasted and brewed well. It warmed his chest, allowing his muscles to relax. He wasn't going to answer her question; there was too much risk in her uncovering his secrets.

Élise shifted in her seat as she took another bite.

"Then tell me of Amée. I saw the love in your eyes when you looked at me and thought of her. Is that why you want to know me, because I look like Amée?" she asked in her blunt fashion, but her face flushed, perhaps realizing the intimacy of the question. Her eyes averted. "I shouldn't have asked you that."

Amée's memory warned him to stop, to get up and walk away. He swiped his mouth, afraid to answer her. He hadn't spoken of Amée with anyone since Cateline refused to be a part of his life after he laid Amée to rest. His jaw grew taut, and he played with his bread and cheese before taking a bite. He swallowed it down with another sip of coffee, debating what to say.

"I have made you uncomfortable," Élise said. "I am sorry. I shouldn't have asked."

He shook his head and leaned back in his chair. "No, it is a valid question."

His gaze flickered to the hearth. "It's been years—felt like several lifetimes. She was my wife, fell sick, and died in my arms. Our daughter passed as well." He fidgeted with his thumbnail as the words came without prompt. "Time has blurred their faces in my mind." He leaned forward, his forearms pressing into the wooden edge of the table.

"Our minds are our best advocate and our worst enemy." Élise chewed her lip. "Thank you for answering, and I'm so sorry you lost them to illness."

"It was a long time ago," he said and took a sip of coffee, hoping he did not give away too much.

Élise studied him. "If I may re-ask my selfish question, do I intrigue you because of Amée?"

The woman liked to ask the hard questions, he mused. His lips thinned. The more he stared at her, the more he realized the answer was no. "I loved her, as you could tell," he began. "I don't know why I thought she was you. It must have been the lamp light or my dream of her the night before. But although you share a resemblance at first glance, I doubt anyone would say you are even kin. Though, you both possess the same kindness and selflessness."

He slowly turned his coffee cup on the table and dropped his gaze into its warm, round black pool. "You intrigue me, Élise, because of your beauty in your own right, in heart, hand, and face—all that I can tell within the little time I've known you." He glanced back up at her. "I hate to see you tied to a man who beats you and withholds food as punishment. But I fear, as you said, there is nothing I can do." His gaze dropped to her rosebud lips, moving as if to speak but no sound emitting, before back to his coffee. He scoffed at his openness. It was a path that would lead him to more heartache, one way or another.

"You represent a possibility that may never be a reality, or rather will never be a reality," he said at last. "These last two weeks, you have been tucked away in the back of my mind." He realized he had slipped from his fabricated navy man character and forced a small, rueful smile, taking a slow sip, letting the warmth settle him and mask his error before meeting her eyes.

She leaned forward. "You have been in my mind as well."

He shook his head with a sad smile. "Don't . . . Don't tell me such things, Élise." He licked his lip and took another sip. He had to end it, there and then. He was too close. "I hate to say, but I received word that I am being called back into His Majesty's service. In the morning, I will have to leave for the port."

Her gaze hit the table, and her shoulders slumped. "When will you return?" Her voice was barely a whisper.

For a moment as quick as his heartbeat, Rollant wondered if he could abandon the endless, purposeless years for a finite life with her. Would the curse end? Would the sorceress' deal be called off? He had tried to leave his duty to the king when Amée was living, but every morning he slit his hand, it healed. Eternity was his prison, just as Gabin was Élise's.

"I don't know," he replied with the weight of his choice six hundred years prior. "I'm not entirely sure what the orders are, but it would have been nice to know they called me back before I spent coin on inns the last two weeks," he scoffed.

The server returned with two bowls of stew and quickly brought their pastries. Rollant nodded in gratitude while Élise sat numb in the chair. Her gaze softened, and he saw her expression shift, mirroring some unspoken longing he did not want to entertain.

"Then I will spend as much time as I can with you today, and when you return, I will be glad," she said. She ate her bread, drank her coffee, and then sent a heavy fist to the table. "Why did you bring me here if you were just to leave and you knew of Gabin?"

Her eyes burned through him. It was a good question.

He cursed his recklessness. Why had he brought her here and allowed himself to slip closer when he knew he'd leave her world before she realized he'd entered it?

"I was selfish," he said. "I beg your forgiveness."

She finished her bread and quietly ate her stew. He sat, watching her eat. He wanted to explain. "I needed to know you. I have spent years alone and missing my late wife. You were in my mind since I saw you last, and I thought if I could find something not to like, then I wouldn't have to return to sea wondering what if. And all I've done is endanger you."

She closed her eyes, and her shoulders shrank. "I can't be mad at you. You are a stranger that I swore was an informant, and I willingly went with you. These past nights, I wondered how life would be if you were by my side instead of Gabin." She shook her head and winced. "I mean . . . " Her voice trailed off as if she realized their weight.

To Rollant, her open vulnerability made her even more desirable.

Her eyes opened wide. "I mean, I still know nothing about you except you seem true and kind. Though you say you are selfish in bringing me here, I would have done the same."

He slid his hand to hers once again. His thumb rubbed her wrist where Gabin's mark lay. Time had stolen fleeting memories, but he would fight to keep the one with her in Le Lys Blanc for as long as he could. "I will remember you, Élise."

"It is better this way," she said with resignation in her tone and said nothing more. "It was wrong of me to accuse you. You have given me a glimpse of something good I can never have." She looked up at him with tears in her eyes. "Thank you for this moment."

The words settled like sediment in a teacup until all that remained was the clarity of what was left unspoken.

It would have to be enough—these few hours with her. He would be back in Versailles by the next evening, and she'd fade to weathered memory as he fulfilled his position as the king's loyal ghost. He sighed at each passing moment that transformed honor into abandonment.

THE SUN CAST its red and purple hue over the westward sky as Rollant and Élise walked the Rue de Faubourg Saint-Antoine. The lamplighters lit the streets and cast the stone pavers in a warm, amber glow. They walked too close with fingers interlaced, hidden in the folds of their coats. Both were aware that their time together was drawing to a fast close. Rollant wanted to say something, possibly even warn her that he was trapped by duty, but she was too blunt, she'd ask more questions than he could answer and not seem deranged.

They came to the bakery, and Gabin's large shadow paced from within. "Where is she?" His voice boomed.

Élise dropped Rollant's hand and began to walk toward the bakery alone.

"No," Rollant whispered, not knowing what brutality awaited her. "I told you I would face Gabin."

"He may kill you, Rollant. I cannot allow that."

"He won't." Rollant put three coins in her pocket. "Don't tell him about these," he said.

"Again, it is too much," she whispered, shaking her head.

"No, as I said, it is not enough." His fingers traced hers before gesturing toward their final destination. They walked into *Au Pain Roux* side by side.

Gabin marched up to her and yanked her behind him as he shouted in Rollant's face. "She is mine! You'll leave her alone, you sea maggot."

Rollant's muscles tensed beneath his coat at the way Gabin handled Élise. He wanted to tear her away from him, take her away, and let her live her life free from his abuse. But he couldn't ensure her safety after he returned to the palace. At the resolve, he quelled the rage into an expressionless façade of his usual outward nonchalance.

"Monsieur Roux?" Rollant asked with eyes as cool as steel, his calm starkly contrasting to Gabin's rage.

Gabin shoved him, but Rollant barely budged. "Monsieur Roux, thank you for your apprentice's time helping me find medical supplies for my return to port in the morning. She was the only face I knew in all the surrounding districts. No one else had talked much to me." Rollant's calm, deep voice diffused Gabin's anger.

Gabin stood upright, his breath steadied.

"You are to return to port?" he asked, dusting the flour off his shirt and into Rollant's face.

"Yes." Rollant held a coin out for Gabin to take. "She was hesitant to help me, but she is a kind soul and agreed after I said I would reimburse her patron for any of her time you lost this day."

Gabin swiped it out of Rollant's hand and peered back at Élise before sizing Rollant up. "I'm glad she was of use to you. Now be gone. Good luck at sea. And should you need my apprentice's time again, you come and ask me first."

Rollant nodded, wishing to give the man a public beating and bring to light how he had treated Élise. "Of course. My error. Have a good meeting this evening. I hope it is as riveting as the last."

Rollant backed out of the entrance and left. He glanced through the window and found Élise's eyes one last time before he disappeared down the Rue de Charonne. The oil lamp light caught her gaze and on the loose strands of her hair. It would be the keepsake he would take with him. It was only one day in an eternity, but perhaps Élise would have the right to live alongside Amée in his memory, not as a love but of what could have been.

CHAPTER 8

The Price of Freedom

FAUBOURG SAINT-ANTOINE, PARIS, MARCH 1788

GABIN BACKED ÉLISE INTO A CORNER. "You left with him?" he sneered.

"He offered coin, Gabin," she said, pleading with her eyes. "We haven't had coin in a long time. Everything has been through barter. I—I thought you would be proud of me. All I did was show him where to find bandages and ointments." She doubted his approval would follow but hoped it would cushion his blow.

He raised his hand, and she flinched at the pending hit. But at the sound of footsteps, he clamped his hand around her jaw and squeezed instead. "What if he was an informant, Élise? You could have endangered us all."

Her head shook back and forth in his grip while her mind raced through every exchange with Rollant, searching for hints of danger, but there were none. Gabin was wrong, yet he always made her believe she was.

Those who had gathered glanced away or watched with cold indifference.

"I wouldn't have—" she began.

"You are a stupid little dove. Now go upstairs and wash his grime off of you. Don't bother joining us tonight. You'll have to pull a double shift in the morning." He shoved her head back, smashing her body into the corner. The evil sneer of jealousy burned green in his hazel eyes. There would be no talking sense to him.

She squirmed from the corner and headed for the stairs, unable to meet any of the gathering crowd's eyes for fear of feeding rumors or the lies Gabin would tell them about her and the newcomer. He had a reputation to regain after the last meeting. She hoped it went well, for maybe she wouldn't have to endure such a harsh beating that night.

Her feet pounded the stairs. She slammed the door behind her and immediately regretted it. Gabin would remember that and give her due punishment. She had to tread lightly and keep her mouth shut to minimize the bruises.

She fell into the bed in the cramped room that reflected her limited existence. Her knees curled to her chest, and tears ran freely down her cheeks.

"Curse this day," she rasped. She had been a fool. Hope was a luxury she couldn't afford, making every day harder to survive. She had allowed Rollant to invade her thoughts against her better judgment. He would leave her like everyone else except Gabin. Rollant would never return. He was a fire that would never warm her, yet she had reached out and burned herself. Her cold life felt even colder against the memory of his kindness. She had no one to blame but herself.

Yet, it was too much of a burden to bear on her own.

She did not believe in God, yet in her despair, she cried to him in a hushed whimper. "Why did you let him come here, of all places? Of all the places in Paris. Do you *hate* me?" Her tears burned the back of her throat.

"It would have been better if I had never met him." The day flashed through her mind: he listened to her, answered all her questions, was kind and gentle, was restrained, fed her without expectation, gave her coin to help her with a future she may never have. Her heart ached at what Rollant represented.

"He won't be back. Why would he come back?" She smudged her tears against the moist flesh of her cheek. "I can't live this life knowing there could be something more."

Her hot whispers fell in the space between her knees and lips. "I survived in my ignorance. Living here with Gabin was bearable and predictable. But these two weeks have been miserable thinking of the possibility of Rollant, and now, all those possibilities have been confirmed." Her breath hitched in her throat. "Why? Why do this to me?" She turned to her stomach and buried her head in the pillow, ashamed she had talked to an empty room. "Why do this to myself?"

At least her belly was full, fuller than it had ever been. For a small moment in her life, Rollant had shown her what it was like in a world where kindness was not born out of favor and power was not wielded with savagery. The glimpse of life in that world was a crueler torment than Gabin's fists.

Her thumb caressed her fingers, remembering Rollant's touch. Just as she hoped for freedom, equality, and food for all, Rollant would be a part of that hope shining out of her dark life. She brought her finger to her lips and pressed a soft kiss at all the ideals he could be.

"I will remember you too, Rollant."

CHAPTER 9

The Shadow of Regret

PALACE OF VERSAILLES, MARCH 1788

King Louis paced the King's Cabinet and fidgeted with a small mechanical lock. The *clack* and *thunk* of the lock opening and closing echoed through the otherwise silent room. The hearth blazed, heating the room to the point of sweat beads gathering on Rollant's brow.

He had given his report and stared beyond Louis to the mirrored wall. Though short in duration, the ride back to Versailles had been long. He should never have stopped again in Faubourg Saint-Antoine. It had done nothing but depress both Élise and himself. More so Élise—her life wasn't guaranteed. He would live on.

Louis muttered about the lies spreading about the Queen, his movements erratic as he crossed the room.

"It's far worse than I imagined," Louis yelled, collapsing into his high-backed dark oak chair.

His body slumped, and the well-fed belly protruded beneath his royal attire. "What do I do?" He turned his eyes, full of disbelief and fear, to Rollant.

"As I have said, Your Majesty." Rollant took a deep breath. "Be the absolute monarch, institute the reforms, and enforce them with military backing. The people will see you on their side and make their voices heard."

"I have not raised taxes to keep their burdens light," Louis muttered, shaking his head.

"My king, I saw poverty in the Parisian streets, and anger fuels their survival." Rollant ignored Louis' impatient sigh. "They don't care that you haven't raised taxes—they want you to hear their concerns and take action. They are crying out because the tax burden is already too heavy, and they are hungry. They think the nobility hoards bread and cattle, unaware that famine, drought, and overseas rebellions contribute to their suffering. They blame you for failing to provide relief. They see their hard-earned wages going to you, with little returned besides the lamplighters and street cleaners, which they hardly care about."

Louis scoffed. "Don't they see I'm trying to make their lives easier? I even gave them the legal right to practice their faith of choice."

"No, they don't because they are starving and sick." Rollant shook his head and said against his better judgment. "You want to be a king of the people, then listen to them. Be their king. Engage with them directly. Show them you will act on their behalf. Tax the nobility and clergy, and use the military to enforce it."

"That is enough, Rollant," Louis snapped. "I will not use the French military to enforce a tax on the nobility and clergy like a reckless tyrant."

"You are king; be a king," Rollant urged, holding his voice steady, knowing this conversation would not have happened even three hundred years prior.

"Leave me," Louis said and hunkered down in his chair.

A rising surge of frustration pressed against his tight chest. He was vested after his day with Élise. The people's struggles and Élise's circumstances had sliced through his indifferent façade. With a deep breath, he settled himself and gathered his thoughts as he walked to the door. This was not him. He was the silent relic, the king's bodyguard. He never wanted to be an advisor. He spun on his heels. "My apologies, Your Majesty. My tone was uncalled for. I beg your royal pardon. I shall keep my silence as I always have."

Louis leaned forward on the table and dropped his head into his hands. "Chevalier Rollant de Montvieux," he said after a sweeping breath. "You will never need to ask my pardon."

Rollant approached the table. His golden rapier bounced at his hip in stride. "The people grow restless, Your Majesty. There is truth in their whispers, but you are not beyond saving."

Louis chuckled. "My passions are in locksmithing, not in governance."

He uncovered his face and massaged his temple with two fingers. "Minister Brienne has already failed again at instituting his universal land tax. He insists on calling the Estates-General."

Rollant shook his head. "My King, if I may," he said, pausing to wait for permission, which came through a small wave of Louis' hand. "Do not call an Estates-General. Instead, engage directly with the Third Estate. Hear their concerns, establish goodwill, and soften their demands. Given the political and environmental conditions, let them see you are trying. Releasing a small amount of power now may prevent an outright revolt and solidify the crown."

Louis' brow furrowed. "If memory serves," he softly bounced a closed fist on his forehead, "You had told me to rule with absolute authority."

"Yes," Rollant said, with eyes lighting up. The king had heard him. "I did, and I still urge the same."

"But engaging directly with the Third Estate would be ceding authority, as you said, 'releasing power'?"

Rollant dipped his head in acknowledgment of the king's hesitation. Had the king done what he had said to do ten years ago, perhaps their predicament would have been nonexistent. "Your authority remains absolute, but power, your power, is influence. By engaging directly with the kingdom's people, they will feel a part of it and respect your authority again."

Louis considered Rollant's words with lips tightly pressed. "But why not through an Estates-General?"

"Because, Your Majesty," Rollant said, resisting the urge to shake his head. "You bypass the nobility by going directly to the people. You present the crown untainted by the nobility's greed. Show the people you are their king and are working for them. Bypass the Parlements and enforce your land tax. Save your people, and they will save your crown."

Louis sighed. "You have been away for too long. I have tried to bypass the Parlements with Minister Brienne, but the reforms are rejected and not upheld."

"Then enforce it with the military." Rollant made a fist. "To show the power of the king."

"Oh, Chevalier, we are past the Crusades." Louis leaned back with weary eyes. "We are not kings of the medieval ages anymore. We are an advanced people of diplomacy and democratic approaches."

Rollant suppressed the urge to yell and kept his voice steady, though his fist rested on the hilt of his rapier. "If I may, Your Majesty, throughout the centuries, I have seen hunger drive the most docile man to violence. Already, your people speak of acting where you fail to provide relief."

"I have not failed. I have prevented further tax raises!" Louis said, slamming his hands on the table.

Rollant bit back a sigh, wishing his immortality came with the ability to rewind time. He had chosen the wrong words to say, and they were back at the beginning of their cyclical conversation.

"You have indeed, my King, and done so mightily!" Rollant said, resigning himself to be just a guard. He took place at the edge of the room, hands by his side, back straight, stare unfocused with a steady breath.

The world of present problems would be gone in a hundred years. It didn't matter.

Louis dropped his head back, his shoulders sagging. "Oh, Father, thou art in Heaven," he prayed. "Show me what I must do."

Rollant closed his eyes as he waited for the king to finish, knowing the path he needed to take was right before him. He only had to decide and proceed on the road to the crown's salvation.

He thought of Élise, and for her sake, he stepped forward once more with softer words and reframed his advice. "Your Majesty, the solution is not simple, and no one has all the answers. But your people, the hungry, the poor, are not enemies. Listen to them without the Parlements' interference and the nobles' interests skewing their needs. Let them see you as their protector. Your willingness to show you understand their plight will prevent far worse."

Rollant paused, holding Louis's gaze with an intensity softened with humility.

Louis's fingers drummed against the table; his gaze drifted below Rollant's shoulder and filled with heavy thought. "I want to be the people's king, Rollant, yet every day, I feel that dream slipping away."

Rollant leaned forward. "Then let it not slip, Sire. With a single decision, you can reclaim it. Engage with the people's leaders sincerely and directly. This is not ceding power—it is ruling in a way they will respect."

Louis bounced his hand on his thigh before folding his hands behind his back. "I will . . . consider it further."

CHAPTER 10

A Time to Break

PALACE OF VERSAILLES, AUGUST 1788

NEARLY SIX MONTHS passed in slow decay.

August came after a bitter stalemate between the Parlements and the crown, and Minister of Finance Étienne Brienne fell. Not from violence but exhaustion.

He had failed to sway the Parlements.

Failed to impose reform.

Failed to revive a dying economy.

The crown's failures were no longer whispered behind fans or muttered in cafés. They were shouted from the street corners.

Then came the Parlement of Paris, which declared in bold defiance that the king's will alone could not make law. They demanded the Estates-General—though they had always accepted taxation without it.

And in a panic, Louis reached for absolutism's last dagger. At Minister Lamoignon's urging, he tried to dissolve the Parlements and replace them with a Plenary Court—a new body loyal only to the crown. Louis took Rollant's advice—six months too late and only half of it.

Rollant had stood in silence as the orders were given, knowing what would come. What might have steadied the crown years ago would instead sharpen its collapse.

Soldiers were sent to enforce the new court. But barricades rose in the streets, and stones rained from windows.

The Plenary Court collapsed before it could even assemble. Lamoignon was dismissed in disgrace. The crown could no longer borrow or bluff. And Brienne, with the coffers hollow at last, suspended payments and vanished from Versailles.

The nobles remained unbent, and Louis refused to raise taxes.

In desperation, the king summoned a name the people had never forgotten.

Jacques Necker.

The Genevan. The banker-turned-minister. The people's idol. The common man's illusion of salvation.

Rollant stood in the corner of the King's Cabinet, silent and still. Duty bound him to Versailles, but his thoughts drew back to the streets of Paris, where hunger bred rage, and rage had learned how to fight back. He feared what would come next.

Necker's blaring banker voice dipped and dove through the air. "The stock exchange has risen suddenly because of my appointment, and we have secured further loans to stave off bankruptcy."

Louis interrupted the man's report. "Our future is brighter with your appointment, that is certain. There is hope yet." The king cast eyes on his newly appointed financial minister as if Necker's words alone might reverse the kingdom's fate and calm the storm rising beyond Versailles' gates.

Rollant blinked long and slow at Louis' fascination with Necker and repeated Louis' word in his mind: *Hope*.

Necker had charmed the people nearly a decade ago with a report that masked the kingdom's ruin behind glittering numbers. His popularity had helped bring down Calonne's reforms—and later Brienne's—yet now he stood triumphant, granted the seat he had always coveted. A savior in the king's eyes. A saboteur, in Rollant's.

Necker's thin hands moved in grand, sweeping gestures—as if puppeteering France itself. His self-assured tone grated like splinters beneath the skin.

Before his reconnaissance trip to Paris, Rollant wouldn't have cared what passed in the King's Cabinet. He would have stood there, as he always had, indifferent, trapped in a monotonous life that would never end.

Necker's voice cut through his thoughts. "I propose we convene the Estates-General to achieve the necessary tax reforms, and the Third Estate should receive equal representation to the First and Second."

Rollant's chin dropped slightly, and a small sigh passed over his lips. Necker was proposing the exact opposite of his advice to the king.

Louis nodded in agreement with Necker.

Rollant tried to remind himself that they would all be gone in a hundred years, and he would be left unscathed. Glancing at the row of kings' portraits on the wall, he tried to return to his prior mindset. He tried to cling to his old callousness, repeating that nothing mattered. That everything was futile.

But the memory of Élise lingered, stirring within the truth: even brief lives left marks. Lives—frail and impermanent—held meaning, and decisions made would echo long after the present generation was gone.

What happened in the King's Cabinet or on the streets of Paris was important. He had known centuries of lives slipping past him, and none had touched him except Élise.

Rollant glanced at the flickering hearth, his breathing steady and even, trying to anchor himself. The room was warm, almost stifling, and he felt the tickle of sweat at his collar as Necker's words continued to stir the urge to take action. Rollant said nothing but shifted his stance toward the king, drawing all eyes—his silent plea not to summon the Estates-General.

Louis met his gaze—and turned away. He'd dismissed Rollant before, brushed off his warnings like dust from velvet.

Louis snapped his gaze back to Necker. Fabric rustling was the only sound echoing in the room as Louis adjusted himself in his seat. "Continue," he finally said, making his decision, and did not look back at Rollant.

Necker's voice droned on, an endless hum of debt and diplomatic promises. It might have lulled any other man to sleep.

The crown was doomed, and centuries of building power through blood and sacrifice would come to nothing. Rollant stood as powerless as the suit of armor in the hallway, and King Louis sat in a trap. They both seemed ensnared by forces they could have controlled but did not.

As he watched Louis hang on to the minister's words, tap his fingers on his chair's armrest, and fidget with his lock in the other hand, he wanted to ask the sorceress—whom he had not seen since the day she cursed him—what would happen if the crown fell. Would the curse lift? Would he become mortal?

The thought eased his shoulders: a world where eternity no longer bound him. But the prospect of release, once enticing, now unsettled him. He had only just begun to feel alive again.

Élise—she out of all those he had tried so hard not to care about—had stirred hope in him, unexpected and unwelcome, and not felt since the day the sun rose over Damascus as they laid siege to recapture the Holy Land some six hundred years prior. But in the back of his mind, he knew for certain that hope had no place in a cursed man's heart.

Rollant's gaze dropped to the polished floor until Louis' voice cut through. "Chevalier." The king appeared before him and shoved him lightly on the shoulder.

Rollant blinked and scanned the room, realizing he was alone with the king. "Your Majesty," he said with a dip of his chin and a stain of embarrassment on his cheeks.

Louis's eyes flickered with an impatient glimmer. "We are promising to hold the Estates-General in May. After the announcement, I need you in Paris once more. Be my eyes and ears. Observe the people's moods, demands, and ambitions. Bring me word of the issues they mean to raise.

Report to me on what stirs the Third Estate so I can be ready for the Estates-General."

Rollant thinned his lips. He quieted the urge to speak. There was still time to engage directly with the Third Estate before the Estates-General, but the King would no longer listen to his advice. The King would deepen the divide.

Instead, Rollant nodded. "It will be done."

THE KING'S announcement came at the end of the month, and Rollant found himself on his horse returning to Charonne in mid-September. He didn't race along the path this time. His horse trotted, and his mind wandered—to Élise.

He wondered if she was still alive and had endured the riots and the hunger that plagued the streets of Faubourg Saint-Antoine. And if she was alive, would she remember him as fondly as he remembered her, or had the relentless grip of survival erased every memory of him?

He'd follow the King's command. But he feared what he might find in Paris. And more than that—he feared what Paris might awaken in him.

CHAPTER 11

The Cost of Jealousy

FAUBOURG SAINT-ANTOINE, PARIS, SEPTEMBER 1788

ÉLISE PULLED the dough and folded it over, pressing her palms into the creamy, gooey mess. The ache in her shoulders told her she couldn't do it anymore, but she pressed on. Her fingers ached as did her feet. She wanted to rub her neck but feared Gabin would return and see the flour wasted. He had taken the day to seduce another woman who wanted to be his. Little did that woman know about his raging temper.

Gabin had never been kind to her since Rollant, forcing her to work double shifts every day while he took off doing whatever it was he did. She believed deep down he knew she was attracted to Rollant and wanted to leave him. It had gnawed at his stomach. She had betrayed him and there would be no forgiveness. She had lied to Gabin, but he couldn't prove it. It ate at his ego, and he took out his frustrations on her. She had to hurry her rounds to the children and the widows and Madame Marie, now forced to the nighttime, which cost her hours of sleep.

The days had turned into months and months into seasons. Rollant had lived with her in her mind and dreams, though his face began to melt away into memory. She knew then what he meant when he had told her Amée's face was a blur. The wish to be able to afford a painter to capture a loved one's likeness in a portrait to keep for all time would have been nothing short of a miracle. Though she mused, Rollant may not recognize her with the dark circles under her eyes and her waist and arms being thinner than they already were. Her lips were cracked from the heat of the oven. She wanted water, but it was empty. There was no time to fill it.

As the world spun around her, she hoped no customers would come in. She fell against the bread counter, pressing the weight of her whole body into her hands on the dough.

"Is Monsieur Roux around?" a man's voice startled her, and she stood up straight. She rolled her neck without looking over her shoulder.

"He is out," she said, groaning and folding the dough once more with considerable effort. "May I help you?"

"I wanted to borrow his apprentice again," the man said, his voice becoming more familiar.

She stopped.

It couldn't be.

It had been more than half a year. The joy in her heart sprouted, but she plugged the spring. She blinked in rapid succession, trying to clear her vision. Her arm dropped to her side as she hesitantly turned around.

Rollant's brow furrowed as his eyes ran down and up her body. She was repulsive to him, she figured. Hollow cheeks and threadbare clothes adorned her once full face and semi-healthy body. He saw the woman Gabin had hollowed out, a shadow of what she'd been. But maybe it was better this way. It was better for Rollant to see how broken she was so he wouldn't stay long enough to get himself hurt. Her gaze dropped.

"You don't want me," she whispered and turned around to the dough again. She expected his footsteps to leave, not come closer. In an instant, he was beside her—his deep eyes staring into her soul.

"Has Gabin done this to you?" he asked. "Because of me?"

She wanted to cry, but there were no tears left to fall. But she wobbled, and he steadied his hand on her lower back. There was his touch, as gentle as always. He hadn't changed. She lowered her head to his chest. Her body betrayed her, a reminder of how little she had left to give. For so long, she had carried the weight of survival, her will being the only force keeping her upright. But it had its limits.

"I've missed you," she said without answering his question. She expected his arms to fold around her, but instead, a rigidity formed beneath his shirt, and his hands remained as they were.

"What has he done to you?" His hand hovered over her cheek.

She wished for his embrace but took his lack thereof as rejection. She was too miserable to be touched. She couldn't lean on him. Depending on anyone was dangerous. If she let herself trust Rollant, she wondered what would happen when he left.

No, she had to stand on her own, no matter how much her body screamed otherwise. She lifted her head from his chest. "Nothing to bother you with. I am just a weak woman, unable to bear life," she said, pushing him away to no avail.

He scoffed and turned her face to him with a soft touch of her cheek. "Élise, if you believe what you just said, then you are not the woman I have been thinking of all this time."

Her eyes softened. She had been on his mind, but she doubted she would take up space in that big, beautiful head of his any longer. She steadied herself against the counter, feeling dizzy. The heat from the oven was too much, though winter seemed to have come early, and its freeze had set in her bones.

Rollant glanced at the dough. "I have eight days until I am on a boat to the port," he said, meeting her gaze that drifted to his. "I have saved enough to take you away from here, give you a home."

A home. She had never had a home. She'd had a bed and a blanket on nights she was lucky.

"Will I live with you?" she asked, steadying her other hand against his chest.

His face pained. "I don't know. Tensions are high, and all military men must be in the service or risk treason." He cleared his throat to signal what the penalty was for treason. "I will be gone most of the time, and I may not come back alive."

Her heart crumbled at hearing she would be alone, and Rollant might be dead. She shook her head back and forth, the pain bouncing between her temples.

"I can't do it." Both hands shot to her head, leaving her body unsteady on her feet. He caught her again with one hand to steady her against his chest. "I've never been on my own before," she whimpered.

His lips brushed the top of her ear. "I think you have always been on your own," he whispered. "You just didn't know it."

Her knees buckled from exhaustion, and he caught her under the arm, swung her weak frame into his embrace, and then studied her face with an intensity she had never seen.

"Why do you stare at me? Is beauty fleeting?" Her head rolled to his shoulder. "I'm so tired, Rollant."

"Can you breathe?" he asked in a timid whisper.

She took a deep breath. "Yes," she said softly.

He visibly swallowed and nodded. "Good. Where is your bed? I'll take you to it."

"I can't. I have to work, and Gabin is out at the brothel."

Rollant's face fell slack. "Gabin is at a brothel, while you work here at the brink of death?"

Her lips drew thin, teeth bared in defiance. "But he feeds me."

"Not well enough," he said. His grip hardened on her flesh. "Do you want another life, Élise? One without me in it but one out of this?"

She might have answered the question differently had she had water or food to think clearly. She shook her head. "This is all I know." Leaving meant freedom, but it also meant facing Gabin's wrath—a wrath that would not stop at bruises. She couldn't disappear, not yet. Not without knowing the streets better, not without knowing who to trust. She had to have a plan, and she had none.

"Say the word Élise, and I will have you a new life," he said, his whispered words fluttering the frizzed strands of hair by her ear. He started for the door, but she held on to his shirt.

"No," she whispered. Leaving seemed as impossible as staying, a life where each day blurred into the next, where survival outweighed freedom. Further, if she escaped, Gabin would indeed find her and make her life even more unbearable, and she doubted he would do her the good service of killing her quickly. The fact she couldn't imagine life without Gabin or Rollant made her feel weak and insignificant, not worthy of Rollant's time or coin. She had to find the independence and freedom she rallied behind without either man, but the path to that reality was lost on her. In frustration, she gnashed at Rollant.

"Leave me here. Live your life. Forget me." She wanted to be angry at him for leaving, but he was only guilty of trying to help. The bitterness in her words was not directed towards him, but towards herself. In her most significant moment of weakness, she found she was a woman of hollow ambitions, tied to a life she knew, a life she had become a shadow within. She didn't know how to leave—hadn't the courage or the strength.

"Élise." Rollant's voice dropped and filled with pleading. "I made a promise to remember you always. I cannot forget you. You are my friend, Élise. I cannot watch you suffer."

"Then leave." She swatted his arm and stared unfocused at the ceiling. "It's what you are good at."

He had left her there. She blamed him, but she didn't. Fear rooted her in a pathetic life. "Now, now, before someone sees you," she groaned and kicked her legs to force him to let her down.

Her words were slurred. Each time she blinked, her vision blurred. The shadows crowded her sight as if the world was darkening. Her heart beat too fast and yet too slow. She still had so much to do. Upon uneasy legs, she tried to make her way to the counter but slumped, and her knees almost hit the floor. Rollant's arms were quick to wrap around her and hoist her up.

"You are in no shape to work, Élise." His hand gingerly cupped her face. "You need rest."

She half-laughed. "Rest shall never be mine," she muttered and regained the strength to stand, knocking his arms off of her. Her life wasn't horrible before Rollant, but it had become unbearable. She only imagined what it would be like after this second encounter.

Her feet carried her to the bread counter. She began pulling the dough again, but her arms shook from fatigue. Rollant stepped behind her and slid his hands down her arms, calming the ache. He was warm and grounding. His fingers interlaced with hers, lingering a second longer than he should have and anchoring her trembling hands. His words were low and almost lost to the sound of the streets just beyond the door.

"This will not be forever, Élise, I promise," he spoke a quiet oath.

At his assurance, she leaned her head back into his chest and gave up her will to stand. He lifted her in his arms and carried her to a nearby chair in the corner by the fire.

The next thing she knew, warm water was at her lips, and she drank freely. Then, warm bread. At first, she refused, muttering, "Gabin will not like me eating his bread."

Rollant's soothing response allowed her to eat. "I paid for it."

Soon, it was gone, and through her eye slits, she observed Rollant snatch Gabin's apron from the wall and take up the dough she'd abandoned. Her eyes closed fully, and for the first time, she believed, even briefly, that true rest was within reach. She only had to be brave enough to take it.

HER BREATHING FELL into an inconsistent cadence as she slept. She was sick. Rollant knew it. He racked his mind, trying to figure out how to help her. Where could he take her? To an inn?

No, Gabin would realize she was missing, and she might be dead the next time the king sent him to Paris.

Could he take her to his home in Charonne? Hide her away from all this madness?

He sighed.

No, she was too headstrong for that, and he risked her discovering his true nature and the lies he'd told. He rubbed his neck after he finished her chores. Making bread was a skill he had learned at one point several hundred years ago when he had nothing else to do, but he wasn't sure how the bread he'd just made would turn out. He licked his lip, hoping Gabin wouldn't punish her for it.

He replaced Gabin's apron and approached her. For the briefest moment, he allowed himself to touch her—but only enough to keep her steady on the chair. It was all he dared to do with the sorceress' curse. She hadn't died in his arms when he picked her up, and it only meant he hadn't fallen in love with her yet.

No, not yet—he wouldn't fall in love at all.

She was just a woman who needed help—a temporary friend in his immortal life.

"I do not love her. I cannot love her," he whispered. He draped his coat over her shoulders and brushed a stray hair from her face.

A customer came in and saw him. "Is she well?" the man asked.

Rollant shook his head. "No. How can I help you?" he asked and took Élise's place behind the counter.

"I don't deal with strangers," the man of about thirty years asked. His clothes were torn and his coat was thin. Two teeth were missing in the front of his mouth.

"I am Rollant Montvieux," Rollant said. "I came here to barter for bread but found Élise near exhaustion and the Gabin Roux nowhere to be found."

The main pursed his lips and scanned Rollant's clothes. "The name's Malo." He narrowed his eyes as he studied Rollant's face. "I remember you." He pointed a dirty finger in his face.

"I have been away at port. I'm a navy man," Rollant offered by way of introduction. He grabbed a loaf of bread and wrapped it in a rag to scoot it across the counter. "What'll it be?"

Malo turned a corner of his mouth up. "You are either stupid working for free or you have a good heart. As a kind word of advice, don't tell anyone you are in the king's navy. People around here don't like people like you." Malo raised an eyebrow and jerked his head toward the bakery entrance.

Rollant chuckled. "Good to know. I appreciate the frankness."

Malo waved off the gratitude and laid three pieces of textiles on the counter. "This is my usual barter. You'll just have to trust me."

Rollant scanned Malo's arms. He wasn't carrying anything else, so he assumed there was no maliciousness.

A shadow loomed in the door as the trade happened.

"Élise!" Gabin's voice boomed, jolting her from her slumber.

She shrunk beneath Rollant's coat. Gabin's head spun to Rollant. "You?!" He marched inside with fists. "I told you to leave, sea rat!"

The counter blocked Gabin's approach, but Rollant stood calm, a fury building behind his eyes. Diplomacy might win this, and if not, he'd knock the man out. No, he couldn't do that. Élise wouldn't leave, and it would only worsen her plight if he did such a thing in front of a customer.

As much as it pained him, the only way was to appeal to Gabin's vanity and pride. He saw the fist coming, but he didn't flinch and let it come. The smack of Gabin's fist against Rollant's cheek echoed throughout the bakery. Rollant overplayed its impact, staggering to the side and catching himself on the counter to avoid a fall.

Malo had stepped back with eyes darting between the three of them.

"Quite the fist there, Monsieur Roux," Rollant said as he maneuvered his jaw to sort the pain. He rubbed the sore spot.

"Get out, thief!" Gabin's eyes were bloodshot, and spittle formed in the corner of his mouth.

"Gabin, leave him alone," Élise whimpered from the corner. Sweat dripped from her brow, and her breaths were ragged.

"Shut your mouth, you lazy harlot!" Gabin spun around with a tightly wound fist pointed in her direction. "I'll deal with you later," he spat between clenched teeth.

"Monsieur Roux," Rollant began. "Élise is sick. I understand it could be maddening to walk in and see a stranger at your counter and your apprentice asleep in the corner, but I assure you, when I came to barter, she was not well and nearly fainted from sheer exhaustion."

Rollant gestured to Élise as he approached Gabin. "She has a fever."

He laid a hand on Gabin's shoulder as a subtle gesture of control, speaking in soft tones but loud enough for Malo to hear. "Now, do you as the bakery owner want to lose business because your apprentice is sick and your customers refuse to buy the bread she made."

"She is not sick," Gabin yelled at Élise and shook his fist at her.

But Rollant continued in his calm, firm tone. "She has a fever. Look at the sweat beads on her forehead."

"That is from hard work by the fire," Gabin said, turning to Malo as if to reassure him Élise was not sick.

"Even still, it might be best if I take her to the charity hospital to ensure it is not a fever. I saw one in Le Marais that is strictly for women and children. You could tend to your bakery in the meantime."

"Get up, Élise," Gabin barked, and Élise struggled to stand upon uneasy legs. "Go see if you have fever, and Rollant, get out. Don't touch her. She is my woman, not yours."

"Are you sure she can make it on her own?" Rollant ignored him and nodded toward Élise, who fell to her knees and hands.

"I'll take her," Gabin said and shoved Rollant's hand off his shoulder.

Rollant asked, "Then who will run your bakery, Monsieur Roux?"

"You will," he barked, pulling Élise by her arm. She moaned at the roughness.

"I will not. I have errands to run and barters to make before my next port call. This is your business. I don't even know how to make bread. I just followed Élise's directions, but I am thick-headed. I don't know how it will turn out, and I don't remember what she told me to do."

Rollant was going to make sure Gabin couldn't argue. He gestured to the customer at the counter. "Malo, here, was kind enough to give me his usual barter, but do you have that much trust in the rest of your customers or the travelers who come here on the bakery's wonderful reputation? Your bakery could be near out of business by the time you return."

Gabin sneered. His eyes slipped to Malo as he thought.

Élise coughed and groaned at the weight pulling on her arm.

Gabin finally made a decision. "Fine, take her to Le Marais. I want her back before sundown."

"With a fever?" Rollant asked with a lifted eyebrow. "And chance spreading her illness to all your customers and friends?"

Malo shook his head and finally piped up after keeping his mouth shut the entire exchange. "I don't need any fevers, Gabin."

Gabin dropped Élise to the floor. "Bring her back as soon as the fever breaks," he barked in Rollant's face and thudded behind the counter. He slammed his apron over his head and yelled at Malo. "Anything else?"

Malo shook his head. "Just leaving."

Rollant grabbed his coat while repeating, *I do not love her*, in his mind. He hesitated before scooping Élise into his arms using the coat as a sling. She weighed nothing, and it squeezed his heart.

Malo adjusted the coat to ensure Élise was adequately covered.

It was a dangerous line he was crossing, holding her so close. At any moment, she could breathe her last, and it wouldn't be due to the fever. His jaw grew taut as he adjusted his internal motto: *I will not love her*.

They left Gabin muttering indecipherable curses while folding dough.

The busy street didn't notice Rollant carrying a woman. But Malo leaned in and whispered, "Got some real nerve on you, standing up to Gabin like that. He ain't the sort to forget it come next time."

Rollant nodded off the compliment and was bitter toward the man for not helping Élise for the last six months. Surely, he was a regular bakery customer, and he said nothing and did nothing until it was almost too late. "When your friends are hurting, it is worth the wrath of a bully."

Malo patted Rollant's shoulder. "It is easier when you don't live here where the bully controls the bread."

Rollant bit back his words. Like the king, he was far too detached to understand what these people lived through. "My apologies, Monsieur."

Malo nodded, accepting it. "You have my respect. Safe travels to Le Marais," he said, then continued on his way.

By the time Rollant reached the charity hospital in Le Marais, three hours had passed—a trip that should have taken an hour at most. Every step sent fire through his shaking calves, and his fingers were numb with pain. The sun was hot overhead, and the burning bite of fatigue coursed down his trembling arms. Though Élise was light, her weight became almost more than he could bear. But he willed his body steady for just a little longer.

"Help!" he called through gritted teeth, and two nuns came from the tent. Their long ankle-length habits bustled around their hurried legs.

"Oh, my little girl," one said, and the other sighed, "Oh, poor dear."

They gestured Rollant into the tent. The strain in his neck was visible, and his vein throbbed from the walk. Light-headed, he swayed in his gait. He could only imagine how Gabin would have taken her—pulled her down the street and might have left her for dead.

"Put her down," a nun said and gestured to the only remaining empty cot, which sat low to the ground. He fell into the thin cushion, his elbows beneath Élise. His head hit her bosom. His chest heaved. He'd made it. He groaned at the stabbing pain in his extremities. His arms were stuck, unable to move.

A warm hand came to his brow. "You are exhausted," a nun said. "Here, lay back, rest until you recover. We will take care of her."

They helped him untangle his arms before he collapsed on the floor, gasping for breath, unable to move. Another nun came with a small cushion and placed it under his head.

"The street is uncomfortable, but we don't have any more cots."

He shook his head with heaving breaths. "I'll manage," he finally spurted on his exhale.

"Bless you, my boy," the nun whispered, dabbing his brow. She tilted his head to give him a sip of water before easing his sweaty head on the cushion. Then she turned her attention to assist the other two nuns, helping Élise. They wrung rags and dabbed her body.

"Grab the mint and the teas. We need to cool the fever," the nun's soft voice intermingled with the other voices from beneath the tent. Children's whimpers and women's wails pierced the air.

So much suffering. Élise was just one small part of it.

He was immortal but unable to do anything about it. The suffering had long been something he ignored, a quiet decision to lock himself away, severed from humanity. But now, as he lay on the cool stone street, the cries around him pricked his heart, a sensation he'd forgotten. It was easier to let others suffer without hearing it. Everyone died except for him. He had not let himself feel for a long time, but Élise had cracked the wall he'd put up, and their wails flooded his soul. Maybe he could not help everyone, but he could help her.

Élise's hand dangled off the side of the cot. Rollant reached for it to ensure she was not dead. He heard her labored breaths as he squeezed her fingers with his thumb and forefinger before his hand fell to the earth once again, spent.

One nun began to pray, "Dear Holy Lord, Father of all mercy, hear our humble pleas. Take this child, this dear soul, in your arms. Like so many, she carries the heavy burdens of life and is bound by trials that test the spirit and, now, the body. In your shining glory, comfort her in this hour, heal her, and give her peace. If this child walks in shadows far from your light, remind her you have not forsaken even the least among us. If she has gone astray, fold her back within your glory. If she has no shelter in this life, may she find it within your mercy. Ease her pain and give her hope, Blessed One. We are certain you see and love all your creations, though they feel unworthy. Amen."

The words of the prayer were not lost on Rollant. God loved him in his self-imposed severance. He doubted the sentiment, but the prayer soothed his soul, if not for Élise's sake, for his own.

After a while, stiffness replaced the fatigue in his muscles. His breathing had calmed, and knowing Élise would be cared for by these gracious nuns sent a wave of peace through his body. And at that moment, he dared to imagine a life free from suffering, even as his curse forbade it.

He regained his strength and sat up to look at Élise on the cot. Her dress had been pulled down, and the nuns rubbed an ointment into her chest. He noted the bruises on her skin, but realizing the intimacy of the care being given, he turned his gaze aside to preserve her dignity. He stood despite the ache and stepped away to grant her privacy. A nun, recognizing his presence, gasped and spread her arms wide to cover Élise before escorting him from the tent. "You are good to bring her. We will take it from here. Come back at sundown, and we will give you a report."

He looked over his shoulder before addressing the nun. "If a man from Faubourg Saint-Antoine arrives for her, tell him whatever you need to make him leave. He's done this to her," he gestured inside. "Make him leave."

Her brow furrowed. "Isn't she your wife?"

He shook his head. "No, she remains unmarried, but don't let a man named Gabin take her. She is sick, and she needs rest from him." He doubted Gabin would make the nearly hour walk, but in case he did, he wanted the nuns to protect Élise if he could not.

The nun touched his cheek. "You are a good soul," she whispered with an understanding nod.

Her words were simple and genuine and left him feeling strangely forgiven.

"I see you care for her." Her hand retreated beneath her gray habit robes. "We shall not lie, but we will do our best to divert this man's attention should he come. She is in God's hands."

Rollant urged. They had the see the severity. "She will not survive if he takes her back too soon. Please, do what you can."

"I will make the others aware, although we all saw her bruises." Her gaze averted, and Rollant grew sick to his stomach.

The nun sighed. "Now, young man, get something to eat and drink if you can find it, and rest your weary legs. I'm not sure how you carried her from Faubourg Saint-Antoine."

Fine lines creased at the corners of her eyes beneath her starched white bandeau. "To be young again," she whispered. "Rest now, my son."

She slipped inside behind the tent flap.

Rollant turned with an unexpected wetness on his cheeks. He wiped the escaped tears away quickly before anyone noticed.

Only one other woman had moved him to tears before—Amée.

With a slight limp, he made his way to a nearby cafe and inn, choosing a seat near the window where he could still watch the tent hospital.

He ordered water, wine, and stew and stretched his aching leg as he listened to the hum of voices around him. At the next table, a group murmured about the recent promise of an Estates-General. His muscles slowly relaxed, and he lowered his head and stretched his neck to relieve the tension. Glancing back at the hospital tent, he clasped his hands over his mouth, gathering his thoughts.

Whatever came next, he vowed he would not abandon Élise to this fate. Perhaps it would be the closest to redemption he could ever hope to find.

CHAPTER 12
Light of the World
LE MARAIS, PARIS, SEPTEMBER 1788

THE SHARP STING of mint landed on her tongue and in her nostrils, forcing her eyes open. Her gaze drifted to the unfamiliar surroundings. Rollant's voice drifted to her from beyond the tent flap, steady and low, a tether she didn't yet know she was holding on to. Faded light seeped through the white fabric walls, casting soft, golden hues over the patients as if angels were overlooking them. The tent was filled with the murmur of women and a child's cough. The faint scent of dried herbs clung to the cool air, and gentle footsteps rustled like whispers against the cobbled street beneath.

A nun placed her hand on Élise's brow. The nun's hand was soft and cool, a stark contrast to the rough treatment Élise was accustomed to. Her low and loving voice soothed more than her fever.

"Steady, child," she whispered. "Allow us to care for your fever and your bruises." The nun's eyes darkened from sorrow as she glanced down at Élise's body. The nun's careful eyes traced the bruises marking her arms, a look Élise had seen before in the eyes of strangers who looked upon her with pity. But the nun didn't turn away. Instead, she lifted Élise's hand, pressing it gently against her robes, and whispered, "You are safe here."

The mint's heat gave way to a dull ache that seemed to pulse through her limbs. Its reprieve filled her nostrils and soothed the throb in her head.

Her mind flashed back to the bakery—the suffocating heat of the oven, Gabin's sharp voice, the weight of flour-dusted loaves in her hands. But the world here was softer, more peaceful, with no need to move. Her throat tightened, unfamiliar emotions welling up at the nun's gentle words. Pity, she understood, but this place was something she'd never experienced before, as if the warmth of kindness reached deep into her soul.

"I can't pay you." The words weakly fell over her lips.

"There is no cost, my child," the nun whispered.

"You may call me Élise," she said.

The nun smiled. "My name is Sister Francine. I will watch your fever and tend to your illness." She cupped her hand behind Élise's head and lifted water to Élise's lips.

"Not too much," Francine said in soft tones before taking the cup away. "Try to sleep, my child. Your body needs much rest." She laid a thin blanket atop Élise's shoulders, swept Élise's hair from her face, and began to hum; it was enchanting.

"What is that song?" Élise asked, the words barely audible. "It reminds me of my mother."

"It is the Song of Mary," she said. "Magnificat. I am singing it for praise and thanksgiving to our Lord that your friend brought you, carried you even, from Faubourg Saint-Antoine, and more so, that we can help you."

Élise relaxed into the cot with her eyes lingering closed. Her fingers brushed Rollant's coat, still draped over her body beneath the blanket. He had carried her and taken her from Gabin to a place like this. It was more kindness than she could remember receiving in her lifetime. The weight of his coat around her shoulders and his old wood candle smoke musk had kept her from falling asleep in his arms. She had tried to walk a few times, but he caught her when her legs failed. She heard his labored breath in her memory, a reminder of his silent, steady presence. The corners of her lips turned up. Gabin would never have brought her so far to be cared for. "Can you thank Rollant for all his kindness if I shall not see the morning?"

Francine's gaze warmed. "You will see the morning, but I shall tell him when Sister Ingrid requested he return for a report this evening." She put both hands on the edge of the cot. "Now, sleep." She pushed off, causing the cot to rock slightly. Then Sister Francine was gone.

Élise turned to her left and then her right. Sleeping women and children were all around, and the tent blocked the sun's warmth, though the stale air reigned supreme within the fabric walls. The nuns moved quietly between the cots, dipping with water and cool rags for their patients. The remnant drops of water still beaded on her forehead.

Such a different place than the bakery, she mused. Her body felt weak and vulnerable, but she relaxed into the cot, letting the tension of the hardships she'd faced melt into the linen beneath her bare shoulders.

She had no idea where she was except that she was in a safe place, as Sister Francine had said. Rollant had brought her there, and she'd be forever thankful to him. Yet as ease settled over her, uncertainty flickered at the edges—safety was as foreign as it was fleeting as she knew Gabin would reclaim her in a few days' time and Rollant would have to leave again.

As she drifted into sleep, Élise clung to her resolve, reminding herself that survival was her own burden to carry. This place, these people—kind though they were—were only temporary. The bakery's hold would tighten again, and she would once more find herself navigating its harsh confines alone.

A FAMILIAR, steady voice broke through the haze of Élise's sleep. It was low and gentle, almost a murmur against the soft cries within the tent.

She blinked.

The edges of her vision still blurred, but her senses sharpened at the sound of her name.

"Élise," the voice spoke again, hushed and close, a quiet insistence in each syllable.

Her eyes darted to assess her surroundings in the dim glow of evening filtering through the tent. A small panic rose in her chest before she realized where she was: in a place of safety.

A sigh of relief rolled off her dry lips. Her gaze followed the sound to its source, and there Rollant stood, just beyond the open tent flap, speaking with Sister Ingrid. He watched her, and his expression softened when his eyes met hers.

"She is improving," Sister Ingrid was saying. "The fever has lessened, and she took water and broth earlier. You were right to bring her. How are your legs and arms?"

Rollant nodded, his gaze never wavering from Élise. The relief in his eyes was plain, and for a moment, she felt the strength of his attention, something solid and settled after days of feverish drifting. "I am fine," he said. "I only worry about her."

"Rollant—" Élise's voice came out weak, hoarse, but his eyes met hers immediately, and the rest of the call faded on her lips. She wanted to thank him, but her throat tightened.

Again, a hand, soft and cool, rested on Élise's forehead and coaxed her attention away from Rollant's gaze.

The gentle evening shadows framed Sister Francine's face as she whispered, "I gave him your message when he first arrived."

From beyond the tent, Rollant's voice rose again, low but insistent. "How long can you keep her?" he asked, the words tinged with concern. It drew Élise's gaze again.

"We will keep her until her fever is gone and she is strong enough to walk back to Faubourg Saint-Antoine." Sister Ingrid's voice carried. "But for now, rest is what she most needs—and perhaps you could do with some rest yourself. Return in the morning. She will be well cared for."

There was a pause before Rollant nodded and said low, "I will return in the morning. Thank you, Sister Ingrid."

Élise reached out in an urge to keep him from leaving. Rollant hesitated to go, but his body was already half-turned. His form lingered just beyond the tent flap for a few moments longer.

Sister Ingrid urged him on. "Get some rest, Monsieur de Montvieux."

Sister Francine pressed gently against her arm, lowering it to the cot. "You are safe here, Élise. He is leaving at our request. Men are not welcome in this hospital, which is meant for women and children. There is another up the street for men," she whispered in reassurance as Rollant disappeared.

A pang of fear struck Élise's heart. He would leave her behind again, but she pushed the thought aside.

Sister Francine reassured her again as if she could feel the sudden tension of his departure. "He stayed at the cafe across the street nearly all day. There is an inn nearby, and I'm sure he will be there until his coin runs out."

The cool evening wind exposed his absence, but knowing he was still close by gave her the calm Sister Francine asked of her.

The rustle of Sister Ingrid's habit sounded in the otherwise quiet tent as she re-entered and secured the flap for the night.

"Sleep now," Sister Francine's voice echoed in her ears.

It was the last voice she heard until the stream of daylight found her eyes in a small slit of fabric in the tent wall.

Sister Francine knelt beside Élise's cot and rubbed a mint oil on Élise's chest. "Good afternoon, Élise. Your fever finally broke, but I am still trying to cool your chest. You've been coughing in your sleep."

Only one memory was fresh in her mind. "Rollant? Where is he?"

"He came every morning and night for the last three days."

"Three days?" Her heart raced as she ran her hands up her face and into the base of her hair. Gabin would be irate. She tried to get up to go back.

But Sister Francine's unexpected strength stayed her with a firm press of her hand against Élise's chest. "Yes, three days. You've had a rough go, poor dear."

"I must get back to the bakery," she said and strained against Sister Francine. Her eyes grew at either the nun's strength or her own weakness.

"No, you must rest." Sister Francine's palm pressed flat against Élise's chest over top of Élise's rapidly beating heart.

"But Gabin," Élise began, but Rollant's coat pressed against her leg as she fought to sit up. Its fabric balled between her fingers.

"Rollant would want you to stay," Sister Francine whispered as Élise emerged victorious in the fight to sit up.

Élise pulled Rollant's coat to her chest at the mention of his name. "But

Rollant cannot protect me. He has to leave again. I should return and reduce any consequences I have incurred for being away."

Sister Francine removed her hand and whispered, "I see." She shook her head. "There are other options, Élise."

Their eyes locked. "What do you mean?"

"There is always God's care, Élise."

Élise scoffed. "I am not going to be a nun, if that is—."

"I'm not asking you to become a nun." Sister Francine's eyes drifted to the bruises littering Élise's skin. "You have endured so much, and from what Rollant has told Sister Ingrid, much of it, you have endured alone. You are strong, with a strength many do not understand, but you don't have to fight every battle by yourself. I ask only that you give yourself the chance to heal. No one will hurt you here."

Élise's fingers curled tighter around Rollant's coat. Gabin's rage loomed in her mind—his fist slamming into the counter, his accusations cutting deep. His cruelty had always been a constant, but leaving for days would surely warrant a punishment worse than any before.

"I can't," she murmured, more to herself than the nun. "If I don't return, it'll only make him angrier. It's better to return now."

Sister Francine's hand was gentle but firm on Élise's shoulder. "Sometimes the hardest choice is to stop returning to the same hurt. Here, you can rest. Just for a little while. You deserve that much."

The tears begged for release, but Élise refused to let them fall. Not again. She had a good life with bread, warm clothes, and a covered place to sleep. And Gabin wasn't always cruel. Sometimes, after a long day at the bakery, he'd leave the last scrap of bread for her. Those moments, rare as they were, had been enough to make her believe she could endure the rest. To think of anything more only made the days harder.

"My child," Sister Francine whispered. "I've seen people rise from the depths of despair. I believe God guides us to where we need to be at the right time with the right people." She paused, offering Élise a small smile and a cup of water. "But whether you believe in that or not, I hope you find a strength of your own to carry you forward to peace in this life."

Élise finally wrapped a loose hand around the cup of water offered, letting its cool underside balance in her lap atop Rollant's coat. She stared at its soft, fluid ripples for a long moment, her chest rising and falling with shallow breaths. The idea of staying in the hospital tent felt absurd, almost indulgent. Yet the weight of her exhaustion pressed harder now, pinning her legs to the cot.

"It appears you have worked your body very hard to this point of illness," Sister Francine said softly. "It has carried heavy burdens."

Élise turned her face away, her jaw tightening. "It's nothing," she murmured, her voice guarded. "I'm used to work."

Sister Francine rubbed a small circle on Élise's back, her touch steady and kind. "We all have our burdens. But even the strongest shoulders can collapse under too much weight. Please rest here, Élise. I believe the Lord sees our burdens. Let us carry some of it for you."

Élise sipped the water until she threw it all back and returned the empty cup to Sister Francine. No one had ever offered to help her carry her burdens. They only added to them. Her brow furrowed as she debated accepting the kindness and facing Gabin's wrath when she returned. She had been gone three, four days? What was one more?

The nuns' calming presence soothed her and wore down her defenses. She reclined on the cot. Her head rested on the thin cushion, eyes fluttering shut. The conversation had exhausted her. She'd been foolish to think she could walk back to the bakery, even if she tried.

Sister Francine dabbed Élise's chest with the cool mint oil. "The world can be cruel, but it is not unkind forever. Here we will care for you. That is a blessing, whether you see it from God or the kindness of others."

"I don't believe in blessings, or curses for that matter," Élise said flatly, her voice cracking under the weight of her exhaustion.

"Belief does not come easily. But know there is always hope. Whether it is in God, or in people like Rollant, or in yourself, you are not without it." Sister Francine's voice softened further, a prayer barely spoken aloud. "Rest now, Élise. You'll need that strength when the time comes to choose your path."

The soft lullaby of whispered prayers and distant hymns filled the tent, a gentle harmony that melted into her mind. Even if she never returned or could escape Gabin, she would remember this place, where people asked for water and rest without being scolded, beaten, or forced to work.

Her fingers still wound around Rollant's coat, its weight a reminder of his silent, strong presence. He'd come back for her in the middle of riots, stood up to Gabin, risked his own safety, and carried her to the charity hospital. He had checked on her every day and still had not requested the return of his coat.

The thought filled her chest—not with gratitude, but with something warmer and, maybe, more dangerous. It was a feeling too foreign to trust completely. Her past had taught her trust meant peril, and safety was a ruse. Rollant would leave again; men always wanted something, even the kind ones. It made her ache. What kind of man did such things without expecting anything in return? Or if he was like all the rest, what would he demand, and would it be worse than Gabin?

Soon, Sister Francine moved on to another patient and left Élise alone to ponder the days' worth of fragmented memories. Regarding the nuns, the hospital was a tent, soon to collapse and be moved elsewhere. They'd quickly forget her and the lofty promises of hope. Promises cost nothing. Kind words were easy to speak.

The bakery, Gabin, was always going to be there. His rules were clear, brutal but reliable: pain for shelter, labor for bread, obedience for life. She'd accepted the costly barter.

Kindness without a cost didn't seem right. It didn't seem real, though it appeared genuine. Rollant hadn't flinched when Gabin's fists flew or wavered when she collapsed on the street. Even now, though the autumn nights were cool, he'd left his coat with her.

Perhaps not all men sought to own what they saved.

She pulled Rollant's coat to her chin and turned to her side. His musk gave her peace in a way only his scent had.

As the faint hum of the Magnificat filled the tent, a tentative hope sparked in her chest, not for others, France, but for her own life. Perhaps survival didn't always have to feel like a losing battle. Maybe, as Sister Francine had told her, there were other options.

Rollant's coat, the hymns, the quiet care of the nuns—all of it hinted at a world beyond Gabin's fists. She didn't trust it, not yet. But for the first time, she wondered if she could, and she allowed herself to sleep deeply, lost in a potential world that could be hers.

mit ihren
umliegenden Gegenden

gezeichnet von Thos. Lantz
gestochen von Joh. Spiegel
1805.

Asnieres
St. Ouen
Clichy
Courbevoye
Villiers
Neuilly
Mont Martre
Le Monceau
Puteaux
Suresnes
Chaillot
Passy
Auteuil
Boulogne
Vaugirard
Issy
Belleville
Montrouge
Chatillon

CHAPTER 13

The Shadow of Desire

LE MARAIS, PARIS, SEPTEMBER 1788

ROLLANT'S GAZE washed over Élise as the sunlight glinted off her raven hair as she stepped from the tent. A youthful glow adorned her cheeks, and the dark circles under her eyes were faded. Though her steps were unsteady, she moved with quiet determination. Seven days had passed since he carried her to Le Marais, yet her resilience and will to live struck another chord of admiration within him. He had already completed the king's mission but needed to stay the full ten days he had been allotted to ensure Élise was well.

That morning, Élise stole his heart even more when she had given up her cot when a young mother came to the hospital, but there were no more beds. However, she was still in no state to achieve the probable hour return walk to Faubourg Saint-Antoine.

Sister Francine stopped her and drew Élise into her arms. A whisper was exchanged before Sister Francine glanced at Rollant with a warm smile.

Rollant had never been jealous of the nuns' path, but that day, at that moment, he wished he could hold someone in love like Sister Francine. He dipped his chin to the nun before she disappeared within the tent, and he and Élise closed the distance between them. Élise pressed her forehead to Rollant's chest, and it took every muscle drawn tight to stay his hands by his side to not chance ending her life.

Instead, his fingers graced her cheek and tilted her head up so their eyes locked. In the brief moment, he wondered if a kiss would bestow upon her the same fate as his embrace. But they were in the middle of the street, already drawing wayward glances due to their proximity.

"How are you feeling?" he asked in a whisper, to keep his lips distracted.

"Better. I have a clear head, and I'm full of hope," she said, covering her hand with his.

"Does that mean you will allow me to help you start a new life?" he asked.

Immediate fearful tears filled her eyes, and it was answer enough for him.

"I see," he whispered. "Then," his voice trailed off, not knowing how to help her. "What else can I do for you within the next three days? I am due to return to port after that."

Élise blinked back her tears and took a half step back. Their hands fell to their sides. Doubt cast over her features. "That is why I cannot go with you. You will leave, and, with it, any protection you so generously offer. And what happens if you die? If you never return? I will be left in a place with no resources and no contacts. No family. No job. Nothing. At least at the bakery, I know I have food and a place to sleep."

"I promise you, I have enough coin for your lifetime," Rollant said, his voice steady, though he knew protection was a promise he couldn't keep from the palace.

"Gabin will find me, and he knows those I have been helping," she said with a bitter undertone. "His anger, I fear, knows no bounds. He will hurt them to hurt me. He is spiteful and is capable of many types of revenge. I'd be abandoning them." She blinked back her tears. "And so, I must go back."

Rollant's chest tightened at her words. The way she spoke, resigned yet firm in her resolve, stirred something deep within him. She would sacrifice a better life to protect others—even those who might never know the sacrifices she made. It was a strength he'd seen before.

He had been the same—brash, headstrong, and willing to carry any burden to shield those weaker than himself. He had thrown himself into battle after battle, never once considering his own safety if it meant saving another life. And for what? Rollant clenched his fists at his sides. Sacrifices like those left him in a shell of the man he once was.

He drew a slow breath, his gaze softening as he looked at Élise. She didn't realize it, but her strength was the same, tempered by a quiet resilience that had kept her alive through unspeakable hardship. He feared she would meet the same end if she didn't learn to choose herself. He needed to convince her, though she had only known cruelty disguised as care.

"Then let me put you up in an inn here in Le Marais before you go back. You can rest and eat as much as you need."

Élise stiffened. Her gaze dropped before darting between to the passing crowd. Her fingers curled into the fabric of Rollant's coat draped around her shoulders.

Rollant noted the tension in her shoulders and the way her jaw clenched as if holding back unspoken words.

He kept his voice even as he guessed at her sudden change in demeanor. "Two rooms, Élise. Separate rooms."

She exhaled sharply, her fingers twisting the fabric of his coat. "Two rooms?" she repeated, barely above a whisper, her eyes darting to his. There was doubt there, and something else—fear, suspicion.

Rollant nodded, softening his tone to reassure her. "I would never ask anything of you. You do not have to be afraid of me."

Her shoulders eased a fraction, but she didn't meet his gaze. Instead, her eyes fixed somewhere over his head, as though searching for answers in the distance. The silence between them stretched, her breaths shallow.

He couldn't blame her for her hesitation. He'd seen too many women broken by the promises of men who claimed to care for them. The thought soured his stomach. He wished he could show her that not all kindness demanded repayment.

When she finally spoke, her voice was fragile and conflicted. "I cannot add to your cost, Rollant. Three days is a hefty expense. I can walk."

Rollant shook his head, willing her to see the sincerity in his eyes. "The cost is nothing compared to your well-being, Élise. And the owner gave me a good deal since I stayed multiple nights. Please, rest in an inn. The road to the bakery is long. You will be tired before you even begin working again."

Her grip on his coat loosened, but she didn't let go. She was weighing something—he could see it in how her lips pressed together and how she shifted her weight. He recognized the look all too well. He'd seen it in women across war-torn villages, women who had learned to fear even the smallest acts of kindness, knowing they often carried unspoken debts. It wasn't mistrust of him; it was mistrust of the world.

"Two rooms, then?" she asked.

"Yes, two rooms," he assured her with a steady voice. "I will never expect anything in return, Élise." The repeated statement caused her to find his gaze. His eyes smiled for the first time in centuries. "Thank you for allowing me to care for you."

The street chatter filled the silence between them as Élise's chest rose and fell with quick breaths. "Why? Why do you care?" she asked. "Sister Francine said the same, but life has taught me kindness is never free."

"It is when the giver truly cares," he said. "Just as you give away your bread to those who need it when you hardly had enough yourself. You do not expect anything in return from them."

Her shoulders lowered, and her eyes fluttered shut. A sigh of relief softened her features. The corners of Élise's mouth turned up, and a soft laugh erupted from her lungs. She shook her head, clamping her mouth shut. She said nothing for a moment before a concession escaped in a whisper. "Well, I suppose you are right."

Rollant's gaze flicked over her shoulder, catching sight of two men loitering at the corner. Their postures were relaxed, almost lazy, but their sharp gazes betrayed their intent. One nudged the other and muttered something, both pairs of eyes locking onto Élise. A chill ran through him. Gabin's grip stretched farther than he'd thought. He should have known Gabin would never let go of what he claimed as his; he would never release his grip on her. The men were there to observe and report back, chained to Gabin's will like Malo and so many others who couldn't intervene, bound by their dependence on his bread. Control was always the same, enforced by brute strength or mastery over survival. Rollant clenched his jaw. He had to act quickly, convince them Élise was still not well, or her life would hang in the balance when she returned to the bakery.

"Gabin sent his men to see about you," he whispered, locking eyes with Élise. "If you want the inn, pretend you are having trouble standing."

Élise wobbled on her knees, her movements unsteady but deliberate as she leaned into him. Rollant wrapped his arm under hers, supporting her as her weight pressed heavily against his side. Her warmth seeped through his shirt, and for a brief, agonizing moment, he wondered if his curse could harm her through such a simple touch. The thought was maddening. His longing for closeness was cruelly twisted by the ever-present threat of the curse that shadowed his every action. Every touch felt like a gamble, the price of which he dared not calculate. He adjusted his grip, careful not to pull her closer than necessary.

"Let's get you somewhere to rest," he said and led her to the inn he had stayed at earlier in the year.

Rollant glanced back. The two men watched them a beat too long before trailing them. He had to let them follow until they were convinced. "Really lean in, Élise. They are following."

As Rollant guided her into the inn, Élise's fingers lingered on his shirt. Her steps faltered, each one slower than the last, her weight sagging into Rollant's arm as though she could no longer bear the effort of standing on her own. For a moment, he thought she might let go, her hand trembling as if the gesture was too vulnerable to follow through. But then her grip tightened, the fabric bunching under her quivering fingers. The silent act spoke louder than words—gratitude, perhaps, or trust beginning to crack through the armor she wore.

After Rollant and Élise arrived at the inn, the two men returned to the Rue de Faubourg-Saint Antione, hoping to report that Élise was still unwell—or at least that was Rollant's wish.

Rollant ensured Élise had all her essentials every morning, including fresh water, bread, cheese, and stew. In the evenings, he heated the water pan to warm her bed and brought more bread and stew, yet remaining true to his intentions, he left her to sleep alone.

On the third morning, Rollant knocked on the door, holding a special gift.

The door opened to reveal Élise standing fresh-faced with an open smile and dewy skin. The ends of her hair were still wet, leaving dark water blots on her threadbare dress.

"Come in, Rollant," she said and side-stepped to allow him to enter. She glanced at the fabric bundle in his arms while he noticed the empty water pitcher near the basin and the wet washcloth.

"I'm glad you felt well enough to wash yourself," he said, putting the gift on the bed. "I brought you a present that I hope can last you through the winter."

She gave him a sly eye with a slight upturn of her lip. "What is it?"

"Open it and see," he said with an unexpected anxiousness fluttering in his belly.

She perched on the edge of the bed, gesturing for him to sit beside her. He lifted a hand in polite refusal, stepping back instead. He couldn't risk being that close.

A soft wave of disappointment crossed her face, but she turned her attention to the first bundle and unrolled it with care.

"A dress!" she exclaimed, rubbing the thick fabric through her fingers. "A new dress?" She gathered the garment into her arms and smiled as bright as the Sun King's City of Lights. "Oh, Rollant, I needed a new dress; I haven't had one in years."

Rollant's lips curved into a small smile at her joy, but his chest ached. Such a simple gift—and yet, for her, perhaps it wasn't simple at all. He had seen too many like her, living hand-to-mouth, scraping by in a world that seemed bent on crushing them.

"Do you like the color?"

Her fingers smoothed over the long skirt, her touch reverent. "I love it. The green is beautiful. So different from brown and gray."

He hesitated, his gaze dropping to the floor. He could have chosen a gown fit for a noblewoman, something rich and fine. But a dress like that would have been a burden, not a blessing. She couldn't return to the bakery in such a thing—or to Gabin. The dress had to be practical, even if his heart wished to give her the world.

"I wanted you to remember every time you wear it that you are unique and have a strength that leads," he said, lifting his gaze. "I chose green because it reminds me of you," he said softly. "No matter what's thrown at you, you endure. You find a way to grow."

Her smile faltered, the glow in her eyes dimming as her gaze fell to the dress in her lap. "I very much doubt that." Her fingers stilled. "But… maybe someday." She glanced at the second rolled fabric on the bed. "Another dress?" she asked, before he could respond.

Rollant shook his head.

She grabbed it in haste, unfurling the length. "A coat?" Her jaw fell agape. "You gave me a dress and a coat?" Her brow furrowed. Suspicion replaced her earlier joy. "Why . . . why would you do this for me?" she asked, her voice barely above a whisper.

He stilled. "Because you deserve it, and you need it," he said, simply. "And because I can."

She smoothed her hand over the fabric, her fingers lingering on its sturdy weave. "They are beautiful," she whispered, but her voice wavered. A shadow flickered across her expression. "But . . . it's too much. I—I'm not used to gifts."

"It is not," he reassured her. "I can give you a life like this. It can be on the other side of Paris or outside the city walls. You can have peace, Élise." His voice held a longing, an urging for her to take his offer.

"Gabin will find me, just as he found me here."

"He only found you because I told him where I was taking you—the charity hospital in Le Marais."

Élise shook her head. "Gabin hates you. He tells me every night. Gabin would find me. I'm sure of it." Her gaze drifted to the door of the inn. "It's not just Gabin," she whispered, her voice thick. "It's… everything. The bakery, the streets, the hunger—it's all I know. What if I leave and fail? What if it's worse than what I have now? I need to go back; I have to return to him. He could hurt my friends to spite me. They've gone days without bread already."

Rollant studied the outline of her profile, envisioning the bruises that would likely migrate from her arms to her cheeks in time. "Choose yourself, Élise. This one time, do what is best for you."

Tears welled in her eyes as she stared at the garments on her lap. Her breath caught in her throat. "Even if I did . . . If I tried, what about you?"

"What about me?" Rollant asked, kneeling before her.

She wet her lips before adjusting her posture. Her eyes closed, accompanied by a deep breath. "Must you go back?" she asked, toying with the fabric. Her eyes opened to slits. "What if we began a new life together?" The question was almost inaudible.

He wanted to promise her the world, to vow he would stay at her side no matter the cost. But the chains of his curse were heavier than the darkest oath he'd ever taken, and the lies he carried—his persona as a navy man, his very purpose in Paris—were a wall he could never let her breach. To protect her, he could only offer her freedom from Gabin, not himself.

"I am bound by oath, Élise, and I am a man of my word." The sting of guilt hit him deep in the belly. He had lied to her. He was not a man of his word, but maybe she would never find out. He would just become a memory to her. Maybe one day, she would find someone who loved her like he wanted to and provide the resources and protection that she needed to feel safe.

Her gaze found his again, and the tears fell from their welling. She touched his jaw, and her lips brushed his cheek, a fleeting warmth that burned through the icy walls he had built around his heart. He wanted to pull her closer, to lose himself in her touch and return her kiss tenfold. But the weight of his curse sat thick between them, an invisible barrier he could never cross, a silent specter that forbade what his heart wanted most —to shield her in the one way he could not.

"If I could leave, I would. If I could have a life with you, I would," he whispered, kissing the back of her hand to satisfy his desires. Slowly, he returned her hand to her lap.

"Even to a king who hates his people?" she asked through clenched teeth.

Rollant rubbed her fingers with his thumb. "I don't think he hates anyone. I think he does not know what to do. It's why he has called the Estates-General."

Her gaze turned inward, and her hand slipped out from under his hand. "Well, it is easy for you to say, you who are paid with coin." Élise pulled the dress and coat into her crossed arms. "You get to reap the benefits of us, don't you, Rollant? And then look like a savior when you come around, throwing coins at all of us miserable people." She jolted up. "Is that it? Is that your fee? Do you have an ego to fill? Are you trying to buy my affection with coin?"

Rollant dropped his chin to his chest and slowly rose to meet her. The proximity to her lips unnerved him. His lies were stones in his chest, dragging him down into silence. If she knew the truth, she would see him not as a savior but as a fraud. His heart beat out of his chest beneath a steady voice. "Do you believe that, Élise?" His gaze bore through hers.

After a moment, she couldn't maintain his intensity and turned away. "I–I don't know what to believe." A quiver in her lip preceded a quiver in her arms. She glanced at him before returning her gaze to the floor. "I know why I give away bread that I need," she finally said and sat down again on the bed. "But I don't know why you are so kind to me." Her voice broke. "I was thirteen when I learned kindness is always a barter."

Rollant, against his better judgment, sat beside her.

Élise's fingers smoothed the edge of the coat. "My aunt had left me outside on a snowy night as punishment for not delivering my quota of stolen items. I knew I was going to die that night."

Pain gripped Rollant's heart as he listened.

"There was a boy, older, named Rene. He snuck me a thick blanket. I thought he cared about me and wanted to save my life." She hesitated, her eyes flitting up to meet Rollant's briefly before darting away. "But I found out he was saving to get away from my aunt. Made me hand over all my coins. I didn't want to. I was stubborn, but I didn't want to be left out in the cold again with nothing." Her voice faltered. "I was afraid to die."

"I'm sorry Élise," he whispered.

"After Rene had saved up what he needed to escape, he did. Never once looked at me after that. Probably never thought of me again. I was just a means to an end. I was hungry and cold, and all he did was exploit me."

"Like Gabin," Rollant said.

Her eyes shut tight. "Gabin saved me from my aunt. He's never made me sleep outside."

"How did he save you?"

"He came and saw me. Gave my aunt a large delivery of bread with no barter and took me with him."

"He bought you?"

"No," she said, shaking her head. "My aunt wasn't going to let me go."

"You could have left with him—"

"Gabin is a lot of things, but he wouldn't buy me. I'm not a slave."

Rollant stayed his tongue as she released a shaky breath and continued. "Kindness always has a cost. I thought Rene cared about my life, but he didn't. Gabin needed help with his bakery. And you?" She shook her head. "I don't know yet."

Her gaze finally lifted to Rollant's, her expression guarded. "That's why I don't believe in free generosity. Even when it's well-meaning, it always takes something."

"Even the stranger who gave you a loaf of bread when you had nothing and caused you to vow to do the same?"

Her brow furrowed. "But he didn't know me. You know me. You have admitted your feelings for me. I—I don't understand you. Spending your hard-earned coin from years at sea and serving our horrible monarchy on . . . me. For what purpose? You've told me we have no future together. For what gain? I am no one."

"Don't speak such lies," Rollant said, placing a hand on her upper back. "You are resilient and adaptable. I admire you, Élise." His mind told his tongue to stop and not drag the poor woman into his doomed life. He pulled his hand away.

"So admiration is your motivation?" she said, her eyes pleading with him to reveal secrets he closely guarded.

Six hundred years of holding his emotions at bay, shedding any semblance of the man he once was, to simply exist in an eternal state, cracked under her silent plea.

"My mother and my wife and daughter, my brothers," he said with a tightening chest. His mind told him to shut his mouth, but he kept speaking. "They all died because I could not save them. My brothers died in wars fought for the king. My mother died because her love for my late father and brothers couldn't be filled by me alone. I lost my entire family by the time I was eight. Amée's family took me in. Ten years later, I was married, a knight—navy man"—he corrected—"with a child on the way. I was off on the king's wars, and I wasn't home to save my wife and my daughter."

He realized his gaze was not on Élise but her coat. "I lost myself," he said, lifting his gaze to hers. "I shut the world out. It was easier to endure each day if I felt nothing. And then I heard you, speaking of freedom and hope with a voice that even the angels envy. You reminded me what it felt like to care. You gave me a spark of life again, Élise. I am indebted to you."

Her lips parted at the revelation, but no words came.

"Kindness may not be free, but it is I who repays you," he said as he let his fingers grace the side of her arm.

His confession landed between them, its weight settling in the silence. Élise's gaze dropped, her fingers curling tightly around the garments in her lap, clutching them as though they could protect her from the truth he had laid bare.

He needed her to say something; he couldn't bear to break it himself. He'd answered her doubt, but whether she would accept it was not up to him.

Her shoulders stiffened as she shifted where she sat.

Her voice, when it came, was barely above a whisper. "I don't . . . I didn't know." The tremble in her words cut through him. Her fingers twisted the coat hem, the motion small but desperate. "I didn't think someone like you could feel so lost."

Rollant's chest tightened. Someone like him. He understood what she meant, though hearing it still stung. A knight. A sailor. A man with coin enough to spare for gifts, but not the life he had pretended to lead.

She finally looked up. Her gaze was raw and unfiltered. It unsteadied him. She shook her head, her breath catching audibly. "You said I gave you a spark of life again," she murmured, her voice again heavy with doubt. Her words sharpened as she continued, almost accusatory. "But what if I can't keep it burning? Will your gestures cease?"

Rollant wanted to reach for her, to soothe the quiver in her voice and the doubt in her eyes, but the curse mocked his desire. His hands rested at his sides, fists clenching briefly before relaxing. He couldn't promise her a future he couldn't give.

"You gave me the spark, it's up to me to keep it burning. That's not your burden," he said, his voice steady despite the turmoil in his chest. His gaze softened as he held hers. "You're stronger than you realize. Even if you don't believe it now, you will."

He watched as her lips pressed into a thin line. "But I did nothing," she murmured.

"You did everything." His soft smile reached his eyes. "The coat and the dress," he said quietly, "aren't just for the winter. It's for wherever life takes you next—because I believe you can and will choose something better."

Élise clutched the coat to her chest, her gaze dropping to the floor. "I don't know what I'll do," she said, her voice barely audible. Her lips pressed into a faint, straight line. "But maybe . . . you're right. Maybe I can choose something better . . . just not yet."

Rollant's heart swelled at her words, though he dared not show it. Instead, he leaned back, giving her space. "Wherever you go, Élise," he said softly, "I will give you whatever I can to support you."

She glanced at him then, her eyes searching his face, as if trying to decode the puzzle of his kindness. And for the first time, she didn't look away.

Rollant felt the weight of that moment—fragile, like the first green shoot breaking through winter's frost. It wasn't in full bloom yet, but time would tell if it would grow to maturity or wither beneath the strain.

CHAPTER 14
A Time to Choose

FAUBOURG SAINT-ANTOINE, PARIS, OCTOBER 1788

AGAIN, they walked too close, their hands loosely intertwined and hidden in the folds of their coats. As they neared *Au Pain Roux,* the sun was on course to set.

Rollant gave her a surge of strength. His grip was steady, his calloused palm firm yet warm against hers. The faint roughness of his skin spoke of labor, but his touch carried a gentleness she had never known before his.

Gabin's grip, like that of her father's and aunt's, had always been rough, cold, like a vice meant to control. Rollant's hand was different—it lingered like an ember, radiating a heat that seeped through her fingers and traveled up her arm. Even as the chill of evening bit at her exposed cheeks, the warmth of his hand made her forget the cold. It made her miss his touch before he even left.

For a moment, she let herself imagine what Rollant had given her for a few days—a quiet room of her own, the freedom to rise and rest without Gabin's fists dictating her every move.

But it was temporary—a dream, and dreams had no place in her life. Every time she tried to escape, she had been dragged back—first by her father, then her aunt. Each return was worse than the last. And what if Rollant held something darker behind his promise?

His deep voice broke through her thoughts. "If I could give you a life without fear, I would," he said softly. "I can still give you another life somewhere else, Élise. You don't have to go back."

Her tears blurred the sight of him as he stepped between her and the bakery down the street. His warmth left her as he withdrew his hand to keep any observers from witnessing their touch. He was a man doomed to be bound to the shadows of her life.

She studied him, searching for cracks in his words, for the hidden cost she'd always expected. But there was only sincerity in his eyes. Her fingers tightened around her new coat. For the first time, doubt wavered—not in him, but in the walls she had built around herself.

A sudden swelling in her chest told her that what Rollant offered didn't have to be a dream. She could still leave, but she had waited too long. Rollant had to return to port in the morning. There wasn't enough time, and even if there were, her hand would be empty as it had always been. She pulled the coat's collar around her chin. Her gaze drooped; the new wool did not hold his scent of old wood and candle smoke.

"I don't know when I will be on leave again, given the current environment," he continued as if reading her mind and assuming her dissenting answer. "But I will provide you a respite again should you want it when I return."

"*If* you return," she whispered, reminding herself why she could not take his offer.

He swallowed visibly. A quiet quiver wrapped his balled hand. "Élise, do you want me to stay away? I will if you desire it. If I—if I am making life harder for you—"

The hot tears burst from her eyes, and she quickly wiped them away. A man who asked such a question could not wish her harm. "Yes, my life has been harder since you entered it, but . . . I can't imagine the rest of my life without you being a part of it in some way."

The weight of her new dress and coat mirrored the dread gnawing in her belly, either at returning to the bakery or at the chance she would never see Rollant again.

"The thought of making your life harder hurts me deeply," he whispered. "Promise me, next time I come, you will not be in the same state I found you in."

She took a chance, grabbed both his hands, and stepped into his space. She wished for him to kiss her lips, her forehead, anything, but he remained a sentinel, protecting her from prying eyes and maybe even heartbreak should he not return.

"I will not let Gabin destroy me," she promised with an ache in the back of her throat. "I will find the strength you say I have."

"You've already found it," he whispered, leaning in. Her gaze dropped to his bottom-heavy lips, but he turned and gestured toward the bakery. "May I escort you in and see to it you are well before my departure?"

She nodded with her lips pressed thin. "Thank you, Monsieur," she whispered and took the arm he offered, embarrassed at her actions. What was she thinking? What if someone saw them and told Gabin? He'd beat her to death.

The wooden sign above the bakery door flapped in the wind. Each hit on the stone façade echoed like Gabin's fists against her flesh, jolting her nerves.

Élise hesitated in the shadow, hearing an inner door slam. Rollant stopped beside her, and she drew his gaze. Her eyes closed. "I have survived worse," she whispered.

"It's not too late," Rollant offered. "You can leave."

She shook her head. Without Rollant there after the morning, what would she do until he came back; *if* he came back?

Shadows loomed from the bakery entrance. Her fingers turned cold; her stomach rolled. The world spun for a moment.

Curse her life.

She only had to choose: certainty with Gabin or uncertainty with or without Rollant. Envisioning the pain and the hunger that awaited her from within the bakery almost made her choose the latter. But her friends needed her if they were still alive.

Madame Marie. The orphans. Their hungry faces haunted her. If she left, who would care for them? But maybe, just once, she deserved to choose herself.

She only had to choose.

Deep within her heart, she knew she wanted to leave Gabin. She spun to face Rollant and opened her mouth to accept his offer, but Malo and Yves approached the bakery's entrance.

Before she could accept, Yves shouted with a glint in his eye, "Élise! Good to see you back. You all well now?"

Her heart sank when Gabin's heavy footsteps ran to the door from inside the bakery. Malo's eyes darted between her and Rollant before Gabin burst into view.

"Élise!" Gabin's voice thundered beneath the setting sun.

Two of the men Gabin had sent to follow Rollant when he first came to *Au Pain Roux*, Olivier and Yanis, approached from behind her.

Yanis leaned close to her ear. "Decided to make our meeting, Élise? Glad to see you well."

She nodded with a tight, polite smile as Gabin pounded closer. He ripped her from Rollant's arm, yanking her away with a tightening grip just above her bicep.

"Be gone, you snake," Gabin threatened Rollant. "None of the king's dogs are allowed here. Be grateful we do not kill you where you stand." Spittle formed in the corners of his mouth.

Élise had forgotten about the riots and the hatred for anyone in the king's uniforms. Rollant had taken such a risk coming there for her. She ducked her head to hide the overwhelming flush of gratitude on her cheeks. The tingle in her chest expanded and reached the inner depths of her soul. The quiet burn of welling tears tickled the backs of her eyes. Her gaze rose from his toes to his perfectly chiseled face. He stood upright and folded an arm behind his back, and the other crossed his belly.

Rollant seemingly ignored the threat and began reporting on Élise's health. "Your apprentice was very ill and worked to exhaustion. Her fever lasted seven days. She would have died had you not allowed me to carry her to Le Marais. The nuns—"

"Shut it," Gabin gritted. He stepped toe-to-toe with Rollant. Each man was similar in height and build.

"Shut what, exactly?" Rollant asked with a lifted eyebrow. "I understand times are hard, but if she continues to be treated the way in which I found her ten days ago, your apprentice will be in the grave."

Élise glanced at the others. Malo's head dropped. Yves nervously looked around. Olivier and Yanis' eyes darted between Gabin and Rollant. More citizens of Faubourg Saint-Antoine gathered at the bakery entrance, watching the spectacle before their meeting. Élise forced the growing lump down her throat. None of them had ever helped her as Rollant had. They all saw the bruises. If Rollant could see them, they could too. She was alone, she realized, just as Rollant had told her. Gabin shook her arm and tightened his grip.

Élise grimaced at the pain.

"You're hurting her," Rollant interrupted whatever Gabin was saying.

"I am not. I'd never hurt my woman, my little dove." Gabin's grip loosened.

The man disgusted her, she realized. Calling a woman—his woman—"a little dove" was supposed to be a term born out of love and honor. Her arm went limp in his grip. He never loved her. Never honored her. And she had thrown away her chance to escape him. She was a fool.

"You all see how I care for her! I'd never hurt her," Gabin barked at the growing crowd and gestured to Élise as if she were a display of his generosity. "I took her in when no one else would, and this is the thanks I get? Letting a sea rat steal her from me for ten days, leaving me to labor alone for all of you?" He turned to Rollant. "You vagrant, listen here, she's well now, and you don't have to worry your pretty head. Get back to the water, sea rat."

Rollant countered again, and she knew Rollant would only leave on his terms. The corners of her mouth dared to rise at his show of calm power, yet worry etched into her brow. No one trifled with Gabin.

"She had a long walk here and is still not fully well," Rollant said. "Élise will need rest and assistance in the bakery to fully recover."

She shook her head slightly at Rollant, hoping to signal him to leave before Gabin turned the crowd against him to take his life. She would survive Gabin, but part of her survival hinged on whether or not she knew there was a possibility Rollant was still alive.

Gabin must have seen her headshake from the corner of his eye, for he growled, "You have something to say to your lover, Élise?"

There was a gasp through the growing crowd. "He isn't my lover," she whimpered at the renewed deathly grip he had on her arm.

Rollant broadened his stance. "We are not lovers," he said with a voice that rose above the murmurs. "And you are hurting her. You should let go of her arm before it bruises." There was an emphasis on his last word, *bruises*. It quieted the crowd.

Élise noticed the turned heads and the pressed lips. Again, they silently pleaded guilty to seeing but saying nothing. They all depended on Gabin for bread. They were all trapped as she was. She resented them for doing nothing, but she understood their plight. Rollant was her only advocate there because he did not rely on Gabin.

She had let herself become entrapped, and if she wanted freedom, she had to take it back, just as she told her community the first night she had met Rollant. It wouldn't happen overnight, but small steps and small actions would eventually allow her to be free of Gabin.

"You are hurting me," she said in a bold voice, its shake only audible to her ears.

"Shut up, woman," he said, shoving her away to square his shoulders with Rollant. He pushed a stiff finger into Rollant's chest. "I know you took three days to bed her at the inn, and she returned to me. So what does that say about you? Are you weak in bed, sea rat? A little limp fish you have?"

Rollant chortled. The high insult brushed past him as if it were nothing. "Oh, Monsieur Roux," Rollant sighed with an amusement perched on his lips. "I did no such thing." He shook his head. "She had her own room. If you can spare the hours' walk, go and ask the innkeeper. Two rooms. She is loyal to you, Gabin, and always has been. There is no need to hurt her. She has no feelings for me. You are the bigger man, the better man. You provide for her, and she admires your generosity."

The words came out with ease. So much ease, Élise thought they were true and wondered what other lies he might have told her that seemed genuine.

Rollant continued. "Don't treat her harshly because of me. It is all for naught. She loves you and only you, Gabin. If she didn't, would she have returned?"

"She knows I'd find her." His voice lowered as he tried to shove Rollant backward. His face flushed red at Rollant's rooted stance. "She is mine," he gritted. "She is my woman! Not yours! And now you know it. So don't come here again, or we will string you from the street lamp and put your little fish on display."

"I don't seek trouble, Monsieur Roux," Rollant said, unfazed by Gabin's threat. He glanced at Élise with an intensity that made her knees weak and made her know the following words he said would be kept. "But if harm comes to her again, I will find my way back here—and you won't like what follows."

A murmur rippled through the crowd at Rollant's bravery. Gabin's eyes swept over their faces before narrowing on Rollant like a predator on its prey.

"I've already told you," Gabin gritted. "I have *never* harmed Élise!" The crowd's hums of disagreement sent Gabin into a rage. He yelled at the crowd.

"You eat my bread every day, don't you? Who else in this entire district has offered you as much? I keep this bakery running for your families, and still, you stand there gawking, letting a stranger mock me in front of my own home!"

Some people nodded faintly, shuffling their feet. Élise's heart sank as she caught their hesitant approval of Gabin's words. She clenched her fists, willing someone to speak out, but their heads dipped, their gazes sliding away.

Gabin released a low growl. "I am the one who ensures you're not starving, and this is how you repay me? This is how she repays me?" He returned his grip on her arm and jerked her shoulder up. The sharp tug drew a gasp from her lips, but he ignored it, his voice building in anger and bitterness. "After all I've done, I am betrayed. This navy man comes here, flaunts his coin, takes my woman, and makes fools of us all!"

Rollant's gaze never left Gabin, and a look of boredom sat heavily on his face. "I already told you, Monsieur Roux, I did not bed Élise. She had her own room. False assumptions are not becoming of such an honored position in this community, such as yours."

"Liar!" Gabin sneered amid the crowd's murmurs and brandished a bread knife from his belt. Élise froze with her eyes wide. The crowd shrank back. The blade glinted from the bakery's inner lamp, its jagged edge as unpolished as Gabin's temper. The knife trembled in his grip as he fought to maintain control.

Élise's breath hitched. She envisioned the cold steel against Rollant's skin, him dying in her arms as Gabin's murderous rage sliced through her fragile resolve at the show of betrayal. It was enough for her to yell, "No! Gabin!"

Olivier and Yanis' hands shot up as they stood next to Rollant, and they shook their heads.

Rollant remained still and asked a simple question, "Are you to murder me with the bread knife with which you cut all the bread for your fellow townspeople?"

Gabin's blade stopped mid-air as Rollant continued. "A knife can never fully be cleaned. You'd be feeding my blood to your friends. I'd never knowingly barter for bread with another man's blood on it."

A murmur swept through the crowd, and flickers of doubt or guilt flashed on their faces. It was the first night Élise had seen any cracks in Gabin's control over them and Rollant had brought the cracks to light.

As Gabin thought about the implications, his knuckles grew white around the thick wooden handle.

"Gabin," Yanis whispered. "We saw Élise after she left the charity hospital. She could barely walk. Rollant took her to an inn and nearly had to carry her; she was so weak."

Olivier put a hesitant hand on Gabin's shoulder. "Rollant didn't mean anything by what he said. He saved your business, ensuring Élise was well so you could tend to the bakery, right? I doubt Élise would have even had the strength for an affair, Gabin."

Gabin snorted and popped his neck. He pushed Olivier and Yanis out of the way and leaned into Rollant's space, who still stood rooted to the spot.

Élise's fists clenched so hard they ached. Her shoulders tensed up to her neck. "Gabin, I love you," she whimpered. "Rollant is a gentleman. He never did anything inappropriate—"

"You didn't have a coat before, Élise?" Gabin asked, glancing back with eyes that ran the length of her new dress beneath her new coat.

"Yes," Rollant answered for her. "I saw she had no coat and a threadbare dress, so I got her a dress and a coat suited for the winter. I thought it would be one less expense for you and her. I know the cost of baking bread is at an all-time high, and I don't want you to lose your apprentice due to the coming winter's cold nor cut into the number of loaves you could make for these good people." Rollant gestured to the crowd.

"If you're so rich, why don't you just buy everyone bread?" Gabin asked and pointed his bread knife at Rollant's face.

Rollant smirked. "I am not rich, my friend. Oh, how I wish I were. I only have two coins left and need them to take the ferry up the river to the port, which reminds me, I must be leaving. The captain is not kind to those who tarry." Rollant dipped his head. "Goodnight, Monsieur Roux and Mademoiselle." He glanced at Élise, but Gabin moved to block his line of sight.

Élise shrank back, knowing Rollant could do nothing more. He had already done so much. She held her breath as she watched him walk away amid the parting crowd, his steps measured and deliberate, his frame becoming smaller the farther he went. It was as if a door was closing, and the warmth shut out. Each step carried away the only light she'd ever known. She should have gone with him.

Gabin spun around, knife still in hand. Red filled his bloodshot eyes, locked with hers, before scanning the crowd. "What is everyone waiting for? Are we to have a meeting or not?"

He pointed the blade's upturned tip at Élise's face. The knife didn't need to move anymore; it spoke in the way Gabin's fingers curled too tightly around the handle, draining the color from his flesh. His breath came hot and shallow, matching the tension of his shoulders as if poised to strike. The promise of punishment held her breath captive, and she only hoped to see the morning.

He slammed the knife back on his belt and entered the bakery. The gathered townspeople slowly followed, not meeting her gaze. Some shuffled their feet, others whispered behind cupped hands. None of them would speak up for her—they never had. Gabin's bread was their lifeline, and her suffering was the price they seemed willing to pay.

Élise felt the world spin as Malo offered her the chair in the corner. Her chin fell to her chest to process everything that had happened.

She took a few deep breaths, wishing Rollant would return for her, but she knew she had waited too long and lost the opportunity. She only hoped he would return soon. She wouldn't turn down his offer a second time. She'd figure out how to help her friends in Faubourg Saint-Antoine and live a life away from Gabin's control. Pulling a knife was the first time Gabin had ever done that, and she wondered if he'd do it again with her in the privacy of their room. Would the bread Gabin sold be tainted with the taste of her blood, her suffering seeped into every loaf?

She lifted her gaze to the people, who were half-listening to Gabin and half-staring at her. Hot tears welled in her eyes and blurred their faces, but she knew them—silent, complicit, trapped. Her neck throbbed, her knuckles ached, and fear had paralyzed her. But she refused to let it win again.

Her fingers slid along the coat's sleeves, hesitant at first, until she hugged herself and pulled the coat tighter around her. Rollant believed in her enough to buy her a coat—a green coat, the color of growth and life. Its thick wool shielded her from despair, buttressed her resolve, and constantly reminded her that this wasn't the end.

She yearned for Rollant's scent of old wood and candle smoke, a trace of him she could readily keep in his absence. Instead, it was a gift, a blank slate, waiting for her to make it her own. She turned her face into its upturned collar. Its wool absorbed her silent tears. She made a promise in the fibers—she'd been saved many times, and one day, she vowed to save herself.

CHAPTER 15

The Path to Destruction

PALACE OF VERSAILLES, DECEMBER 1788

SNOW CLUNG to the gilded windows of the Hall of Mirrors, but the December wind's howl was muted within the King's Cabinet. Within, the voices of royal ministers droned on as if the unrest in Paris were a distant tale instead of a storm about to strike. The lack of urgency turned Rollant's blood cold.

The King's Cabinet was a world unto itself—removed from hunger, from revolution, from reality.

"The Assembly of Notables refused to double the deputies of the Third Estate, but they decided to follow the traditions of the old ways," Minister Necker said with a despondent undertone.

Another Assembly.

Another path to failure.

Rollant's frustration simmered beneath his indifferent façade. His time in Paris had given him a growing sympathy for the people. He had pleaded with the King not to follow tradition, to meet with the people directly, to address their demands for equal representation, social justice, and fairness in law and taxation. But his words had landed like stones in a pond, rippling against the stillness and subsequently forgotten.

Instead, the King, persuaded by his ministers, had called another gathering of the nobility not to discuss changes or reform but to determine how to run the Estates-General promised in May of the coming year. They all clung to tradition like a raft in a storm, blind to the tide pulling them closer to ruin. The worst of it, Louis clung to the illusion that the people wanted a king, wanted him, and even liked him.

Louis rapped his fingers on the table. The sound echoed, firm and deliberate, in direct opposition to his character. "I voided the Paris

Parlement's order to double the deputies at your urging," he said, a trace of hesitation creeping into his voice. "But now you ask me to overrule my own veto? To stand against the Assembly of Notables? To alienate my nobility?" He paused, glancing at Necker as though seeking reassurance. "How will I not look the fool?"

The new Minister of Justice and Keeper of the Seals, Charles de Paule de Barentin, shook his head. "No, my King. That order should have come from the throne, not the Parlement."

Necker interjected with a cautious tone. "The nobility will retain their traditions, as they have insisted. But I fear their decision to adhere to the old voting system will make passing the tax reforms nearly impossible." He hesitated, glancing at Barentin before continuing. "Perhaps the Third Estate's grievances deserve more consideration than we've given. It may prevent worse disruptions."

"Minister Necker's 'considerations' have already weakened the crown's authority, emboldened the Third Estate, and increased his ever-growing popularity among them," Barentin said with a pointed glare. "Now he would have us bow to the mob in the name of reforms that will never satisfy them, only to grow his wealth and favor."

Necker shook his head. "I have done no such thing. The whole objective of this council is not to let the state go bankrupt. I am personally funding the state affairs as of current. We must have the tax reforms passed one way or another . . . and soon."

"Then we are back to where we started," Louis sighed and glanced at Rollant. The King wanted his guard to shield him from the decisions that needed to be made. The pamphlets about the Notables decision had already begun circulating throughout France, and outrage was felt in the streets. But Rollant clenched his fists at his side.

As Louis' attention returned to those seated at the table, Rollant focused on the portraits on the wall. He had never been so immersed in the king's affairs in several centuries. Only since meeting Élise had he cared one way or the other. Rollant owed his encounter with Élise to Louis's missions—a fact he could neither resent nor celebrate. Yet, the King's senseless decisions remained a bitter frustration. He had sent Rollant on these missions to Paris, and then ignored his detailed reports that held clearly worded actions and direction. He leaned on Rollant for his centuries of knowledge and experience, but failed to take any of his advice each time. Rollant was a pure royalist; however, the monarch had chosen time and time again to undermine his own authority, generation after generation, squandering absolutist power.

Rollant didn't mind the trips to Paris; in truth, he longed for another, if only to see Élise—see if she was still alive. Yet every departure left guilt gnawing at his chest for leaving her with that wretched man. He was torn between duty to the crown, wanting to see it upheld, and Élise, suffering because food was too expensive.

A soft sigh escaped.

Her time to die would come, and he would live on with a second heartbreak for another six hundred years, watching kings squander their birthright for indulgence and luxury.

King Louis tapped his fingers on the large oak table again and rolled one of his hobby locks in the other hand. Rollant noticed the hesitation in his movements and the glance at Necker for reassurance. It seemed the king was to answer a question, but words eluded him.

"Captain of the King's Bodyguard," Louis called to him, breaking the tension.

Rollant stepped to attention, his leather boots clacking softly on the polished floor.

"How do you feel about the traditions of the Estates-General?" Louis asked.

Rollant did not want to revisit the same report ad nauseam. The king was well aware of how he felt about the old traditions in the present situation, so perhaps Louis wanted the council to hear.

The fire crackled in the hearth, but the room remained indifferently cold. Rollant scanned the ministers' faces, each marked by arrogance or dismissal. The council had clung to old traditions, reinstated the Parlements, did not act a decade prior at the first overstep of Parlement power, undermined each other to gain fame, legacy, and riches, and promised an Estates-General, leading the crown into its current predicament—a storm even royalist ideals could not weather. The council had already decided, Rollant realized, that whatever words he spoke would be unwelcome.

"If you cling to tradition, Your Majesty, it will not anchor you—it will drag you under. Paris is already stirring, and another tradition will not silence the mob. Vote by headcount, not by social status. It matters not if the Third Estate is doubled when their vote counts the same weight as each of the First and the Second."

Barentin gestured to Rollant. "Am I the only one hearing this? Even the Captain of the King's Bodyguard is not loyal to the absolute authority of the King. Advocating for the mob?"

"I heard it," La Luzerne, the Minister of the Navy, said.

Rollant puffed his chest at the man rumored to be keeping the price of flour inflated.

"I am loyal to the crown," Rollant declared. He should not have said anything more, but the new Minister of Justice had inflamed the very reason for Rollant's turmoil of eternal life, and the Minister of the Navy spoke of hypocrisy if the rumors were true.

Rollant's focus turned to King Louis. "If you do not give voting equality to the Third Estate—"

Barentin interrupted. "We are giving them voting equality. Their vote counts the same."

Rollant shook his head. "With all due respect, Minister, their vote counts less by proportion. As Minister Necker stated, if the goal is to pass tax reforms, the Estates-General will vote two to one and override the Third Estate's vote. If you vote by headcount, the tax reforms will pass."

"Voting equality by headcount? If we do such a ridiculous thing," Barentin said, standing up and leaning on the table, "the Third Estate will have great power. They would strip the clergy and nobility of their voice. The First and Second Estates are the bedrock of this crown's legitimacy."

"I have been in the streets of Paris," Rollant said, glancing at Louis to see if he needed to close his mouth, but found the king studying his lock. Rollant realized Louis had wanted Rollant to state his position for the council and leave the decision with them rather than making it himself.

With a soft sigh, Rollant continued. "If you do not give the Third Estate power or at least a voice that can make a change, they will march to your palace door and drag you all out to publicly answer for the perceived crime of luxury amid famine and silk among rags."

Barentin scoffed again. "How will they get past the French Guard Regiment, the most elite and prestigious warriors in France and Sweden?" he sneered, as though the question itself was an answer.

Rollant folded his hands behind his back and spoke, his voice cutting through the condescension. "The Third Estate numbers well over 20 million, Minister. The King's Bodyguard, barely three hundred. The French Guard numbers about three and a half thousand, but per my observations, most of them would defect should an uprising occur. Lastly, the Swiss Guard, about nine hundred. Even if there were no financial crisis and you did not have to disband the Door Guards, the Gendarmes, Provost Guards, Musketeers, and the Calvary-Lancers, by the sheer size of the mob that will come to pound down the door, the Military Household of the King of France would be reduced to nothing in a matter of moments."

"Let's not over sensationalize the situation, Monsieur," Louis Pierre de Chastenet, the newly instated Secretary of State for War, leaned forward and said with a hint of amusement in his tone. "The mob would never reach Versailles. The French Guard alone would crush them before they stepped past the city gates. I doubt any good soldier would defect. And twenty million, you say? The King commands a quarter-million troops. Do you truly believe the mob can outmatch the might of His Majesty's military?"

Rollant slid a sideways glance at Chastenet. "If they responded in time. Though the bird may fly at a great speed, horses, men, and boats cannot match its pace. You would have barely organized the soldiers into marching formations by the time the Queen's head was on a pike being paraded out of Versailles."

"You dare dismiss the might of the French Royal Army?" Chastenet slammed a fist into the table. "You speak of mobs as if they are organized armies. Peasants with pitchforks will not overthrow the might of His Majesty's forces."

La Luzerne added, "Will you let your guards speak in such a way?" He directed the question to Louis, but the king held a tight grip on his lock and a finger tracing the intricate engravings. His head was down. Rollant was not sure the king was even listening.

Barentin flicked his hand in Rollant's direction, dismissing the conversation. He turned his attention to Louis. "Your Majesty," he said in a voice that caused Louis to jump. The King jerked his head up and listened to Barentin. "Your Majesty, this is not the place for outrageous conjecture. To defy the nobility and clergy now would fracture your crown. The Estates-General alone will pacify the Third Estate."

Necker chimed in. "Yes, I believe the Estates-General will give the Third Estate the voice they so deservedly desire. It will be a first step to reform and mend the—"

La Luzerne cut Necker off. "The people want structure, not chaos. The Estates-General will restore order. The Captain of the King's Bodyguard paints a grim picture, but such an outcome is highly improbable. They will not act against their divine king."

Rollant sighed as most people he encountered in Paris no longer believed in God.

Chastenet stood at the table. "I propose a vote by a raise of Minister's hand if His Majesty agrees."

Louis glanced at Rollant before giving a short nod.

"Very well," Chastenet said. "Those in favor of voting by headcount."

The room stilled. Rollant scanned the table of rich men. They would not, could not understand.

"I cannot alienate the nobility, not any more than I have," Louis finally said, his voice rising in uncharacteristic firmness. "Without the clergy's and nobility's support, the crown would collapse, and I would lose my family's throne and possibly my life. The Third Estate must see the Estates-General as enough. Tradition has held this monarchy for centuries through war and discontent—it will hold again. I have not raised taxes. I have sold fine fabrics. I disbanded entire divisions of my royal house to help the Third Estate. I will not gamble the stability of my reign on a path unproven."

Though his words were firm, his hunched posture and shaky glances around the room differed.

"The starving rarely see clearly, Your Majesty," Rollant said as he returned his hands to his side and stepped back into his position, resigned to say no more. As the ministers debated words in the king's forthcoming decree that would placate no one, Rollant focused on the gold leaf on the walls, shimmering like the last light of a setting sun, fragile and fleeting. Monarchs fell when their thrones became blind to the world outside their walls.

Again, the question plagued him: if the crown crumbled, would his curse crumble too, or would it bind him to eternity amid the ashes of another to-be fallen kingdom?

Élise's face lingered in his mind, a vision of what he could never have. Duty had bound him for six centuries. Perhaps, one day, he might be free—but hope was a luxury for mortals. He had no such claim.

CHAPTER 16

The Call of Change

BASTILLE, PARIS, JANUARY 1789

Élise pushed through the crowd to swipe a copy of the latest pamphlet. The Bastille loomed on the horizon. People were shoulder to shoulder. The stench of the poor mingled with the perfume of the *bourgeoisie,* the middle class, the uppers of the non-aristocracy.

A man wrenched her already bruised arm.

"I doubt you know how to read. Give it here," he barked and yanked the pamphlet out of her hand before shoving her away. She bounced back, grabbing it from his hands and dashing off. Years as a child thief gave her the upper hand. Her lithe, petite frame squeezed between bodies until she lost the irate man and found Gabin standing at the forefront of the Faubourg Saint-Antoine community, who had come to hear of the King's latest decree.

"There she is!" Malo said, pointing at Élise. His hand was quickly pushed out of the way by the growing mob.

Gabin grabbed her wrist and pulled her in close. His eyes had never regained what little warmth they had when he gazed at her. Apathy had taken residence there every single day since she had gone to the little cafe with Rollant. The bruises had migrated to her neck and forearms. He still had not hit her cheeks. She assumed it was because he liked looking at her. His hot breath blew in her face.

"You took too long," he gritted and plucked the pamphlet from her hand. He spun around, and the business owners took to the pamphlet, trying to decode the writing. She maneuvered around the huddle, pressed by the crowd moving around them, before finding a place to peer over Malo's shoulder where Yves blocked Gabin's sight of her. She only knew a few words and letters from running the bakery and dealing with suppliers and customers. She tried to make out the title. Her fellow townspeople were struggling as well. Eventually, they would be able to read it.

"What is the Third Estate?" Gabin finally read the title after all the inputs.

"We are the Third Estate," Élise said, but immediately regretted it. Gabin pushed Yves out of the way to glare at Élise. He had not been expecting Élise to be a part.

"This is no place for a woman. Go back to the bakery and stay there," Gabin shouted over the crowd's roar.

Élise scoffed and glanced around at the women in attendance. "No place for a woman?" she yelled, hoping to garner at least some support from the strangers, but to no avail.

"Yes, that's right," Gabin said through his teeth. "Now go."

Élise crossed her. "No. I am fine right here."

Malo turned to her and shook his head, and his eyes begged her to go. Yves let out a shaky breath with eyes darting between Gabin and Élise. The others froze amid the crowd's pushing. They wouldn't help her or stand up to the man who enabled them to feed their families. She was alone then as she had always been. Only Madame Marie asked if she was well during her last absence, and was the only one worried about her. The others she had given her bread to were only mad that they had not received a free meal; they cared nothing about her. Madame Marie would be the only family she would help if Rollant did as he offered. In her isolation, especially after Rollant had instilled hope in her life for something better, defiance had fueled her mission to take control of her fate, whether it be death in Gabin's grip or freedom from his oppression, just as was the goal of those gathered in the square.

Gabin's eyes narrowed. He wouldn't dare beat her in the middle of a freedom rally, but she'd wear a new layer of bruises by the morning. It didn't matter. If Rollant lived, he'd be back and offer her a new life, and she'd take it, not for him, but for herself. She wasn't going to have his pity, and she wasn't going to treat him as a savior. And if Rollant died, then Gabin would most likely kill her one day in her own attempts to escape. But one thing was certain: Gabin would not beat a silent woman, not anymore. If there was a God, as Rollant and Sister Francine believed, the deity had given her the gift of speech, and it would not be wasted.

Gabin's lip curled. "The paper states the answer is, 'Everything,' you stupid woman."

Her eyes slid down to the pamphlet. There were three lines below the title; the first line had the title repeated, so she assumed the one word after it was "Everything." She would remember that. She knew the word for the answer to the second line. "I see that, Gabin. I am not so stupid. The answer to the second question is 'Nothing.' But I would wager you don't know what the second question reads, do you?"

A low growl came through bared teeth.

Malo's eyes grew wide as his gaze fell to the floor. The others with them shared glances. Yves held up his hands in an attempt to diffuse the situation. "I don't think any of us know the second question the pamphlet is asking, Élise. We could all try to figure it out together?" He nodded, and the others did, too.

Gabin sneered at Élise but took the lead on Yves' suggestion. "The first word is 'What.'"

Élise almost let herself say, "I knew that as well, Gabin. Are you as stupid as I am?" But she bit her tongue. He could only be pushed so far until he wouldn't care what her face looked like.

A drum beat echoed through the air, followed by a drumroll. A soldier from the French Guard Regiment stood in the center of the town square. He bellowed, but his voice didn't carry as far as Élise and her community members stood. They had to wait for the echoed sentiments. It finally came.

"What is the Third Estate? by Emmanuel-Joseph Sieyès."

Élise's eyes dropped to the pamphlet, still in Gabin's hand, and followed the words as the echo came. "We have three questions to ask ourselves: What is the Third Estate? Everything. What has it been up until now in the political order? Nothing. What does it ask for? To become something."

The crowd erupted in chants to show agreement with the message: "What is the Third Estate? Everything. What has it been until now? Nothing. What will it become? Something!"

She'd remember those written words. The soldier beat his fist in the air, in rhythm with the chant. The crowd mirrored until he signaled the drum roll to silence the crowd.

The echo came.

"And yet King Louis XVI says this in his decree: The number of deputies for the Third Estate shall be doubled."

A cheer arose but was silenced at the drumroll. The soldier continued. "And the traditions shall be observed for the Estates-General. Deputies must be members of the *bourgeoisie*, and a list of grievances must be drafted."

Élise's jaw fell agape. The *bourgeoisie* would lead the Estates-General. The rest—the bakers, blacksmiths, farmers, and seamstresses—would remain unseen, unheard.

"What of the working class, the farmers, those who starve?" she yelled without another thought. An angry echo took her question to the soldier. Head nods and murmurs showed agreement with her question, all except Gabin, who glared at her. He would likely tell her she stole his question and took his opportunity to speak and lead.

She ignored him.

"What of us?" a voice finally echoed, an older woman clutching a threadbare shawl. Her face was weathered, lined with years of labor and hunger. "Do we starve while the deputies speak for us?"

Soon, the plaza was filled with questions asking, "What of us?"

"The *bourgeoisie* are nothing more than merchants with finer boots," another man spat, his fists clenched. "They will speak for their own profits, not for us."

Divisions among the middle and lower classes rippled through the crowd.

"Necker!" Someone yelled, and a great cheer rose at the minister's name. "Minister Necker will introduce the social injustices and gross inequality."

Gabin approached her.

But she couldn't stop. "If we are the Third Estate—if we are everything —then we cannot settle for deputies who won't even look at us."

Malo shifted uneasily beside her, his hand brushing her arm in warning.

"That's enough," Gabin growled, grabbing her arm in the crowd's uproar. "It is time to close that pretty mouth of yours," he gritted.

Élise's hands clenched into fists. She wanted to scream, to lash out, but the crowd's attention was already turning to others who were shouting for plans, for action. It didn't matter. Gabin would not control her.

"Let me go, Gabin." She yanked free from his grip, leaving red streaks down her arm, sure to bruise.

He gripped her tightly right under her shoulder joint and armpit. If she yanked, he'd break her arm. "Close your mouth," he whispered in her ear with no further threat needed.

A wiry man stepped onto a crate, raising a hand to command attention. "We must draft our grievances, as the decree allows. Every district is to send its demands to the Estates-General. If the *bourgeoisie* won't speak for us, we'll ensure they have no choice."

Cheers broke out. Gabin shoved Élise aside to join the growing knot of men discussing the logistics. She stumbled back, her breath hitching as Malo caught her elbow.

"You shouldn't have done that," he whispered, his face pale. "Gabin won't forget."

"Good," Élise said, though her voice wavered. "Maybe it's time someone didn't forget."

She dusted herself off and turned over a crate of her own. She had a voice—a gift—and no one would silence her.

CHAPTER 17

Rise of the Beaten

FAUBOURG SAINT-ANTOINE, PARIS, FEBRUARY 1789

JANUARY ENDED with a bone-chilling cold that blurred Rollant's view of the streets of Paris. Duty pushed him onward to carry out the crumbling throne's request, yet desire pulled him along. Fear of what became of the woman who had captured his thoughts slowed his steps. The King's Decree had come two weeks earlier, and Louis was worried how the Third Estate would react before the Estates-General. Rollant volunteered to go again to Paris, to which Louis agreed.

Rollant rolled the coat's collar up around his neck and narrowed his eyes to slits. His breath became foggy in front of his face. The liveliness on Rue de Charonne paled in comparison to the prior year. Its inhabitants were bundled in rags with pitiful sneers. Hate lingered in their eyes at the stranger in a thick, unstained coat walking along. The whispered disgust was tangible. Rollant ignored them and walked faster. He would have to do a better job of blending in if he wanted a good report to the King that would ultimately fall on deaf ears and inactive hands. Louis desperately wanted the people to love him, but because he was so detached, he couldn't see that they did not and would not, at least not anymore.

Fragments of conversation blew past with the wind. Élise's name emerged. His heart settled. She was still alive. He drifted toward the conversation: two men huddled around a fire outside a closed-up woodshop.

"Pardon me," Rollant interjected.

They looked up and examined his untattered clothes and nicely kept leather boots. "What do you want?" one man growled.

"I heard you mention the name Élise. Would that happen to be the Élise at *Au Pain Roux*?"

They shared a glance. "And who are you to be asking?"

"Rollant Montvieux."

One of the men smiled a toothy grin. "Ah, we've heard of you too. The rich man."

He shook his head. "Not rich. I am usually on a ship in a uniform, being fed with ship gruel. I only wear these clothes and spend a few coins of my wages a few days a year."

The other rubbed his fingers through a scraggly beard. "I'll only tell you this because the rumor is you are a nice man, but I wouldn't be telling people the king employs you. It probably isn't safe if you like your life. Come up with a different story."

Rollant gave a short nod, remembering Malo's same advice. "Appreciate it," he said, scanning the people staring at him with narrowed eyes. "Could you please tell me what you were saying about Élise?"

"What is your interest in Gabin's woman?" Toothy Grin said.

"She has become a friend, and Gabin beats her. I only want to make sure she is well," Rollant said.

Scraggly Beard shushed him. "Everyone knows it, but Gabin is dangerous, and we need him to keep things running. We've no choice. So don't say anything."

"So you let her suffer?"

"Some of us don't get to run off to the King's ships," Toothy Grin sneered.

"Is she well?" Rollant asked again.

"I suppose," Toothy Grin answered. "She has more bruises these days, but she's made a little name for herself across these districts. Lots of women have been following her because they like what she says, and she's been more defiant, too. Told Gabin 'no' the other day in front of us all," he sniggered. "I have never seen that man turn so red. I thought for sure he'd kill her there on the spot."

Rollant clamped his teeth. The news sharpened both Rollant's fear and admiration. Élise had become a hero in the community, but it put her in greater danger from Gabin and any remaining French Guard Regiment royalists.

He nodded, murmured, "Thank you," and continued to *Au Pain Roux*.

The cold nipped at his fingertips as he stuffed his hands into his pockets. Ignoring everyone else on the streets, he envisioned Élise's face with black eyes, cut cheeks, and irises lit with a flame for freedom. She was in sharp contrast to Louis' weakness and indecision.

He hadn't seen the sorceress since she'd cursed him on the battlefield at Damascus, but he wondered if eternity always meant he must serve the French monarchs blind to the truth. What if they didn't deserve the crown? He'd run the dagger over his hand that morning before he left his Charonne home. It healed as it always did; thus, it didn't matter. He was still immortal and cursed. Why had he let himself get attached to Élise? She was just a woman, but not any woman. After six hundred years, he was ready to love again. He wanted to love again. He desired to be with Élise and live a mortal life with her, maybe even in his Charonne home, free from his oath.

He swallowed the hard lump as the worn wooden *Au Pain Roux* sign appeared at the corner of Rue de Charonne and Rue de Faubourg Saint-Antoine.

But he was cursed, so he decided if she came with him this time, he would leave her in Charonne. It was a perfect, peaceful home with a nice single man her age who lived down the street. He would never return there so she could live her life, and if the king sent him back, he would stay in royalist inns. He hoped she would leave the unrest behind in the city and heal in the sanctuary he provided for her. Otherwise, he wasn't sure he could return to *Au Pain Roux* again. Every appearance put Élise further into harm's way. Gabin would surely kill her if she stayed a third time.

A child dashed out of the bakery, squeezing a big loaf of bread. He took off down Rue de Faubourg Saint-Antoine. Gabin's shadow and heavy footsteps pounded behind him.

"Thief!" Gabin's yell defeated the wind as the husky-built man charged into the winter cold, holding his long bread knife. He pointed in the direction of the child. "I'll kill you if I see you again, boy! Stay out of my bakery!"

Gabin swung at the wind, slashing it in rage before re-entering his business.

"Élise!" he roared.

Rollant peered in through the frost-streaked window and saw Élise back away, using the counter as a barrier. Her chin lifted in confidence, but the quiver in her hands betrayed her façade.

Gabin advanced and jutted the knife in her direction. "You saw that boy, and you didn't stop him. That's the third one this month!" The fury in his words blasted past clenched teeth.

"I did no such thing, Gabin!" she yelled back, dropping her hands as fists to her sides. The defiant stance masked her fingers' tremble.

"Don't lie to me!" he growled, slamming the blade's handle across her jaw. She crumpled to the floor, clutching her face.

"Get up and work, you lazy, lying whore!" Gabin screamed as he leaned over the counter.

Rollant had seen enough and would not tolerate the injustice. He knocked on the wooden post and stood within its open frame.

"I heard something I should not have heard," he said, his voice low and steady. His silhouette drew a long shadow in the interior room. The bakery's firelight illuminated the red rage in Gabin's bloodshot eyes as he turned to face Rollant.

"You!" Gabin pointed the blade at him. "I warned you to stay away, and now I'll gut you like a pig!"

Rollant stepped inside, kicking away the door stand and allowing the doors to swing shut behind him. "I came to see if you had killed Élise or not. Looks like she was one bad decision away from death." The warmth from the bakery did little to thaw his tone.

"She is my woman!" Gabin bellowed, stabbing the air between them as he stepped toward Rollant. "I can do with her what I please."

Rollant glanced at Élise, crawling toward the door with blood spots marking her path from behind the counter. "A man who treats his woman this way is no man at all."

Gabin snorted like a bull and charged Rollant with his baker's knife in the air—a madman bent on killing. Rollant stood like a sentinel and waited until the blade was ramming down. Rollant caught Gabin's fist mid-swing, his reflexes honed by centuries of battles against men far deadlier. The familiar surge of power in his grip reminded him of the curse he carried, making mortal brawls too predictable.

Gabin yelled and put another hand atop his own, trying to force the blade down, but Rollant's grip didn't falter.

"I will kill you!" Gabin screamed. "You disgusting sea rat!" His face grew red with effort.

Rollant chuckled. "You will try." He yanked the knife out of Gabin's hand with a twist of his wrist and sent it clattering across the floor before shoving the brutish man away. Gabin shuffled backward into a table and chair, with his chest heaving.

Gabin yelled with teeth bared and spittle forming in the corners of his mouth.

"You want me gone?" Rollant asked. "Fine. But Élise's life is her own. If she chooses to leave with me, you'll let her go without retaliation. She doesn't belong to you."

"Élise is free to go whenever she wants." Gabin spat. "I am not holding her captive, and yet she stays of her own free will. She wants me. Needs me. I am everything to her."

"Is that so?" Rollant asked.

Élise slowly rose, her fingers slipping from her bruised jaw. Her tongue caressed the gash on her lip. Gabin's wild eyes focused on Élise, whose gaze darted between Rollant and Gabin.

"Tell him," Gabin ordered. "Tell him!"

Élise's voice, though quiet, carried the weight of her past. "Six years, Gabin—"

"Élise," Gabin gritted in a hoarse voice, interrupting her. "You go with him . . . you don't come crawling back to me."

"Six years, Gabin," she continued as she grabbed her coat off the hook on the wall. "Six years of bruises, beatings, bedding others, broken promises, and brash lectures. Six years I stayed, and not once did you think I deserved better. Tonight, I choose better. I won't be crawling back this time."

"You ungrateful wretch!" he yelled, lunging for her.

Rollant stepped in between Gabin and Élise, blocking the path. He deflected Gabin's blow, then punched Gabin in the stomach and delivered a powerful uppercut to his jaw. Gabin's head snapped back. He stumbled into the table, upending chairs and sending bread loaves tumbling to the floor. With a guttural groan, his legs buckled, and he collapsed in a heap, his chest heaving faintly as unconsciousness claimed him.

"Sleep well," Rollant muttered and turned to Élise. He dipped his chin. "May we depart, Mademoiselle?"

"Before we go, I want you to know I'm leaving for myself. Not for you. I didn't need anyone to save me," Élise said with a voice full of conviction as she folded her arms across her chest one at a time.

He nodded. "I understand that, Élise. You chose this. Not Gabin, not me. You don't have to come with me if you have somewhere else to go, but my offer still stands: a place to bathe, fresh food, and a warm bed that will be all yours. It's a place you can call home."

His gaze lingered on her resolute expression, and for a fleeting moment, admiration for her courage to leave Gabin warred with the weight of his curse. He reached for the door.

"I do not owe you anything," she said, her arms still crossed.

Rollant peered back. "I never said you did."

Her arms lowered. Uncertainty still weighed on her shoulders. Caution remained in her eyes, yet the allure of freedom prompted a reluctant nod of acceptance.

"Then, let's go. You deserve more than this place. It's time to leave it behind," Rollant said, letting her step into the biting cold with her chin high. Rollant followed, closing the door firmly behind them.

CHAPTER 18

The Road to Trust

CHARONNE, PARIS, FEBRUARY 1789

SHE WALKED alongside Rollant down the uneven cobblestone street. Time seemed to slow the longer she walked on Rue de Charonne. It was farther down the street than she'd ever gone before.

The houses were spaced apart, each featuring a lit lantern hanging on the doorpost.

Quaint was the word that came to mind. It felt like a whole different world compared to just on the other side of the city wall. The scent of paint and wine replaced the acrid smell of the city to which she had grown accustomed. The frigid night wind whipped through her coat, causing her to shiver as she drew the collar up and slipped her hands back into her deep pockets.

Her attention shifted to Rollant, who had remained silent for most of the forty-minute walk. Unlike the two times he had escorted her back to *Au Pain Roux*, he hadn't taken her hand. His brow was furrowed, and he walked with his eyes fixed ahead, never glancing at her. A small sense of foreboding gnawed at her stomach. Had she left Gabin's lion's den only to walk straight into Rollant's viper pit? He had played her well if he had something other than what he promised waiting for her. She swallowed hard, the lump in her throat growing.

"I had said you'd find cheaper rent outside the city," she murmured, hoping to elicit some conversation.

"Yes," he said with a nod, but nothing further.

"Have I upset you?" she asked straightforwardly.

He stopped with a sigh and squared his shoulders to her. "No," he said curtly, his gaze lingering in her eyes. He took a deep breath and rubbed his forehead. "I am upset that you have even more bruises." His attention dropped to her mouth. "And a bloody lip. At least you aren't near death this time." His jaw grew taut as he shook his head. "Don't go back to him," he said. "Please. I'll make it to where you can stay in this rented house forever."

She scoffed. "Don't make promises you can't keep, Rollant. If something happens to you, I'll have no way to pay the rent."

Rollant ran his hand over his mouth, letting it drop. He sighed and scanned the lush landscape. "I promise," he said, nodding her down the road.

"But how?" she asked, keeping up with his brisk pace.

He stopped again and lowered his face to hers. Her heart skipped at the closeness. Something about him scared her, but he settled her, drew her in as if she belonged with him, yet pushed her away for safety.

Rollant's whisper made her breath hitch. "I will provide for you, Élise. You will never have to worry about food or a place to sleep. I promise you, and I am a man of my word. Surely you know this."

She kept her lips pressed tight and gave a quick nod. He had left her with Gabin for months to fulfill his oath to the king. She dared not ask him again how he could keep such a promise. Her chest tightened. Breaking the king's oath would lead to death or imprisonment. Breaking an oath to her meant nothing; there were no consequences there. He had only ever been kind to her, but the fear of the unknown haunted her. She had always known how to survive, and it meant trusting no one. Though Rollant had explained why he was helping her at the inn in Le Marais, it felt odd and out of place now that they were walking the cobblestone path. What was he planning for her?

She followed him until he reached a modest one-story home with a low-pitched roof. Beyond the small garden, a short path led to a tall wooden door flanked by a window and secured with a simple iron padlock and hasp.

The smell of the morning's bread and the fading fire graced their entry into the rented home.

Élise stepped inside, and her jaw dropped. She quickly closed it. Wooden planks spanned the length of the small entryway, leading into the main room beyond. She took three steps to survey the main area. A large hearth was positioned against the northern wall, while a small kitchen counter extended along the rest of its length, with a barrel for water tucked into the corner closest to the door. A small wooden table for two stood near the center of the room, and a simple yet sturdy merchant sofa occupied the corner opposite the door. An open doorway was located on the east side of the room, suggesting a private bedroom or storage space beyond.

"You live here?" Élise asked, disbelief staining her tone.

"Yes," he said.

"And you can afford the rent even though you are on a ship?" She crossed her arms. Education had never been afforded her, but his story did not add up. Was he a noble spy, as she had suspected from the start?

"Yes," he answered as a hint of unease flashed in his eyes.

"How?"

"It's a long story, Élise." He glanced at her, the corner of his mouth twitching into a faint smile, though his eyes gave nothing away. His gaze fell briefly to the ground. "Perhaps another time."

But she wanted an answer. "How long did you say you were in the King's Navy?"

He brushed past her into the main room, softly answering, "I didn't." He straightened and met her gaze with something unreadable in his face. "Some things are better left unsaid."

Maybe he didn't understand her question, she mused as he walked toward the hearth.

"I'll ask you once more," she said, staying rooted to the spot with the locked door at her back. The walls of the grand main room started closing in on her. "How can you afford this home on a navy man's wage, even outside the city?"

He stooped and threw another log onto the nearly exhausted flame in the hearth. The crackle covered the sound of her grumbling stomach and growing fear. Her mind raced through all the reasons why he would have wanted her alone and outside the city. Why try to win her trust unless he had planned something sinister? Had he brought her to squeeze information from her? Picked her as the most vulnerable, naive, gullible of the bunch?

"Did you hear me?" she asked again at his silence.

He took off his coat and tossed it on the sofa. "Yes, Élise, I heard you." He lifted his chin as he stared at her. His eyes were calculating. It seemed as though he wouldn't answer her, at least not that night.

"I don't want your pity, Rollant. I just want an answer." She hoped she could have the upper hand if he were truly a foul man like all the rest. "I will not treat you as my savior. I did not leave Gabin to enter another poisoned promise under your control." She planted her feet firmly beneath her weight, keeping her arms crossed and head raised.

Rollant nodded. "I've already told you—I want nothing from you. If you don't want to live here, you may leave anytime. This neighborhood is filled with good people who tend to the garden and the stable and are ready to share whatever you need, provided you do the same for them. I thought this home would allow you to start over in peace. You don't need me. I won't even be here. I only have a few days every few months, sometimes even years." He gestured toward the city. "With everything happening within the gates, I'm not sure if this will be the last time I'm here, but I know I have enough for you to live here without earning a wage for at least three years. If you earn a wage or barter with the owner, who, according to the neighbors, hasn't been around in decades to collect rent, you could stay here forever if you wanted."

Élise glanced around the house, her brow furrowing. "You know the owner hasn't been around for decades, but you only now rented it?"

Rollant paused, then shrugged. "The neighbors told me. That's how I found it."

She wanted to believe him, but something about the ease with which he explained didn't sit right. It was the same when he lied to Gabin after Le Marais. There was no hesitation in his voice, but she saw this time there was something unnatural in his eyes, but it soon was gone.

"Élise, all I am offering you is this home. If you want to fall in love and start a family, you can do that here. If you want to paint or garden and live alone, you can do that here, too. If I ask anything of you, it's that when or if I return, I can at least sleep on the sofa or a pallet on the floor."

Rollant's offer of hope seemed genuine, sincere, and too good to be true. "But why? Do you expect nothing from me? I don't deserve any of this, Rollant. I half-expected you to take me to a dingy apartment with holes in the walls and floors and rats in the bed, so as not to burden you too much. But this?"

She looked around at the plastered walls and polished wooden floors. The comfort of the hearth fire had already reached her. The counter held a small cheese wheel and bread, along with a few wine bottles.

"A new dress? A new coat? I thought that was too much, and yet"—she swallowed her disbelief—"you tell me that I'm free here, free to stay, free to leave. I don't work for you or anyone. I only have to be kind to the neighbors?" She shook her head and waved her hands to dismiss it all. "What are your terms, Rollant? I don't believe for a moment that this is the new life you promised."

He approached the table and pulled out a chair. They locked eyes, and he spoke with his voice low and raw. "You are gold, Élise—precious and valuable, with a rare beauty worthy of admiration. I'm sorry you've been treated as the utilitarian and undervalued iron all your life. I want you to see your worth. You deserve all of this and more." He gestured to the seat. "Please sit, and I will make us dinner."

Her arms fell to her side. "What?" she asked in a breathless whisper. No one had ever made her dinner, much less a man offering to do it for her. Her jaw remained ajar.

"Please," Rollant pleaded. "I am hungry and don't wish for my stomach to speak in your presence."

Her muscles grew tight. Her gaze found the bread knife on the counter. Was Rollant a murderer—a man who lured women into this place, killed them, and disposed of their bodies in the garden? Who was Rollant?

Where did he come from? Why did he pick her out of all the women in Paris?

His third "please" drew her attention to his frame. Her gaze darted between him and the open chair. Why was he helping her to sit? She knew how to sit. Her mind finally processed what he had said about gold and iron. It was the most kind sentiment anyone had ever given her. She forced one foot forward and then the other until she stood before the chair. Her breath caught in her throat. There was still time to run, but there was nowhere to go. Rollant knew it, too. Her eyes lifted to meet Rollant's.

Patience waited for her in his gaze. He had never hurt her before.

She steadied her heartbeat, shook her head at her likely bad decision, and turned to sit down.

He pushed the chair just before her bottom hit the wooden seat, seating her perfectly at the table. "What was that?"

His brow furrowed. "I pushed your chair in for you as a gentleman would," he said before heading to the counter.

She folded her hands on the table as she observed him, still not fully understanding what he had done, but he called it a gentleman's action. "No one has ever done that before," she said.

"Well, that is a shame." Rollant kept his back to her as he cut cheese from the wheel. "Monsieur Roux left a lot to be desired. I never once liked him. It is all vanity with that man." He finished with the cheese and sliced the bread. "I want you to know something. I was elated to have knocked him senseless tonight."

The corners of her mouth immediately rose at Rollant's last comment, but she forced herself to say nothing. She watched him pour the wine and plate their dinner on small wooden plates. He grabbed a wooden bowl and emptied the kettle's contents into it. The aroma of long-boiled stew filled the room. It made her mouth water. He gingerly placed the bowl before her.

"Are you not to have any?"

"I only prepared enough for one person this morning. Tomorrow, I will make enough for two."

She grasped the rim of the bowl with both hands. "But Rollant. You made this for yourself. This is yours."

"And I want you to have it," he said, finishing setting the table. He then sat opposite her, and they locked eyes in silence.

Was it poison? Did he mean to kill her? He wouldn't have been expecting her, or had he been prepared to have her come? She wanted to believe him, but belief was a dangerous thing. Belief kept her in Gabin's grasp for years, clinging to promises that had turned to bruises. Belief was a poison she couldn't afford to swallow again.

"Why is there fear in your eyes, Élise?"

She averted her gaze and stared at the bowl of steaming stew. It looked so good and smelled even better. "I am afraid of you," she said, not lifting her gaze.

As if reading her mind, he leaned forward, took a spoonful of her stew, and emptied it into his mouth. "I made it for myself, as I told you," he said after he swallowed.

She picked up her spoon and dipped it into the thick, meaty stew. Her mouth watered. Her back crumpled, and she lifted her gaze once more. "Rollant? I can't believe . . ." Her voice trailed off. Her sight blurred from tears. She licked her wounded lip and rubbed her forearm over her moistened cheeks.

His soft, but firm croon came. "Go ahead and eat, Élise, while it's still hot."

She nodded and did as he said. The stew stung the cut on her lip, but she didn't mind. She last had a stew of this quality at the inn in Le Marais and the cafe in Bastille, both times with Rollant.

"I apologize for my curtness earlier," Rollant said between bites. "I was angry at Gabin's increased violence and directed my frustration at you. I'm sorry if that was what gave rise to your fear."

"Rollant, stop. Please." Élise let her spoon drop into the empty bowl. She sat back with her hands folded in her lap. "Are you treating me this way out of pity?"

Rollant shook his head. "I told you why in Le Marais."

Her brow furrowed. "But I still don't understand why you would give me three years' rent just because I inspired you to overcome your grief?"

He shook his head again. "No. You inspired me to love again, Élise, and life without love, in any form, is numb and painful." His eyes glimmered in the firelight, and his Adam's apple bobbed as he swallowed the agony that surfaced in his words.

The affliction in his tone could have torn Élise's heart from her chest.

He adjusted the collar of his shirt and recomposed himself. A soft haze replaced the glimmer in his eyes. "I want you to have the same peace that you have given me."

Her chest released the captive breath of relief. She bowed her head, feeling almost ashamed of her cautious thoughts, and continued to eat.

Rollant swirled his wine before sipping, watching her. His gaze went to her neck and focused. She shifted, and his gaze averted.

"Why are you staring at me?"

"I'm staring at your bruises." Rollant dug something out of his pocket and placed a small tin on the table.

Words were painted on its top—words she couldn't read. Her brow furrowed. "What is it?"

His finger ran over the words. "Arnica balm." He found her eyes. "It helps heal bruises and cuts, sometimes overnight. I bought some on the way to see you today if you didn't come with me again. I wasn't sure what state I'd find you in." He pushed it toward her.

"You've done all this for me," she said, arms folded tightly. "But what happens when you decide I'm not worth the trouble? Men change their minds, Rollant. What makes you any different? Are you going to bed me and then kick me out? Get your fill and be done with me?"

Rollant coughed at the blunt question, clearly taken aback. "No," he said with a bitter chuckle. "Where did that question come from?"

She didn't want to tell him. It was too much—all of it. With Gabin, any gratitude was taken as indebtedness. With Rollant's offer, she got out of Gabin's debt. She didn't want to step into any more debt with Rollant than what she had already. Debtors were never treated kindly. He was trying to trap her after she had finally learned to stand up for herself in the face of violence. He was trying to drag her back. She shrugged in response to his question, and they finished eating in silence.

He stacked her plate and bowl and carried them to the large basin on the counter. She jumped up. "I will wash the dishes," she told him, grabbing the pail to fill with water.

Rollant spun around and gently laid her hand atop hers on the pail. "Allow me. I'm sure you have done the dishes every night of your life. Rest."

"If I'm staying here, I'll earn my keep. I won't just sit around waiting for your charity." She sneered, hating herself for doing it. He had been kind, but part of her needed him to have an ulterior motive. She needed him to lie or mistreat her to justify in her mind that he was like all the rest. There was nothing special about him. He was going to be leaving anyway. Leaving her. Abandoning her. Giving her hope and taking it away.

"It is not charity. I've told you before," Rollant said, gently pulling the pail toward his chest. "Let me do this while I'm here."

Her fingers twitched before she finally let go. "It's your home," she said. "That you have three years' rent for, somehow."

His head fell to the side, and a sigh escaped his lips.

She couldn't bring herself to say thank you lest she be trapped again. "Well, what should I do while you hand me a perfect life?"

He turned and pointed to the open doorway on the East wall. "You could start the fire in the bedroom so you are not cold tonight, or rest on the sofa and relax."

The sofa was enticing, but she walked along the room's perimeter instead, running her fingers over the polished wooden counter. Her eyes flicked to the shadowy corners, searching for something—a crack in the wall, a trapdoor, or perhaps a flaw in Rollant's perfect façade.

"Did you want me to leave you alone? You could have told me never to return as Gabin ordered you to," Rollant said as he filled the pail with water and dumped it into the basin.

She spun to face him and bit her lip. She couldn't lash out any more than she had. Her chest felt tight, the weight of the evening pressing down on her. She needed a moment to think—to breathe—away from his kindness that felt too big to bear. The open doorway pulled her into it, and she shut it behind her. She took a deep breath and scraped her nails down her face until they made tight fists beneath her jaw.

She hated herself. Rollant was a kind man, and that was all. He was a kind, beautiful, honest, and hard-working man she had treated like dirt due to fear. The backs of her eyes ached as they withheld tears.

Light from the large gap under the door allowed her to see a spacious bedroom with an actual bed with bedposts and a much smaller hearth nestled in the corner. She traced her hands along the wall, discovering the flint and stacked wood near the hearth. She could see her breath in the dim light. Her fingers trembled and fumbled with the flint. The chill in the room wrapped around her like a blacksmith's vise and gnawed at her fingers, but her pride burned hotter. She ran her hands along her coat's sleeves to warm them before getting to work and lighting the fire. She couldn't ask for Rollant's help—not after all her sharp words and doubts.

Sparks flew on her third attempt, and for a brief moment, the spark caught. A soft glow lit the damp kindling, teasing her with hope. She exhaled in relief, carefully cupping her hands around the fragile ember to coax it to life, but the wood hissed, guttered, and extinguished. She bit her lip hard, forgetting the cut and stifling a cry out of frustration and pain.

She knew how to light a fire; why wasn't it working? Again, she struck the flint, her hands succumbing to the cold a little more with each attempt. A few more sparks. The faintest wisp of smoke. Once more, the wood refused her. Her breath quickened; her chest tightened. It wasn't fair—nothing ever was.

Tears pricked her eyes, hot against the cold air, but she swiped them away with the back of her hand. Her fists clenched around the flint as she tried again, each scrape of the stone growing more frantic, more desperate. Still nothing.

She heard Gabin's mocking voice: *Pathetic. Worthless. Weak.* Her shoulders slumped as she tucked her numb fingers under her arms and shivered.

The faintest shift of light caught her eye. She glanced over her shoulder at the door. Rollant's shadow moved across the gap, pacing—then stopping. Then, pacing again. She pressed her lips together, resenting that he might know she was struggling. Was he waiting for her to admit defeat? To call for help? Her jaw clenched as her pride flared once more. She wouldn't call for him.

But she didn't need to. The door creaked open.

She froze, her heart racing. She braced herself for the impending rebuke, certain of the scornful disdain for her ineptitude that would surely follow.

But Rollant said nothing.

He stepped inside with a lit log. Its flickering light cast calm shadows on his unreadable face. He didn't have to come to help the damsel in distress; she could light the fire herself. She'd done it a million times before. He would mock her or lord it over her that he could do it while she couldn't. A scowl crept across her lips.

"It's tricky," he said softly, crouching beside her. "The wood's damp. Here—allow me."

His voice was steady, as though she was no inconvenience at all.

Words eluded her at his unassuming manner. She couldn't look away as he skillfully coaxed the flames to life. Within moments, the fire began to crackle and leap, casting warmth into the room. She stared at it, her hands still frozen at her sides.

"Hopefully, this will warm you quickly," Rollant murmured, his gaze falling to her hands tucked under her arms. He paused, and when he looked at her, there was no triumph in his eyes, no disappointment.

She averted her gaze and focused on the fire as it danced to life. Shame and relief warred within her. How many times had Gabin called her useless? Was he right after all? A lump rose in her throat, but she swallowed it back as she tried to speak.

Nothing came.

Instead, she simply nodded. Warmth spread through the room, but it wasn't just the flames that chased away the cold. It was him. He thawed the knot in her chest. And she hated how much she needed his warmth, how much she needed him, and wanted him by her side.

"I'm sorry, Élise, I didn't return for you sooner. I'm sorry I didn't urge you to come with me more after Le Marais. I hate that you've endured that monster for so long, needlessly. I'm sorry if you feel I abandoned you. I will do my best to ensure—"

"Stop. Rollant. I—" Élise's chin fell to her chest. "It is I who should be sorry. I am so afraid. I—" What was she trying to say? Her mind emptied.

"I'm not going to hurt you, Élise." His gaze found hers. "From your comments tonight, it seems you think I have some ulterior motive, but it is as I told you." His fingers ran along the collar of his shirt until they fell into a fist on his lap. "I wish I could live this life with you." His eyes traced her face like an enamored boy. "But I have already made an oath to the king." He coaxed her hand into his. "And I am afraid of how I feel for you, knowing I cannot live this life with you."

Affection exuded from him as he warmed her hands with soft strokes. She noticed the calluses on his palms. A noble spy wouldn't have calluses, but a navy man would. Tears welled in her eyes as her earlier doubts dissolved into shame. Of all the lies she had concocted to protect herself, the thought of him as a spy now felt absurd. He was nothing like Gabin or the others. Rollant had given her no reason to doubt him—only reasons to fear what his kindness might cost her.

"I want you to have a happy life, Élise, a life I should have given Amée." His gaze dropped at the mention of her name. "I never should have married her. I should have let her live her life and find love with a man who was there for her."

Her breath hitched at the grief woven into his words. "Rollant, don't say such things," she whispered, half-wishing that if everything he said was true, he would break his oath to the king—the miserable scoundrel. How could a man so kind serve a crown that had let millions like her starve? She wouldn't think less of him if he reneged. She cradled his cheek and prepared to tell him as such. His gaze softened at her touch, but something flickered in his eyes—regret, or maybe guilt—before he pulled away, leaving her hand cradling air.

"Do you wish to bathe this evening?" he asked, changing the subject. His tone was deliberate and controlled as if erasing the weight of his confession with practicality.

The question caught her off-guard. "You have ... a bath?" His sudden recoil had left her mind spinning. She pulled her hand back and pressed her fingers against her coat's thick wool to ground herself.

He gestured to the bin behind her.

"Oh," she said, glancing at it and dropping her hand to her lap. "I—I would appreciate a bath," she said, and added quickly, "But I can draw my own water."

"I can do it. The pail is large and heavy." He jumped up and took a second pail by the bath, filled it, heated it, and returned without a word as she warmed herself by the bedroom fire. She observed him, each muscle drawn tight. She yearned for his touch but despised relying on him.

As he finished the bath, small sweat beads formed on his brow. He went to the chest of drawers, pulled out a garment, and laid it folded on the bed.

"If you prefer clean clothes to sleep in, here is one of my long shirts," he said and stepped back.

His steady patience wore down the walls she'd built brick by brick over the years. She hated how much she wanted to believe him—hated how the warmth of the fire and his presence dulled the sharp edges of her fear.

She stood up and approached him. She took a chance and placed her forehead on his chest and grasped his shoulders as though anchoring herself. For a moment, she allowed herself to breathe him in—the strength of him, the calm he exuded.

"Thank you, Rollant," she whispered and lifted her face to his, afraid of the vulnerability in her voice.

He nodded with a tight jaw and stepped back again, creating a space between them she wished to cross but knew he wouldn't allow her to. He gave a half-bow before exiting the room with a soft, "Goodnight, Élise." He lingered in the doorway for a moment, his hand brushing the frame and eyes glancing back at her before he stepped into the main room. The quiet click of the door closing felt like a finality she hadn't anticipated.

She focused on the empty spot he had left behind, her heart in contradiction. He had provided her with hope only to walk away, and now he had offered her a home before departing again. He had given her warmth and space, kindness and quiet, yet her heart was adrift. How could she long for someone she wasn't sure she could trust? If he spoke the truth, if his promises were good, if he was the man he portrayed himself to be, then she'd beg him to stay. They could have the peaceful life he wanted her to have—they could have it together. France was in turmoil. She doubted anyone had the time or resources to come looking for a deserter in Charonne, of all places.

She collapsed onto the bed's edge and stared at the door, overwhelmed by a confusing mix of gratitude, yearning, and doubt.

She glanced at the bath and realized it would soon be cold, so she stripped off her clothes and stepped into the oblong wooden tub. The warm water embraced her body like a glove. She curled her knees to her chest, forcing the water beneath her chin. Her mother had bathed her once as a child, laughing and singing as warm water washed away the day's grime. It was the last time she had truly felt safe, cocooned in a love that seemed unshakable. But like a flickering flame in the wind, the memory faded, leaving only the ache of its absence. Perhaps the memory was her mother telling her she was safe there with Rollant or in Charonne.

The water cradled her, and Élise sank her tense shoulders deeper into its warmth. Rollant's act of care felt foreign. She wanted to shed the grime of her past along with the chill into the water, but her scars would not wash away so easily. Rollant's words echoed in her memory, tugging at emotions she dared not name.

She had left the bakery to escape promises turned to chains, yet Rollant's home felt different—less a chain, more a lifeline. Yet lifelines could fray. Could she afford to trust him, to believe in someone who would leave just as easily as he had arrived? Was hope worth the risk of heartbreak?

The warmth of the water seeped into her bones, loosening muscles clenched tight for years. Luscious, tallow soap awaited her, its surface smooth and slick against her fingers. She had never bathed with soap before—a wet rag was all she could afford. Her aunt had hoarded the one soap shard, she remembered, though even that had seemed like a luxury out of reach.

The soap bar slid over bruises, leaving a thin film of cleanliness behind.

She wanted it to strip away more than dirt—the bruises. If Rollant saw her entire body covered in black and blue, he'd be disgusted. They were disgusting to her. Her fingers cradled a tender one on her neck before sliding to the cut on her lip. Dried blood flaked off. She stared at the black dots on the pad of her finger before curling it into her fist.

"Curse Gabin," she muttered and slammed her fist into the water. "I hate you."

Her gaze dropped to the ripples as though they reflected the turbulence in her heart. The hearth light made her skin glow, and its crackle soothed her brow.

She finished with the soap and cupped the water to wash her face. She removed the grime, water alone had missed all twenty years of her life.

Twenty years.

She wondered if she was the same age Amée had been. The war in the Americas started ten, twelve, years ago. If Rollant was twenty-six when she met him the prior spring, it meant he was either twenty-seven or almost, and he would have been eighteen or so when he joined the Navy and married Amée. She ran the numbers through her mind. Years of dealing with suppliers and customers had taught her basic mathematics. He said it had been years since Amée died. His voice had wavered when he spoke of Amée. Regret clung to his words. Maybe he still loved her. Maybe he loved Élise too, and that was why he pushed her away. Maybe in his mind, Élise was destined to become just another name in the litany of his guilt. Yet she wondered if she could ever become something more.

If Rollant carried such a heavy weight in his heart, it was strange how little it showed. Unlike her, with bruises on her skin and weariness etched into her soul, Rollant seemed untouched by time, as if the months apart had left no mark on him—no weariness, no signs of strain, no complaints of hardship.

He had been a year at sea since they'd met, only returning once to Paris, yet he bore no signs of the salt or wind. Time passed differently for him, it seemed. He had the same sharpness in his eyes, the same steady gait. The world had left him physically unscathed.

She shivered at the thought but also realized the water had turned cold. The oil in the lamp flickered, and she sighed. Her time in the water had to draw to a close. She dried off and slipped his shirt over her head. The hem brushed her at the mid-thigh, and she pushed the sleeves to her wrists. The smell of old wood and candle smoke embraced her, and she turned her nose into its collar. Odd how a navy man could smell of land and not of brine.

She washed her dress and hung it to dry near the fire. She filled the bedpan with bathwater before heating it and placing it under the mattress. She was excited to finally sleep in a bed alone in such a warm room.

She glanced back at the door and wondered if Rollant would be comfortable on the sofa and if he could stay warm. The urge to go to the door and see how he fared came over her, but he had said, "Good night." He had everything else figured out for the evening, so he probably had his sleeping arrangements in order. The bed invited her in. The feather pillow molded to her head and shoulders. Her body, once tense with fear or anxiety, relaxed.

But a slow knock came at the door. She sat up, her shoulders once again around her neck. This was it—the true test of Rollant's word. She was half-naked in his bed, allowing her to bathe first. She sighed and shook her head at the ridiculous notion. He was a kind man, she reassured herself.

"Élise," Rollant said through the door. "I found the arnica balm on the table—the balm for your bruises. Did you want it for tonight?"

Élise didn't move. Was it a ploy to get her to open the door? To see her half-naked? So he could finagle a reason to force her to bed?

"Stop," she told herself in a whispered mutter.

"If you are already in bed," Rollant continued." I can walk it to you, or if you prefer, I can push it under the door, and you can retrieve it if you want it."

She looked around the room. It was larger than anything she had ever lived in. Her belly was full, and he had not hit her. She rolled her shoulders back and took a deep breath to settle her quickening heartbeat.

"Come in," she said and balled her fists beneath the sheets to hold back her fears.

The door creaked open, and she held her breath.

He kept his gaze on the floor as he entered. "Would you like me to walk it to the bed or leave it on the chest?"

She rationalized her answer as a test. "Please bring it here."

His sock-covered feet made no sound as he approached. Without his hat, soft brown curls fell to his ears. He extended the little tin jar of balm but kept his eyes averted. She slipped it off his fingers. "Might you have a mirror?"

He nodded and pulled a small handheld mirror from the nightstand. She took it again. His eyes had never left the floor.

"You are not going to try to bed me?" The question came out before she could stop it. He had already told her his answer, but there was his chance again.

His brow furrowed, and his jaw grew taut. "I honor women, Élise," he finally said. "I'm sorry you have never met a man who lives by that virtue." His eyes closed at the curt tone in his voice.

She shrank back.

"I am not angry at you," he clarified. "I am angry at the men in your life." He turned his back on her. "Is there anything else you might need before I turn down the lights?"

Her shoulders relaxed, and the breath she had been holding blew in a sigh of relief.

"No," she said.

He began to walk toward the door. "Then goodnight."

"Wait." She winced. She hadn't wanted to say anything more.

He stopped and waited for her to speak, his head turned perched over his shoulder, but his eyes still downcast.

Hesitation surfaced again in tight shoulders. "I . . . I have bruises on my back." She pressed her lips together, wanting them to stay closed. Her belly twisted into knots. "I cannot reach them."

She watched his body language. He did not jump at the chance to help, but rather waited for her to finish her request.

Her head shook, hating herself for inviting a night of probable pain. At least, she hoped Rollant would be gentle with her. "If you truly honor women," she began as tears welled in her eyes.

Was it wise? Was she asking too much—or was she simply trying to confirm he was different? Her chest tightened as the request tumbled from her lips, unwelcome but not undesired.

"Will you apply the balm to those bruises and . . . and . . . not do anything further?"

"I will do as you ask," he said.

As he approached, she shifted on the bed, bracing herself for the worst while willing away the tears threatening to spill. It had always hurt with Gabin. She faced the wall as Rollant came to stand behind her.

"I won't hurt you, Élise."

Her jaw ached from clenching her teeth. She slid the shirt up to reveal her back. The cool air kissed her exposed skin, but it was nothing compared to the heat of her fear, curling low in her belly. Silence and stillness ensued until finally she peered over her shoulder to see if he was even there.

"Does he kick you as well?" The question sliced through the air as a swift knife.

"Yes." She heard herself say. "Please, they are tender. Some of them are new."

He snatched the balm she had placed by her side. A measured sigh came through his clenched teeth. The balm's lid hit the nightstand. She closed her eyes and dipped her chin to her chest. She expected his fingers to roam, but they stayed on each tender spot, softly rubbing the tallow over the wounded flesh. She wasn't used to the softness, to a man's hands that didn't demand or bruise but soothed, as if her pain were something precious enough to cradle.

"I believe that is all of them," he said after a while, returning the balm to her side. He gently replaced the shirt over her skin. The tightness in her shoulders and chest dispersed. He had not harmed her, but he hadn't moved either once the cotton had slipped down her back.

"Thank you," she said, returning to her seated position with her legs under the sheet.

Their eyes locked, and he bent over. The knots in her belly came back with a vengeance. The sheet was her only ally and protection. She should have known better. Men always wanted something. Why should he be any different? And yet, he hadn't taken advantage. Not when he could have. His hands had only carried care, no trace of the cruelty she had braced herself for.

His eyes darkened the longer their gazes locked. Anger swirled behind the windows to his soul, just like Gabin. Rollant could hurt her if he wanted.

Rollant's nostrils flared. "I'm sorry you've endured so much," he whispered as he pulled the blanket up to her hands. He spun around to his chest of drawers and slammed two fists atop it. His jaw tightened, and a low growl escaped his throat—a sound of anger, of helplessness to change the past, almost feral in nature. He yanked open the drawer and pulled a dagger free. He set it down beside Élise's coat with a reverent motion. His movements were sharp and precise, as if they were the only thing he could control. The blade gleamed faintly in the lamplight—its hilt worn smooth from use but sturdy in its purpose. She stared at the dagger, the weight of its meaning pressing against her chest.

"If anyone touches you, kill them. I will teach you how in the morning," he said.

No one had ever entrusted her with anything, let alone a weapon meant for her protection. The responsibility it carried felt immense. Could she use it if it came to that? Her fingers twitched, aching to grasp it, to feel the power it offered. Rollant had not promised her safety but would equip her to ensure her own.

He stepped away, eyes averted, and dipped his chin. "Good night, Élise."

The tenderness in his voice and his offer rendered her mute. She thought Rollant would have at least let his hands roam on her bare back. The oil lamp dimmed, and the door opened and closed. In the stillness alone in the room, her voice then managed a whisper.

"Good night, Rollant."

Élise's gaze fell to the dagger, where the hearth light reflected a sliver on its blade. Trust had always been a concept for fools and dreamers. Yet, Rollant's actions spoke louder than any of the hollow promises she'd been fed before.

Her back caved, and she fell back into the feather pillow. Maybe trust wasn't foolish, but a type of strength when put in the right person.

The balm's tin warmed in her palm, a reminder of his touch—soothing, intended, and entirely without malice. It grounded her in the unfamiliar reality. She finished applying the balm to her arms, face, and neck, but didn't have the strength to use it on the bruises on her legs. As she slid the balm to the nightstand, she paused.

Survival had always been an immense burden, and, in one night, Rollant had lifted it from her shoulders, offering to carry it in her stead.

The tears came slowly at first, warm trails slipping past the walls she had so carefully constructed until they flowed freely, carving paths of relief down her cheeks and soaking the pillow beneath her head. Her chest ached from the tension she had carried all night and rose and fell with a deep sigh. For the first time in years, the darkness felt less oppressive, the silence less threatening. She sighed into the pillow, her tears washing away the last traces of fear. Her eyes fluttered shut as a faint smile lingered on her lips. For the first time, she dared to believe that the kindness she'd glimpsed in Rollant might not be fleeting. Perhaps, the home, the dagger, the night—it was a start. A promise she didn't have to fear.

CHAPTER 19
The Choice of Redemption
CHARONNE, PARIS, FEBRUARY 1789

THE DOOR SHUT with a soft click, yet Rollant's heart thundered in his chest. The blind revenge that had consumed him six centuries before surged again, flooding his veins. The image of Élise's ghastly bruised back seared into his mind. Small yet ashamed, her whisper echoed in his ears: *"I cannot reach them."*

His fingers trembled with a desperate and immediate urge to act, to repay blood for blood, like a demon prodding him to the edge of fury. He pressed his nails into his palms to contain the dark tide coursing through him. He paced the room, the weight of his immortal curse pressing against him. He had once unleashed the savage bloodlust against Arnoul, and it brought him to this lonely, eternal perdition.

But Gabin deserved death. The man's cruelty demanded it. Rollant shoved his boots on and examined his hands in the hearth light, flexing and curling his fingers, testing their strength. They would be as steel bars around Gabin's throat.

For Élise, he would put the man in the grave in the same brutal way Gabin had handled her.

The heavy weight of his coat felt like the armor he once wore as he threw it over his shoulders. He strode toward the door, the resolve of centuries hardening his steps. He stepped into the small entry room, and the cold pressed against him, stopping him mid-stride.

It wasn't winter's bite paralyzing him, but the familiar absence of life. The chill swept over him like a wraith, thrusting him to the last fateful moment when his hands had been drenched in blood and vengeance outside the walls of Damascus.

Life drained from Arnoul's wide, unblinking eyes. The iron stench of blood pressed against his senses harder than the sword in his hands. The moment of justice arrived, yet it did not bring him peace. It had not erased his pain but had only carved a steep punishment for his soul. Blood begat blood, and revenge spawned a curse of eternal solitude.

Standing before the door of his Charonne home, he faltered in his resolve to release death upon Gabin. His fist struck the wooden beam barring the door, and the sound reverberated through the room like the toll of a bell. He hit it again and again, each strike an attempt to pummel the memories from his mind—the bruises on her body, the pleading look in her eyes, the helplessness of his own restraint. He wanted to be her shield, her sword, her justice. The world had hurt her, and yet he feared causing more harm to come to her.

Her voice came. "Rollant, is someone out there?"

He swallowed his anger and took a deep breath. He glanced over his shoulder and said in the calmest voice he could muster, "No. I'm just cleaning up. Go to sleep. You are safe here."

The bed squeaked, and then silence.

Rollant sagged against the door, his forehead resting against the wooden planks. "Curse you, Gabin," he muttered. He clenched his fists, envisioning Arnoul's blood on them as if it had never dried. The sorceress' warning left him, replaced by the soft hum of the winter's wind forcing through the small cracks where the door met the doorpost.

The room was silent except for the crackle of the hearth. Rollant turned around and stepped toward the main room. The home was a mirror of his life—sharp, precise, but empty. He threw off his coat onto the sofa and sat by the fire at the table, letting its warmth seep into his skin as his gaze got lost in the dancing flames.

Élise was safe. She lay beneath his roof, tucked in his bed, well out of Gabin's grasp. That assurance should suffice, he reasoned while taking a deep breath through his nostrils and releasing it over his lips. He wanted to heal her wounds and give her a life of peace. Killing Gabin in cold blood would do neither. He had engaged in wars for monarchs and navigated political courts seeking honor, but this—this self-control—proved the most difficult.

"Vengeance is the Lord's," he whispered, pulling the words from the oral citation from his youth, six hundred years prior. It was the only soothing thought that came to him in his powerless state.

Rollant leaned back, pressing against the chair. He closed his eyes and exhaled another slow breath. He gripped the table's edge until his knuckles whitened. "She will have peace here, even if I do not," he whispered.

The words calmed him. His fingers relaxed as he leaned forward, his elbows on his knees, and rubbed a hand over his face. It took six hundred years for him to feel again, but in some way, he sensed it had been a test—

a second chance—and he chose not vengeance but peace. And his choice, fragile though it felt, brought with it a glimmer of something he thought he'd lost long ago—honor. Maybe the curse could be lifted since he had chosen well the second time. Perhaps the sorceress would grant him the ability to hold love in his arms again.

He flicked the notion away. Her dark celestial being hadn't come to inform him that the curse was lifted, and he doubted she would ever do so.

The firelight danced across the ceiling as his thoughts churned. He had two weeks in Paris, due back to the King's side by mid-February. The king's command echoed in his mind. The same as it had been for a year: gauge the reaction to another faulty decision.

Élise was a voice among the districts, her words reaching further than she realized. She understood the people's needs, their anger, and their hopes. He could stay here, ask her, and deliver the king's answers without ever stepping into Paris again. Two weeks to make sure she wouldn't look back toward the city or fall prey to its cruelty again and still glean what he needed to answer the king.

"The king. The king. The king," he muttered. All the royal houses had used him as the perfect instrument of power—his purpose and punishment—from the day the sorceress cursed him. Eternal life, eternal servitude. His loyalty was not born of respect or admiration but by force, an irrevocable deal he wished would end.

The quiet creak of the house enveloped him as his gaze drifted toward the closed bedroom door. He had glanced back at Élise before leaving the room; their connection was real and raw.

Despite her fear, she had trusted him to see her body, trusting him to do nothing more. Her silence spoke louder than any words. She hadn't expected him to follow her request. His blood began to boil again at the notion and evidence of abuse in her life. He swallowed the growing lump in his throat and relaxed his fist to calm himself.

"Two weeks," he whispered and focused his thoughts. But the words were hollow. If he fell in love or had already fallen, could he pull himself away at the end of two weeks?

The thought lingered, tantalizing and dangerous, paralyzing him between two equally difficult futures: a life where she resented him for leaving and a life where she suffered for him staying.

He had lived this story before, watching Amée turn gray and fragile while he remained untouched by time. Amée's gaze had brought him joy. Her laughter was his strength. He had witnessed her light fade at arm's length, and in its absence, he'd been left in endless shadow.

Staying meant condemning Élise to Amée's fate, and he wouldn't allow it. Élise would live, thrive, and die in peace, never tethered to his curse. If he loved her, he had to leave after two weeks and never return. There was no other way. He thought of the neighbor family down the street; he'd invite them over—they had a son her age. They were good people.

He closed his eyes, imagining Élise in his Charonne home—her laughter filling the house, her hands tending the garden in the spring, her face framed by sunlight streaming through the windows. She deserved a life unshackled by fear, a life free to bloom. He glanced at the floorboards beneath the table, a spot worn smoother than the rest.

He knelt, his hands brushing over the worn wood. Beneath it lay centuries' worth of gold and the deeds to his Charonne and Chartreuse estates. He had carried them through wars and dark nights, but now, for the first time, he felt their true purpose. They were not for him—they were for her. The gold would last much longer than the three years he told her. He would leave her everything but himself.

He would pour the weight of his years into the next two weeks, equipping her with every tool she needed to build a life without him. Even if it meant carving out pieces of his own heart to leave behind, he would ensure she had everything she needed.

His throat tightened as he imagined saying goodbye. Would she plead with him to stay? Would she see through his calm façade to the sorrow that would surely linger in his eyes? He exhaled slowly, willing his resolve to harden. He would make her understand that this life—this house, this freedom—was for her. It was never meant to include him.

His mind emptied as he shifted to the sofa. He slipped off his boots and pulled his coat around him like a blanket. The fire crackled as he adjusted his head in the crook of his arm. For the first time that night, the tight chains of indecision did not wrap around his chest.

"One day," he whispered, allowing some of his thoughts to escape. He might return to find her grave nestled among the wildflowers, her grandchildren playing beneath the trees she had planted. Perhaps her name would linger, spoken with love by those who carried her fire. It was a hope as fragile as it was bittersweet, but it was the only gift he could leave her.

His gaze drifted from the bedroom door to the flames as though they might burn away the ache in his chest. Perhaps, in letting her go, he might find a shred of redemption for his past sins and give her the life she deserved. And that, he decided, would have to be enough for her, if not for him.

CHAPTER 20
The Pull of Desire
CHARONNE, PARIS, FEBRUARY 1789

THE ARNICA BALM had already started healing the gash on Élise's lip, and the bruise on her eye and neck had turned a ghastly yellow-brown, a sign of healing. Élise's gaze drifted to her eyes in the small mirror's reflection. The dark circles had diminished. She had slept well, better than any night previous.

The smell of eggs filled the home, making Élise's mouth water. Eggs had been few and far between. She placed the mirror on the nightstand and checked on her dress. She didn't dare walk out in Rollant's shirt, but she was hungry, and her dress was cold and damp. Her stomach grumbled.

Her fingers dug into her temples before slipping up into her scalp. She took a deep breath and decided to wear only Rollant's shirt, and her coat over it, with the belt tied. She'd be showing her calves and ankles, and she hoped Rollant would not think less of her for it. Her stomach roared and sealed the decision. She opened the door to see Rollant spooning the freshly boiled eggs into wooden bowls.

His attention shot to her. A pressed smile arose on his lips. "Good morning."

She nodded and shrank, hoping he didn't notice her legs. But his gaze slipped down to her bare calves. He straightened his back and turned his attention back to the eggs. His muscles drew tight.

Before he could say anything, she pulled her coat tighter across her chest.

"My dress is still damp, and it's cold. I hope you do not think less of me after seeing—" She closed her eyes. He had seen her back bare the night before. Her shoulders rose to hide her neck in the coat's collar.

"I made breakfast," he said, keeping his eyes on the eggs. "Please sit and eat with me."

Her tongue dabbed the gash in her lip before approaching the table. He had cut bread and cheese for both of them. She stared at the prepared wooden plate as she sat. "You are so kind."

He glanced over his shoulder as he moved the pot to cool from the hearth. "I have two weeks until I have to return to port. I need to make sure you are well before then." He placed their two bowls of boiled eggs on the table before returning to pour hot water into their cups.

"The neighbors grow herbs and raise chickens. I bartered for eggs and some dried mint and sage," he said, pouring the herb dust into the cups. The steam rose from the herb-infused water. He swirled each before bringing it to the table and sitting down. "This will help heal your wounds and clear any headache you may have."

His words were right, but the tone lacked his usual kindness. She should have worn the damp dress. Her chin lowered as shame's stain rose on her cheeks. She pulled the cup into her grasp, letting the warmth seep into her fingers and the minty steam curl into her mouth. She felt Rollant's gaze fixate on her, so she risked a glance up.

"I am sorry I am not dressed appropriately," she said, knowing that if a neighbor turned up to see her, they would think her a woman of the night and think ill of Rollant.

But Rollant shook his head. His gaze fell to his eggs. "No need for apology."

"I'll go put on my dress," she said and stood up, but Rollant reached over and grasped her wrist.

"Please sit and eat, Élise. Let your dress dry. There is a miller down the road. We can go later today and order a few more dresses." His tone was straightforward. He was clearly uncomfortable.

"You don't have to do that, Rollant. I can see I have upset you. I will go put on my dress."

He stood as her hand slipped through his. "I don't want you to be cold and wet," he said. "You will need at least two dresses anyway. One to wear while the other is hanging to dry." He gestured to her empty chair. "Please sit and eat, especially while the food is warm."

He sat down and refused to touch his food until she returned to her seat. He dipped his chin to thank her, but said nothing more.

She sipped her tea and let the cool bite of mint chase away the shame on her cheeks.

"You didn't have to make breakfast as well," she finally whispered. "You've done so much already." But her heart silently begged him never to stop and never to leave.

He swallowed his bite of bread. "It is my honor to care for such a woman as yourself," he said.

The world beyond the walls faded as she observed him eat in the quiet room. The plaster walls enveloped her like a safe cocoon. In a fleeting moment, she envisioned Rollant, an old man, and her, with gray hair, eating their breakfast peacefully. With a slight smile at the passing image, she took a bite of bread and cheese.

"I heard your name whispered in the streets as I was going to the bakery," he started with a quick glance. He stopped to gauge her reaction. "But we can choose another topic if you'd rather not discuss the burdens of the city."

The murmurs of the people in the district, their talk of food shortages and growing unrest, pressed against her thoughts like an unwelcome draft. With it, the vision of their advanced years was whisked away in its current. The corners of her mouth fell flat. "Yes, at Gabin's disapproval, I have been leading angry women, supporting them, encouraging them to be free from oppressive masters and men. Their anger doesn't fade quietly. Many have starved and are no longer willing to die without a voice."

Rollant nodded and averted his gaze to his half-eaten egg. "Their fight is yours too, then," he said. As he studied her, his brow furrowed. "Does this mean you will not stay here in Charonne?"

She shifted in her seat, understanding that all he had done for her was to keep her safe. But she had earned her bruises and shed her blood to be one of Paris' voices. "The prisons are full of men, women, and soldiers like me, who have spoken out against our king." Her words came out softer than she intended, almost fragile against the steady crackle of the flames. "I doubt I will stay away for too long."

She turned her gaze back to the fire, fingers tracing the rim of her cup. "Everyone is suffering. The women, especially. We've gone too long without answers, and we are demanding them now." She took a deep breath, not wanting to snub the massive generosity offered to her but knowing the deep pang of hypocrisy would eventually smother her will to live should she stay out of the movement she had helped inspire. "You are asking me to abandon them. Staying here would be a betrayal to—"

"What if you end up killed or in prison and are worse off than with Gabin?" Rollant asked, lowering his cup without taking a sip as if he had lost his appetite.

"Then," she lowered her head and licked her busted lip, feeling the torn, delicate flesh with her tongue. "I hope I can find the will to survive or die quickly."

Rollant placed his cup on the table. He stood up and wrapped his hands behind his back. The sound of his booted steps fell in a soft cadence as he paced the main room. He stopped and looked out the window.

"Why do you care whether I stay here?" she asked.

He hesitated. "Because someone needs to." His gaze met hers, a pleading look in his eye. A gaze that told her she was everything to him, not the look of love he had when first mistook her for Amée, but one of great care and affection.

"Can you at least promise me"—he began with a measured breath—"you will stay in Charonne until the Estates-General is adjourned? Maybe the people's demands will be met and their questions answered. All through a more peaceful venue, and you can avoid prison?"

She couldn't outright refuse the plea in his eyes. "Do you believe anything will come of the Estates-General?" she asked, her heart growing heavy.

A flicker of uncertainty crossed his face. "What are the people demanding?"

"We want equality with the nobility and the clergy," she said with a lifted chin. "We want the law to be fair. We want the wealthy to share the tax burden. We want accountability with the state's finances. We want democracy. We don't want a king."

Her hands balled into fists as she remembered the rallying cry of the gathering at the Bastille. "We want to be something when we have been treated as nothing, though we have done everything."

A shadow settled over his features.

"Don't you want the same?" she asked.

He nodded. "Of course, Élise." But his focus shifted to the view out the window.

"Are you not willing to fight for it?" she asked, leaning forward.

His arms crossed, and he leaned back with a sigh. "Fighting does not always bring peace. I've seen what fighting leaves in its wake: widows, orphaned sons, broken families living with a cost no one expected." He glanced back at her. "It breaks people. Twists their minds. Perverts judgment."

He winced and returned to the table. The affection in his tone resurfaced. "Please, Élise. Stay in Charonne until the Estates-General adjourns. I know, or rather, I hope it will improve the conditions."

She chewed the inside of her cheek, debating everything she would trade for a peaceful life in Charonne. It would be someone else's fight. The Third Estate's *bourgeoisie* representatives had heard the people's demands. They were crafting their list of grievances. Maybe she could stay.

No, she told herself, not after finally finding her purpose. Her fingers cradled the cup of tea, and her attention fell to her breakfast in thought before returning to Rollant's intense gaze. He had given this life to her. He cared for her, the only man—the only person—in the world who did. Tears welled in her eyes. It was his only request: to stay in a safe place while the world burned.

At her silence, his eyes begged her. "Please, Élise," he whispered.

She sat back, running out of excuses and short on willpower. "What of

Madame Marie? She was the only one who cared for me when I was ill. I can't leave her with nothing. I must go back and give her bread."

"I will ensure she has enough to buy bread until the Estates-General adjourns," Rollant promised.

The question from the night prior pounded on her mind's door until it blurted out. "Are you rich, Rollant?" she asked. "How can you afford this home? How can you afford to make promises to feed a family for months, perhaps even a year? Tell me I can live here for three years without paying so much as a *livre*?"

His hand slipped to hers. His thumb slid up and down her forefinger. His eyes held no deception, and his words were deliberate. "If I told you how I can afford such a place,"—he leaned forward with the sear of agony branded in his gaze and a whisper on his lips—"you would not believe me."

His words reached her heart and squeezed. "What did you do?" she asked.

"If you stay in Charonne, I will tell you when I return," he said. "And hope you believe me."

"You have not given me a reason to think you would lie to me," she replied. "Tell me now."

He shook his head. A glint crossed his eyes. "You would never look at me the same way again," he whispered.

He was ashamed, she realized. Whatever it was, it could wait. He gave her so much. Yes, it could wait. She turned her hand in his and squeezed in affirmation. "If you provide for Madame Marie, I will stay in Charonne until the Estates-General is adjourned and agreement on reform is reached."

He blinked back the glisten, and a soft sigh of relief forced out of his chest. "I'm glad," he said and sat back, returning to his breakfast.

She ate her eggs in silence, wondering what he had done to secure such an allotment of coin and if she would have to stay alone in this place. But did she have to stay alone?

But before she could ask him to desert the king's navy, he scooped up the empty bowls and plates. "I will teach you to survive the fight you may find yourself in should the Estates-General fail or if a man tries to harm you again." He placed the dishes in the basin. "Bring the knife I put by your coat. I will ready the room."

She finished her tea and brought her cup to the basin as he washed them all. She did as he asked but stopped to look at him in the doorway. He was a mystery, one she wanted to know. The need to unravel his secrets made him more desirable. Because in his secrecy, he dangled nothing in front of her out of ill gain. Everything was her choice.

The dagger was where he had placed it the night prior. Its weight felt different than the baker's knife. The dagger was a weapon meant to kill rather than feed. Dark blood stained the hilt. She swallowed the lump in the back of her throat, envisioning the men who'd been stabbed with it. A deep breath filled her lungs as she settled her nerves.

The screech of furniture sliding across the wooden floors brought her back to the present. She returned to the main room to find Rollant standing in the cleared room, with the table and chairs next to the sofa.

"Please, come stand here," he said, gesturing to the spot beside him.

She obeyed.

"Now, face the bedroom door, and place the knife in your coat pocket."

Rollant stood, facing her profile, with one hand tightly wound behind his back. His posture was unwavering professionalism. Her gaze lingered on his handsome face. The shadow of stubble on his chin plucked him from perfection. His jaw tensed when he stepped closer.

His hand covered her hand, his fingers laying atop hers—warm, calloused, steady.

"If a man attacks you, you will first pull your blade up." His breath, edged with mint and sage, brushed her temple. She resisted the urge to lean into Rollant's presence, to anchor herself in the moment.

He reached her hand into her coat pocket. The dagger's handle fit perfectly in her palm. The blade felt heavier in her grip, as if weighted with purpose.

He moved her hand in a swift, fluid movement to brandish the blade. "Anticipate he will attempt to hit you in the face, so you must either stab him first or block his blow."

He moved her hand again as if it were a dance or a soft beat in a rhythm as he guided her to practice both movements. "And again," he said, releasing her hand. "Return the dagger to your pocket," he said with a quiver in his voice.

She glanced up to find him looking at her as if searching for something. His hand overlaid hers. "Pull the blade up," he said again, guiding her hand through the motions. Her heart thrummed louder with every deliberate movement. His fingers tightened over hers, gently insisting that she follow his lead. She tried to focus on the blade, on the imagined threat of Gabin, but the weight of his presence pushed all else from her mind.

His breath faltered when their gazes met. Their faces were too close, but neither pulled away. His eyes lingered in her hold, spilling all his secrets into an indecipherable pool for her to swim. But as quickly as the vulnerability appeared, his eyes shifted and returned guarded once more.

"Now you," he said, his tone cool, the warmth stripped away again. "Without my aid."

Her grip on the blade tightened as Rollant stepped back. The weapon felt foreign in her hand, yet in its weight, she felt a flicker of something unfamiliar—control. It was the culmination of the gift he'd given her:

control over her life. He'd become her refuge from pain, where no one dared to harm her.

Rollant narrated the scene. "A man grabs you by the shoulders; he intends to assault you."

She pulled the blade up, slicing upward as Rollant had shown her.

"His right hand is winding to punch you in the face."

She turned the blade to stab first.

"Too late." Rollant's voice cut through the room. "You've been hit." He stepped close and grasped her elbow with precision, sliding his hand to her wrist, and redirected her movement in a firm but careful grip. "Like this, Élise."

She tried to focus on the movements, but his closeness and his familiar, comforting scent clouded her thoughts. Her pulse quickened, and her grip faltered. She wanted to turn into him and beg him to give up his career as she would relinquish her fight to stay in Charonne together. Never had she met a man such as Rollant. Never would she let him go. Never would she find another man such as him.

"Focus," he said as if reading her mind.

She countered with frustration's stain upon her cheeks. "It is hard to fight an imaginary man."

He stepped in front of her with squared shoulders and a challenge. "Then fight me. I am Gabin. I've already hit you, and you fear what I might do to you."

He grasped both of her shoulders, firm but far from pain.

"I am going to corner you," he whispered, guiding her backward and pressing her against the wall with a gentle hold. The plaster cooled her body and slowed her racing heartbeat.

She leaned her head back against the wall and exposed her neck to him. The weight of everything he had done and was doing crashed over her. The hot sting of mint touched the gash on her lip, but she wanted to draw him in. The man had killed before; he was dangerous and deadly, yet with her, she knew he'd never raise a fist. He had earned her trust, her complete trust. No one had ever done such a thing before. She slipped the dagger into her coat pocket and placed a hand on his belly and the other on his chest. They locked eyes. His gaze dipped to her lips and lingered in silent hunger. His words ceased. His breath slowed. Her stomach fluttered. Desire charged the space between them. She wanted to erase the distance between them. His fingers slipped to her neck and cradled her cheek, weakening her knees. His thumb stroked the fatty flesh of her bottom lip with a tender touch. Her heart thundered as she waited—hoped—for him to close the distance.

Her mouth parted to receive her first kiss born in love, but Rollant stepped back, letting his hands fall away in fists to his sides, taking the moment with it. The blaze of his touch lingered on her skin, a ghostly imprint that faded too quickly. She blinked in rapid succession, trying to mask the sting of disappointment.

"You need to raise your blade." His voice lowered, and regret laced his words. He jerked one hand behind his back as if to keep from reaching for her again. His brow furrowed, and fear lived in his eyes.

Élise shook her head as she tried to determine what he feared: losing her, leaving her, loving her like Amée. She let her hand drop to her side, her gaze fixed on the empty space he had left between them. What had she expected? For him to close the distance, to press his lips to hers, to shatter the careful distance he had maintained since their paths crossed? Of course not. Rollant wasn't like other men. He held himself apart. Whatever kept him from her, she knew it was tied to the sorrow that haunted his eyes. She swallowed hard, willing herself to let the moment go, though the ache in her chest refused to fade. Her throat tightened.

"I cannot raise a blade to you, Rollant." Her voice broke. "Even though you pretend to be Gabin, you are nothing like him." Tears brimmed her eyes, and the truth slipped free. "You are my sanctuary."

Rollant stilled. His lips parted as if to speak. Instead, he turned away before any words came. His broad shoulders tensed, mirroring the wall he'd built around his heart rise once more. Once he faced her again, he spoke in his usual steady tone, though his affection faded. "If you can't raise a blade to me, how will you survive should you find yourself in a fight, especially if you return to the city?"

Her gaze met his, unflinching. "Because I will remember that all men are not like you." Her words carried the weight of conviction.

His expression grew unreadable, but his weight shifted. His tight shoulders loosened.

"Again," he said, his tone faltering in the truth he tried to ignore.

She pulled the dagger from her coat pocket.

His hand brushed against hers once more as he adjusted the weapon in her grasp with the same precision as before. He guided her next movement, deliberate and impersonal, as if he sought to erase the intimacy that had passed between them.

Yet Élise couldn't forget. Her chest tightened with each touch and every whispered instruction. His words barely registered, drowned out by the thrum of her pulse and the lingering ache of what might have been. She wanted to ask why he had pulled away, to demand answers to the questions swirling in her mind. But his tone had shifted, and the admiration in his voice was stripped away.

It seemed it was merely training for him, yet his glances lingered a moment too long. For Élise, though, she resolved to break through his defenses and find the man she saw in his rare moments of vulnerability, even if it meant risking her heart.

CHAPTER 21

Walls of the Cursed

CHARONNE, PARIS, FEBRUARY 1789

THE NEXT DAY came and went, as did the third and fourth days. Rollant had taught her how to chop firewood, tend to the garden, and defend herself. He made her practice every morning, though he never let his resolve waver as it had on the first day. He'd nearly come close to kissing her that time, almost wrapping her in an embrace and letting her succumb to the sorceress' curse. Night fell once more, and once again, he wished Élise good night after tending to the faded bruises on her back.

He stoked the fire before sitting on the sofa and slipping off his boots. Her trust in him was fragile, too precious to shatter with the truth. Yet, the memory of standing so close, her breath mingling with his, and her hands on his chest and belly, made him ache to tell her everything—to let her see the man he once was and the immortal monster he feared he had become.

He lay down, closed his eyes, and thought of Amée's rose in the dresser drawer in the bedroom. From memory, he stroked Amée's aged, blurry face as he pulled her close, hoping the sorceress had lied. But Amée gasped for air, and the life slid from her eyes. Her silver hair cascaded over her shoulder, loosely woven into a braid. A silk green dress clung to her frail frame.

His lips lowered to hers, and after forty years, he kissed his beloved. The corners of her mouth turned up before her soul left her body.

"God be with you," he whispered and closed her eyelids. He buried his head into her chest and wept. He had brought the curse upon himself. He had no one to blame but himself. A lifetime away, not able to go home, and never to hold Amée until she asked to be let go of this life in his arms.

The day he buried his wife was the day he vowed he would never love again. He didn't deserve love—a penance for murdering Arnoul in cold, vengeful blood.

After six hundred years, he had kept his vow. No woman had tempted him. No woman had pulled on his heart. Cateline had wanted nothing to do with him after he had killed her mother. It didn't matter to Cateline that she was already sick and dying. He had continuously monitored her and his lineage, ensuring they were safe. But all of his descendants were among the first to perish with the black plague that had swept across the lands. He loved his last living granddaughter, ten generations gone. Ninette was her name. She had been orphaned at seven years old, so he took her in only for her to run into his arms and perish. He had cursed the sorceress, for he could love no one in any form.

Tears ran down his cheeks, remembering the hazy visage of his last heir, running to him with a smile on her face and her subsequent lifeless eyes beneath his same chocolate curls. In a moment of neglect, he became the unwitting bearer of cursed love's fatal blade. The curse lived and held him captive. He was alone—no blood relation left in the world—only an oath to the French crown. The world became cold and numb. There were days he thought about killing the king and ending his oath, but he knew the sorceress would not simply let him die an easy death, nor allow him to see his family with the Lord. Her dark magic kept him from plunging the blade.

But Élise had seized his stoic heart and compelled it to beat with life again. Despite the hardships and traumas, she had not lost the fire and vitality of life—something Rollant once possessed. She had awakened something in him that he believed was dead long ago. She was unlike anyone he had met in six centuries. Her resilience shone brightly, a flame undimmed by the storms of her life. That fire, reminiscent of his own before Arnoul, drew him to her against his will. Amée was his anchor in the tempest, and Élise was fire—filled with a passion for justice cradled within a sharp mind.

Rollant shifted on the too-small sofa, the coarse fabric scratching his cheek. The fire crackled in the hearth, a steady reminder of the life that moved around him even as he lay still. Its warmth was a poor substitute for the chill leaching onto his bones. The faint scent of ash lingered in the air, mixing with the leather of his boots lying nearby. He clenched his jaw against the tightening in his chest, staring at the bedroom door.

"I will not love her," he whispered, shifting on the sofa to stare at the ceiling. Yet he could not doubt his deepening connection with her. But life was nothing without death to make it sweet and vibrant. He threw his arm over his eyes and relaxed on the sofa. "Each day comes and goes just like the next," he told himself. "Protect the king and the king after. That is your oath. Do no more, for there is nothing more."

He pushed Élise from his mind and tried to remember Amée's last smile as she died, as if to remind himself why he would not kiss Élise, hold her, or be a part of her life after eight more days in Charonne. He stole forty years from Amée. She did not find love with another because she had made a marriage vow to him. She was involuntarily celibate and raised Cateline on her own. No, he did not deserve love. He did not deserve happiness. He did not deserve joy. Because if he loved and was loved in return, they could never be together in any sense of the word. He would not steal another life that could have been happy with someone else. He would help Élise, but he would not, could not love her, and each day with her made him long for death—a mortal life—but he knew she too would pass, and he would not.

His body turned slack before he wiped his tears and turned on the sofa, facing away from the fire, away from Élise. He did not deserve either's warmth. He focused on the dark, unyielding shadows dancing on the wall, chasing each other into the long night.

By the light of each day, her laughter chipped away at his resolve. Its sound was so pure in its timbre. He'd imagine a life where his curse was lifted, and he could spin her into his arms and lay passion upon her lips while holding her tight. But night always brought clarity. The curse. The vow. The pain.

He had to leave her.

He would leave her.

The same decision followed each night after debating the time spent in sunlight. The memories of the day were pushed away but lingered stubbornly in the back of his mind. He retreated beneath the steel armor he had placed around his heart. Yet, as his thoughts drifted to the woman asleep beyond the door, he feared the steel might soon crack.

ROLLANT AWOKE to a rapid knock and the smell of warm bread. The knock came again, forcing him to sit up as Élise handed him a cup of tea.

"You always look fresh, Rollant," she whispered, tousling his hair as if her fingers could command his unruly curls. "I'm jealous." She glanced toward the entryway. "There is someone at the door."

He sipped his tea and stood up, adjusting his pants and stepping into his boots. "It is the neighbor family," he said with the minty tea refreshing his breath and memory.

"Ah, yes," she said. "I'll warm more bread. I had forgotten they were coming."

Answering the door, he forced a smile at the family of five. They came bearing gifts. The two girls, about fifteen and thirteen, the son, twenty, and the parents stood on the porch.

"Good morning," Rollant greeted them. "Please come in." He eyed the father, hoping he would keep their exchange from a few days earlier a secret. "Jacq," he said his name, and led them in.

Jacq hesitated at the doorway, his hand brushing the frame as though he needed the solid wood to steady himself. "It's strange," he said quietly. "Being back in this old house. I was here with your father as a child and grew up thinking of this house as, well, a symbol of your family's generosity. Now that I'm standing here again with his son, once more in your favor, we are doubly blessed."

Rollant opened the door wider to let them in. "Take care of each other in these hard times, is all I ask," he said with a pointed stare at Jacq.

Jacq nodded in unspoken agreement, stopping in the entryway as the rest of his family entered the main room. "My wife knows you are the landlord and of Élise, but my children do not," he whispered. "They only know she was beaten, and you found her and brought her here."

"Good, they shouldn't know I have asked you here to introduce Hugo to Élise," Rollant whispered while his gaze lingered on Hugo's eager smile as he kissed Élise's hand. "Does your wife know of my intentions as well?"

"Yes," Jacq said, "but I asked her to act without pretension."

His gut twisted at Élise's gentle surprise with lifted eyebrows and parted-lipped smile. He told himself it was for the better—for her sake. She deserved happiness, companionship, and a life untouched by curses or eternal oaths. But as Hugo's blue eyes sparkled at Élise, Rollant realized he was tearing out his own heart, piece by piece.

Jacq placed a gentle hand on Rollant's shoulder. "You and your father, rest his soul, have been so kind to our family. Are you sure you want to go through with this introduction? I have just witnessed regret in your eyes."

"Regret, yes. It gnaws at me, but it has to be this way. I cannot stay, and even if the introduction does not end in love over time, I ask you to still help her find her way here," Rollant said as he caught Élise's glance, discernment brewing in her gaze. "I hope Hugo can at least allow her to see a different future and be a friend when she has none."

"She has you," Jacq said, patting Rollant's shoulder.

"Not for much longer, I'm afraid," Rollant glanced at Jacq. "I have other matters that require me elsewhere for years. I won't lie to you; Élise and I are fond of each other, but I cannot be the man she needs and wants. My resolve is firm." Rollant forced a smile, but even he could hear its hollowness. He hoped seeing Élise with another man would lessen his longing to love her, ease his return to a numb existence, and allow her the opportunity to live a normal life.

"My, what a beautiful sofa," Jacq's wife said as she ran her hand down the curved wooden arm. "Though you haven't done anything with the walls?" Her gaze darted from bare wall to bare wall.

"Camille." Jacq addressed her, entering the room and shaking his head at her unfiltered conversation. Then he turned his attention to Élise. "Thank you for having us for breakfast, Mademoiselle. Your new home is lovely, a blank slate to make it your own," he assured her.

Camille waved him off. "If she is going to be our neighbor, she might as well know I speak my mind."

Élise laughed. "I have been forward and blunt as well. Why act with assumption when you can just ask the question?" She glanced at Rollant. "Monsieur Montvieux knows all too well the questions I have asked him."

Jacq shifted and peered at Rollant at the informality of her address to Monsieur *de* Montvieux, but Rollant ignored him.

Camille raised her eyebrows. "Oh, did you hear, Jacq? I like this young woman. She'll fit right in." She drew near to Hugo. "And I taught my boy to respect a woman's mind and to answer the questions she is courageous enough to ask with honesty and tact." Her head bobbed with each spoken virtue.

Hugo chuckled with a too-wide smile as his cheeks turned rosy pink. "I—I have good parents," he said finally with a nod of his own.

Élise smiled at him, glanced at Camille before turning her attention to Rollant with a pressed smile. She was wary.

Rollant forced the corners of his mouth to lift. Camille was giving it all away.

"Of course you do, Hugo," Rollant said, patting Jacq's back. "Élise, this is the family that bartered for your mint and sage tea, and Hugo gave an extra amount out of his heart's kindness."

Élise turned to Hugo with a new appreciation. "Thank you so much, Monsieur." Élise's smile lingered, but her eyes searched his face as if weighing his and his mother's intentions. "I believe it helped my stomach and my bruises."

"I—I'm glad to hear it," Hugo said, tracing her face with his eyes. "I—I had only heard Monsieur de Montvieux had found a woman who had been attacked in the city and wanted to help her. I thought I—I could help in—in that way."

Élise had taken the poor boy's words. Her eyes shifted at Rollant's name, but Hugo continued before she could throw Rollant a questioning glare.

"I—I'm an herbalist," Hugo stammered, his cheeks flushing as he glanced at Élise, then quickly away. "For the community. It's . . . it's just a small way to help."

Camille patted his shoulders. "Hugo is the best herbalist around. Any malady he can cure with the right mixture. He is smart and kind and generous. His care for his common man and woman is unparalleled."

Hugo's smile froze as his mother tried too hard to paint a picture Élise would have seen for herself in due time. Rollant glanced at Jacq, who stared wide-eyed at his wife, shaking his head in a silent quiver.

Élise's head tilted to the side as her gaze darted between mother and son. "I'm so happy to hear I will have such a kind neighbor."

"Gabrielle, Giselle," Jacq interrupted the exchange and addressed his daughters. "Give Élise your gifts."

Gabrielle, the younger daughter, handed Élise a jar of honey, while Giselle gave her a small wheel of cheese. "These are for breakfast," Giselle said. "May we assist you?"

Élise smiled and nodded. "Hugo, Rollant, could you move the table and the chairs to the sofa, so we can all eat together?"

Jacq and Camille shifted at the informality of Élise calling Rollant by his first name, but Hugo smiled widely with a sparkle in his blue eyes. He was smitten already, tongue-tied as well.

Rollant couldn't blame the young mortal. He, himself, had fallen under her spell after a single glance at *Au Pain Roux*. Even bruises couldn't hide her beauty or her fire. Rollant clenched his jaw as he scooted the table while Hugo got the chairs. It was for the better, he told himself. The few times he had returned over the past year, the family had been good to him. Jacq's father was a compassionate soul. Hugo would be a friend, if not more, to Élise.

"It is ready!" Gabrielle said as she spun around with plates in hand. The table was set, and they found seats.

Élise's smile was gracious but guarded as Hugo pulled out a chair for her. Her warm "Thank you, Hugo," was a dagger through Rollant's resolve, but Élise's glance darted toward him as she sat with a knitted brow. He wondered if she noticed how Hugo's manners mirrored the gestures he had once offered her in an attempt to show her not everyone was like her abusers. There was still good in the world.

Rollant sat on the floor with his back against the sofa leg, focusing on the morning's hospitality, knowing they'd all be in their graves the next time he passed through Charonne.

Hugo moved quickly to pull out his mother's chair, but he bumped into the table's edge in his eagerness, sending the plates and cups teetering. He laughed nervously as his frantic hands steadied the dishes. He gave an apologetic glance toward Élise with a shaky breath and the stain of embarrassment still on his cheeks. "Ah, forgive me, Élise. It seems my hands are less graceful than my mother boasts."

"Your hands are fine, Hugo," Élise said as she steadied her and Giselle's teacups.

Camille piped up. "Sit here, my son, across from Élise."

Rollant closed his eyes, wishing Camille would close her mouth.

"Father and Monsieur de Montvieux should sit on the sofa, Mother," he said.

Rollant waved his hand to quickly overlook Hugo's comment. "Your father and I are already seated. Take the sofa."

Hugo dipped his head, tiptoed past Rollant, and sat on the couch, his knee by Rollant's head. His sisters sat beside him, and his father sat beside the opposite sofa leg.

After Jacq led the small group in a prayer of thanksgiving for their meal, the table silenced, all eyes on Hugo and Élise.

Rollant swallowed his piece of bread and began the conversation, "An herbalist? Is that a family tradition?"

"No, Monsieur," he said. "I did not want to raise chickens like my father, and the prior herbalist did not have any children, so it was a natural inclination for me to study with him and become his apprentice, rest his soul."

Camille leaned over to Élise and said loudly behind a wall of fingers, "He also learned to read. Had to read so many books. I'm grateful because we could not afford him an education, but the Good Lord has blessed him in his endeavor."

Élise's gaze shot to Hugo. "You can read?" Her eyes lit up. "Could you teach me?"

Hugo chuckled with raised shoulders. "I—I am no teacher, Mademoiselle, but I—I'd love to help you best—the best—that—the best I can."

Rollant took a bite of cheese to distract his tongue from his contribution to the conversation. He knew how to read as well—in seven languages. He could stay and teach her to read. He swallowed the cheese and took a bite of bread to stay silent.

"Hugo!" Camille whispered in a harsh tone. "Why are you talking like you need the healing hands of our Lord and Savior?"

Jacq sighed loudly. "Let our son make his own way, Camille." He dipped his head to Élise. "I apologize for any discomfort we may have put you in, Mademoiselle."

Élise smiled with her eyes darting between Hugo and Rollant. "None whatsoever," she spoke as a true lady of the house, but tension laced her words.

"We could start today, if—if you wanted, Élise," Hugo said. "I've read over ten books and anything I can find. I've memorized most of them. Well, I—I had to in order to be an herbalist, and a good one, if—if I can boast. My master said I surpassed him at my age. He believed I'd become one of the best in the region if I kept studying."

Rollant couldn't bear to look up and see the zeal flaming in the boy's eyes; his tone was enough. He sipped his tea with his gaze on the worn spot on the floor.

"Well, Rollant is only here a few more days, and he still has much to teach me before he leaves."

Hugo's eyes dropped, the spark dimming. "Oh, I—I see."

It was in Rollant's interest to speak if his resolve was firm. "I think you should begin now, Élise," he said after another sip. "You seem more excited about reading than any of the other topics I had lined up for us." His smile did not reach his eyes.

Her brow knitted again, and her head twitched in confusion. Her mouth opened and closed as if words fought to escape but failed. At last, she nodded. "Well, what book shall we start with?"

"Oh, the *Book of the Apothecary*"—Hugo's voice steadied, the stammer gone—"It's very old and written by a monk. It tells of all the ailments and what to pluck, how to prepare, and what to do. My favorite is one on how to soothe coughing."

Élise's gaze softened as Hugo spoke of his remedies, but when her eyes flicked to Rollant, her smile faltered with a question hidden in her glance.

Rollant shifted, averting his focus to Hugo. The boy zealously spoke of his trade, a lifeline of compassion and skill. The craft was admirable and quite a feat to master. It was one of the many professions Rollant had dabbled in over the centuries until he realized he would never require it. His thoughts bittered his tea, heavy with truths he could not speak.

The confidence in Hugo's discussion of his trade grated against Rollant's resolve as he realized Hugo reminded him of himself long ago, before the Crusade, before the oath, before the curse stripped him of his innocence. He, too, spoke with certainty in all things before God as he trained as a squire and became a knight. Hugo, he assumed, would be suitable for Élise as a husband, provider, father, and friend, for Hugo would never be calloused by unending time.

Hugo's boyish enthusiasm lit up the room. He must have told a joke; Élise laughed a genuine laugh. Everyone chuckled in the room, and Rollant followed suit, as if he had been listening intently. But he sipped the last of his tea soon thereafter to soothe the sharp sting in his chest. How many generations had he seen come and go on this land? How many lives had flourished under his care while he remained unchanged?

He'd watched Jacq's ancestors grow from struggling farmers to the respected neighbors they were now. He could take pride in that, at least. His gaze lingered on Élise's guarded smile, growing soft under Hugo's attention. He'd given his heart away, only to see another claim it. That was his curse—the curse of revenge.

Breakfast ended, and Hugo agreed to come over with his sisters after Rollant left. Élise cleaned up while Rollant walked the family to the door. Camille and the children exited, but Jacq stayed behind to speak with Rollant.

"I know I was a child, but from my memory, you look so much like your father," Jacq murmured with nostalgia. His gaze lingered on Rollant as if the resemblance unraveled decades.

The weight of the man's words settled on Rollant's shoulders. "*You look so much like your father*"—the same sentiment came more times than he cared to remember, spoken with reverence and gratitude, only to be met with countless lies in return.

Rollant forced a smile and spoke the lie. "I've heard that once or twice."

Jacq chuckled, shaking his head and studying Rollant's face. "The resemblance is uncanny, though. Same eyes, same chin. I suppose good deeds and strong features run in the family."

Jacq remembered a man who never existed, an illusion crafted by Rollant to account for his unchanging face and decades of guardianship. To the people of Charonne, he was a legacy—a dutiful son who continued his father's work before him. They didn't see the truth: there was no father, no passing of the torch. There was only him, pretending to belong to a mortal world that would never be his.

Rollant cleared his throat. "A family trait, I suppose." His tone was careful. He patted Jacq's shoulder as he passed over the home's threshold.

Jacq leaned in and whispered, "I do apologize for Camille. I asked her not to say anything, and I hope she hasn't ruined the introduction."

"No need for apologies. I'm sure she wants to see her son happy. Not too many young women here, I suppose."

"No, not many, and she refuses to let him go to the city. Too expensive and too much turmoil there."

"Yes, I agree with her on that. Don't let your son go to the city for his safety."

Rollant ended the conversation and closed the door behind Jacq. The bar lowered into place. He took a deep breath before spinning around and finding Élise with her arms crossed.

"What was that?" she asked.

He swallowed the lump in his throat and hid it with a shrug. "What?"

"Did you bring them here to have that poor woman showcase her son as a suitor?"

That was exactly what he had done, but he shook his head. "He gave us double the mint and sage I had asked for, Élise. I asked them over to thank them and to introduce you to their family and the community's herbalist. His mother had another agenda, it appeared."

She stepped closer, her eyes blazing. "You let her build up hope for her son. You didn't say anything. You almost pushed me into his arms."

"I will be leaving in a few days. It is better if I do not let my feelings for you complicate whatever life you have ahead of yourself. You should not see me as anything other than a helping hand. But Hugo, he will be here. He is your age."

"And you are not?"

"I'm almost seven years older than you."

Her arms fell to fists by her sides. "Do you think I'm not mature enough? Or is it that you've already decided my life for me? That I'm better off with someone like Hugo because you're too afraid of what we could be?"

"No, Élise, that's not—"

"You want me to believe this is about what's best for me, but it's not." She crossed her arms, her chin lifting in defiance. "It's about your poor decision to follow a king that cares nothing for anyone."

Rollant flinched, her words cutting deeper than he thought possible.

She continued, unrelenting. "I'm not broken, Rollant. I'm not some fragile piece of glass you can protect by walking away. I want you in my life, and I won't apologize for it."

"Élise, stop." His stomach turned. "You only care for me because I have cared for you. Did Hugo not show you the same care I have shown you? He is a kind, good man, better than I am. He is innocent and doesn't have blood on his hands. He heals the sick, and I kill the hardy. A man like him would never leave you. He would make his oaths wisely."

Tears brimmed her eyes. He regretted speaking the last statement. He rubbed his mouth and dropped his gaze, unable to see the pain he'd caused with his words.

"I am only saying there are other good men, Élise." He found her gaze. "Men you can have a happy life with, should you choose to want a life with one."

She spun around and marched across the main room. After she entered the bedroom, she yelled, "I want you to stay, Rollant! Is that clear enough for you?" before slamming the door.

"I want to stay as well," he murmured, rolling his sleeves to finish washing the dishes. "But it cannot be."

CHAPTER 22
The Will to Leave
CHARONNE, PARIS, FEBRUARY 1789

THE PALE MORNING sunlight cast a golden glow over the room. Dust motes danced in the beams, and the faint scent of smoke from the hearth lingered, mingling with the earthy aroma of mint from the main room. Élise's smile widened as she stretched in bed, her body still aching from the quiet pleasure of tending to the garden while the sun warmed her winter-chilled skin the day before. She hummed with the satisfaction of accomplishment.

The past fourteen days had been nothing short of transformative—a blur of discovery, learning, and warmth that felt like a lifetime of joy compressed into a few moments. She'd learned to trust herself again—to believe that happiness was still possible. And through it all, Rollant had been there, as steady as the earth beneath her feet.

Élise's fingers brushed her lips, the memory of Rollant's thumb still fresh as it was the first day she'd woken up in Charonne, and he'd almost kissed her. Heat flushed her cheeks. She wanted to pull him back every day since, to demand why he had retreated. But every time she saw him, the answer was evident in his eyes—a barrier of sorrow and duty shielded his heart. Yet even his silences spoke of care, of the pain he carried and the love he dared not touch again.

Her own heart warred between accepting his distance and defying it, yearning to be the one who could draw him back into the light. But anger mixed with her yearning—a simmering frustration that he could give so much, yet hold himself back from her entirely. She knew his reasons, and she understood his duty. But she also knew her own heart.

Every shared glance and every quiet moment with Rollant had deepened her sense of belonging. Today, her heart was resolute. She would confess her love to him as a plea for him to choose her and to share the life she had begun to dream of in this place. She would confess what she could barely admit even to herself—that she trusted him completely and wanted him by her side for as long as she lived. She'd hope it was enough, though doubts pressed against her heart. He'd already told her he was leaving, though she said she wanted him to stay, but if he knew he held her heart, he might reconsider. The thought sent a flutter of anticipation through her chest. With only hours left before he was to leave, she hoped it would be enough time for him to give her the answer her heart longed to hear.

She got ready for the morning, washed her face, and donned her newly made dress—a perfect fit. The mirror showed her face fully healed. She bit her lips and pinched her cheeks to bring forth a pretty pink color, as Giselle had taught her. Her hair swept down her back, and she'd leave it that way for the day. Her red scarf lay unused on the dresser. She stood before the door, steadying her breath with her eyes closed and her head down.

"This is it," she whispered.

She opened the door to find Rollant sitting at the table, about to take a sip. He glanced up and stopped, rooted still, with the cup hovering mid-air. His eyes traced her figure from head to toe to commit her to memory, lingering on her face with awe that made her pulse quicken. He slowly placed his cup on the table and stood up as she approached him.

When he finally spoke, his voice was reverent, and he whispered, "You're beautiful, Élise." He cleared his throat and pulled her chair out for her, but it remained empty.

Her heart pounded as she stepped closer, the weight of her words pressing against her chest. What if he turned her away? What if he still chose the serviceman's path over her? Yet even the thought of silence, of never telling him what burned within her, felt like a betrayal to herself. She could endure no more half-measures, no more half-spoken truths. It was now or never.

Her hand trembled as it covered his, the warmth of his skin sending a wave of reassurance and fear through her. His fingers stiffened beneath hers before relaxing, their touch grounding her as tears of bittersweet joy rimmed her eyes.

"Élise." He whispered her name as a prayer on his lips. His free hand rose as if to touch her cheek, but stopped mid-air, hovering between them. He read her mind. "You don't know what you're asking."

She stepped closer, her tears spilling over as she shook her head. "I know exactly what I'm asking, Rollant. I'm asking you to stay—not because I need you, but because I love you."

His shoulders slumped as if he wanted to wrap his arms around her. His gaze dipped to her lips. He shifted closer but pulled his hand away, remaining silent.

"Not because you saved me, or because of everything you've done for me, but because of who you are." She pressed on despite his silence. "Because I see the goodness in you, despite what you say you've done. I see the strength that carries you through every burden you bear alone. And I want to share it with you—not to take it away, but to bear it together."

She grabbed his hand. "I trust you, Rollant, with everything that I am. I want you by my side for the rest of my life. I want to grow old with you. I want a life with you."

The silence stretched between them, fragile as an old spider's web. Rollant's gaze darkened, his eyes swimming with emotion. He opened his mouth, then closed it again, his jaw tightening.

"You could stay," she whispered, her voice breaking with the hope she couldn't contain. "I doubt the king would notice a single navy man absent, or even where to look for you. I would not think less of you if you did not return even though you gave your word."

Rollant's lips pressed into a thin line, his eyes flickering with regret. "I would think less of myself," he said. His voice was firm, yet it carried the weight of sorrow and deception. He was making an excuse.

Tears spilled over Élise's cheeks, but she didn't let herself falter. "I would not think less of you," she said again, softer, pleading, not calling him out on his lie. "You've given so much. What more could they ask of you?"

"They ask everything," Rollant said, his voice bitter yet resigned. "And I am bound to give it. It is who I am, Élise. It is the oath I took, and I cannot break it without breaking the man I have struggled so hard to remain."

There was no deception that time. That was the truth, and it angered her. "Why reveal your feelings for me if you were going to leave?" she demanded, her voice trembling with frustration and pain. "Why give me hope if you knew it would only end like this?"

His eyes softened, and he shook his head, his hand falling away from hers. "I am sorry, Élise," he said, his voice thick. "I am sorry I revealed my feelings for you. I was wrong to do so, knowing I cannot be in your life."

"You are in my life now," she countered, her voice fierce with determination.

"I will not be any longer," he said, shaking his head again, his expression hardening with resolve, but his voice betrayed his façade. "I know it feels as if I am not choosing you, but I am, Élise, and that choice forces my absence from your life. I'll not be returning. You deserve more than I can give. You deserve peace, love, and freedom—not the shadow of a man bound to a duty that will never end."

Her breath hitched as the truth of his words sank in, leaving a hollow void in her chest. But she refused to crumble. If this were the last time she would see him, she would not let him leave with only her tears.

She stepped back, her hand falling to her side as well. The space between them felt like a chasm, one she didn't want.

"Then go," she said, her voice steadier than expected. She didn't understand his logic, but he had told her from the beginning he wasn't to stay. Her chin lifted to keep her tears from falling. She had been a stupid girl, a stupid, stupid girl.

Her lip quivered. "If you've made your choice, I won't beg you to stay anymore. But know this, Rollant: If I can't make you stay, I'll prove I don't need you to."

Her eyes burned, but she didn't flinch, her resolve building with each word. "I will survive. I will fight. And I will honor the sanctuary you gave me. Not because of you, but for me."

For a moment, Rollant stood frozen as though her words had struck a chord of admiration in him. He reached out, his hand brushing her cheek, but stopped just short of touching her. Instead, he swept his hand around a lock of her hair, letting the ends glide off his fingers. They twisted into his palm, and his fist dropped to his side.

"I know you will, Élise," he said. "I told you in Le Marais; you are stronger than you know."

He withdrew his gaze and scanned the hearth and counter before letting a finger brush the top of the table. "Would you like to have breakfast one last time together?"

She shook her head. She said what needed to be said, and there was nothing more. Her arms crossed at her belly to keep the pain inside.

"Then I shall get an early start to port. It may be beneficial since the river is likely frozen." He took a last sip of tea before walking toward the bedroom to pack his bag.

Her eyes shut tight, and she called out, still facing the table, as his footsteps neared the bedroom door. "Will you leave your long shirt?"

The wooden planks creaked as his weight shifted as he likely debated an answer.

Her voice quaked with justification. "I've found it comfortable." She drew a deep breath and stared at his empty cup of tea. "For sleeping, that is." The request was small, almost trivial, but it carried the weight of her longing—something to hold onto when he was gone.

He hesitated but finally said, "Of course, Mademoiselle."

A while later, he emerged with a packed sack slung over his shoulder.

Élise was seated at the table, sipping her mint tea. She had not touched her bread and cheese, as her appetite had vanished.

He lingered in the doorway between the entry room and the main room with his hand firmly on the post as though it were the only sturdy frame to keep him upright. He turned to face her. "Don't tell anyone in the city about this place, Élise," he said quietly. "They'll tell Gabin in exchange for bread, and then he'll come for you. Keep this place a secret, please."

Her lips pressed thin as the corners of her mouth pinched tight. Those were his last words to her? She pushed the thought aside and instead spoke her feelings. "Always the protector, Rollant." He remained silent, so she agreed. "To honor your gift, I promise this home will be a secret to everyone in the city."

He nodded in gratitude before his façade dropped. The desire to run back to her, take her in his arms, and stay forever flooded his eyes.

She stood with a fluid grace, hoping for him to do so.

"Goodbye, Élise," he whispered, straightened, and turned from her sight. The bar lifted. The door opened. Deliberate footsteps echoed. The door closed. He was gone.

She didn't watch him go. She didn't trust herself to.

Instead, she spun toward the hearth, the embers still faintly glowing from fresh wood. The scent of mint and smoke filled her lungs, grounding her in the nightmare.

The air shifted—both lighter and heavier all at once. Élise allowed herself to cry, raw and unrestrained. She sank to her knees, wrapping her arms around her belly as it heaved. Her heart broke, giving rise to a burning ache in her chest. Every word he spoke, every moment they'd shared, every smile on his lips when he thought she wasn't looking, and every time his voice softened when he said her name—those fragments felt like sunlight slipping through her fingers.

WHEN no more tears were left to fall, she drew a shaky breath over trembling lips and grasped the chair to help her stand. Her legs wavered, and she swayed against the wood of the chair. The fire blurred in sight as the silence pressed in around her.

She had a choice now, and she would make it.

If Rollant chose to leave, she would make sure her own life, her own fight, would be something worth living for. Something worth loving. Something worth dying for, in the end.

"This isn't the end, though," she whispered to the empty room. It couldn't be. The embers caught a glimmer of new light. She wiped her cheeks. "Not for me."

But the day had already been long, and she turned toward the bedroom, her body heavy with exhaustion but her mind refusing to let go of him. She rounded the doorway and found his shirt neatly folded on top of the dresser, next to his dagger, and a coin in place of her red scarf. She placed her hand over the coin's cool metal. Her heart clenched at the unspoken message it carried. He took a reminder of her as she had asked for one of him. The coin was more than a means to replace it with another—it symbolized what he believed she could build without him. Practical, like he always was, yet so achingly personal. She clutched the coin tightly, her tears threatening to fall again.

She grabbed his shirt and collapsed onto the bed with the collar pressed against her nose. He truly loved her, believing he was doing what was best for her. But if he took her scarf, maybe, maybe one day, he would return. Perhaps after the Estates-General adjourned, he would be free from duty and could come back to her. She clutched the soft cotton and held it tight.

If he ever did, she would be ready. She promised herself she would make this place a sanctuary, not just for him, but for herself too—a home she could be proud of, one built with her own hands and strength.

CHAPTER 23

The Land of Secrets

CHARONNE, PARIS, APRIL 1789

THE WINTER WAS the harshest Élise had ever witnessed, forcefully bleeding into April. The crops failed. Her garden was devastated. The price of bread tripled from the year prior. She crossed her arms and shivered as she stared out the window at the snow on the ground. She sighed at the injustice beyond the window and approached the sofa where Giselle had given up on her supervisory duties and fallen asleep. Élise pulled the blanket over Giselle's shoulders before returning to Hugo at the table.

Admiration lived in his eyes. "You are so kind to my sister."

She shrugged and took her seat next to Hugo. "Anyone would do as I did."

Her gaze fell to the pamphlet from January in Hugo's hands, but his eyes remained on her profile with a soft smile on his lips. He pulled himself away at her insistence on the pamphlet by way of a soft nod.

"Are you able to read this line?" he asked. His blistered finger pointed to the third row of text.

She traced the worn edge of the *What is the Third Estate?* Pamphlet.

She remembered the first time she held it in Bastille, and Gabin told her to leave because she was a woman. To read all of it by herself was a dream come true.

The words danced on the page, but finally, tracing each word, the sounds came to her in a broken harmony: "The privileged orders make everything burdensome, even their own uselessness." The waver in her voice mirrored her lack of confidence. She glanced at Hugo to see if she'd read it correctly.

His broad smile reassured her. "Well done, Élise. You are a quick study."

"But do you know what this means?" she asked, her confidence growing sullen.

His smile faded, and a sigh escaped his lips. "Of course I do, but this is a reading lesson."

"But how can you read this and not be angry?" Élise demanded, slamming her hand atop the pamphlet. "Uselessness. That is Jean-Baptiste Réveillon, the scoundrel. He deserved what came to him." She saw the smoke rising from his burning business and home from her Charonne window in the days prior. "That scum built his fortune while telling his workers they deserved less wages."

Hugo slid his hands off the table and leaned back. "Why does it anger you so much?" Hugo asked, his voice gentle but curious. "Réveillon isn't the only wealthy middle-class business owner in Paris, nor the worst of them. I'd even say he was far from the worst."

"Because he said we should be grateful to eat scraps! Because men like him build fortunes on our backs and call it charity!" Her cheeks flushed, and her chest heaved. "How can you stay so calm, Hugo? How can you not care about what is happening in Paris? Across France?" Élise shook her head, not understanding how the man before her was content with meager meals and high taxes.

"I do care," Hugo replied. "But anger isn't the answer. Twenty-five people or more died in the riot at Réveillon's place, Élise. And now? Families are worse off than before. Bread is still expensive, and many now have no homes or work. I see the pain you feel, and I understand it. But I know rage leads to violence, and violence only breeds more suffering. It doesn't fix what's broken; it only carves deeper scars." He sighed. "I want to heal bodies. I want to give people their lives back, Élise, not take them away."

Hugo's logic warred with her fury, leaving her angrier than before. Élise slammed the pamphlet onto the table, unable to refute him. Rollant had said something similar. At the thought of the man who'd left her, her cheeks flushed. Her teeth clamped down on the hurt.

"I can see you are upset again. Do you need to look out the window once more to calm your mind?" Hugo asked, his voice steady, like Rollant.

She closed her eyes and tried to push Rollant away. She wished Rollant were there teaching her to read rather than Hugo. It seemed her anger had two fuses, one short in reading the pamphlet and the other two months long at Rollant, though he said he would leave from the beginning.

Her racing heart settled as she rubbed her neck. She wouldn't let Hugo see her lose control a fourth time. Her back straightened, and she pressed her hands into her lap. "Perhaps you have something else to read?"

Hugo smiled and plopped a thick, old leather-bound book on the table. "This is the *Book of Simple Medicines*."

The sheer size of it made her breath hitch. Her mind froze like the dead plants in the garden.

Hugo gently stroked the cover before opening the book to the first page. "What does this line say?"

Her forehead balanced in her palms. The line eluded her. But rather than look a fool again, she asked in a much calmer voice, bringing the conversation back to where it was before. "Before we begin again, why are you not angry at how we've been treated by those richer than us?"

Hugo sighed and shook his head.

"Please, answer me, Hugo. I've only ever known suffering."

His hand hovered over her shoulder before letting it rest, and he slowly rubbed her back. "I'm sorry you've had a difficult life. I'll probably never know your experiences."

At her stiffness, he removed his hand. "I'm not mad that you are angry at what's happening, but all I see is people gone mad with rage. Outside of the four families in our little community on the Montvieux land, neighbors have nearly killed each other over disagreements. I don't feel it's worth it. It doesn't fix anything."

She lifted her head and furrowed her brow. Hugo's words echoed in her mind against her own. *Montvieux land. Fighting for what was right. Sacrificing everything for change.* The thoughts clashed against each other—thunder against thunder—leaving her struggling for what to say next.

Hugo shifted on his seat at her silence. "I am surprised you are so against the *bourgeoisie,* considering Rollant de Montvieux is one of them, or maybe more. His name signifies he is nobility," he chuckled.

She froze. Her head twitched as if she hadn't heard him. "What? What do you mean?" she stuttered. Élise frowned, her thoughts stalling at the unfamiliar phrase. "Montvieux land?" she repeated, the words catching in her throat. "Nobility?" It dawned on her: Hugo's entire family had called him Monsieur *de* Montvieux since she'd met them.

Hugo tilted his head, his brows knitting. "Well, yes. You've lived here for months. Didn't you know? The land belongs to Monsieur de Montvieux."

She froze, her breath catching. "Rollant?" she whispered, the name tumbling from her lips. Why had he lied about his noble status? Because she was a revolutionary, and she was supposed to hate him.

Hugo's eyebrows raised, clearly confused at her reaction. "Well, Mama, at least, says he's the landlord," Hugo said, smiling faintly. "Father says he and his father were always so generous, never asking for rent. They must come from a wealthy family, at least."

Élise's heart pounded. Rollant, the landlord? The one who owned all of the land, who had given it to the community freely? It made no sense. Her mind reeled with questions. Why hadn't he told her? Why had he lied about being an orphan, about living off a sailor's wage? Each thought pricked at her heart, unraveling the trust she'd built in him.

She tried to speak without letting her words falter. "Rollant told me he was orphaned at eight. His future wife's family took him in before he married Amée and joined the Navy. Why would he lie?"

Hugo shrugged, oblivious to the storm brewing in her thoughts. "I don't know, Élise. Maybe it's not a lie. Maybe his father passed away years ago, leaving Amée's family to raise him. Maybe he didn't find out about the inheritance until later. But if he doesn't collect rent, I don't know how he pays his taxes unless he is of the nobility and exempt from taxes." He shook his head and shrugged again at her dumbfounded expression. "Maybe he pays out of a navy man's wage. Or maybe he's an officer in the Navy. Most wealthy sons are usually officers, that is," Hugo said, licking his lip.

She sat dumbfounded.

He fidgeted and tapped his knee until he finally asked, "Would you like to get back to reading?"

But his words fell on Élise's deaf ears. She stared past Hugo. Her hands gripped the table's edge until her knuckles whitened. The man she had given her heart to—the man she trusted above all others—was a stranger. Whether he'd lied or simply withheld the truth, she didn't know. But her heart ached with longing, even as questions burned within her. Why had he left? And who, truly, was Rollant de Montvieux? Why was he ashamed to tell her how he could afford the home? Was it because he was nobility and he knew how she felt about the rich? Their conversation rushed back to her. But why had he given her a common name? Why was he at *Au Pain Roux*?

Her chest tightened as the pieces began to fall into place. The land she'd come to see as her sanctuary, the home he had given freely to her and others, was his. Rollant's. Rollant's land. *His* home.

Why hadn't he told her? Why had he let her believe he was just a sailor, scraping by on navy wages? Every memory of him shifted, twisting into a mystery—like the shadows stretching long after sunset. And yet, her heart ached with the longing to see him again.

She willed Rollant's return, unsure whether to slap him across the face or fall into his arms. But one thing was certain: there would be no peace until her questions were answered and she uncovered the true identity and motivations of the man wrapped in mystery.

CHAPTER 24

The Tinderbox of Change

PALACE OF VERSAILLES, MAY 1789

ROLLANT STOOD a sentinel behind King Louis, scanning the room. The Estates-General was a stage, and the actors followed pre-written scripts, none of which addressed the primary grievance: social inequality and injustice. The same tired premise of noble support dominated the agenda, ensuring the king's reliance on the First and Second Estates remained unshaken.

Even if Louis had the best intentions, they were lost on the Third Estate. It didn't help that delegates were forced to wear black while the First and Second Estates paraded into Versailles with their best clothes, uniforms, and vestments. Worse, they waited hours to bow before the king. When Louis finally appeared, the Third Estate had kept their hats on in silent protest, forcing him to remove his own in return. Rollant had scoffed under his breath. For a king so unwilling to concede power, Louis seemed not to mind shedding it in public spaces.

The opening speeches were as dull as expected. The king and the new Keeper of the Seals delivered platitudes that drew only polite applause. But the mood shifted when Jacques Necker, the Third Estate's beloved celebrity minister, took the floor. Delegates leaned forward in their seats, eager for substance.

It never came.

Necker's voice failed early, leaving a moderator to drone through his words for three hours, stripped of the minister's zeal. The delegates wore scowls for lips and daggers for eyes. There was no mention of social injustice, no acknowledgment of the grievances Rollant had outlined in his report—ignored again, tucked away for some undefined future.

He understood why Louis and his advisors were reluctant to order the nobles to do anything. They were the generals and the bankers with families boasting a long history of support for the king. Still, the issues at hand were not adequately resolved in the decades prior, slowly building under the heavy weight of financial burden. He tried to tell Louis and his Cabinet again in February, but the fools brushed him off as they had in December. Mocked him even: *What did the Captain of the King's Bodyguard know about economics and government?*

Their taunts echoed in memory, as did their chortles. They had dismissed him as a soldier who couldn't comprehend the intricacies of governance. Perhaps they were right. But Rollant didn't need their numbers and charts to understand suffering. He had seen it in Élise's haunted gaze, in her fury at a world that ground people into dust. Her beautiful face came to his mind, but he immediately pushed her away, unable to bear his love for her. Every instance where she came to mind was a harsh reminder of the life he could never have. He straightened up and focused on the room to distract himself from the agony of his decision never to see her again.

Half the soldiers in the room also appeared disgruntled, their gazes fixed on the Third Estate delegates as though weighing allegiances. He doubted any of them would give their lives to defend the palace if the crowds outside rebelled.

He hated standing idle, watching history unfold in gilded circles. Yet, despite his frustration, he knew his place, his eternal loyalty to the throne. He was the king's shadow, his ageless weapon, bound by duty even as cracks formed in the crown they both served.

The first day adjourned with no further progress. Rollant escorted King Louis to the Cabinet, where they waited for the advisors to follow. Louis paced alongside the long table while Rollant stood in his usual position.

Unable to contain himself, Louis whispered, "How do you think it went?"

Rollant shook his head, eyes still on the wall across the room.

Louis pursed his lips. "That bad?"

Rollant sighed, knowing Louis' request for advice would come; he would give it, and it would be ignored.

"What should I do?"

Rollant's gaze shifted and met Louis'. "Your Majesty, you have nearly six hundred delegates from the Third Estate and the crowds outside in their support. If you command the First and Second Estates to give up their privileges and demand equality, the people will agree, and you will earn some favor with them."

Louis gritted with a tight jaw. "I've already told you. This is a meeting to pass the tax reforms. We cannot risk bringing up other grievances."

"That is what they have done, however. They expect you to hear their grievances and act accordingly."

"The Estates-General wasn't called to address grievances," Louis said, his voice sharp. "Its purpose is to solve the financial crisis and advise on tax reform, nothing more."

"From my time in Paris, I can firmly say the original purpose no longer matters. Your people's support is on its last breath. Your noble's support is built on favors, and it is not likely to withstand much more. I—"

The door swung open, and the ministers waltzed in as if they had outstanding accomplishments to share.

Louis glanced back at him and shook his head. "Let's just see what happens," he murmured.

Rollant's eyes hit the floor. He already knew what would happen. The Estates-General would falter, its divisions too deep to heal. But for Élise's sake, he allowed himself a brief, foolish hope—that this time, the call of the people might finally be answered. Perhaps, for the first time in centuries, history might prove him wrong.

After a month of bickering about names, titles, and voting procedures, the Estates-General produced nothing. The Third Estate demanded to be called the Commons. Some members of the First Estate sided with the Third Estate, and all of the nobility disregarded every grievance and course of action proposed by the Commons. Louis demanded a swift resolution, but the Dauphin fell ill and perished, taking the king away from the chaotic and futile Estates-General.

With the king absent, the Estates-General devolved further into chaos. Every resolution crumbled beneath the weight of infighting, and no one dared enforce unity in the king's place. Rollant doubted Louis would have succeeded even if he were present—but in the private royal chapel, kneeling in grief, Louis seemed more kingly than he ever had on the throne.

Rollant had seen every monarch kneel in prayer in a chapel of their royal residence since the day he died. Louis was no different as his pleas for the Lord to take his son's soul into heaven echoed against the gilded walls.

"An innocent child…for such as these, theirs is the kingdom…" he whispered. The weight of the crown seemed to bow Louis lower than his prayers.

The king's tears pricked at Rollant's long-buried grief. He had knelt as this king did, begging the heavens for mercy—for Amée, for Cateline, for his descendants, until the last bright-eyed Ninette. Time had dulled the sharpness of loss, but since he'd met Élise, moments like the one before him tore open old wounds, bleeding into his eternity. He closed his eyes to focus his thoughts. He had secluded himself from the world once, and he could do it again. He pushed Élise and all the others away, for the pain was too much to bear. It was difficult enough to have Élise live in his dreams; he couldn't endure the pain of having her in his waking thoughts as well. He drew a deep breath and opened his eyes with a clear head.

Louis whispered, "Amen." His voice cracked, raw with anguish. For a moment, he was not a king but a father, fragile and mortal; his crown rendered meaningless in death.

But the country was failing, and the king's ministry had been paralyzed amid the chaos beyond the doors of the royal quarters. He wanted the king to have his time to grieve, but urgency was at hand if there was to be any saving of the monarchy.

"Your Majesty," Rollant began.

"Not now, Rollant," Louis gritted and buried his forehead atop his knuckles. The rosary looped through his hands.

"It has been three weeks since the Dauphin's passing. As your friend and confidante in our time alone, I must reluctantly provide this warning. The Estates-General has spiraled out of control. The people, the Commons—they will not wait for a mourning king. They have also mourned their loved ones due to the famine and high cost of food; they do not share your sorrow."

Louis' shoulders shrank. "Leave me," the nearly inaudible command followed.

He was on shift with a royal oath never to leave the king's side. "You know I cannot do—"

"Leave me," Louis ordered.

Rollant shifted his weight. He ran a hand over his mouth as he debated. "I will be outside the doors."

When Louis finally emerged, his red eyes betrayed his grief. His voice carried a brittle resolve. "Shall we see to the Estates-General?" he asked in a rush of words.

Rollant's jaw grew taut. Never had he seen Louis act like a king until that moment, though his heart ached for him as a father. Rollant lifted his chin in respect before doling out the news he had withheld from the king in his time of mourning, an error perhaps, given the state of things.

"The First Estate joined the Third Estate and called themselves the National Assembly. It began conducting its business outside the Estates-General, declaring all taxes illegal. Minister Necker has been offering concessions in your name, but the others haven't been much help. The National Assembly has claimed authority on behalf of the people. The crowds outside the palace gates are growing more uncontrollable. And apparently, no one told the National Assembly of our next royal session, which would be today, and they were outraged when they arrived three days before to find the door locked."

Louis' mouth twisted into a frown, and for a moment, Rollant thought tears would again fall down the man's cheeks. "Well," he said, adjusting his cravat and blinking back his tears, "It looks like quite the predicament. God help us," he muttered.

The king stopped before he entered the royal session and sighed. He stood silent before the grand double doors. His jaw twitched, and his gaze was downcast. "I never wanted the crown," he whispered. "I've never been good for it, but I'll show the people I am the best king I can be."

As the doors swung open, Louis entered with Rollant at his side. The King's steps were measured, and his expression was a façade of authority. But Rollant could see the cracks—Louis' hand trembled, and his breaths were too shallow.

The grand hall was stifling. Tension thickened the air as the Estates convened once more. The Second Estate was in full regalia, their seats a sea of silks and powdered wigs. The deputies of the National Assembly sat clustered together, their black attire stark against the opulence. Their silence was a weapon, their unmoving presence to greet the king louder than any shout. Rollant couldn't shake the thought of Élise. Her belief in change, her speech at the *Au Pain Roux*, shouting, "Take it back!" empowered the people. When the news spread to Charonne, she'd be elated at what was transpiring, though he feared what would come if the royal session did not go as intended.

Louis took his place before his throne and addressed the Assembly. He announced, "We shall begin again. We have made mistakes, and we shall reset our proceedings. Any decisions that have been made in my absence are null and void. As a gesture of goodwill, I hereby decree that no future taxes will be raised unless the Estates-General consents."

The deputies sat unmoving, with a quiet, dissatisfied murmur rippling through the room. It was not the cheer Louis had hoped for, so he glanced at Rollant as he paused. He drew a deep breath and spoke again with a slight waver. "Additionally, as the monarch of the Kingdom of France, I advise the Second Estate to relinquish its privileges to allow for equality among the estates."

Rollant scanned the deputies, noting the only murmur came from the Second Estate. The king hadn't commanded the Second Estate to relinquish privileges as Rollant had suggested, only advised them. As such and as expected, the National Assembly remained stoic with eyes locked in a deadly glare at the king with expressions of contempt or hate.

At their silence, Louis began again, his voice straining, "In the present company, I must state as a reminder, the crown is the ultimate authority; nothing the Estates do is valid without the king's approval. Let us adjourn to our separate quarters for the day."

As Louis turned to leave, Rollant's gaze swept the hall. The National Assembly deputies sat rigid, their inaction loud with open defiance. A shift in the air arose. The king's words were like ants to the elephant. Louis left without noticing, but Rollant knew their refusal of the king's command to leave was only the beginning.

Louis had executed Rollant's advice half-done again, and again, the king would find it to fail. What might have appeased them in May only fueled their rebellion in June. But as it were, they were past anything Louis had to offer other than approve what they gave him.

The sun dipped below the horizon, leaving the palace bathed in restless shadows. The murmurs of discontent outside the gates swelled into a nasty roar as night fell. The crowds stormed the palace, and the soldiers, as Rollant had expected, did nothing. He had warned Louis, the advisors, and anyone who would listen, but never once had they heeded his warnings in all the long decades.

It was the tipping point—a people who would not be subdued by order but by chaos. They felt they had nothing to lose and forced the king's hand to order the Second Estate to join the new National Assembly. The crown, once absolute, had been slowly drowned and clung to life in the latest form of government.

Rollant watched it all unfold and remembered it would be just another day in his immortal life. But if there was one sentiment he cared to retain for the reign of King Louis XVI, it was this: too little, too late. He'd seen it all before, and he knew history had a knack for repeating itself—kings falling to their knees, killed, and perhaps burned, and the victor placing the crown upon their head, becoming a new master for Rollant to serve. From his experience, time usually worsened before it was ever better. The people would rebel again and crown a new king. Always a king, it seemed.

And yet, even as he resigned himself to history's unbroken cycle, a part of him held to an ember of hope in the imminent pyre—hope that Élise, with her vitality and courage, could find something better in the ashes of this crown.

THIRTY THOUSAND TROOPS were garrisoned in Paris at the discreet order of the King. His newly replaced ministers had insisted on it, except for Minister Necker, warning that the National Assembly's defiance and new constitution could spiral into rebellion. The presence of soldiers, their uniforms crisp and their muskets gleaming, did little to quell the unrest.

Rollant stood in his palace attic room, his gaze fixed on the city on the distant horizon. Paris was a tinderbox, and the King had struck the match. The Assembly had offered to extinguish the flame by passing a motion requesting King Louis withdraw the soldiers. Minister Necker suggested His Majesty accept the motion as he continued to make greater and greater concessions on behalf of the king.

Rollant advised Louis not to replace Necker, though he never liked the Genevan banker and even suspected it was he who told the Assembly of the King's order. Louis had paced at the foot of his bed while Rollant stood at the door.

"I want him gone," Louis had said, but Rollant shook his head.

"He has done nothing for dismissal."

"I thought you wanted a king with absolute power," Louis said, marching up to Rollant.

Rollant's gaze had met his king's. "We are past that now, Your Majesty. Minister Necker is your last lifeline to the people. Cut it, and you will sever your own head," Rollant advised. He hoped, for once, the king would listen to him.

But he didn't.

That morning, July 11th, Louis dismissed and ordered Minister Necker to be deported in a fit of frustration over the latest constitutional draft, which reduced the king's role to that of a figurehead. As the Cabinet departed, Louis ordered Rollant to go to Paris to assess the reaction to the dismissal. It wasn't a request, as it had been before, but Rollant obeyed, as he was bound to.

"Always the tinkerer," Rollant muttered regarding the king's locksmith hobby as he stuffed his pack of clothes again. "Tinker too much, and it breaks."

He wasn't sure where to stay as no royalist inn would take him in. They were all closed up, afraid of the mobs. He dared not return to his Charonne home and face Élise again, knowing he'd have to leave, and the king had no place for him to stay in the city and keep his spy's disguise. He slipped out of the palace and into the forest the grounds butted up against to avoid the eyes of the National Assembly. He took the long way to Paris, a four-hour horse ride turned five.

The countryside was eerily quiet. Villages were shuttered, their streets empty, as though the inhabitants had vanished into the shadows.

As Paris neared, the air thickened with smoke, sweat, and desperation. He circled the city's edge with the city walls in far sight, not daring to enter with a horse. A horse was status, and status was the enemy in the streets. Chaos lay in wait. Paris was restless, hungry, and livid. No one in Saint-Denis would take him in. No matter what tale he told, no one in the rural districts offered him lodging until finally he came to Charonne. The uneven cobblestone clacked beneath the mare's hooves. She shifted beneath his indecision, her breath huffing in the humid air.

"Dare I go back?" he asked.

Élise's face flashed in his mind, her voice sharp and full of fire.

She won't forgive me, he thought, *and maybe she shouldn't.*

He could already hear her sharp questions, her anger at his return after so long. But it wasn't just her wrath he feared—it was the pull of her presence, the longing that had no place in his cursed eternity.

"Maybe I could stash the horse and sleep in the stable without her knowing." The heat of July was no comfort, but at least he wouldn't freeze.

With a heavy sigh, Rollant dismounted and led the mare toward the familiar path to his Charonne home, off the main road to hide his approach.

CHAPTER 25

Resolve of the Broken

CHARONNE, PARIS, JULY 1789

THE HOUSE WAS dark when he arrived in the late evening. He hadn't anticipated it would feel so alive. He heard light footsteps within. Though he hadn't seen Élise, her presence permeated the surroundings: the garden, though wilting, showed traces of her attention, and a dress was drying on a line by the house, and chopped firewood stood stacked by the door. Her life had grown in his short absence, though he wanted to be a part of it. Maybe Hugo had taken his place. He hoped for it but hated it. The thought of Hugo taking her hand knotted in his chest, but it had to be. At least she was flourishing and would only grow at home more. It gave his bittersweet thoughts peace.

The mare nudged him as he led her into the stable as if wanting him to return to his home. But he stroked her neck and whispered, "I wish I could." He patted her mane. "For a few nights, though, might I be your bunkmate? If you'll have me, of course."

The mare pawed the ground and nodded her head with a snort. Rollant stroked the underside of her muzzle. "I appreciate you," he said, putting her up for the night in one of the two stalls. As a token of his gratitude, he gave her a nice big carrot from his bag before making his bed of hay in the other stall.

The stable remained silent, interrupted only by the rhythmic swish of the mare's tail against the wooden walls. Lying in the shadows on a bed of hay with a belly satiated with dried venison and berries, Rollant rubbed the sweat off his brow. The heat of July, thick in the air, made the cramped space feel oppressive. His eyes wandered to the small home, visible through the wooden slats. The moon illuminated the roof line. Élise's smile rose in memory. The way she moved in his shirt. He closed his eyes and pushed that dangerous memory away. He envisioned her inside the back room, asleep with the fire subdued for the night, maybe dreaming of him as he dreamt of her. No. Not him. Hugo. "She dreams of Hugo," he muttered.

A sigh escaped. He hadn't planned to return to Charonne, and yet there he was. He longed to see her face once more and hold her in his arms, but the latter was a futile wish. It was all futile.

It was foolish to be there, mere paces away from her, hiding like a thief under the dark veil of night. His gaze fixed again on the silhouette of the house. A budding light in the back room cast a moving shadow against the window. Élise was preparing the bedroom hearth.

Knowing she was thriving, safe within the walls of his old home, should have been enough for him. But each pulse of Rollant's heart betrayed him and rippled reminders of the ache that had grown unbearable since he'd left her behind.

"Lord God, heal my heart," he muttered his first prayer in ages as the weight of his eternal curse pressed down on his chest. The stifling July air swallowed his voice as he doubted his divine creator would even listen to such a man as him.

The mare shifted in her stall as if mirroring his unease. He reached out and ran his fingers along the worn leather of the saddle he'd propped against the wall as a pillow. This was where he belonged—in shadows, in transit, never lingering long enough to disrupt the lives of others. The ache was too great to endure for eternity.

A silhouette crossed the light—a figure he would know anywhere. His heart raced. She paused, her hand brushing the curtain aside as if sensing something beyond the glass.

He froze, his hand hovering over the saddle. His heart quickened, torn between the yearning to see her and the instinct to remain hidden. Rollant pressed his back against the hay, his breath shallow. Did she feel his presence?

"No," he whispered, shaking his head. "She's only checking for the night," he mumbled.

The curtain fell back, and her silhouette vanished. The light in the window flickered once more before fading dim, as did his heartbeat.

Relief and regret warred within him. She hadn't seen him, hadn't come searching. Yet, that small part of him, the selfish part he despised, had wanted her to sense him, find him. To step into the stable and confront him, to demand answers he couldn't give.

He ran a hand through his hair, damp with sweat. His promise to himself to keep his distance was as fragile as the hay beneath him. But he knew what he had to do.

Over the next few days, he would venture into Paris, fulfilling his duty to the king and staying in the unused, unattended stable each night. He would confirm whatever chaos was sure to ensue and deliver the reports as expected. Perhaps it would distract him from the pull of Élise, the magnetic force that quickened his pulse.

But for tonight, he allowed himself to linger on the edge of her world, a silent shadow among the hay. He closed his eyes, daring to dream—not of the eternity that stretched ahead of him but of a fleeting life that might have been, a life where her fire warmed more than the corners of his imagination.

THE EARLY MORNING sun crept through the cracks, and the slight change in darkness forced Rollant's eyes to slits. The crick in his neck sent a painful wave rippling through his back. He sat up and massaged the crick out of his neck with a sigh.

He hopped up and set to work. After he'd poured water and shoveled hay for his bunkmate, he slipped out of Charonne before the rooster crowed and any prying eyes were out in the fields.

The clatter sounded louder as he approached Paris, as if the very threads of the city itself were unwoven. Not taking any chances of running into Gabin, he went north once he entered the city walls into the district of Popincourt. Anger crackled in the air like thunder after a lightning strike. The feeder roads allowed him to see what took place on the main streets, and so that was where he stayed and observed the storm brewing like the pelting rain before the flood. He did not want to stay in one place too long and risk anyone asking questions. So he cut over to Le Marais and Les Halles before heading south to Bastille. Every district was the same: mobs gathered in the streets, spewing hate for the king in dismissing Jacques Necker. They rioted and tore into the wealthy's homes and businesses, parading busts of the former minister and shouting curses against the monarchy.

Nothing surprised him. It was all as he had expected. He'd come back for another few days and see the people settled, but given the tensions and centuries of abuse, he felt the tides turning. These people had their children out, destroying property and stealing from the slightly better off. He wasn't sure when their backs would break, but it seemed Necker's dismissal had fractured the spine of the Third Estate.

As he turned north toward Popincourt to avoid Faubourg Saint-Antoine, a voice he knew too well caught his ear. He stopped mid-stride and turned to see if his ears had betrayed him.

Élise stood on an overturned crate, her fiery gaze sweeping the gathered workers and tradespeople as she spoke. Her audience cheered.

Desire and dread clashed in his chest. She had promised to remain in Charonne, away from the growing chaos in the city, but it was clear her fire would not allow her to stay. Paris called to her, and she had answered.

She spoke with conviction, denouncing the injustices that had driven Paris to the brink of self-implosion.

"The time for waiting is over," she boomed. "The king dismisses the one minister who dared to listen to us, who dared pull back the curtain on the royal treasury, who dared reveal the filthy liars and fat pigs who sat on us and lied, saying, 'We are all starving.'"

The crowd roared in agreement.

Pride and apprehension filled his heart as he listened to her and watched the light in her eyes flame. Her words held power, but power was dangerous.

He glanced at the King's Guard Regiment, scanning the crowd, likely searching for the most egregious offenders. Yet they did nothing. The shadows of the Bastille loomed over the mob, as if the king was about to squash their revolt with the five thousand royal soldiers encamped on the Champ de Mars. Still, the troops did nothing.

Élise's voice rose as the soldiers did as ordered: nothing.

"The king commands military force to subdue us, to take back the National Assembly at Versailles. He will oppress us not! We shall take it back!"

The audience chanted with her, "Take it back! Take it back!"

He lingered at the edge, keeping to the shadows, hoping the guards would not find her speech "egregious."

Rollant kept a steady distance as Élise wove through the chaos. He did not let her out of his sight. She moved north to Le Marais with purpose. Her fire and beauty drew people to her like moths to a lantern. Embers of revolution remained in her footsteps. Stolen pamphlets leaked from her arms as she slipped them to workers and tradespeople.

Rollant singled out her voice as the riot's racket faded in his ears.

"The Bastille still stands; its walls are a prison for our voices!" Élise shouted, her words igniting shouts of agreement in the crowd. "Will we let them silence us, or will we make them listen?"

Rollant's chest tightened. The city was an inferno waiting for a single spark, and Élise was a match. He watched from the side streets trailing her as the shadows of the crowds grew bolder, louder. He had seen this city change over the last year, and Élise transform from a passionate speaker into a revolutionary leader. The girl who had once sought justice now stood at the heart of the chaos.

He hadn't planned to stay all day in the mobs, but he needed to ensure Élise was safe. Just as the sun dipped below the horizon, Élise headed to Popincourt and then south to Charonne. Rollant chuckled as he lagged far behind. "I'm glad we thought alike," he mumbled.

From a distance, he saw Élise's steps grow heavy as she neared his Charonne home. She didn't notice his mare neighing in the stable behind the house. The door swung open, and she stepped inside.

Rollant continued off the main road and into the stable. His stomach growled, and he pulled a hard biscuit and some cheese from his pack. He didn't dare buy anything in the city and show his coin. He could have stolen food, but it didn't feel right, stealing in the middle of chaos. Night fell, and there was no movement in the house. Curiosity got the best of him, so he snuck up to the window to find Élise collapsed on the sofa; exhaustion had claimed her.

THE NEXT MORNING, Rollant awoke to soft footsteps on the cobblestone path outside. Peering through the stable slats, he saw Élise leaving the house before dawn. Her coat was slung casually over one shoulder, and her stride was purposeful, carrying her toward Paris with unshakable resolve. She didn't glance back or notice his figure hidden in the shadows.

The morning air had a crisp edge, but it wasn't cold enough to warrant a coat. "Where are you going so early?" Rollant muttered under his breath, his brow furrowing as her silhouette grew smaller in the distance. He lingered, caught between following her and sticking to his mission.

By the time he saddled his mare, he was determined to follow her.

"I'll be back shortly, girl," he whispered to the horse.

Charonne was stirring with the faint hum of morning life, and he slipped by unnoticed. He took the road toward Popincourt, hoping to catch sight of her again, but Élise had vanished into the labyrinth of Paris. The city was eerily quiet. The usual clamor of carts, merchants, and restless mobs had stilled.

Yet, something was in the air—a low rumble, a vibration that seemed to come from the stones beneath his feet. It was a harbinger, the quiet before the storm. He pressed on toward Le Marais. The streets were also empty, except for a few watchful faces peering behind shuttered windows. The rumble grew louder.

It wasn't until mid-morning, as Rollant entered the Bastille district, that the city revealed its true state. A mob of nearly a thousand surged through the streets, an ocean of bodies and weapons raised high. Some carried muskets; others brandished scythes, swords, and even makeshift clubs. Their voices were a thunderous roar, a call to arms against the Bastille. The crowd's roar echoed in his ears, drowning out reason. This wasn't just a riot; it was a reckoning.

And then he saw her.

Élise marched among them, pistol in hand. Her face was fierce, her jaw set, her steps in rhythm with the revolt. Rollant's heart stopped.

"Élise," he whispered, his voice lost in the cacophony. She didn't hear him. She didn't even see him. She was part of the wave now, swept along by its tide.

"Do not go," he muttered, his voice hoarse with desperation as he watched her venture deeper into the crowd.

Duty and love warred within him. He was the king's shield, bound to deliver the news of this uprising to Versailles without delay. Every second counted. The crown could not afford ignorance. The king needed to act immediately to save his throne. He needed a decree by noon to resolve this revolt. Yet how could he leave her? How could he ride away knowing that Élise, with her fire and fragile mortality, stood on the precipice of death?

His fist clenched at his side. He stepped back, the sorceress' supernatural chill pressing into his bones as if urging him to turn away. Do as he was bound. The eternal weight of his existence pressed down on him, a constant reminder that his loyalty to the throne had been paid for in blood and sorrow. But his heart, long numbed by centuries of duty, thrashed against its chains.

Élise would never forgive him if she knew he'd been there and done nothing. But perhaps it was better that way. Better to let her fight, even die, without the shadow of his cursed presence looming over her. Better not to endanger his secret or his mission or return to someone with whom he would never share a life. To someone who did not keep her promise of staying away.

But none of it mattered; he loved Élise. He chose her, and he'd choose her again after the king. The king always came first. The crown had shaped him, bound him, and molded him into its covert weapon. But as he saw her figure vanish into the sea of people, he realized the blade had been dulled by a love he could never claim.

"It is a two-hour ride at a fast speed; I can make it there by noon, and then I will come straight back with the king's decree in hand and take Élise to safety," he mumbled to himself. He turned on his heel and ran toward Charonne, his heart a battlefield of regret and resolve.

But as he reached the stable, the mare waiting anxiously, he hesitated. His hands trembled as he gripped the saddle, and the image of Élise marching with the mob burned into his mind. He cursed under his breath, knowing the moment he chose the king over her, no redemption awaited him. He mounted the mare, the reins twitching in his hands. He spurred the horse forward with a sharp kick, but Élise's face lingered, vivid in his mind. The fire of rebellion was not new. Countless kings were toppled, thrones burned, and lives lost in the name of justice. Yet, despite all his years of witnessing history's cycles, Élise's face haunted him then. She had become his rebellion, the tether binding him to a world where he no longer belonged.

The mare cantered easily along the road, and the morning summer breeze pelted his cheeks. Each stride carried him farther from her and cemented his doubt of her well-being upon his return. The crown had already cost him everything, and now he feared, as he glanced at the Paris city walls, that by the time he came back, the Bastille would be in ashes, and Élise would be among them.

CHAPTER 26

The Urgency of Time

PALACE OF VERSAILLES, JULY 1789

ROLLANT PUSHED OPEN the double doors of the King's chambers. His boots struck the polished floor, sending an echo through the room. The sharp ends of two guards' rapiers crossed before him, halting his entry. His eyes locked on Louis, seated with his midday meal.

Louis's eyes widened at Rollant's lack of uniform, sensing the urgency. He stood immediately and ordered, "Guards, leave us and shut the door."

They did as commanded, and the doors clicked behind Rollant, leaving the room in tense silence.

Rollant straightened, his breath still heavy from his arduous ride to the palace. He pulled his shirt down to smooth its wrinkles.

"Sire," Rollant said steadily despite the storm brewing within him. He bowed and rose.

Louis' brow furrowed. "What is it, Rollant?"

"Your Majesty, a revolt at the Bastille is underway."

"What could they possibly want with the Bastille, the relic of no purpose?" Louis scoffed. "It's due to be demolished. There's nothing there," Louis said as his fingers massaged his temple, trying to understand the people's reasoning.

"Yesterday, Sire, I witnessed the transfer of gunpowder from the Hotel de Invalides to the Bastille. The mob is armed, likely with the weapons from the Invalides."

Louis collapsed into his chair. His gaze was fixed on his half-eaten meal in front of him. "Gunpowder and muskets." The murmur repeated. His fingers fidgeted as if playing with an imaginary lock. "How many in the mob?"

"Almost a thousand men and women were marching, from my estimates."

"A thousand?!" Louis grabbed his head. He leaned over his food and balled his hands by his ears. He paused, and Rollant said nothing to let his words sink in.

Finally, Louis asked, "You said they were marching, but were they shooting? Were they revolting? Or is this just another display of anger? Sometimes, mobs burn out before they meet their purpose."

Rollant slumped with a sharp exhale with the sound of a low growl. "Your Majesty, I have lived through enough wars to know when a crowd is on the brink of violence. Yesterday's street riots should further testify to the mob's purpose."

Louis lifted his gaze and met Rollant's. "Then what should I do?"

"Reinstate Necker immediately. They were rioting yesterday and using his bust as their flag. I'll take word to Paris this very hour that is what you have done, but you must do it," Rollant urged him.

But as Rollant spoke, Louis shook his head, pushed back the chair in opposition, and rose. "No! Absolutely not. Necker was going to be the ruin of the crown, of the monarchy. He panders to them, to their grievances. He undermines the king's authority in every sense of the word. It's no wonder he is the banker turned savior."

Rollant shook his head at the king's folly. "And if you lose the people entirely, there will be no monarchy left to ruin," Rollant said, stepping closer. "It is a time game now. Who concedes first will hold the upper hand. Reinstate Necker, or the revolt will take everything. Send the troops on the Champ de Mar to settle it. If the mob starts shooting, it will not end well for the crown, no matter who wins the scrimmage."

Louis' jaw clenched, his gaze flickering with indecision. He paced the room, with each finger moving with a mind of its own. "Governor de Launay is at the Bastille," he said finally. He nodded to reassure himself of his words. His hands accentuated each statement. "Yes, I trust Governor de Launay's decisions. His father managed the fortress well, as Launay has done. Born there, raised there—he knows the Bastille better than anyone. Launay will not surrender it, nor will he order a massacre. He is a man of peace, and I believe he will do whatever it takes to ensure peace."

"And if the mob doesn't care for peace?" Rollant asked in warning. "If they force his hand?"

Louis sighed. "I do not want Necker returned nor the notion I sent five thousand soldiers to put down a protest." He stopped pacing and folded his hands behind his back. "We shall see what happens by morning. If there is a revolt, I'll consider reinstating Necker."

"Your Majesty, by then, it will be too late," Rollant said with a clenched jaw.

Louis leaned back and lifted his chin to stretch his neck. "It is in God's hands now."

Rollant's gaze dropped. The silence thickened, punctuated only by the faint footsteps echoing outside the room.

It was not in God's hands but in the king's, as it had always been. And like every decision Louis faced, this one had been postponed. Rollant knew the price of such hesitation and delay. Some battles could not be won, and some sacrifices left scars too deep to heal. But he refused to let Élise become a casualty.

Rollant straightened his shoulders. "Your Majesty, if you are to take this stance, may I request leave to return to Paris?"

Louis turned with a knitted brow and crossed his arms. "Why, Rollant?"

"I have a personal matter there that I need to attend to," Rollant said, choosing his words carefully. "One, I must address before the situation worsens."

Louis studied him, his gaze narrowing. Then, with a slow nod, he approached him and gripped Rollant's shoulders. "My friend, you have given me your every day since I became king. I grant your request, but due to our predicament, I request you return tomorrow before sunset. The days ahead will be critical."

"I will return as you command," Rollant said, bowing his head and his heart beating fast. Another grueling ride awaited him, but the stakes demanded it. Élise's face swam before his eyes. He had to reach her in time.

Louis released him, and Rollant turned sharply on his heel. With every step, his resolve hardened. By the time he mounted his mare, his thoughts were clear.

He would save her, no matter the cost. Eternity could wait.

CHAPTER 27

A Spark to Ignite

BASTILLE, PARIS, JULY 1789

THE STREETS of Paris were a cauldron, bubbling with rage and desperation. Smoke curled into the skies, mingling with the distant rumble of rushing feet and angry cries. Rollant cared not about appearances and rode straight through the city gate at Faubourg Saint-Jacques, crossing the Seine and cutting eastward past Notre Dame. He weaved through narrow streets until he found a place to hide his mare. From there, he ran toward the Bastille.

The fortress loomed over the city as a monument to the king's long-held royal authority. Smoke clouded the air, obscuring the streets at its base.

Rollant shook his head at the ignorance of the rioters who dared think they could penetrate a medieval fortress. If they had tried to overrun the Bastille a few hundred years prior, the few soldiers in the fortress could have massacred the entire mob in a mere hour. They would not have cared about the loss of life and thought it their righteous duty to defend the king's fortress against anyone who threatened it. But for Élise's sake, he was glad the year was 1789, and Governor Launay was a man of peace.

Gunshots ripped through the air. The resounding boom of a cannon shot blasted. The acrid smell thickened with each step closer to the medieval monument.

"Where have they got a cannon?" he muttered. The sound of a second blast made him wince. "Must have been mutinous soldiers. Where are the royal troops? They should be here by now." His eyes darted westward, but there was no sign of reinforcements coming from the Champ de Mars. He shook his head at the lack of help. The King had not ordered them, and so they would do nothing.

An ox cart hurtled toward him with its bed of hay set alight. He jumped out of the way, barely dodging it, and coughed against the smoke as it engulfed him. The cannon deafened his ears once more. The chaos was maddening, but he hunched down, scanning the street for Élise. A few lay dead, some wounded, as he moved closer to the fighting.

"Élise!" he yelled. The cacophony swallowed his call. He searched until the summer sun started its descent.

By evening, the Bastille's shadow stretched long over the throngs of angry Parisians. His heart stopped. He spotted her near the front line, pistol raised and firing toward the gates.

"Élise," he whispered. She stood among the chaos, fearless and resolute, her jaw set with determination.

The mob surged forward, battering the gates of the Bastille with whatever they could find. Gunfire cracked in the distance, and Rollant's instincts screamed at him to pull her away, to drag her from the chaos.

But Élise didn't flinch. She held her ground, her courage a beacon to those around her. Rollant fought men to get to her before the mob crushed her against the Bastille's impenetrable gates.

A musket ball whizzed past her, striking the gate. She screamed and tore her face away from the blast. Rollant's restraint snapped. He surged through the crowd, his height and strength parting the mass like the knight he once was.

"Élise!" he bellowed.

She turned, her wide eyes locking onto his. Shock flickered across her face for a moment, but there was no time for questions. A bayonet gleamed as a reckless attacker charged toward the gates, heedless of her position. Rollant moved with each action precise and calculated, intercepting the weapon and wrenching it away before driving the man back with a single hard-pressed shove.

But his action earned him a musket ball that ripped through his back shoulder. Pain flared, but he gritted his teeth, knowing it would soon pass. He fell toward Élise, grabbing her arm and pulling her through the melee to the safety of a fallen cart away from the Bastille's entrance. He forced her down behind it and sank with her.

"What are you doing?" Élise asked in a shout, and he finally let her yank her arm free.

Another shot rang out, silencing her protest.

"You were nearly killed," he said, his voice steady despite the madness around them. His gaze lingered on her face before raking her body, searching for blood or injury. "Are you hurt?"

"I'm fine," she snapped. "I'm going to finish what I started," she said, trying to rise, but he pulled her down.

"Stay low. You don't expose yourself in battle," he said and gestured to a man lying behind her, lifeless with a bloody hole in his head.

She turned and shuddered at the sight.

"Unless you want to end up like him," Rollant said.

Her face paled as she nodded, and he wished he hadn't brought the body to her attention.

"I'm just glad you aren't hurt," he said.

"What are you doing here, Rollant?" Élise asked with a tremble in her voice. She leaned forward and covered his hand with hers.

Rollant stroked her hand.

"I was worried about you," he admitted. "I wasn't sure you would stay away, given everything that has transpired," he said, turning her hand in his. "I couldn't bear the thought of you . . ." His voice trailed off, and his throat tightened. "I needed to know you were safe."

Cries of the mob roared to life: "They've opened the gates!"

Élise's face lit up, her jaw dropping wide. "We did it! We—!" She almost jumped up, but Rollant kept her down.

She shook her head, pulling against him. "I'll be safe now. We won."

"You don't understand," he said, peering one eye over the cart. The riot spiraled out of control. The mob spilled into the Bastille's gates with shouts of victory. Rollant knew the danger wasn't over—victory often turned to bloodlust.

"You did win; now let's return to Charonne," he said.

"What? No!" Élise tried to pry his iron grip off her wrist. "Let me go, Rollant. We won!"

Rollant shook his head. "I've seen it before, Élise. More will die. Please," he said, removing his grip. "Please, let me take you home."

Her gaze flicked to his hand before looking down at the spot he'd held on her wrist. Admiration flickered in her eyes. "You didn't bruise me," she stammered.

Rollant's chest tightened. He knew why she'd said it—knew the weight her words carried.

"I will never hurt you, Élise," he whispered. "I only aimed to restrain you from seeing things that will haunt you for a long time."

A flash of fear leached into her eyes before she glanced back at the dead man.

"Please, Élise," he urged. "I'm not supposed to be here but came for you. I had to make sure you were safe."

Her gaze fell back on her wrist. "You didn't bruise me," she whispered.

A tear ran down her cheek before she wiped it away. She lifted her chin and studied his face before giving a slight nod. "You can take me home, Rollant. I trust you."

Relief swept through him as she took his outstretched hand. Before doing anything further, he kissed the back of her hand just to feel her soft skin against his lips.

"Thank you," he whispered.

He kept Élise close, careful not to let her fall into his arms. His broad frame shielded her from the frenzied crowd as they pushed through the streets. The crowd had already beheaded a garrison soldier and dragged Governor de Launay into the streets, beating him as they paraded him toward a likely execution. Élise froze at the sight, her fingers squeezing Rollant's.

They reached his mare and escaped through side streets, avoiding the worst of the violence until they crossed the city gate. Black smoke marked the large chateaux in the countryside.

Rollant's heart sank. The revolt was not as isolated as he had thought; it was something much bigger: a revolution.

Élise sagged against Rollant, her breath coming in ragged gasps. She scanned the spots of black smoke. "Why have they set homes on fire?"

"Because they belonged to the rich," Rollant sighed as he gripped the mare's reins in one hand and adjusted her hand in his other. They walked the cobblestone path to the quiet, contented village living on his land. It was a stark contrast to the chaos they'd left behind.

"I don't understand. Did they say horrible things like Réveillon?"

"Doubtful." Rollant opened the door. "They only had too large a home."

He held the door for Élise. "Can you make dinner for us? I will put the mare in the stable."

When he returned, she was waiting with a plate of cheese and dried meat. "I'll wash up," he said, pouring water into the basin.

"Were you shot?" She must have noticed the blood stain splattered on his back.

He remembered the bullet. Answers raced through his mind.

"Must be another's blood," he finally answered. He washed the grime from his hands, face, and neck in the basin, leaving the ends of his hair dripping with water. He sat down, exhausted. Élise did not look well either.

They ate in silence, and when she was done, her voice was soft, and her shoulders sagged. "I was so excited earlier, and now I can barely stay awake."

"It was courage surging through you, but those acts usually leave you exhausted after the surge is gone. Believe me, I feel the same after today."

She stood using the table to support her. "I'm glad you're here, Rollant. I've missed you so much," she said, though her eyes drooped.

"And I, you," he replied. Unspoken truths pressed against him. He wondered if she would ask him to stay again. How could he refuse her a second time?

"I want to talk to you in the morning, but I am so tired tonight," she said.

"Go, sleep. I promise I won't leave until we have spoken." He stood to respect her exit.

She lingered in the bedroom doorway, glancing back at him with a faint smile. He smiled in return, watching as she disappeared into the bedroom.

Alone in the dim light, Rollant slipped his shirt and boots off, grateful to have a basin of water to wash the rest of the grime and sweat from his body. The water cooled his muscles after the day's many trials. He sank against the too-small sofa. The ache would dull with time, but the memory of seeing Élise again—after swearing never to return—would haunt him far longer.

CHAPTER 28
The Dance of Death
CHARONNE, PARIS, JULY 1789

THE DOOR CREAKED as Élise opened it, its sound too loud in the quiet morning air. She froze, her breath hitching at the sight before her. Rollant's hand fell away from his head, revealing the broad, scarred expanse of his bare chest. The early sunlight caught the fine hair running down his belly where his breeches buttoned. For a moment, she thought she was dreaming again—his return, the day before, had been too surreal to trust.

He stirred and opened his eyes, breaking her trance.

Rollant rolled to sit and let out a groan as he rubbed his neck. He stopped upon seeing her in the doorway. He jolted up.

"Forgive me," he stuttered, looking around the floor and finding his shirt. He stooped quickly and threw it over his head. Élise could not look away from the soldier's perfect body and left her to wonder about the scars that marred his skin. The soft fabric rolled down, and he adjusted it in haste.

She swallowed the lump in her throat as Rollant's eyes met hers.

"You wear my shirt still?" he asked with a straight face and a neutral voice.

"Oh," she said and looked down. She usually paraded around the house and slept in it instead of her chemise. "It is comfortable and . . . well, I'm so used to being alone here, I forgot you were here."

He nodded, his lips tightening into a straight line. "I see," he murmured, lowering himself to the sofa. His hands moved methodically, tugging on his boots, though his focus seemed somewhere far away. His jaw clenched as if to keep anything more from coming out.

He finished with his boots and walked past her to prepare a simple breakfast of bread and tea, and sat at the table. With a silent wave, he invited her to join him.

She fidgeted with the fabric around her thigh. She watched him, wondering what had happened to the man who had saved her from Gabin, who had offered her his home with a smile, and the man who had taken her to safety only the day before. The man before her was polite and curt at the same time.

"I apologize if I—" she began, but he interjected.

"I apologize for not rising before you, ensuring I was appropriately dressed, and having a meal ready for you." His voice was monotone. He said all the right words, but somehow, their affection was stripped again.

"I've seen men more inappropriately dressed at the taverns," she chuckled, though none of those men had a body like Rollant's. "And still, no one has ever made my meals before except for you." Her voice trailed off at his lack of interaction and eye contact. "I can change out of your shirt if you'd rather me not wear it."

He raised his eyes to meet her gaze. "As I've told you, it's yours now," he said. "Do as you wish with it."

She sat across from him, a faint smile playing on her lips, though the unspoken tension lingered between them.

His attention returned to his food. She wondered if he was still upset at her involvement in Paris, so she asked. "Are you upset with me?"

"Yes, and no," he nodded without looking up.

"Why?"

"You promised to stay in Charonne until the Estates-General adjourned," he answered, his tone tight.

She placed her hands on the table and leaned forward. "And I did until the king dismissed Minister Necker. That was the end of it."

Rollant shook his head, his brow knitting in frustration. "You could have been killed."

"What did you expect me to do? Ignore the king amassing troops to take back the National Assembly?"

"Stay out of harm's way like you promised," he said.

Her cheeks grew red. "What do you care? You left, remember?" She pushed her plate away. "You discarded me like I was nothing."

"I did not discard you," Rollant said, slamming his hand down. "I wanted you to build a life here, Élise!"

"I can't build a life here when Paris burns a few steps away," she yelled, standing up.

"Yes, you can." His tone was more restrained. "You chose to go into the city. You chose to incite the people. I'm sure you even helped plan yesterday's actions."

"And why were you there, Rollant? Were you not supposed to be on a ship? How did you leave the ship, return to the mainland, and come to Paris? All in a day? Just for me?" She crossed her arms.

He stopped eating, lofted an eyebrow, and averted his gaze. "I—I told you—"

But she cut him off before he could answer. "More secrets . . . landlord."

His eyes shot to hers.

"Who told you that?"

"Does it matter if it is true?" She leaned back as he stood and stepped closer to her. Her belly knotted at his approach. She stiffened. Her body recoiled from instinctual fear, but her mind soothed it. Even though Rollant was a mystery, she knew he would never raise a hand to her.

But she was angry and had a right to be. "So you are at least a member of the *bourgeoisie,* if not the nobility, Monsieur Rollant *de* Montvieux. Did you leave me because I am beneath you? Did you stop me at the Bastille to keep your privileges over us?"

He leaned into her space, locking eyes with her. Her knees weakened at his intensity.

"Do you believe that?" he gritted.

She licked her lip, remembering the gash and his touch there, her first in Charonne. If he thought she was beneath him, he would have taken what he wanted from her and then left. Her shoulders slumped, knowing the answer. "Then why did you leave?"

He leaned back and sighed. "I already told you. Would you want a life with me, knowing you'd only see me a few days out of the year for the rest of your life?"

Her arms flew to her sides. "But you own this land. You don't collect rent, so I assume you don't pay taxes, which means you are nobility. You could stay here." It didn't matter if he was nobility, though she hated the Second Estate. He was different. He cared about her, she was sure.

He grumbled and muttered, "I didn't know about the land until after I signed my life away to His Majesty's Navy. I am not nobility anymore, though I have the name and must work to pay the land tax."

Her heart sank. Part of her sensed deception, but maybe it was regret. Either way, she wanted him with her. She stroked her arm, clawing through every solution to let him stay. "Well, didn't the National Assembly declare all taxes illegal? You wouldn't need to pay taxes anymore. You could stay."

A gleam came over his eyes. His fingers grazed hers, trembling for a fraction of a second before he withdrew them. "I'm not even supposed to be here. They pulled us off the ship because of the rampage in the streets—"

Again, he brushed her aside, and she was tired of his lack of answers.

"Then where is your uniform?" She nodded to his civilian coat on the sofa's arm.

His shoulders rose and left her question unanswered. Deception flashed in his eyes.

She had him; she had caught him in a lie. What was he hiding from her?

"As I said, I'm not supposed to be here." He gathered the empty plates in a clatter. "Promise me, you'll stay out of the city." His back was to her as he walked to the counter to wash the dishes.

"I can't make that promise," she said, folding her arms across her chest. More secrets he refused to tell. More deflection.

"Shots have been fired, Élise. Men have been killed. It will never be the same. If the crown is abolished, tyranny will rule until stability sets in. Please stay out of the city; stay safe."

He threw the plates down. Droplets flung from their edges. He spun around. "Please do not speak to anyone about your beliefs, especially in this turmoil; you don't know which side will win and what enemies you may make."

"We already won," she said. "Remember yesterday at the Bastille?"

He shook his head. "You won the first fight, and if they happen to abolish the crown, a new king of sorts will rule and kill anyone who threatens his reign."

"No," she said, shaking her head. "We all want the same thing: freedom from hunger."

"What if Gabin is given a prominent position in the new order? Do you think he will let you live just because you have the same ideals?"

She could feel the crack of Gabin's fists strike her jaw, reliving his abuse. It froze her belly, and she pulled her arms tighter across her chest, as Rollant continued speaking.

"And if the king somehow takes back his authority and re-establishes his regime, you will be tried and executed for treason," he said, again stepping closer to her. "No matter who wins, there will be so much death, so much blood. I have seen it!"

She let out a frustrated sigh. He was trying to scare her, to control her without bruises. "Where have you seen all of this wisdom play out, Rollant? In the Americas? We are the French. It is different here."

He shook his head. "Do you remember King Henry III? War between Catholics and Protestants left millions dead. It is no different now: Catholic versus Protestant or Royalist versus Revolutionist."

Élise squinted her eyes in defiance and dug in her heels. "If you are not for us, you are against us."

"That is not true," he said.

"You speak of treason against the revolution."

"Élise, stop." He approached her with pleading eyes.

"I trusted you. I cared for you. I loved you." She backed away. Her voice faltered. "But all you do is keep lying to me."

His hands found her shoulders, his grip firm but gentle. "I am trying to show you the danger of your path. Can't you see that?" he asked. "I don't want to see you hurt again, but it is your life, Élise. I have no claim to it."

Her heart warred with her mind. She didn't want to see his face twisted with worry, but she couldn't let him control her, even if through pleading and not force. She shoved his hands off. "You want to keep me safe, but I'm willing to die for this. You are not!"

His eyes narrowed as he shouted, "I would give anything to d—" His voice trailed off. His hands balled into fists. He rubbed his forehead and swallowed hard. With his tone much softer, he said, "You don't know what you're saying, Élise."

Her temper got the best of her. She could have asked another question to allow him to open up to her, but instead, she spat, "I know what I'm saying. How dare you tell me I am ignorant of fighting because of a struggling life you clearly have never lived?"

"It's not about that." He looked up at her. His fist bounced on his thigh as if he debated the unsaid.

"Then what is it?" She stepped closer, catching the slight tremble in his hands and the way his gaze darted away. What was he so afraid of? Maybe he wanted to tell her his secrets. Maybe she just had to ask again. "I deserve the truth, Rollant, don't I? Who are you, and why do you care what I do if you're never here?"

"Because, Élise, I . . ." His voice wavered, his hands flexing at his sides. A flicker of pain crossed his eyes—hesitation, fear. "Some truths," he finally murmured, gaze dropping to his hands as though they carried the weight of centuries, "are crueler than silence."

He wasn't making any sense.

"I don't care if it's cruel; give me the truth." She jabbed a soft finger into his chest.

Rollant scoffed and shook his head. "Everything I love about you is frustrating me in this moment."

She blinked a few times to process what he said. "You love me, or you love qualities about me?" She tightened her arms across her chest in case he again rejected her.

His shoulders lowered. "Always direct; I would expect nothing less."

"Then tell me the answer so I don't have to guess."

He brushed her upper arm with his fingers, stroking the shirt sleeve. "I've told myself countless times I should not love you," he whispered. His gaze traced her face longer than propriety allowed. Her chest tightened as she saw the flicker of a battle in his eyes—one he seemed to be losing.

The intensity in his expression faltered, so despite her anger, she stepped closer. Her fingers brushed his stomach—tentative, testing—as if daring him to deny what they both felt. His sharp intake of breath beneath her touch told her enough.

"That does not make any sense," she whispered, tilting her head to meet his gaze. "Do you, or do you not?"

A battle raged behind his eyes, the struggle between restraint and longing etched into every tense line of his face. "I . . . Do," he whispered, his voice hoarse with surrender as his gaze dipped to her lips and lingered.

Her eyes smiled as she rose to her toes and pressed her lips to his, granting his unspoken wish. For a moment, she hesitated, afraid she'd gone too far with the proper Rollant. But instead of retreating, he leaned into her, cradling her cheek as his lips crushed hers in a kiss that revealed the raw, unguarded truth—she belonged with him, and he with her.

His restraint gave way. Both hands, rough and strong, cradled her face, pulling her closer. Her heart thundered as his touch melted the space between them and ignited a fire that spread to the tips of her toes. His lips were hungry, and she fed them with a willing offering. They spoke a language his words had never dared. The faint bitterness of mint tingled her tongue.

His hand slipped to her waist, gathering the fabric of her shirt and pulling her against his contours as he deepened the kiss.

The world faded until there was only him. It was her first kiss born of love, and she knew she wanted him by her side for all time. The truths he so desperately tried to hide would come forth eventually, but they wouldn't matter. They belonged together. His hand on her cheek slipped into her hair, gently tugging her head back so his lips could kiss where bruises once lived on her neck. She wrapped her arms around him and held him tight, relishing every moment.

The flat of his hand slid and pressed against her lower back, his fingers gently dug into her flesh as if never to let her go. A tightness bloomed in her chest, forcing her breath to hitch. It was as if someone reached down her throat and pulled the air from her lungs.

"Rollant—" she gasped in broken speech, her voice barely audible as her hands clutched the fabric of his shirt. Darkness rimmed her vision. Her heart beat fast in panic. Her knees went weak.

He froze, his eyes darting to hers as panic flared in their depths. "Élise?" he said, his voice a rasp. His hands yanked away, and he stepped back as though the moment had broken him. His breathing turned ragged as did hers. Fear shadowed his gaze. "Can you—" His voice broke. "Can you breathe?" His eyes gleamed with tears ready to fall.

Her hands gripped her throat and chest. Finally, fresh air swept through her lungs. Her body heaved as the pressure lifted, leaving behind a coughing fit. She bent over to settle herself. Her lungs burned. Her body shook. Her throat pulsed. Her head throbbed. She sank to her knees to preempt a fall.

Rollant stepped closer to her, his hands hovering but daring not to touch.

After a moment, she stood and adjusted the collar of her shirt. The burn in her chest loitered, but her breath was finally her own again. "I'm fine," she managed and glanced at Rollant with a sheepish gaze. The stain of embarrassment rose on her cheeks. She ruined a perfectly good moment.

"I just—" Her words faltered as she met Rollant's eyes, which were full of horror and shame. But it wasn't for her.

"I'm sorry," he said with a thick voice. "I shouldn't have—" He shook his head, backing away again. "I must . . . go," he stammered, his chest heaving. He ran a hand through his thick, curly locks. His eyes darted to the door as if it were the only lifeline he had left. "I—I must."

He quickly threw on his coat and turned to the door.

Her brow knitted in confusion as she watched the man stagger as if intoxicated. She forced a rebuttal through her aching chest. "Why, why must you go? Why?"

But his response was scattered. "Why did you—I lost . . . control—Now I must—" He stopped, his breath hitching as panic darkened his features. "I—I'm sorry, Élise, for—for everything." For an instant, his mask slipped with guilt laid bare before he turned and strode to the door.

"Rollant, wait—" she started.

"Forgive me," he whispered as he yanked the door open. He hesitated for a moment, pulling his shoulders taut as his eyes traced her figure as if committing her to memory before he disappeared, leaving the door swinging closed in his wake.

Élise stood in silence, wrapped in his shirt, unable to follow—not for lack of will, but for fear of what the neighbors might think. She stared at the door, her nails digging into her palms.

Rollant was a man of secrets, of burdens she couldn't yet fathom. She pressed a flat hand to her heart, thudding against her ribs as if she had chased after him, and took a sweeping, shuddering breath. The tightness was gone, but it left a strange bitterness on her tongue.

She collapsed on the sofa, letting Rollant's faint scent of old wood lingering in the fabric envelop her. It was a cruel reminder of his absence.

Her fingers brushed her lips, where the spark of his kiss still burned. A fleeting moment of honesty—the taste of truth she'd begged for—left her aching for more. He had kissed her like a man drowning in love, desperate for her touch, yet he had fled as if she were the tempest, a danger meant to kill him.

Her mind reeled as she replayed the moments. Something had stolen the air from her lungs, or perhaps her heart had dared to beat too fast.

Rollant remained in her mind: his eyes wide with fear and his touch retreating as though she were poison. Maybe there was more to his words that he should not love her. But every touch, glance, whisper, and trembling breath told her otherwise.

So why did he run? Because of her or something he feared within himself? Whatever it was, the truth was in his kiss—he loved her. He had told her as much. But it seemed love wasn't enough to stop him from running, telling her any more truths, and soothing the fear in his eyes.

"Why Rollant?" she whispered to the empty room. "Why are you cursing me?"

The golden light streaming through the window appeared cruelly serene, as if mocking the storm raging in her mind. The house felt impossibly still, as though the walls themselves held their breath, unwilling to answer her question.

CHAPTER 29
The Hour of Reckoning
PALACE OF VERSAILLES, OCTOBER 1789

TWO DAYS after Rollant's report, King Louis reinstated Necker and promised to live in Paris to live closer to the people as the National Assembly requested, but the damage was done.

Paris had become a furnace of rage, its streets choked with barricades and smoke from burning homes. Officials swung from ropes in the public squares, landlords were dragged into the streets and beaten, and the nobility fled like rats from a sinking ship, leaving the king to fend for himself. Rollant had seen it with his own eyes, and yet, there at Versailles, the palace clung to its gilded serenity as though the revolution could not breach its walls.

But the cries for bread had turned into cries for the Queen's head. In the eyes of the people, no one was more indulgent than Marie Antoinette, and their hunger for reckoning burned hotter than their need for food.

Pale light preceded the sun and crawled across the early October morning sky. Not hearing the growing rumble in the distance, Rollant sat on his bed in his attic room, with Amée's rose and Élise's scarf in each hand.

How cruel a punishment the sorceress had given him. It struck not at his vices, but at his very nature—to love, to protect, to hold—turning his greatest virtue into a death sentence.

The last memory of Ninette clawed at his mind, her small hands clutching his clothes, her gasping cries fading to silence. Ninette could have lived—if only he had let go as he had done with Élise. If only he'd known that love, when held *too long* in his arms, meant death. Every heartbeat spent in his arms was a breath stolen by the curse. The truth had come too late—three centuries too late—and now Ninette's death hung over him like a freshly woven noose.

His stomach churned. Bile rose in his throat as he clutched the rose and scarf tighter.

He was a monster, unworthy of anyone's memory or love.

With a heavy sigh, he returned the rose and scarf to the drawer. Their weight was heavier than any weapon he'd wielded. Beneath them lay his knight's surcoat, a relic of another life, yet the duty remained.

Death would never claim him, no matter how much he invited it. His dagger, his instrument of futility, was now Élise's. He hadn't bothered to replace it. He slammed the drawer shut, turned to the mirror, and stared at the unchanging face bound by a curse—immortal, untouched by time, and yet burdened by centuries of failure. He forced composure as he adjusted his uniform before descending the stairs.

Faint drumbeats echoed through the halls, joined by angry shouts. He stopped to listen. "Paris has come for their king," he muttered with a scoff, wondering how they would dispose of Louis.

He hurried to the King's Chambers to relieve his post for the day, though he doubted the poor guard would get much sleep or even live to see the day.

"Captain," the guard addressed him before Rollant dismissed him, took his place, and knocked at the king's door. Louis opened it and rushed Rollant inside, taking him to the balcony. Rollant's chin dropped at the sight.

"They've walked all the way to my gates?" Louis muttered, his pacing quickening. "This is unthinkable. Unheard of!"

"Yes, and with the newly formed National Guard as well," Rollant muttered, lofting an eyebrow, remembering when he told the king and his cabinet about the possibility of mobs attacking the palace with rebellious soldiers. "At least, Commander Lafayette is sympathetic to the crown."

"If they stay behind the gates, they shall tire and leave," Louis muttered, pacing the room as his fists clenched and unclenched. "I will reconsider the decrees vetoed only yesterday. Yes, and I will move the Assembly to Tours tomorrow, so we won't have to worry about the Parisians."

Rollant stared at the king, unmoving. He had heard such hopeful delusions before—kings clutching at the last threads of power, blind to the tide rising around them. He strained to hear the mob's shouts beyond the gate. "It sounds like they're here for the Queen's head, Sire."

Louis stopped, his face pale. "No . . . No! They wouldn't dare."

But at Rollant's expressionless gaze telling him otherwise, Louis sank onto his bed.

"Father in Heaven," Louis whispered, his voice trembling. "What have I done to deserve this? Help me in my time of trouble." He clutched his temples, rocking slightly as the shouts of the guards grew louder, more desperate.

Rollant had seen palaces breached before and their kings slaughtered, but his heart raced every time, knowing he could not save the king from a mob even in his immortality. He'd always been killed, and by the time his body revived, the king was dead, and then he'd be killed again, thought to be a demon, enduring relentless death until he found himself reborn at the feet of the new king to explain himself. He rubbed his neck, remembering the few times he'd been beheaded; at least the later beheadings had been easier to bear.

"Sire, I hate to interrupt your prayer, but the crowds have found an entrance point through the Chapel," Rollant said as he observed the crowd kill two bodyguards in their haste to the palace doors in the Royal Courtyard.

He walked to the door and ordered the bodyguard to block the entry to the King's Guardroom and ensure the Queen and the children were in the antechamber immediately.

The first crack of splintering wood echoed like a gunshot through the halls. Frantic shouts rose over the clash of steel. The mob's rage crawled closer every second. Rollant's pulse quickened. He'd trained the bodyguards for this moment, but their number was too small.

The mob poured into the palace like a flood—men and women wearing the red-white-and-blue tricolor cockades, their pikes glinting in the morning light.

"They are spilling into the Great Hall," Rollant advised the king.

The clamor of weapons mingled with the angry shouts and sharp cracks of doors splintering.

"Curse my grandfather for tearing the iron gate down to build an opera. Yes, Grandfather, a wooden gate will keep the masses away," Louis mumbled with clenched fists. His fingers popped and dug into his forehead before he stood up with purpose. "If they want my wife's head, they shall not have it."

At that moment, they heard frantic knocking. Soon, the Queen burst into the room, her petticoat barely clinging to her frame, a single cloak thrown over her shoulders in haste. Her face, pale as porcelain, shone with sweat and tears. Her chest heaved as she clutched the Dauphin in one arm and held Madame Royale's hand with the other. Behind her, the muffled thud of pikes striking wood and the rising shouts of the mob filled the halls. Each sound was a countdown to catastrophe.

Rollant stepped aside as she rushed to Louis.

"Save me!" she cried, her voice cracking.

"Mama, I'm hungry," the Dauphin whimpered, tugging at her sleeve, oblivious to the threats at the door. Queen Marie Antoinette knelt, smoothing his hair with trembling hands. "Be patient, my love," she whispered, though her voice wavered with fear. "Be patient."

Rollant's heart tightened—a sensation he came to despise over the years—watching history devour the innocent time and time again.

Louis tended to his children and ran a hand down the Queen's arm. To calm her, he said, "They will not harm you, not while I'm alive. "

Rollant walked past their family, suppressing his desire for a wife and children as he had always done. Commander Lafayette awaited Rollant in the antechamber. He approached the commander, noting his stiff posture and carefully measured expression. Rollant asked, "Is this how you run your guard, Commander? Through chaos and mobs?"

Lafayette smirked and cast his eyes down. "There wasn't much of a choice," he admitted, running a hand over his tricolor cockade. "Surely, Captain, you understand it is better to concede a little than to lose everything."

His eyes met Rollant's, steady, though his hands held an almost imperceptible tremor. "I serve the people as much as the crown," Lafayette said, his voice tight. "Do you think I like this, Captain? The monarchy won't survive the day if we don't meet their demands."

Rollant narrowed his eyes but said nothing, his jaw tightening at Lafayette's pragmatic stance. The commander continued, his voice softer but more urgent, "They want to see the Queen. Her presence may calm them enough to save her life."

"And what happens if it doesn't?" Rollant shot back, stepping closer, listening to the shouts clearly state they wanted her head. "You cannot guarantee her safety, can you?"

"No," Lafayette admitted, the word heavy with resignation. "But I have men among the crowd who will try to prevent further violence. That is all I can offer." He gestured toward the shouts beyond the door. "If she doesn't go out there, they'll tear this palace apart. We have no time."

Rollant's gaze flickered to the door and back to Lafayette. "The people may call for her, but you'll be the one sending her to her death."

Lafayette's face hardened, but his next words carried an edge of desperation. "And if she doesn't go, they'll take her anyway—along with the king, the children, and anyone else they find. Would you have them butchered like animals instead of standing as symbols of dignity for what little time remains?" He paused, his voice dropping to a near whisper. "I've seen what they do to those who resist."

The commander's words hung in the air, and Rollant let out a slow breath, his gaze locked on the man before him. Whatever sympathy Lafayette held for the crown, it was clear the commander's loyalty had become a balancing act on a crumbling bridge.

"Very well," Rollant muttered at last. "I will take you to her."

The Queen stood by the window, her shoulders taut and trembling as the mob's chants grew louder. Rollant opened the door, gesturing for Lafayette to enter.

The commander knelt before her, his hat in hand. "Your Majesty, the people demand to see you." He hesitated, glancing at Rollant. "However, I cannot promise your safety. But your presence may be the only way to calm them so that we can decide the next actions peacefully." The slight tremor in his voice betrayed the gravity of his plea.

Marie Antoinette lifted her chin, her gaze darting between Rollant, Lafayette, and Louis. "If I refuse?" she asked, her voice steady but brittle.

Lafayette's jaw tightened. "If you refuse, they will break through, and I will not be able to stop them."

Marie Antoinette directed her next question to Rollant. "What are the chances of our family surviving if they break through successfully?"

Rollant did not want to answer. He shook his head and pressed his lips thin. "I would hope they would at least spare the children," he said, knowing sometimes they did not. The weight of his words told her all she needed to know.

The Queen blinked back tears. "Then, I'll do it," she said with renewed vigor. "Even if it costs me my life."

Rollant tilted his head back in admiration. Despite her fear, she held a firm resolve, in contrast to the king's hesitation and Rollant's own grim practicality.

Lafayette rose, offering his hand to the Queen. His voice softened, carrying his burdens. "Please know, Your Majesty, I ask this of you not as a traitorous soldier but as someone who wishes to save lives—yours, the King's, your children's."

She nodded and placed her fingertips in his hand.

Louis stood. "I will go with you."

But Rollant put his hand up to stop Louis. "Sire, if they kill both of you, your four-year-old son is king, with your eleven-year-old daughter as his regent. Do you want to leave them in this situation?"

"So I am supposed to sit here and let my wife face a murderous mob on her own?"

Rollant steadied Louis. "You are the king," he said, implying her death would not be as impactful as his.

Lafayette bowed. "Sire, I will accompany the Queen, but we must not delay."

Louis grunted as Lafayette escorted Marie Antoinette to the balcony beyond the antechamber alone.

The king paced the room. "I can't believe I let my Queen go alone," he muttered.

Rollant stared at the children, the sister consoling the brother. Louis Charles rubbed his belly. He pulled a piece of hardtack from his pocket and unwrapped it for the boy. He knelt before him.

"It doesn't taste very good," Rollant warned, "but it is food."

Louis Charles looked at it, looked at his nodding sister, and then plucked it out of Rollant's hand. He took a bite, and his face contorted. He handed it back.

Rollant stifled a chuckle. "Well, that one bite will help your belly," he whispered.

Lafayette re-entered the room as Rollant stood. Louis stopped his pacing.

"They want the king in Paris as he promised," the commander said. "The only way to calm the disorder and save your queen is to agree and reside in the capital."

Rollant shook his head. More demands would lead to more demands. More violence would lead to more violence. He thought the era of savagery and brutish antics was over. The heathens. But he fooled himself. Humans were animals in their basest form; all it took was a raving herd to strip away civility.

Lafayette pursed his lips and directed his attention to the king. "What say you, Your Majesty?"

"This is the last demand," Rollant said in Louis' silence. "And Sire, I suggest conditioning your response. You will move to Paris only if your family is unharmed and accompanies you."

Louis nodded. "Yes, and to spare the lives of my bodyguard."

Lafayette agreed. "Then I will urge the people to meet such conditions."

He left and returned moments later. "They agree if the members of the King's Bodyguard disarm themselves for the journey to Paris."

Louis nodded in agreement and motioned to Rollant. "Captain, will you see to it?"

"As you command," Rollant said, and he walked out to gather his men. "Throw your bandoliers down," he said, and was the first to take off the white and gold shoulder belt full of ammunition. He held it over the balcony and dropped it. The others followed. Forty bodyguards led the king and his family to the royal carriage at the stables beyond the gate. A body of men armed with pikes and swords escorted the unarmed mass.

Once the royal family was secured in the carriage, Rollant ordered the wounded to follow first. Two of the national guards held each of the wounded bodyguards. Rollant ensured every guard member was accounted for on the remaining horses, save for the two beheaded guards in the Royal Courtyard.

Rollant muttered as he approached his mare, remembering the former Minister of War, "Well, General Chastenet, it seems your matter of moments was six hours. Where is the might of the Royal French Army you spoke of to save the king?"

He hated being right, and he hated it even more when no one listened.

He turned to mount his horse with the National Guard cavalry behind him, but Élise stood before him.

He stopped mid-stride. The thought hadn't occurred to him that she'd be among the masses, though there was no reason for her not to be. She might not have cared about her life, but he did.

"So, was it all a ruse?" she asked, her voice trembling and hands firmly on her hips. Her wide eyes glistened with unshed tears while the sting of betrayal burned her cheeks.

Answers flew through his mind. Not everything was a ruse, but the words stuck in his throat. He doubted she would believe him. He doubted she would believe the reasons. The thought of ending everything with her then amid chaos broke his heart, but maybe it was for the best. She was in too deep, leading marches on the palace and having spotted him. He grabbed the reins and patted his mare's mane, keeping silent.

"At least have the decency to answer me," she said, crossing her arms. "The truth, this time."

He turned his attention to securing his saddle. He did not know how to respond. If he pushed her away, she would never allow him in her life again, which is what the rational mind told him he wanted anyway. If he told her the full truth, she would think he was deranged. She may or may not accept the half-truth if he told her that.

However, the curse weighed on his mind. What difference was there if she loved him as he loved her? He could never hold her in his arms, never give her a life of love and happiness. Her aching gasp when he pulled her close resounded in his memory. It had shattered the space between them. He'd frozen; his blood ran cold. He'd heard it twice, first with Amée, then with Ninette. He wouldn't do it again.

With the resignation of cutting out his humanity once more, he said in the most monotonous tone he could muster, "Of course, it was all a ruse."

Her arms dropped to her side. She pressed close to him. "Everything?" The whisper brushed his cheek.

Her question cut deeper than any pike. He wanted to tell her that no part of her had been a ruse. That she had become the only light in centuries of darkness. But the curse weighed heavier than her accusations. Loving her would only bring her ruin.

The words burned his throat as he forced them out.

"Yes, everything."

Each syllable was a dagger in his chest, but it was better this way. Better for her to hate him than to die because of him.

Élise sneered and punched him in the side. "You're a pig," she spat. Hate and hurt warred in her voice.

"The fattest kind," he said, not acknowledging her but looking straight ahead like a good guard would do. He could feel her recoil from him, but it was for the better. Eventually, time would claim her like all the rest.

She shoved him and then spat at his feet. He recovered with ease and mounted his horse. He did not look at her; he couldn't, or he'd jump down and beg her forgiveness.

She hit his leg with a closed fist. "I hate you," she gritted.

"Move aside, Mademoiselle," he said, pulling himself into the eternal stasis that had kept him from losing his mind for the last six hundred years.

He clicked his heels into the mare's sides, and the horse jolted forward as the carriage rolled down the long road on the path to the Tuileries Palace in Paris with two bodyguards' heads on pikes leading the crowd.

It was done.

She was free.

The carriage creaked forward, its wheels grinding against the cobblestones as the crowd surged around it. Shouts of "Vive la Nation!" rang in Rollant's ears, mingling with the crude insults hurled at the Queen. Ahead, the pikes swayed like grim banners, their grisly trophies dripping blood under the noon sun.

Rollant gripped the reins tighter, the leather biting into his palm. The end was coming for Louis, for the Queen, for them all, but not for him. He would remain a relic of another time, a silent witness to history's endless cruelty.

Alone.

Always alone.

And once again, Rollant would remain—an eternal witness to the fall of kings and the slow, painful decay of love. And as he rode on, Élise's final words echoed in his mind, sharper than the jeers of the crowd: *I hate you.*

mit ihren
umliegenden Gegenden

gezeichnet von
gestochen von
1805.

Asneres
S. Ouen
Clichy
Courbevoye
Villiers
Neuilly
Mont Martre
Le Monceau
Puteaux
Chaillot
Passy
Auteuil
Vaugirard
Boulogne
Issy
Belleville
Meudon
Chatillon

CHAPTER 30

Betrayal of the Forgotten

FAUBOURG SAINT-ANTIONE, PARIS, NOVEMBER 1789

ÉLISE CLUTCHED her coat tighter around her arms as she walked the Rue de Charonne, the November air biting her cheeks. Her neck ached from the tension in her jaw, and hot tears burned behind her eyes. "How could I have been so blind?" she muttered.

All she had ever wanted was to be loved, yet Rollant—his smile and kiss—had been nothing more than a calculated lie. He'd played her, left her to feel the fool. The harsh truth clawed at her: that was why he hadn't stayed after their kiss. It meant nothing to him. He wasn't on a ship. He was in the palace and probably had women stashed away all over the city.

Her feet scuffed against the cobblestones as doubt gnawed at her. Would he even let her stay in the house now, knowing what she'd seen and heard? Or was that a lie, too? Perhaps it wasn't even his home.

"Not a landlord," she scoffed at the bitter thought, her fists tightening in her coat. "Just a loyal dog of the king. A bodyguard. An informant." The words were ash in her mouth.

She hadn't seen him once in the month since she'd been at Versailles, but his absence only deepened her anger, like a wound that refused to heal. He'd betrayed her—and worse, made her believe that, for a fleeting moment, she had meant something to him. She clutched her heart to hold it together.

Her pace slowed as she turned down the narrow path leading to Madame Marie's apartment. Guilt settled like a rock in her chest, constricting her throat as the street constricted to her shoulders, walls on each side.

"If I'm such the fool he played me to be, then why does any of it still matter? Why does he still matter to me?" she whimpered, shaking the notion away. "No, others matter now, like Madame Marie."

It was her first time venturing into Faubourg Saint-Antione since she'd left, but she had to check on her last remaining friend. She doubted Rollant would have given her enough to last this long. She imagined the children's hollow faces, their swollen bellies from hunger, and the thought made her feet move faster. In her arms, she clutched a loaf of bread she'd baked that morning—her only offering, but hopefully enough to keep them alive until she could find more.

She happened upon the familiar main door, entered, and walked past the pungent aroma of the shared bathroom, down the hall, and knocked on Madame Marie's door.

The sick woman rasped, "Come in!"

Élise opened the door and smiled upon seeing her only friend left in the world.

"Élise?!" Madame Marie yelled as she struggled to sit up in bed. "Come in. Come in!" she said, gesturing to her with a wave.

Élise smiled with a brightness she hadn't felt in a long time. "Oh, Madame, I am so happy to see you. My friend said he would give you bread while I was away, but we are no longer friends, so I had to make sure you were taken care of," Élise said as she put her loaf and coat on the table.

One of Marie's children dashed through the door before Élise turned to close it.

"Where is he going at this hour?" Élise asked.

Madame Marie frowned and shook her head at the click of the door. "Dear child, they never stop working. Your friend gave us much coin, which was fine until the summer. We were using it to pay for everything, but the people started threatening us for being rich. I didn't want to endanger my family, so we had to stop. The children returned to their jobs, and the coin sits useless under my bed."

"I'm so sorry to hear that," Élise said and hugged Marie, wondering why Rollant would have kept such a promise if she meant nothing to him.

"Well, I have been afraid of Gabin since I left him," Élise said. "But I needed to know you were well. I'll come this time every night to give you some bread or whatever I conjure up during the day."

"No need, Élise." Madame Marie's gaze averted when Élise mentioned Gabin. "We are fine." A slight tremor in her voice spoke of deception.

Élise chuckled, brushing it off. "No, your children go out to work in the evening when riots and barricades occur. You are not fine. But I am here, and I will help you. What do you need to be done?"

Madame Marie's smile faltered. She looked down, wringing her hands. "Élise, you have to understand. We were starving," she murmured. "I never meant for it to come to this, but—" her voice cracked—"you need to leave. Now."

"What do you mean?"

Madame Marie grasped Élise's wrist. "I've made a mistake, Élise. You are a kind soul. I merely forgot in my misery. But you need to leave now."

"What?" Élise's voice rose. "What do you mean?"

Madame Marie fell back onto her pillow. "Lord, forgive me," she prayed. "Leave now, Élise, before Gabin comes."

"Gabin?" Élise staggered backward. "Why is he coming? He—he will kill me."

"No, he won't, but he wants you back. He offered bread, a lot of it. We were starving, Élise," she repeated. "I'm sorry. Go now. Don't come back to this district. You have no friends here," Madame Marie warned. She waved her off. "Please go."

Élise's heart beat out of her chest as she spun around. She grabbed her coat and ran out the door. The bakery was not that far. She flung herself through the main door, knocking into Madame Marie's child as she exited.

"Why?" she whispered.

"You left us to die," the child said with a hate-filled glance and entered the building with a hard slam of the door.

The ache of another betrayal nearly tore her heart apart. She pushed down the narrow road, running back to the Rue de Charonne as fast as she could. But a large frame blocked her way home. The evening sun was sinking low and fast.

"Coming home, are you Élise?" Gabin's voice bellowed.

She stepped back and turned to run, but he caught her by the hair and pulled her back until he gripped her arm. He dragged her and threw her into the Rue de Charonne.

Pain shot through her knee as it struck the cobblestone, but it was nothing compared to the terror twisting her insides. Gabin's grip burned like a brand, dragging her back to a nightmare she'd thought she'd escaped forever. She bit her lip to keep from crying out, refusing to give him the satisfaction.

"Become weak, have we, Élise?" Gabin asked, hissing her name. He pulled her up again by her hair and marched her back to the bakery.

In the November wind stinging the tears on her face, she realized she had lived free of Gabin's fists for the greater part of the year. She had never seen her body without bruises until Rollant lent her his rented home in Charonne. Why had he done it? Why had he rescued her, carried her to Le Marais, and given her coin, bread, tallow, and a bath? Had it all been a ruse, as he said? Why continue treating her with such kindness? Had her march on the palace obliterated any feeling he had for her?

He was a royalist. She was a revolutionary. Maybe their paths were not meant to cross. She swallowed the lump in her throat as the harsh

November winds swept past her legs. The thick wool of her coat collar fluttered against her cheek. Maybe he was just trying to run for good. Another lie meant for her benefit. But none of it mattered. Gabin was going to kill her, one way or another.

The brute shoved her in the back, forcing her to stumble into the bakery. Gabin's heavy arm wrapped around her and squeezed as he announced to the men gathered for the night's meeting. "Behold—my little lost dove has come back to roost!"

Malo and Yves' faces dropped before faint smiles perched on their lips.

"Welcome home, Élise," Olivier said with a nod.

Silence reigned as Gabin paraded her to the back wall. "Is that how you treat my woman on her grand return?"

Applause and whoops sounded immediately.

But Élise squirmed out from under Gabin's arm. "No, Gabin. I am not here to stay. I will not stay with you!" she yelled and tried to run to the door, but Gabin caught her and threw her into a chair.

"You'll do as you're told," Gabin growled. "The streets aren't safe for a little dove like you wandering alone."

Élise rubbed her elbow and fought back tears. "I don't care. I'm not staying with you. I'm never staying with you again." She got up to leave, but he shoved her back down. Her shoulder cried out in pain.

"Stay like a good little dove, unless . . ." He smirked before throwing his hands wide to his audience. "Unless I should let the streets teach you a lesson instead! Let's round up a few rich men and show them what it's like to be beaten so far down they can't get up?"

A shout raised in the air.

Élise's eyes opened wide at the deliberate purpose of their escapade.

Gabin pointed to Malo and Yves. "Are you coming this time, boys?" They glanced at Élise and nodded, raising a tentative fist.

"Good," Gabin said. "Get the others," he barked at a few attendees Élise had never seen before. Gabin grabbed the hair at the back of her head and pulled her up. "You want to leave, then we can leave, my little dove," he whispered in her ear as he led her out.

"What is the Third Estate?" Gabin bellowed.

"Everything," was the cry.

"What is the Second Estate?" Gabin bellowed.

"Nothing," was the cry.

Men and women joined the small party turned large as they marched through the district of Bastille, where charred remnants of barricades lined the streets, a grim reminder of the July uprising. Residents peered out from cracked shutters as the mob thundered past. Many joined them with guns in hand as they continued to Les Halles.

Gabin's voice dropped to a hiss as he marched her forward. "See how they cheer for me, Élise? You should be grateful. Without me, where would you run? Back to that royalist lover of yours? Back to your lies? No, little dove. You belong here. With me."

The smell of rotting vegetables from the abandoned market stalls filled the air in Les Halles, mixing with the bitter tang of torch smoke as more men and women joined their ranks. They marched until they came upon Rue Saint-Honoré. The street unfurled before them, lined with Paris' oldest homes, standing like fortresses of wealth. It stretched before them, its cobblestones gleaming in the dying light. Grand façades adorned with wrought iron balconies and gilded shutters stood like silent witnesses to the mob's fury. The Tuileries Palace loomed in the distance, its shadow stretching long and dark over the scene, a stark reminder of the power they sought to tear down.

Gabin passed Élise to a pair of men. "Hold her," he ordered, and their grips intensified on her neck and arms as Gabin took his place at the head of the mob. His gaze swept the crowd until it landed on a young man near the edge with torchlight dancing in his nervous eyes.

"What's your name, boy?" Gabin called.

The man stammered, "Jean."

Gabin pointed at him with pride in his eyes. "Tonight, you fight for justice. For bread! For France!"

The crowd roared, and the young man's hesitation melted into a raised fist.

Élise's stomach twisted as Gabin's words whipped the crowd into a frenzy. She'd marched before, shouted slogans, even dreamed of change—but this was different. This wasn't about justice. It was about destruction.

The houses loomed ahead, their golden windows catching the last rays of sunlight, and for the first time, she wondered how many innocent people were trapped inside.

"Let's show these pathetic scum they have dared step on the wrong estate!" Gabin yelled. The crowd's shout shook the perfectly maintained cobblestone street.

"Tear them from their silken beds!" Gabin roared. "Let them feel what it's like to bleed on the streets they've ignored! And if the cowards aren't hiding inside—burn it to the ground!" Gabin's voice rose above the clamor, a sharp command that sent the mob scattering like wolves scenting prey.

Screams of families littered the night, and Élise shut her eyes tight, wishing to forget the curdling sounds.

Gabin slowly walked the street with the two men holding Élise behind him, admiring all he had accomplished. She tried to squirm free, but the two men's grips only tightened.

There was a shout. "Gabin! We found someone you would want to see!"

Gabin bounded to the edge of the road, where they dragged a man beneath the street lamp and forced him to his knees. One pulled his hair back.

"Rollant?" Élise whispered.

Gabin grunted before he laughed. "Ah, Monsieur Rollant Montvieux. Do you live here?"

Rollant sighed and laughed with Gabin. "No, Monsieur Roux, I do not."

"Then why are you here?"

"I had a job to do to pay for bread," he said.

Gabin walked up to him and punched him hard in the face. Élise flinched.

Rollant spat blood before looking up at Gabin.

A woman's scream took their attention. "I saw him riding at the palace! He is a King's Bodyguard!" She yelled and pointed with a knotty finger. "And she was with him!" Her finger swept to Élise.

Her heart sank. The two men holding her threw her to the street and kicked her.

Gabin turned to the crowd, his voice rising above their murmurs. "Do you hear that? Traitors, both of them! One a spy for the king, the other a traitor who dared to lie to us, to all of you. Will you let them escape justice?" The roar of the mob shook the street, and Élise felt the ground shift beneath her feet.

"Tie her up too," Gabin barked. The two men grabbed her hands and started to drag her on the street as she screamed, reconstituting the crowd.

But Rollant bellowed, "She's innocent. I lied to her."

The men paused, and Rollant directed his next comments to Gabin.

"And how ironic the command to kill her comes from the man who made her wear bruises and bloody marks of his dominance. She left you, Gabin, and now you want revenge on her. They should tie you up as well. We all saw her bruises and marks. None of us is blind."

Gabin sneered, grabbed Élise, and pulled her to stand.

A murmur rippled through the crowd at Rollant's words. A few faces turned to Gabin, their expressions wary.

"Lies," Gabin snarled, raising his arms to reclaim the crowd's fury. "Lies from a royalist dog! Will we believe him, or will we take back our justice?"

The hesitant murmurs dissolved into roaring chants. Gabin wrapped his arms around Élise and brandished his baker's knife. "If I recall, Élise, when we first met Rollant, I suspected him as a spy, and your words were that if he were a spy, you'd draw first blood and kill him," he said loud enough for the crowd to hear.

"Now kill him." Gabin shoved the dagger into her hand and pushed her into the space before Rollant. "Show us where your loyalty lies."

Élise glanced back at Rollant before turning to Gabin, frozen in fear.

She scanned the angry mob; their shouts dimmed in her ears and gave way to her pounding heart and shaky breath.

"He said he is a navy man, but is now a king's guard as well? He lied to all of us. He doesn't want our freedom." Gabin spoke to the crowd. "He wants the king to oppress us! Death to him!" Gabin yelled. "Death to Rollant Montvieux!"

The cheer erupted into the night.

Élise glanced at the dagger in her hand. "I can't do it, Gabin," she whispered.

Gabin sneered at her and answered her publicly. "Your words were 'Take. It. Back!'" He pumped the air for each word. "Take. It. Back."

The crowd chanted in unison while Gabin closed in on her.

"You said, if you remember, little dove, that if he were an informant, you'd be the one to take his life. Did you not say that Élise, that night he first came to my bakery? Well, it turns out, he was an informant," Gabin gritted. "He betrayed you. I have never betrayed you. He lied to you, but I have never lied to you, though we've had hard times. Be good to your word, Élise, and kill him like you said, or I may be unable to save you from this crowd."

Gabin forced his hand around hers so much that she felt she would have a permanent indentation of its hilt in her palm.

"You can feel it, can't you?" Gabin whispered, his breath hot against her ear as he tightened her grip around the hilt. "The weight of justice. Go on, Élise—be the hand of the people. Take back what he stole from you."

He shoved her into Rollant's chest. "Gut him—make it slow. Let him bleed. We'll string him up too as a warning for any royalist scum," Gabin ordered.

Her heartbeat thundered in her chest, each pulse a countdown to the unthinkable as her gaze locked with Rollant's. The bruises on his face, the quiet resolve in his eyes—it was too much. The crowd's chants of vengeance swirled around her, muffled and distant, as if the world held its breath. Could she do it? Could she destroy the one thing that had felt like kindness, even if it was a lie? Her hand trembled, but Rollant's eyes were steady as he gave her a slight nod.

"Everyone dies, Élise," he whispered, his voice deep in a calm command. "Put the blade through my belly. Leave it in."

The men, holding his arms, wrenched them back so his head dropped.

She grabbed his shoulder and leaned her mouth to his ear. "I am afraid. I can't do it."

"They will kill you if you don't," Rollant said, his lips brushing against her cheek. "No sense in having us both die. Do it quickly. Don't give them reason to doubt."

She pulled back, letting his lush brown curls give them some privacy. He stared at her like he had when he first saw her—with all the love in the world. It was the look she had always wanted. The look that confirmed it was not all a ruse, confirmed his kiss, his care, his love for her.

"I can't take your life," she whimpered.

Rollant's lips curved into the faintest of smiles, his voice low and steady as it had always been. "You've already saved me—let me save you too." His shoulders straightened, and he met her gaze with quiet determination. "You can do this. For both of us."

Her breath hitched, and her head shook.

"I cannot save you if you don't," he whispered.

The crowd chanted, "Kill him!"

The air reeked of sweat, smoke, and fear—the heat from the torches pressed against Élise's cheeks, making her shiver. The mob's chants pounded like war drums, shaking the air and drowning out her frantic thoughts.

"Do it, Élise," he coaxed her. "Quickly."

"I'll die with you," she whispered.

"No," he shook his head. "No," he repeated through clenched teeth.

But Gabin's hand wrenched hers. "It will be easy, Élise. A quick push" —Gabin yelled and thrust the blade into Rollant's belly for her—"and we rid France of one more royalist dog!" The crowd erupted in joyous cacophony.

Gabin whispered, "There you go, little dove. Hold steady. Let him feel the length of the blade."

The knife hilt was slick in her grip, damp with sweat and blood. Rollant's breath hitched—a sound so brief, so quiet, yet it shattered her more than any scream could. Pain etched into Rollant's brave face.

Gabin spun around with arms in the air to show victory.

Rollant's blood oozed on her fingers as they still clutched the blade. Her jaw fell agape, and she forgot to breathe. Her fingers popped off the handle. The words spilled from her mouth: "Forgive me."

His groan sounded in her ears as the hollers of the crowd doubled.

"Best not let the men see your tears," he whispered in a stammer, echoing her words from their first meeting.

"Rollant," she whispered. She had just stabbed him and sentenced him to death. Her hands slid to his chest, his neck, his cheeks, leaving a bloody trail of guilt.

"What have I done?" Her breathy words were lost in the cheers, and before she could say more, Rollant was yanked back and a rope thrown around his neck. Gabin shoved her aside, barking orders to hoist him on the streetlamp. "Easy does it," he said. "Leave him on his toes, let him really suffer and feel our plight!"

Rollant's gasps came out in spurts as Gabin walked up to him. "I told you she was my woman," he murmured and spat in Rollant's face. Gabin twisted the blade Élise left in his belly with a hard wrench of the handle.

Élise's vision blurred with tears. Her fists clenched at her sides, nails digging into her palms. She wanted to scream, to rip the knife from Gabin's hands and stop this madness—but her legs refused to move, frozen by fear and the weight of her betraying hand. She should have thrown the knife down and been killed alongside him. She had allowed Gabin to force her hand.

Rollant's face contorted as Gabin twisted. The rope tightened around his neck as they tied his arms with the same rope that hung him. He stood on his toes to keep breathing. His arms were strung up behind him at an awkward angle. To lower them meant to lift his toes off the ground and die.

"Let's see how strong this royalist is, shall we?" Gabin said as he spun to the crowd. "Let's see how long the king's dog can last. Who's betting he'll still be breathing by sunrise? Or if he took the weak man's way out and fell to his heels during the night?"

Élise's breaths grew heavy as she watched Rollant. Their eyes met. What had she done? Rollant was dying before her eyes because she had caused a scene at Versailles. He was the man who had taken every chance to protect her and care for her, even until the end. He told her it was all a lie, but deep down, she knew at least his feelings for her were not false, though maybe everything else was. And she'd thrown it away. The urge to vomit overcame her, but her belly was empty.

Gabin grabbed Élise under the top of her arm and dragged her behind him, back into a life of torment. Élise peered over her shoulder at Rollant, who was hanging onto life and perched on his toes beneath the lamplight. There was a glint in his eye, a shimmer of hope in his coming end. His coat blew in the winter breeze past his calves. She blinked back the tears from her eyes. This time, he wouldn't be coming back.

"You see, little dove," Gabin murmured as he dragged her away, her focus still on Rollant. His grip bruised her arm, and she winced. "There's no one left—not your lover, not your friends, not even God himself. You're mine to do with as I please, just as you always were."

CHAPTER 31

A Promise to Live

RUE SAINT-HONORÉ, PARIS, NOVEMBER 1789

IN A MURDEROUS HORDE, the mob rounded up anyone they did not like and killed them on some unfounded basis of lending sympathy to the monarchy or for being wealthy. They stole barrels of ale and started a bonfire in the middle of Rue de Faubourg Saint-Antoine outside the bakery. After Gabin had drunk a few mugs, he belched and stood up, still with Élise in his firm grip.

"Stay here if you wish, but we will retire for the night," Gabin said.

Élise tried to pry her hand off her arm.

But Gabin laughed. "See my little dove is anxious to get to bed."

The men roared at the crude humor as Gabin dragged, half-pulled her into the bakery, up the stairs, and threw her on the bed.

But she hopped up and dodged him as he lunged for her. "Where are you going, dove?" he yelled, catching her by the hair again.

She jerked backward, her hands on her head. "Leave me alone, Gabin. I don't want to be here."

He threw her against the door and pressed his body against her, holding her wrists above her head with one hand, before pressing his mouth to hers. The malt in his breath made her gag. "I missed you," he gritted and bit her lip hard.

She squirmed to move her legs, but he had her pinned.

"I hate you," she whispered.

He punched her in the jaw. She fell to the floor with blood falling from her lip. He yanked her back up. "Looks like we will need to reteach the rules here, Élise," he said with eyes red from the rum.

He wound up to punch her in the face once more. He had hold of her right hand, but Rollant had taught her to use her left. Rollant. His dagger.

She reached into her coat pocket. Her fingers brushed the blade—a lifeline she'd never thought she'd use.

Gabin's fist swung toward her, but instinct—fear, fury—took over. She twisted her wrist the way Rollant had taught her and struck upward. The blade sank into the underside of Gabin's jaw. His punch never landed. His hands fell limp at his side as he staggered back, gurgling in disbelief.

He fell to the floor in a growing puddle of his blood.

Élise stood still, the knife still clutched in her trembling hand. Her heart beat out of her chest. The blood pool crawled toward her feet, staining the floorboards in dark crimson. Gabin's eyes stared blankly at her, wide with the shock of death. She wanted to feel triumphant, but all she felt was the weight of the blade and the bile rising in her throat.

"I killed him," she whispered, her voice shaking. But there was no time to think. No time to mourn. If they found her there, they'd string her up alongside Rollant.

A cloud of laughter rose to the window.

She stared at the blood-stained blade, wrapping the handle tighter in her grip before transferring it to her right hand. All she knew was she couldn't let Rollant die alone if there was a chance he was still alive. She grabbed the water pail and hid her weapon in case she had to fight her way back. She exited the room and snuck down the stairs, out the bakery door, and slid into the shadows.

Malo caught her gaze.

She froze.

Yves looked up and saw her too.

She swallowed hard.

Malo and Yves shared a glance before Malo tipped his head north, and the two men dipped their heads to take another drink and rejoin the conversation as if they'd hadn't seen her. Maybe she had a few who still cared for her.

Though her breath was shallow, she walked to the well as if Gabin had asked her to get water. Lightheadedness became her enemy. She put the pail on the well's rim, dropped the knife back into her coat pocket, and began to run.

Her boots clacked on the cobblestone, and she ducked her head, hoping no one heard her or cared. She rounded the street corner to Rue Saint-Honoré. Rollant stood there with his hands in front, untying himself from the lamppost.

"How?" she whispered, her voice breaking as she saw him—slumped but alive, his hands working the rope that bound him. Her feet stumbled forward, driven by relief and disbelief in equal measure. How could he still be standing after everything she'd done?

"Rollant," she choked out, her tears spilling freely. He paused at the sound of her voice, his head turning slowly toward her, and for a moment, she thought he might collapse.

"Élise? What are you doing here?" he asked with a groan of pain.

"I had to come back for you," she said. "Here," she reached out and hoisted his hands up so he could roll down to his heels. She unwound the rope from his wrists and began untying his noose.

"How did you get away?" His eyes scanned the bruises on her face and the gash on her lip.

Images of Gabin's slit neck appeared in her memory. "I had to kill Gabin. He was beating me," she whispered. Her voice trembled, but she didn't elaborate.

Rollant gave a small nod, his expression empathetic.

She removed the noose, and he collapsed to the street.

"Well, it serves him right," he said, leaning back and to the side, likely to ease the pain. She knelt next to him, propping her leg beneath his back to support him.

"I'm sorry you had to do that, Élise. I gave you the dagger, hoping you never had to use it, but I'm glad you could get away." He winced, and lines of pain carved into his brow. "If anything, I hope you stay in Charonne. The city is not what you thought it was."

She glanced at her hands, studying the dried blood stains, one from Rollant, one from Gabin. Tears ran down her cheeks. "I should have listened to you," she cried. "I should have—"

His fingers grazed the sleeve of her coat, silencing her. He rested his head in her lap. "I kept the truth from you," he said.

The blade stuck out from his belly and moved with each straining breath. His hand wrapped the handle.

"Don't pull it," she said, gently placing her fingers on his hand.

"It will be faster that way," he said.

She started weeping. "I am so sorry, Rollant. I killed my only true friend."

He cradled her cheek. "I am not dead yet." He smiled and chuckled with the sound of searing pain ruining its glee. The lamplight glistened in his eyes.

"Oh, Rollant," she whispered. She pushed his chestnut locks over his forehead and gripped his coat, balling the fabric in her hands. "How will I live without you?"

Tears filled his eyes. "No, how will I live without you?" he repeated her question.

As he slumped against her, she reached to brush his hair from his face, but stopped. The bruise that had darkened his eye was gone. The gash on his lip had vanished, leaving no trace of injury. Her breath caught. This was no trick of the light—his wounds were healing before her eyes, or had she imagined it?

"Rollant?" she asked in a trembling whisper.

The sound of heavy boots striking cobblestones broke the stillness of the night. Élise's breath caught in her throat. Shadows flickered at the edge of the lamplight, growing larger with each step. Her pulse quickened as two figures emerged from the darkness, their faces twisted with drunken rage. They were men from the riot. She saw them join in Les Halles. They must have followed her.

A man's shout pierced the sky. "What's going on here?"

"Why're you crying over the royalist, wench? You a sympathizer, too?" The other barked and drew closer.

Rollant yanked the blade out of his stomach with a groan.

The attacker kicked him in the gut as she screamed, "No!"

The second man kicked her in the side. Air expelled from her lungs as she gripped her ribs. She moaned in pain with an open mouth against the cobblestone.

The man grabbed Élise's hair and yanked her along as the second punched Rollant while he was down.

"Stop!" she yelled.

Rollant caught the man's boot and shoved it backward, sending the man down beside him. He raised the baker's knife and plunged it into the man's chest.

She had both hands on her hair to keep it from ripping from her scalp as she watched in horror. She screamed again. Rollant staggered to his feet, clutching his stomach, his breaths shallow but determined. Élise's eyes widened as he lurched forward, slamming his shoulder into her attacker. The man fell back with a grunt, but Rollant's strength faltered, and he barely kept himself upright. Even injured, he fought with the desperation of a man who refused to let death claim him.

"Run!" Rollant yelled to her as he took another punch to his face, already bruising again.

She scrambled backward and to her feet.

"Go home!" he yelled.

Rollant was still trying to save her even after she stabbed him. She picked up a nearby rock and threw it as hard as she could against the attacker. He screamed as the skin was ripped.

"I'll find you," he growled as he took a blow from Rollant with his head turned toward her.

"Run!" Rollant yelled again as he landed another punch. But he took two subsequent hits to the stomach and doubled over.

The man yanked the dagger from the dead one's chest and stabbed Rollant through the ribs.

Élise's insides turned and knotted. Her heart stopped beating and cracked. The tingle of devastation streaked down her limbs. She staggered backward.

"Run!" Rollant yelled with a faded breath as he grabbed the man's neck.

That time, Élise ran with tears streaming into a spinning world. Rollant was saving her. She didn't want him to die in vain. She vowed never to return to Faubourg Saint-Antoine or Paris. Fear kept her legs moving, and she hoped that if there were a God, he wouldn't let anyone follow her.

Stumbling through the garden gate of her Charonne home, Élise collapsed to her knees, tears soaking the cold earth beneath her palms. She dragged herself inside, barring the door behind her as though it could lock out the horrors she'd left behind. Throwing herself onto the sofa, her cries filled the empty house, echoing off the walls like a prayer unanswered.

"Forgive me, Rollant," she sobbed, her voice breaking with each word. "Forgive me."

She clutched her arms, her nails biting into her skin as guilt pressed down on her. She didn't deserve life. She didn't deserve anything. Hate seethed behind her ears and on her cheeks. She had run, but there was no escape. Not from the hate, not from herself.

CHAPTER 32

The Fate of Truth

CHARONNE, PARIS, NOVEMBER 1789

A SUDDEN POUND at the door shattered her sobs, twisting them into silence. Her head snapped up. Her breath hitched. Her chest tightened as the sound echoed through the room. Another pound rattled the doorframe, more insistent, more demanding. Her gaze darted to the window. Escape? No, she couldn't outrun them. Her trembling fingers sank into her coat pocket, clutching the blade she'd used to kill Gabin. She would fight if she had to—there was no other choice. But, a voice cut through the dark.

"Élise!" Rollant's voice shattered her fear, and the blade slipped from her grasp.

She ran to the door and unbarred it. She slammed into his chest and tried to help him inside, but he walked in more or less without help. He barred the door and led her to the main room.

"Thank you for letting me in," he mumbled and sank on the sofa.

Élise blinked rapidly, her mind racing to make sense of the impossible. She had seen the blade plunge into his chest and felt the warmth of his blood on her fingers. Surely, he was hurt and bleeding—dying even. Yet he had walked in, steady on his feet, alive. Was her memory failing her? No, she knew what she saw.

She hurried over to him. Her hands grabbed his bicep and forearm. "You are hurt," she said, but Rollant kept his body from her.

"I am not hurt."

"I saw him stab you." She stooped to grab the edge of her dress to rip it for linen. His hand gently grasped her wrist. She locked eyes with him. "I—I stabbed you."

"I'm fine." He smiled. "Didn't even leave a mark."

But she didn't believe him. She saw him bend over and groan like he had been stabbed. She yanked him up, ripped his blood-stained shirt open, and ran her hands over his chest and belly, searching for bloody wounds in the hearth light.

"I saw." Her voice trailed off. "I know I stabbed you. I did! I felt the blade. I felt . . ." His belly was covered in blood smears, but there was no wound.

He grasped her wrist and pressed her palm flat against his belly. "I'm fine." His fingers caressed the back of her hand.

He took her hand and guided her fingers to the hole in his coat. "See? It went through the fabric." His tone was light, almost reassuring, but something unsaid flickered in his eyes.

"But I saw Gabin . . . He—he twisted the blade. I heard you . . . in—in pain," she said, grabbing his coat to examine it more closely. "I saw the blade in your belly after I untied you." Her fingers smoothed the spot where the baker's knife had protruded.

"I am fine, Élise," he said softly, but there was a tension in his voice as if he were choosing his words carefully. "A little sore in the neck, perhaps, but nothing that won't pass." He smiled faintly, though it didn't quite reach his eyes. "I am alive, and that is what matters." He cradled her cheek. The look of love again lived in his gaze. "You don't need to fear or worry or cry. Not for me."

She blinked in disbelief, her hands trembling as they traced the unbroken skin of his chest. It was warm beneath her palm, solid, real—but unmarred. No wounds. Only the scars from a long time past. She pressed harder, searching for anything her eyes might have missed, but there was nothing. She remembered the blade plunging into him, the resistance as it pierced his flesh, the sticky warmth of his blood on her fingers, and his groans of pain. Had she imagined the entire night?

No—she couldn't have. She had seen it, felt it, heard it. It had all been real. And yet, there he was, whole and untouched, standing before her. She didn't trust her eyes. Her heart raced, fear and wonder twisting into a knot in her chest.

"Impossible," she whispered.

"It was dark, Élise," he whispered. "See, I am fine." A soft, polite smile came over his lips. He took her hand in his and opened his mouth to speak.

"How?" she asked, her jaw agape in wonder.

"Did Gabin find this place?" he asked at the same time. "Do I need to find you another home?"

She broke through her trance. "I'm sorry," she stammered, her voice cracking under the weight of her shame. Tears streamed down her cheeks as she clung to his hand.

"I didn't want to go back to Gabin. But Madame Marie—she sent her child to fetch him. I didn't know, Rollant. I didn't know." Her chest heaved as the words tumbled out, each heavier than the last. "He dragged me back. He said I was his. He beat me—humiliated me. He started a riot just to show me that I belonged to him. And I—"

Her voice cracked, and her sobs overtook her. "I didn't know how to stop him. I didn't know what to do."

Rollant closed the distance between them. She closed her eyes, thinking surely his backhand would come after the night she'd put him through, but instead, he cradled her face. "There is nothing to apologize for," he whispered. His hand curled around her fingers on her chest.

Her brow furrowed, and her gaze dropped to the ground. "Regardless, I still stabbed you. I didn't die with you. Then I ran."

"Élise. If you hadn't stabbed me, they would have made me watch you die a painful death before killing me as well." Rollant lifted her chin. "I'd rather die alone than be made to witness such a thing. It was just lucky Gabin didn't make sure I was dead in his haste to punish us."

He had watched Amée and Cateline die, she remembered. Tears streamed down her cheeks. She nestled into his chest, but his arms stayed by his side. How could he hold her? Twice, she'd almost been the cause of his death.

Though his thumb smoothed over hers on his chest, and his cheek lay atop her head, silence lingered for a long time.

"It's been a long night, month, for both of us," he finally said.

She glanced up, and he tilted his head to the bedroom. "I have men's blood on me, and I'd like to wash it off."

She nodded. "I'll be out here," she said.

He returned a little while later in clean, damp clothes, holding his blood-soaked coat, while she was trying to replay the evening in her mind, given Rollant's recent additions.

"I can't do much about this," he said with a half-chuckle and left his coat next to the hearth to dry. He walked up and sank to her feet with a basin of lukewarm water and a cloth. He dipped the cloth, gently wiped her face, and patted a few blood spots from her neck. The heat from the water soothed her chilled skin and pulled her from her thoughts.

"I saw . . ." Her voice trailed off.

He smiled. "But I'm here. You're here. We are fine. Please promise me, you'll stay in Charonne, though," he said as he dabbed away Gabin's dried blood on her left hand. When he reached for her right, she pulled it back in hesitation. She stared at her fingers and thumb. The red outline-turned-black stained them.

"I felt your blood, Rollant," she said with a knitted brow. "I felt its warmth. I felt it on my fingers."

He shifted. "It was . . . a very scary time," he stammered. His gaze averted. He moved to the sofa, sitting close to her, placing the basin to balance on their thighs. He threaded his fingers in between hers and washed the blood from them.

She watched the water turn muddy brown as he cleaned the blood from her fingers. It didn't make sense. It was his blood. Whose else would it have been? But his belly, his chest, perfect. Not even a bruise. Bruises. He had been beaten. She had seen them, but then they were gone. She looked him full in the face.

"Where are your bruises?" she asked while touching the tender spot on her cheek from Gabin's hit, knowing at least part of the night was certain.

His lip twitched. "I'll answer all your questions tomorrow," he said. "But for now, sleep is your best remedy."

He helped her into the bedroom and pointed to the shirt he'd left for her on the bed. He left a basin of clean water and another cloth for her on the dresser.

"I'll sleep out here," he said. "Good night, Élise. I will see you in the morning."

After she cleaned herself, Rollant's long shirt slipped over her head and fell just above the knee. The winter tickled her legs, but his scent of old wood and candle smoke warmed her. She breathed in his scent as she wrapped her arms around herself and pulled the shirt's collar over her nose, thankful even after all the months he had been away and all the washes she'd put it through, it still smelled of him. The fabric gathered in her fingers. The cold wrapped around her legs and made them shiver. She wondered how Rollant was going to sleep with damp clothes. The fire flickered low, casting light but offering little warmth. She hadn't cut enough firewood. Even though she shivered, she opened the door, and the blast of cold air weakened her knees.

"Are you well?" Rollant said, lifting his head. His coat draped over him as he curled up in the fetal position on the small sofa.

"I am thinking you are going to freeze out here. I would sleep better knowing you at least had a blanket." Her lip quivered from the cold. He got up and draped his coat around her shoulders. It chased away the chill, but the iron stench of blood clung to the fabric, pungent and metallic. Her knees stopped shaking, but his shoulders twitched seemingly from an icy tendril. His shirt hung open since she'd ripped the buttons.

"You will be freezing all night if I take the blanket," he said. "I will be fine with my coat."

"You will not sleep well curled up like that with a coat." She glanced at the sofa.

"It's almost dry," he said. "As are my clothes."

"You'll still freeze out here," she whispered, her gaze dropping to the floor. Her fingers twisted in the hem of her gifted shirt. "And I—I'll sleep better knowing you're warm too." She hesitated, the words catching in her throat before she forced them out. "Could we—could we share the bed? Just to stay warm?" Her cheeks flushed, and she couldn't bring herself to meet his eyes. "That way, we'll both have good sleep."

"If that is what you wish," he said softly, his voice heavy with restraint. "But I will not hold you, Élise. I will not touch you. For your sake—and mine." His fingers brushed her chin, lifting her gaze to meet his. For a moment, his eyes lingered on her lips, and she felt the weight of all the words left unspoken. "Please, Élise," he whispered. "Do not tempt me further, for I have already failed once before."

"We all fail," she said to comfort him. Though it pained her that he would not kiss her, she whispered, "But I promise it."

They returned to the bedroom. She took one side of the small bed, and he took the other, pulling the blankets up. His weight caused her to slide into his back. He didn't move, and she didn't want him to. His warmth put an instant spell on her. She ran her hands down his long shirt and pulled it over her bare legs.

"Rollant?" she whispered, curious.

He hummed, already half asleep.

"If you are unwounded, then why did you groan? Why did you moan in pain?"

He shifted a little on the bed and scratched his neck. "I don't remember, Élise. Everything happened so quickly. I'll speak of it tomorrow."

It was impossible. No man could bleed without a gash, cry out in pain, yet bear no wound. The memory haunted her as she lay in the dark, her mind repeating the night's events again and again. She knew what she had seen—what she had felt. It didn't make sense. And as Rollant slept beside her, steady as a stone, Élise stared into the dark, her mind racing. She wasn't mad—she couldn't be. She had seen the blood. Felt it. Heard his pain. Yet there he was, whole, untouched, breathing softly beside her. The impossible truth settled over her like a shroud: either she was indeed mad, or there was more to Rollant than she could ever comprehend.

DAWN'S pale light seeped through the shutters, cold and gray. She stretched her arm across the bed, her hand meeting only emptiness where warmth should have been.

Her heart seized.

She bolted upright, the sheets tangling around her legs.

"Rollant?" she whispered, her voice catching in her throat. Had she imagined it all? Had it been his ghost that had tended to her, whispered to her in the dark?

Her trembling hands rose to her line sight. Faint specks of dried blood stuck to her skin. His blood—or what she thought was his. A cold dread knotted her stomach. She flung herself out of bed, stumbling as the sheets dragged her down, and slammed into the dresser. Ignoring the sting, she scrambled to the door and threw it open, her breath lodged in her chest.

He was there. Standing by the hearth, tending to a pan of eggs. The amber glow outlined his form, casting his long shadow across the floor. His shirt hung loose, and his dark hair curled from the lingering moisture of his wash. He turned, his steady gaze finding hers with quiet concern.

"Are you well?" he asked, his voice low and warm, like the fire crackle.

An audible gasp and sigh followed as her knees went weak with relief.

"Yes," she managed.

She pressed her hand to the doorframe, and her body sagged as the weight of her panic lifted. He was alive. Not a ghost. Not a phantom conjured by her grief-stricken mind. Rollant was there, standing before her.

She closed the door and slid down, curling her knees to her chest and leaning her head back against the wood. Relief swelled in her chest, but it was tangled with confusion.

A knock at her door came. "Are you certain?" Rollant asked.

"Yes," she said again, crawling to her drawer. Questions raced through her mind: How could he be here, standing upright and whole, after what she'd seen? The blood, the groans of pain, the dagger pulled from his own belly—it burned in her memory like the glow of the fire in the hearth. But the more she thought, the more her memories blurred, tangled by the impossible. Shaking her head, she pulled out her dress and prepared for the day.

When Élise finally emerged with her hair unkempt and her dress wrinkled, she found Rollant standing at the small table. He pulled a chair out for her like nothing in the world was amiss. The scent of warm eggs mingled with the faint smoke of the dying hearth. Her stomach grumbled, but her mind wouldn't let her relax.

"You are too kind," she murmured, but before she sat down, she paused. Her fingers curled around the back of the chair, and her gaze averted. "At Versailles, you said everything was a lie. Everything." Her voice was quiet, but the words trembled with accusation. "Was that a lie as well?"

Rollant stilled, his hand brushing the sleeve of her dress as if grounding himself. Slowly, his fingers reached beneath her chin, tilting her face up to meet his. His eyes softened.

"Of course it was," he said, his voice barely more than a whisper.

Her breath hitched at the touch of his hand, the warmth of his skin against hers. "But why?" she pressed. "Why would you say that? Why would you—" her voice faltered, breaking on the word "lie."

He leaned down, his forehead almost touching hers. For a moment, he hesitated, his hand cradling her cheek as if weighing the cost of what he was about to do. Then, he kissed her—a fleeting, feather-light touch that was gone as quickly as it came. A promise, not a possession. An apology, not a demand.

"I will tell you everything today," he promised with a gaze solely and steadily on her. "But for now, let us enjoy a quiet breakfast."

ROLLANT DEBATED how to tell Élise all through their meal. And after they cleared the table, Rollant led her to the sofa and lowered his hand to hers.

"I'll answer all your questions, Élise," he said softly. "But let me start from the beginning."

He closed his eyes, drawing in a deep, steadying breath, bracing himself for what was to come. She waited, quiet and poised, though he feared the truth might shatter her. He could have left her to think he'd died, could have let her grief bury the questions—but that would have been a guilt he could never tame. She deserved the truth, however cruel it might be.

He kissed her hand, hoping it was not the last time he kissed her. "I couldn't tell you I was Captain of the King's Bodyguard," Rollant admitted, his voice low, "so I told you I was a navy man."

Élise blinked, her brow furrowing. "So, you're nobility?" she asked, her tone edged with curiosity and suspicion.

"Forgotten nobility," he replied.

"Then how did you rise so high?" Suspicion sharpened her voice.

He hesitated, his gaze falling to the floor. "Through service. Loyalty. And proving myself when it mattered most."

"Were you an informant?" She leaned forward, pleading to know. "Did you throw any of us in prison?"

"I informed the king of the city's reactions to his decrees per his command," he answered, meeting her gaze evenly. "I was on Rue Saint-Honoré last night, seeing where loyalties lie. And no, I never threw anyone in prison, nor did anyone ever go to prison from my reports to the king."

He paused, waiting. He knew there was more she needed to ask, more she had to understand before she could forgive—or condemn.

She nodded slowly, as if weighing his answers before her voice softened. "Then what about Amée and Cateline? Were they lies?"

A shadow passed over Rollant's face. He smiled, but it was a smile touched with sorrow. "Everything I told you about them is true, except they passed from life as old women with silver hair."

Her brow knitted, and her eyes closed, processing his words. "How could they die old women," she whispered, her eyes narrowing, "when you're only twenty-seven?"

"They lived a long time ago, Élise,"—his voice grew heavy—"and . . . I will always be twenty-six."

She rubbed her neck, her head tilting as if to shake loose the growing knot of questions. A chuckle escaped her lips, full of disbelief. "What do you mean?"

The bitter truth stuck in his throat, reluctant to emerge. But he forced it out. "I was born in the year 1122."

Her brow furrowed. "Eleven?" Her tone was incredulous, her eyes narrowing as though she were trying to decipher some cruel joke. "You mean 1762, surely."

His silence was her answer. Her lips parted, but no words came. Finally, she shook her head. "I don't beli—"

"Please," he interrupted, his voice almost a plea. "Let me tell you the truth, all of it, and then you can choose to believe it or not."

"I hoped you thought me deserving of the actual truth, Rollant," she whispered as tears glistened. "Not another lie—"

"You are," Rollant crooned. "And I will tell you."

She slid her hands into her lap, her shoulders stiff with distrust. A slight, curt nod signaled for him to continue. Her face was carved with indifference, but her quivering fingers betrayed her.

"My father fought in the First Crusade," Rollant began. His words were slow and deliberate. "He was a knight for the Kingdom of France. He died when I was a boy. My older brothers died in subsequent feudal wars. My sister perished as a child. My mother . . . She lost her life to illness, or as the physician said, a broken heart." He looked away, his jaw tight. "I was not enough for her to want to live."

"Knights?" she scoffed, her lips curling with disbelief. She threw her hands up in exasperation. "Rollant, that's impossible. They've been gone for centuries. Whatever story this is—stop. Please." Her voice trembled, torn between anger and fragility.

But Rollant continued, undeterred. "I grew up training as a knight. I won many awards and favors. I was King Louis the Young's favorite warrior. In the Second Crusade, in 1148, I was murdered."

Her scoff was immediate. "Murdered," she repeated, her tone dripping with disbelief.

"Slain by a brother-in-arms out of greed and jealousy," Rollant continued. "The King's sorceress offered me immortality to serve the king. I accepted, Élise."

He paused, but Élise was still and silent.

"I accepted because I loved Amée and Cateline. I did not want them at the mercy of the man who killed me. And so when I was restored to life immortal, I took my murderer's life in cold blood. The sorceress cursed me for I had cursed myself—a life of disciplined virtue gone in an instant."

Élise sighed with a slight shake of her head. "And what was this curse?" she asked.

Rollant paused, hoping the words would make it out. "If I crossed the threshold of my home, Amée and Cateline would perish," he said, his voice breaking. "And as long as I remain immortal, anyone I embrace in love will draw their last breath."

Élise froze, her arms tightening across her chest as if shielding herself. Her breath hitched as she stared at him, her disbelief warring with fear. Her gaze turned inward, perhaps remembering when he pulled her close and she'd lost her breath, but she snapped back.

"Do you really expect me to believe that?" she asked, her voice shaking. Anger flickered in her tone, but it couldn't mask the fear shadowing her gaze. "After everything else you've lied about?"

"Believe it or not, it is true." He tapped a fist on his thigh. "Amée was my wife when I was murdered. After I returned with my curse, I could not cross the threshold of my home nor hold her. She chose to remain my wife, bound by her vows, though it meant forty years of solitude. She raised our child alone and, when illness finally claimed her, she chose to die in my arms. It was the first time I was able to hold her, and no sooner had my arms wrapped around her, holding her tight, she gasped and drew her last breath just as the curse foretold."

Élise's eyes watered, though a wavering sneer perched on her lips. "I will give you this, Rollant; you are an excellent storyteller."

"My daughter, Cateline, wanted nothing to do with me after that."

Élise squared her shoulders to him. "And this story just keeps getting stranger, doesn't it?"

Rollant ignored the question. "I watched over my descendants until the Black Plague took them all except my seven-year-old granddaughter, ten generations removed from me. Her parents had died, and I took her in, but she ran to me and jumped into my arms."

The memory of Ninette's face, twisted with panic as she gasped for air, haunted his dreams. He scratched his neck, unable to bear the weight of what he'd done.

"I buried her with the rest of my family. I locked myself away in whatever room the King had me in and cut myself off from everyone and everything except the duty I was bound to serve."

"Then why did you not try to end your service for the king and die?" Élise asked with disdain.

He sighed. "I tried many times to desert or not do my duty, but somehow fate forced me back. It was the sorceress' deal, and it wasn't allowed."

Élise stood up. "Well, that is the most colorful story I've ever heard. But may I ask you, what did you hope to gain by spinning these lies to me?"

Rollant looked up at her and met her gaze. "It is the truth."

"Prove it," she said in a whisper, though her voice was hard with scorn.

"Have I not already? You stabbed me, Gabin twisted the blade, hung me from a lamppost."

Her lip and eye twitched. "But you said—"

"Do you think a mortal man would have been alive by the time you came back after being strung up on his toes?"

Her eyes darted to the items around the room as she took a small step backward. She shook her head and ran her hand over her brow and through her tresses.

"Could have," she said, her voice shaking.

His heart hurt for her. The reality she lived in unraveled before her. But he asked again, "And survived being stabbed in the chest?"

"But," she whispered and took another step backward.

"And survive a bullet at the Bastille?"

"You said it was another's blood." Her voice trailed off as she remembered.

The newly issued dagger was heavier than it should have been as he drew it from his boot. He hesitated, staring at the blade. His thumb brushed the hilt, his jaw tightening. Would proving the truth ease her doubt—or drive her further away?

He thought of her fear, the way she'd recoiled from him only moments ago, and it twisted in his gut. But he couldn't bear for her to think him a liar. Not about this. Not when it mattered most.

"I can show you," he whispered, laying the knife across his thighs. "But there will be blood."

She backed up a few more steps. Her eyes focused on the dagger. "What do you plan to do with that?"

"I plan to slice my hand and show you I am immortal. It will heal before your eyes after a moment."

He took it in his hand and waited for her rejection, but curiosity must have tamed her tongue. The blade slid across his palm. Centuries of repetition had dulled the pain, but it still burned, as always.

Élise stood with arms crossed tightly over her belly, leaned forward, and gazed intently at the gash on his hand.

Blood ran freely until it didn't, and the wound was stitched up from within.

Élise's jaw fell agape. Her breath shaky, she spewed, "What sorcery is this? Are you a demon? Who are you?!"

He laid the dagger on the sofa before meeting her gaze. "I've already told you, Élise."

Her hands balled into fists, and her arms spastically fell to her side before crossing again. "So what was your plan with me? How many Amées have there been? Did you plan to kill me all along? Get what you needed and be done with me?"

Rollant shook his head. "There has only been Amée, and now you. I never wanted to hurt you. I never wanted anything from you." His chest constricted at seeing her afraid of him. "I never meant for our relationship to go this far."

"But why me?" Her voice cracked, and she pressed a hand to her chest as though to hold her heart together. "Why did you do this? Why fall in love with me? Why let me love you? Why did you not stay away?" She stepped back, trembling fingers brushing the wall as if needing support. Her breath hitched. "You should have stayed away."

Rollant had asked himself the same questions many nights. He stayed rooted to the sofa, not wanting to scare her further. "Because I was selfish, Élise. You opened something in me that I had long since buried. You are the essence of life. You reminded me of the man I once was—a man of honor and virtue and passion for what is right and true. You are the fire of life that I was and lived for. I found the same passion I had in serving my God and my king in your words at the *Au Pain Roux* that night. I couldn't stay away; no matter how many times I told myself to stay away, I always ended up back at your doorstep."

He rose and leaned toward her, wishing to hold her. "For six hundred years, I found immortality was easier to bear if I lived alone, isolated, never caring about anyone or anything but you . . . Élise . . . you made me care. I feel like I have a soul again because of you."

Tears streamed down her cheeks. "So what does this mean?" she stammered.

"It means I am afraid I may never hold you in my arms for fear of taking your life and letting the curse again rear its dark head. I tried to give you a good world where you could find love in return. I tried to right my selfish, vain desires, and I'm sorry it wasn't enough."

She shook her head. "You dare love me and leave? Push me away?" she choked, her voice shattering as tears streaked her cheeks. "You took my heart, Rollant. You have it, and now I want it back. Leave me! Leave me alone. You're a monster. I never want to see you again!"

Her voice cracked on the last word, and her tear-filled eyes softened for a moment. She turned her head quickly, as though ashamed of whatever emotion had flickered across her face, and pressed her lips into a trembling line. "Just go," she whispered. "Please."

Her words struck him like the blows he had taken the night before. They cut deep, but were expected. She was scared and wanted nothing more to do with him, though at the softness in her eyes, maybe she did. He hung his head and dusted off the futile hope.

He responded in a hollow whisper. "I'll do as you ask, Élise. You have my heart as well, though I fear it's worth little to you now."

"I don't want it," she said, tears blurring her eyes.

He swallowed hard and glanced at her, feeling her fear and heartbreak mar her words. "Whether you want it or not, I love you, Élise. Find love. Find life. Forget me, though I'll carry your memory forever. I have Amée's rose, and I have your scarf. They'll remain with me until the end of time, and that will have to be enough."

He paused at her silence, taking in her hitching breaths.

"I'll not intervene again." He wiped his hand on his shirt, leaving a new trail of blood, and threw his coat and boots on. Each step to the door was heavier than the one before. He could feel her trembling breaths behind him, the weight of her tears pulling at him like a tether he could not break. But he had to.

The November air stung his face as he stepped into the street, the sound of her tears clinging to him like frost. He told himself it was for the best—a necessary pain to spare her from something far worse—but the truth was as hollow as the endless, empty years ahead. He had tried to leave every time before to be fair to Élise, but their paths kept crossing. With the violence growing every day in the city, he hoped their paths would not cross again. He would make sure they didn't, not because of her words spoken out of fear and heartbreak, but because it was the right thing to do.

Part Three

CHAPTER 33
Cry of the Heart
CHARONNE, PARIS, MAY 1791

THE BLOOD HAD long since faded from her hands, but its stain lingered on her soul. Sixteen months and Élise still couldn't forget the men she had stabbed—the one she'd killed and the one she had cast away. The ache was intolerable, a constant knot in her chest. Her hand still shook at night, remembering Gabin forcing her to drive the blade into Rollant's belly—Rollant, the only person who'd ever truly cared about her.

She was a wretch.

Sixteen months. It had been sixteen months since she'd screamed for Rollant to leave. Since he'd walked into the cold night and disappeared from her life. Sixteen months, and he had not returned.

She tried to bury him in the past, but he lingered in her dreams, her thoughts during monotonous tasks, or the quiet moments before slumber. Though he lied to her and betrayed her, she understood why. His lies, his departures—they were all to protect her from Amée's fate, from the curse that haunted him. And yet, she had thrown him away, screamed at him to leave, and called him a monster. He never would have shown himself after she thought him dead if he hadn't loved her and trusted her with his secrets. And she threw him away like a fool.

If only to apologize and beg his forgiveness, she wished he would return at least once more in her lifetime. Rollant was only an hour's walk away, but fear kept her rooted in Charonne. She had killed a man, and all the murderous rioters knew she'd done it. If they found her, they'd kill her without hesitation. She didn't want to die, not for that. She hated Gabin, but she didn't want to become him.

Paris had scarred her soul.

Life in Charonne was peaceful, even if it was small. The four families who lived on Rollant's land were kind. They helped her, helped themselves to her garden, and she took from their shops and farms in return. It was a quiet community, one without debts or obligations.

The long grasses tickled her ankles as she lay in them, looking up at the sky. Hugo lay beside her. Élise's hands were behind her head, not allowing Hugo to hold her hand. Though Hugo was a good friend, kind and devoted, she did not feel for him what he felt for her. His infatuation weighed on her like a growing shadow, impossible to ignore but equally impossible to embrace. But as the months went on without Rollant, she wondered if it would be fair to Hugo to marry him as he had hinted or to let him go.

Giselle's shout echoed across the hill. "Hugo, Élise! Mother says dinner will be ready soon."

Hugo chuckled. "That means we have a while," he said, rolling up. He waved to his sister and gazed at the city walls in the distance. "Do you ever want to go back there?" he asked.

"No," Élise said, rolling up beside him. "Never."

Hugo focused on her profile. "Does that mean you wish to stay in Charonne?"

Her chin dipped. "Yes, Hugo."

"You're beautiful, Élise," he whispered and smoothed her hair off her cheek. "I am getting older now," he started. He glanced back over his shoulder to ensure there were no prying eyes. "I've been trying for two years to win at least a slice of your heart."

He smiled, but Élise thinned her lips. She had tried to fall in love with him. It would have been easy, but her heart betrayed her, always pulling her back to the memory of Rollant, alive like the first spark of a flame.

She turned to face him. "You have. You and your sisters are my closest friends."

He leaned back but turned his shoulders to her. "See, Élise. That's what I mean. Friends. I want my wife to be my friend, but if that is all she ever sees me as, then maybe it's not meant to be."

She met his gaze, not wanting to reveal the truth, afraid it might damage the relationship with his family.

His cerulean eyes softened, pleading. "May I at least try to kiss you, Élise? Just once—to see if there is anything between us?" His voice was low, careful, as though he feared her answer.

She pulled her knees to her chest. It was an improper question, one she should refuse. But Rollant's kiss lingered in her memory, its spark unmatched. She glanced at Hugo's lips, soft and full, and forced herself to consider it. She felt she owed him that much, to at least try. At least, as his friend.

"That seems to be acceptable," she said.

"Really?" he asked with lifted eyebrows and surprise etched into his wide smile.

She nodded.

"Alright," he said, shifting in the grass closer to her. "Well," he said with a boyish grin.

He took her hand and cradled her cheek with the other.

He leaned forward, but before he placed his kiss, he whispered, "I love you, Élise. You are the most beautiful, vivacious, protective, and loyal woman I've ever met."

His lips pressed against hers. She forced herself to give him a chance, so she returned his kiss. She closed her eyes, hoping, willing the spark to come. Rollant's kiss had been fire—sweeping, consuming. But Hugo's? There was only tenderness, a flicker compared to the inferno she remembered. It wasn't enough. It wasn't Rollant. Her heart ached as she pulled away, her eyes brimming with unshed tears. Rollant had ruined her for any other man.

Hugo's eyes grew wide, and his fingers quivered against her skin. "Are you hurt? Did I do something wrong?" he asked in a frantic rush.

She looked past Hugo at the house Rollant had given her, where her heart had been left behind.

Hugo cradled her cheek. "Are you alright, Élise?"

"Yes," she whispered.

Hugo leaned in to continue the kiss, but Élise turned her face, leaving him to kiss her cheek.

"I do not love you, Hugo." Her voice broke. She turned back to face him, and her chest tightened at the hurt in his eyes. Hugo deserved a woman who loved him wholly, not someone who pined for a ghost. "I love your family. I love our friendship. I know you would be an extraordinary husband and father, but I do not love you."

His hand fell away from her cheek. "My parents didn't love each other when they were married, but they grew to," he said, his voice flushed with hope. "Maybe—maybe that could happen for us too." The plea in his voice cut through her, but she couldn't give him what he wanted.

She glanced at him, having turned away from her. Silence was her answer.

"At least I'm here," he said before shooting up and walking to the edge of the field with his hands on his belt. He paced at the border.

She slowly got up, walked over to him, and embraced him. "I'm sorry, Hugo," she said, her voice breaking. "Maybe one day, I could fall in love with you. But if Rollant returned, I can't promise I wouldn't find my love for you was only a façade—a remedy meant to heal but destined to fail."

She hurt for him, not wishing to be the one to deliver rejection. She released her arms around him. "And that is not fair to you or your family."

Hugo gripped the edge of the fence, pulling back and pushing forward, figuring out his next words. "He may never come back, Élise."

"I know that," she sighed with a break in her voice. "And I am fine to live a life alone if that be the case." A tear ran down her cheek that she wiped away. The motion drew Hugo's attention. He said nothing but rubbed her back before pulling her into a second embrace.

Élise laid her head on his shoulder. "Only allow me to be the fiery aunt to your children," she chuckled.

Hugo chuckled as well, but his was edged with sorrow. He lifted her face to his and pressed his forehead against hers. "I love you Élise," he whispered. "You're my first love, and likely my only one."

"Don't say such things, Hugo. How you feel about me is how I feel about Rollant. One day, he may come back, and if he does, I want to go with him." Tears welled in her eyes. "I know it's not a nice sentiment, but you should know the truth."

He nodded and pulled her closer, digging his nose into her neck in a bear hug. Then he released her and stepped back. "Well, either I suppose I shall try harder to make you forget Rollant or live my life alone." He smiled. "And I'm not quite content with living alone just yet."

She laughed. "Is it a challenge?"

"A challenge I've already accepted," he said with a sly smile. "Come, dinner is probably ready now."

"I'm looking forward to it, but I'll be there soon. I need to gather my thoughts and compose myself," she said, adjusting the neckline of her dress.

His cheeks turned red as he bowed his head. "Of course, Mademoiselle." His sheepish grin left two dimples on either side of his cheeks before he turned to go.

She glanced over the vast open lands with the city wall just beyond.

"Could I marry Hugo?" she whispered a few moments later. "Could I love him more than I love Rollant?" She wasn't sure.

She leaned on the fence with her elbows; her gaze followed a rider as he trotted east in the distance. Something about him drew her—the way he sat, the familiar tilt of his shoulders. Her heart leaped before her reason could catch it.

"Rollant!" she cried, the name tearing from her throat like a prayer, raw, unthinking, and full of want.

Her voice echoed across the meadow. She hoped, wished, willed, and longed for the stranger on the horse to turn around, but fate did not hear her silent pleas. Her call was left unanswered, and she hung her head, shame burning her cheeks. Foolishness. She peered over her shoulder to see if anyone was outside. She was alone and hoped they did not hear her.

Why did Rollant have any business returning to Charonne after she'd told him to leave? He had told her he would not intervene again. She looked up to the sky, drenched in blue and purple with streaks of gold from the evening sun.

Curse her mouth.

Curse her heart.

ROLLANT WATCHED THEM FROM A DISTANCE, sitting in the meadow. Hugo's arms around her and their lips meeting, Élise returning his kiss—Rollant's heart twisted, a vise tightening in his chest. He gripped the reins, the leather creaking beneath his hands as he forced himself to look away. He'd told himself to let her go.

He'd come the long way against his better judgment for a chance to see Élise once more as he plotted the King's escape route amid rising violence and opposition against the crown. It was reckless and foolish, and yet he couldn't help himself.

As his horse trotted off, a scowl drew heavy on his lips. He had wanted one fleeting glimpse of her—just one. He had convinced himself it would be enough to see her in the garden or hanging laundry, but the image of Élise's mouth on Hugo's burned into his mind. Her closeness, her laughter—it was everything Rollant wanted with her. A life of love. A life he could never give her.

Sensing his tension, his mare shifted beneath him, but Rollant remained rooted in the saddle.

"This is what I wanted," he mumbled to himself. "This is what she deserves."

But watching her embrace another man, the hollow ache in his chest flared into a storm he couldn't calm. He wanted her to be happy, and he meant it.

He wanted Élise to be with Hugo, to find love with someone kind and good, to live a normal life, and to be held in love far from his curse. He would rather endure his own torment than see her fall victim to his sins. He had made his choice long ago—her happiness over his own. Yet what he had just witnessed burned like ash in his heart. He hadn't realized how much it would hurt to see it.

His shoulders slumped as he fought the instinct to turn his horse around, to ride back to her, to pull her into his arms. But what then? Wrap her in his embrace and kill her? Curse her to Amée's fate?

No. He'd already lied and betrayed her trust. She didn't want him. Not anymore. Clearly.

His knuckles whitened as he clenched the reins, forcing his gaze forward and away from the stretching meadows.

"At least I will be in exile with the king," he whispered. "And I can go knowing she is happy, safe, and with a good man like Hugo." His whisper was thick with sorrow but faint at the mention of Hugo's name.

Rollant urged his mare forward, his back forever to Élise. The distance between them stretched into the unbearable.

Yes, he had told himself this was for the best—for her—but he couldn't silence the small, desperate voice in his heart that begged him to turn back. But he couldn't go back. She deserved a future, even if it meant tearing himself from the one person who had made him feel alive. He just needed one more glimpse. To see her smile. To hear her say his name. But what could he give her except heartbreak?

"Take me away, girl," he whispered to the mare, his voice thick with sorrow. "Far from her, far from the pain."

He patted her neck absently, his mind a thousand miles away. But no matter how far he rode, he knew he could never silence the image of Élise in Hugo's arms.

CHAPTER 34

The Flight of Royalty

TUILERIES PALACE, PARIS, JUNE 1791

ROLLANT STIRRED IN HIS SLEEP. Flashes of Élise haunted him in a cruel nightmare: her in Hugo's shirt, sitting on Hugo's lap, her arms draped around Hugo's neck as she kissed Hugo. His fists clenched as he watched from a window, pounding on the glass.

"Élise!" he shouted, his voice desperate, but she only turned to him, her lips curling into a bitter sneer.

"Monster," she mouthed.

The tolling bells in the background grew deafening, louder and louder until Rollant woke with a start, a thick paste coating his mouth. The supper bell echoed through the Tuileries Palace, but it felt as though it rang only for him.

He rubbed his face, wiping sweat from his brow.

"Tonight is the night," he muttered, regaining his breath. He swung his feet out of his bed and rolled the ache out of his neck. "Finally, in two days, maybe the dreams will stop."

Yet even as he spoke the words, he doubted it. Distance wouldn't erase her. Élise would haunt him no matter how far he went—a shadow he could never escape. He longed for the days when dreams—when feelings—were nothing more than faint whispers lost in his eternal monotony. He'd felt nothing—no joy, no pain, no love—and it had been easier to endure.

He had accepted his plight in the past, but with the Revolution slowly crushing the crown, the sorceress tightened the noose around his neck. He wanted out of the deal. He'd called for her to show her face, to remove it, but it was all vanity. She never came.

Rollant ran his hand through his hair, frustration simmering beneath his calm exterior. Every moment spent with Élise had left an imprint on his soul. Her smile and her laugh lingered in his memory like a forgotten melody. But the more he thought of her, the more she became like a ghost he couldn't reach, yet she had become his greatest longing. Her rejection cut deeper than any wound, much more than expected. Maybe beyond the borders, far from Élise and the turmoil of Paris, he could finally find peace. Or perhaps he was lying to himself again.

He dressed methodically, ate his supper brought by a servant, and steeled himself for the secret mission to remove the king from the palatial prison. By the time he mounted the black Berlin carriage, seated at the back as an attendant, the royal family was already inside, disguised and anxious. King Louis held his young son tightly, while Queen Marie Antoinette clutched her daughter, her lips pressed into a pale line. The King's sister, Madame Élisabeth, sat across from them, murmuring reassurances that felt hollow even to Rollant's ears.

Rollant glanced at his pocket watch in the moonlight. They were already half an hour late. The Queen's delay in the palace, nearly discovered by Commander Lafayette, had cost them precious time. It was an ill omen for their journey.

The carriage lurched forward.

He had urged the King to stay in Paris, to negotiate directly with the revolutionaries, and to embrace his symbolic role as a constitutional monarch. But Louis had faltered under the weight of his wife's fears and the mounting hostility of the city, especially the riot that kept the royal family from attending Easter mass. Rollant had tried to convince him that hostilities would pass and concessions could temper the growing tide. But the decision was made, and now they were fleeing like thieves in the night, clinging to a fragile hope of counter-revolution.

The king asked Rollant to come with him, and of course, Rollant had to say yes. But the more he thought about leaving France, the more the idea of distance healing his heart soothed his mind, or, at least, would give him peace. He'd been the one to meet with the royalist allies along the path to the Austrian-Belgium border and set up royalist troops for a counter-revolution, but it was a tricky endeavor. He doubted the king could recover any of his authority if anything went wrong on the two-day ride there and he had to return to Paris.

Outside the city, they met with an intimate Swedish friend of the Queen's to exchange carriages and faster horses and took off riding all night. The carriage rolled through the darkened countryside, its path lit only by the dim glow of lanterns and the moon's silver. Rollant's eyes stayed sharp, scanning for threats. Night was their ally, a cloak for escape, but the dawn would expose them.

As the sun's preceding light entered the sky, the coachman slumped as they came to a bridge.

"Maxime!" Rollant yelled at the coachman. "Stay alert," he ordered.

Maxime straightened up, but his inattention proved costly. The wheel struck the stone post, jolting the carriage and throwing Rollant from the back. He landed hard on the ground. His bones knit themselves back together with an aching crack as he pushed himself up. His ears rang from the impact as he moved quickly to assess the royal family and the damage.

The family was shaken but uninjured; however, the wheel was broken. Maxime and the postilion, Pierre, were already pulling the spare wheel out.

The hard part would be removing the broken one. Rollant pulled the leather straps and ropes from the repair bag.

Every second spent fumbling with the ropes and axle was another moment of escape lost. They were already late. The receding shadows of the dawn seemed to conspire against them. He yanked at the ropes, his fingers sore, the broken wheel refusing to come off the axle. Time was slipping away. He glanced at the royal family standing outside the carriage—Louis with his son, their lives in his hands—and his heart raced. They couldn't afford any more delays.

At last, they were moving again, another half hour later. An hour behind schedule, Maxime and Pierre pushed the horses faster.

When they reached their next checkpoint—a rendezvous with a young royalist Duke and his soldiers—they found it abandoned. The Duke had fled, and Rollant's stomach twisted. Their allies had been spooked, perhaps warned by criers who had already spread news of the King's absence.

The sun had already risen and with new dangers. The towns along their route were waking, and their disguises could only protect them for so long. Beady eyes stared at them as they passed through, and his stomach sank like a rock. They were not safe. The Queen wanted to stop, but Rollant ordered Maxime to keep going and fast.

They had the advantage of knowing the route. Even if there were criers who went ahead, they didn't know to which city the royal family was headed. Rollant's shoulders softened as they passed through towns with no incident, but his unease resurfaced with a vengeance as they entered Varennes-de-Argonne. The streets were eerily quiet, the narrow alleys and dark windows seeming to watch their every move.

Rollant ordered Maxime to keep going. They had to make up time, and Varennes felt like a trap closing in.

As the carriage rolled through the town, Rollant noticed the faces of the townspeople peeking out from behind doors and shutters. Their eyes were sharp, calculating, and he couldn't shake the feeling they were watching for more than just a passing coach.

The horses stopped at a man standing in the middle of the street, flanked by members of the town's National Guard.

The man approached the Coachman, Maxime, and greeted him with an icy welcome. "Good day. I am Maître Lucien Barreau, the town's prosecutor. Where are your passengers going, Monsieur? May I see them?" It was more of a demand than a question.

But before Maxime could respond, he snapped, and the guards surrounded the carriage. Rollant tensed.

The prosecutor approached the carriage window. His eyes narrowed as he swept the faces inside the carriage. His lips pressed into a thin line. There was something in his gaze—suspicion, curiosity—but he made no move to open the door.

For a moment, Rollant feared that the charade was unraveling. Rollant held his breath, waiting for the verdict.

With a subtle tilt of his head, the prosecutor gave a small nod and opened the door as though he had already made up his mind.

"Out," he ordered.

Rollant jumped down from the back but was met with two guards barring his path.

He looked around them at the prosecutor. "I was paid as a guard for these good people. Let me do my job."

The prosecutor paid him no heed as he kept his focus on Queen Marie Antoinette. "Your services are no longer needed, Monsieur."

But Rollant shook his head. "A job is a job. I've already been paid. You're interfering with my duties."

The prosecutor chuckled. "Loyal servant, are you, Monsieur? Very well, you may assist them."

The royal family stepped out one by one, their trembling hands and forced smiles betraying their fear. Rollant offered his hand to the Queen, nodding at her in silent reassurance. But the prosecutor's gaze lingered on her pale face, his lips curving into a knowing smirk. He knew. They had been caught and cut off.

"We must have a record of your passing," the prosecutor said after receiving the family's aliases. "You are free to lodge in our local candlemaker's attic while I prepare your records," the prosecutor said. "I do apologize for the delay, but with an increase in violence, we have to ensure everyone who comes and goes through our town is proper."

Guards confiscated the carriage, led the horses away, and were stationed at every exit of the candlemaker's home.

Rollant conferred with Louis, Maxime, and Pierre as the family huddled in the cramped attic that night. They whispered in hushed tones, debating their options.

"They know who we are," Rollant said bluntly. "The Duke is gone, and we're hours behind schedule. The longer we stay, the more danger we're in."

Pierre piped in. "You suggest we continue? How? They took the carriage."

"I could get it back," Rollant said with a tight jaw, "but the men guarding it will die." He glanced at Louis, who had sat silently through the entire night's exchange.

"But we would not have any soldiers to protect us the rest of the way. It is another day and a half ride to Montmédy," Maxime said.

"And that's if we don't have any more events," Rollant interjected. "Some towns may not be as civil as this one."

Louis glanced at his sleeping family. "Do I put them in harm's way, more so than I already have?" he muttered.

Rollant leaned forward. "They will be in harm's way in either decision."

The king closed his eyes. "Are we sure the town's prosecutor knows who we are?"

Rollant, Maxime, and Pierre glanced at each other. Maxime answered, "No, but we are also not sure they don't know."

Louis leaned back in his chair and lifted his face to the ceiling. "We will wait until the morning, pray they only require paperwork, and we can be on our way." He sighed. "No more bloodshed. We will be civil until we can no longer be civil."

Rollant dipped his head, knowing Louis' hope was misplaced. "Then, my king, you will need sleep."

Once Louis was in bed with his family, Rollant turned to the two men.

Maxime's face was pale, but his eyes were wide. Pierre shifted and looked around the attic room. Rollant didn't need to hear their words; he knew their fear of being found out and dying a traitor's death. But they also knew—it wasn't just about them anymore. "I will take the blame if it comes to it," Maxime said quietly.

Rollant shook his head, his voice cold as steel. "No. I am Captain. It is my responsibility. Now, get some rest. I doubt much will transpire this evening, but be alert in the morning."

Maxime and Pierre retired to the floor and tried to sleep after a full 24 hours without rest. Rollant nestled by the door, his back against the frame. He closed his eyes, but Élise found him there.

Her red scarf framed her dark tresses as she leaned close and brushed her lips against his.

"Monster," she whispered with tears glistening in her eyes.

"I'm sorry," he whispered, trying to reach for her as she faded into the shadows of his dreams.

MORNING CAME with the arrival of the Paris National Guard and constituents of the National Assembly. The royal family was discovered, their aliases meaningless. They were forced into the carriage to be returned to Paris as guards seized Rollant, Maxime, and Pierre.

The town's prosecutor's verdict was swift. "Hang the conspirators," he ordered once the royal family had departed.

But Rollant smirked with a bitter grin as they threw the noose around his neck in the town square. "Let these men go," he told the prosecutor. "These two are hired help. They didn't know the royal family was in the carriage, nor the truth of its mission. I acted alone. They are innocent."

The prosecutor hesitated as the noose was tightened around Rollant's neck. The townspeople who gathered to witness the executions murmured among themselves about killing innocent men until, finally, the prosecutor relented.

"I will believe you for now, Monsieur, but you two will be held for further questioning," the prosecutor said. Maxime and Pierre were untied and escorted elsewhere. They both glanced over their shoulder at Rollant as if to thank him.

"Any last words?" the prosecutor asked.

He smiled in sorrow. He'd never have to worry about last words. The ache and burn in the chest always lingered after hangings. He much preferred a bullet to the head or heart and, if bullets were not available, a swift and sure blade to the neck. He just hoped they would put him in the coffin after his body healed. Clawing out of a grave would take a long time.

The lever was pulled at his silence, and Rollant fell through the trapdoor at the crowd's cheer.

It all faded, and his chest burned with the memories of many deaths. His body still ached with the aftershocks of the noose tightening around his throat, and for a moment, he thought he was still trapped in the suffocating darkness.

But then, the air—cool and damp—flooded his lungs in jagged breaths. A streak of sunlight slipped through the coffin lid, cutting across his face, but stopped cold at his throat as though mocking his execution. The coffin lid was ajar, not yet nailed shut.

He pushed against the cold wood, his hands shaking, his heart pounding as he gasped for breath. Still recovering from a full rebirth, his limbs were stiff as he freed himself. He slid the lid back into place and pressed it close before slinking into the shadows with slow and silent steps.

"Let them bury an empty box and celebrate their so-called justice," he muttered. They'd see that swift trials and executions would leave many innocents dead. He'd seen it before, and it was bound to happen again.

His mind clung to his mission: return to the king, his eternal duty, and

Élise. The thought of her flickered like a dim lantern in his chest, faint and far away. He would be closer to her now—close enough to see her, close enough to remember what he could never have. But as he disappeared into the darkness, he realized with grim clarity that eternity was not the curse.

The curse was living forever without her.

CHAPTER 35
The Crown of Death
TUILERIES PALACE, PARIS, AUGUST 1792

THE KING RETURNED to Paris in disgrace after Varennes, his carriage surrounded by his people's silent, unrelenting sneers. Two years of labor by the National Assembly—two years of cautious progress toward a constitutional monarchy—had been thrown away by the king's ill-fated flight. The nobility had fled, and what remained of Louis' support in the Assembly crumbled alongside his credibility.

The people would never accept a citizen-king allied with Austria and Prussia against the revolution. War loomed on the horizon, and when it arrived, the National Assembly's poorly trained militia army collapsed against the disciplined Austro-Prussian forces. Meanwhile, nobles and royalist officers who had fled France rallied to support the invading armies, determined to restore their king. Yet Paris braced itself, summoning militia from the surrounding provinces within its city walls. It only worsened the king's plight.

"Treason!" was shouted across the divided Assembly: the former *bourgeoisie* and the poor. Among the most radical group, a new leader, Maximilien Robespierre, arose and saw anything related to the monarchy as a serious threat that should be eliminated.

Rollant watched as the armed crowds swelled outside the Tuileries. Month by month, their numbers grew, their chants rising in anger, growing louder and more ferocious, until Paris seemed ready to rise and devour its own. The thin line holding them back broke when the king issued two final vetoes.

The crowds stormed the city hall, seized control of the government under the name of the Commune, and focused their fury on the Tuileries.

With an intent to overthrow the king, they massacred what remained of the King's Bodyguard, though the King had ordered them to stand down.

Rollant awoke in a pool of blood—his own mingling with others. A summer draft swept through the shattered windows of the Tuileries, carrying with it the acrid stench of burning flesh and smoke. He groaned, phantom pain rippling through his back and belly where a pike had impaled him. His hand flew to his gut, but his skin was smooth and unbroken. Once dead, but reborn, as always.

He rolled to his side, pushing himself upright as his gaze swept over the carnage. The Swiss Guards lay still in their gleaming scarlet uniforms, their bodies hacked and mangled, their faces frozen in the grim rictus of death. Gunsmoke choked the air and clung to the back of his throat. He bowed his head and whispered a prayer for the souls of his fallen comrades, should the Lord listen to him.

His head sank under the weight of anguish—exhaustion born of dying. Every death and every forced resurrection tore a piece of his soul. It was unnatural. It was wrong. He just wanted it to end. His chin rolled to his chest. But it was no longer his life to control. He had traded the natural and the right for the eternal bond with the relentless yoke of time. His hands fisted on his thighs, for he had to bear it. With a calming breath, he pushed the thought aside.

He focused on the motionless soldiers. The people of Paris had killed the Swiss Guards—the Swiss who were in charge of the banks. Rollant scoffed at their stupidity, given the dire financial crisis.

Rollant closed the eyes of a nearby Swiss Guard and muttered, "If this does not anger the neutral Swiss to the point of declaring war, I'm unsure if anything ever would."

Rollant moved over the bodies and glanced out the window. Guards from the Temple prison goaded the royal family into a prison carriage amid the angry rebels. Rollant knew his next move; he needed to become a Temple Guard. He stripped the Captain's uniform, put on the blue uniform of a dead National Guard, and slunk into the streets.

Carnage reigned triumphant. Men lay dead, hacked to pieces, still burning, or fed to dogs. He covered his mouth and nose against the stench, his thoughts drifting to Élise. God help her—she had to be far from this nightmare. He prayed she hadn't been swept up in the bloodshed, her courage drawing her into a fight she couldn't survive. The city he had once walked with pride now churned with filth and death, a cesspit of its own making.

At the crossroads, Rollant hesitated. One path led to the Temple, where duty awaited. The other led to Charonne—to her. He wondered if the bonds of his service had been severed, if the crown had been overthrown, and the royal family lay in chains, as commoners. Could he live the life he wanted?

He drew the stolen dagger from his belt and slit his palm with a swift, practiced motion. Blood welled and spilled, but within a few moments, the wound stitched itself closed. He let out a bitter breath. As long as the crown endured, so would his curse. The war's outcome was still uncertain, with the crown's fate dangling by a thread. And so, too, was his. Eternity stretched before him with no end in sight.

Despite all his miraculous rebirths, the crown had once again failed. He was just a man, a man who could never stay dead. He went with the king, and that was where he resided.

Fate pulled him toward the Temple, the weight of his immortality pressing on his shoulders like a yoke. Élise was with Hugo anyway. He thought the notion would soothe the ache, but it only worsened its cruel bite.

He gave his commoner's name, Rollant Montvieux, and exchanged the bloodstained National Guard uniform for a new one as a Temple Guard. As long as the war sided with the king, there was a crown no matter what the insurgents from Paris declared, and he was subject to it, though his heart wished to die.

CHAPTER 36
Crossroads of the Soul
CHARONNE, PARIS, OCTOBER 1792

IT HAD BEEN three years since Rollant left. Élise no longer counted the days but the seasons. When the monarchy was suspended and the royal family imprisoned, she had thought—hoped—Rollant would finally come to her as a mortal. The crown was gone, and his immortality with it. But he never came.

For weeks, she debated, almost packing a bag to search for Rollant, but Hugo had begged her not to return to the city. Reports of bloodlust and anarchy poured in like whispers of a nightmare. Paris was devouring itself—a war within a war. To appease him and his family, she remained content with the distant view of the city's skyline, wondering if Rollant was dead or alive and, if he was alive, where he was. Her fire dimmed the more she stayed in Charonne, as every question went unanswered, and every hope flitted away.

At twenty-three years old, Élise knew Charonne had softened her edges but had not silenced her heart. Giselle and Gabrielle taught her grace and patience—virtues her mother had never been able to impart. Hugo, the ever-steady man, tried every day to win her heart and affection. He was the only eligible bachelor in their close-knit community, and she, the only unmarried woman of age. She appreciated him and loved him in a quiet way, but it wasn't the same.

They all wanted her to marry him and have a family to work Charonne's soil. But Élise's heart remained frozen, trapped between a past she couldn't release and the faint, flickering hope of the future she had once imagined. She saw Rollant in her mind, aged but strong, sitting across the table from her, eating breakfast together in the golden light of morning. Try as she might, she couldn't picture Hugo the same way.

And yet, her life in Charonne had taken root. The seasons passed, her garden flourished, and the ache in her chest dulled but never disappeared.

A knock came at the door. Élise glanced up from the bread dough she was kneading, brushing flour from her hands. Her thoughts would have to wait.

Hugo and his sisters stood in the doorway. Giselle and Gabrielle were dressed in their best, clean, pressed dresses and braided hair with ribbon. Hugo's hair was slicked back and curled at the edges, framing a face freshly shaven. Élise couldn't help but chuckle at the parade before her.

"What is the occasion?" she asked, peering up at Hugo with a wide-brimmed smile.

Élise wiped her hands on her apron and motioned for them to come inside. Giselle and Gabrielle slipped past her, giggling and whispering as they set a basket of herbs on the table. Hugo lingered at the door, his gaze soft but hesitant.

"Hugo?" Élise tilted her head, smiling softly. "You're looking very serious today. What is it?"

He stepped inside and glanced at his sisters. "Gabrielle, Giselle, could you please go into the bedroom for a moment? I would like a moment alone with Élise." He glanced at Élise. "I hope that's acceptable; it is quite cold outside."

She nodded. "Of course." Her hand rose to her hip at the close of her bedroom door, knowing his sisters could easily hear whatever they discussed.

"You've intrigued me. What is all this about?" she asked, waving toward the herbs and his pressed vest and coat.

His blue eyes sparkled, and he pulled out a small wooden ring. Though not ornate, it was smooth and carved with care. He held it between his forefinger and his thumb.

Her heart sank, though she kept a smile on her lips.

"I made this for you," he whispered. He transferred it to his palm and held it out for her. "It's not much, but I wanted it to be special." He cleared his throat and adjusted his coat.

"Thank you, Hugo," she said. "What is it?" She played dumb, hoping to draw the event out so she had time to think.

"Well," he said, but faltered before taking a deep breath with a soft grin. "You know how I feel about you, Élise," he began, sure in his words. "I've loved you for years. I've worked hard to build a good home, a place for a wife and family to thrive. I've done my best to build a good name. I want to share it all with you. I want to be your husband. Will you marry me?"

The world fell silent, except for the giggling coming from her bedroom. Her eyes rimmed with instant tears.

Hugo was safe, kind, and giving. He was everything she needed in a man, a husband, and a father to any children they may have. He was a respected herbalist, a healer, educated, and well-read. He'd generously given his time to further her quality of life. His boyish charm would have wooed any other woman.

She was a fool if she said no.

"I don't know what to say," she whispered, her voice thick with unshed tears.

"Say yes, Élise," Hugo said, his azure eyes pleading.

Her gaze dropped to the ring, and her chest tightened around a slowing heartbeat. Her hands twitched at her sides, knowing the prudent girl would take it.

She met his gaze. Hugo's eyes searched hers, hope mingled with fear. "You don't have to say yes right now," he added quickly, his voice thick with nerves. "I just . . . I needed you to know how I feel. We're getting older. Time is passing, and I—I want you to know I'm here, Élise. I'll always be here."

A few tears escaped the well and ran freely down her cheeks. She looked down at the ring, then back up at Hugo's face—earnest, kind, and filled with a love she wished she could return in full.

Her voice trembled as she spoke. She wanted to treat Hugo fairly, for he was her friend. "Hugo, you deserve someone who loves you as much as you love them. Someone who can give you their whole heart. I don't know if I can be that person."

He stepped closer, his hand still outstretched. "I don't care," he said softly. "You're enough, Élise. Whatever part of your heart you can give me, it's enough."

Giselle and Gabrielle gasped, their joy so immediate and overwhelming that Élise felt trapped beneath its weight. She wished social protocol allowed them to leave—anything to give her space to think. Everyone wanted this union. If she said no, they might ostracize her, and she'd be alone in a world that did not forgive loneliness. How would she survive?

But if she said yes, she'd be lying to Hugo. And Rollant—Rollant had been gone for three years. Three years of silence. Was she a fool to cling to a memory? Was she still just a silly girl, infatuated with the impossible dream of a man who had likely already moved on?

She was a woman now, and women should want stability and security with a man who showed up every day, not pining for the ghost of a first love. Rollant was the passion she yearned for, but she had to accept he wasn't returning. Perhaps Hugo's steady love was enough, if not the love she had once known.

Her fire for life had already faded. Maybe it was time to put the girl's heart aside and extinguish it altogether. As Rollant said, maybe it was easier to live life not feeling when you are torn from those you love.

She slid her hand into Hugo's, still unsure of her answer. Her heart screamed for her to wait—wait for the ghost of a man who might never return. But silence had been Rollant's only answer for three years. Her gaze met Hugo's patient eyes. Her breath hitched, her fingers trembling in his warm, steady grip.

If Rollant was gone—if he was truly gone—then wasn't it time to move on? To stop clinging to the ashes of a love that had burned so brightly it had consumed her?

Hugo was here.

Hugo was real.

Yet, her hand trembled as she forced a smile and nodded.

Both eyebrows lifted high over his wide eyes. "Really?" he chuckled. "Really?"

The broad smile on his face was contagious. She laughed, too, and nodded more at his excitement.

He slid the ring onto her finger—a fit nearly too loose, but it stayed without further adjustment. It was everything he was—solid, simple, and made with care. He picked her up and swung her around, but as he pulled her close, his smile faltered for the briefest moment. It was gone in an instant, replaced by laughter, but Élise felt it—a hesitation, a question he didn't dare ask.

"You are going to be my wife, and I couldn't be happier," he shouted. Giselle and Gabrielle slung the bedroom door open and rushed to them with peals of glee.

Élise kept the smile plastered and laughed with Giselle and Gabrielle as they hugged her tightly.

Giselle squealed, clasping her hands over her chest. "We are going to have another sister!"

Her heart beat faster, and the room spun.

Gabrielle grabbed Élise's hands, squeezing them. "Oh, you could have a Christmas wedding!" she shrieked with eyes full of excitement.

The sisters' joy was a stark reminder of what was expected—what she had chosen. She forced a smile, hoping they couldn't see the cracks.

But Christmas was only two months away. Her ears rang, and the edges of her vision blurred.

Hugo pulled Élise in for a chaste kiss. "With the snow and the fire—"

"No," Élise said quickly, silencing and stilling the room. "I—I don't like the cold," she said, offering no other timeframe.

"Oh," Hugo said and bit his lip. "Well, how about the summer?" he asked.

She wanted to say, "Or next," but refrained and said instead, "That sounds wonderful. A summer wedding would be perfect." She swallowed hard behind a wide smile.

Hugo, Élise, and his sisters visited each house to announce their marriage promise. Each community member's face lit with elation at the news.

Night fell, and Élise barred the door of her Charonne home, shutting out the community's happiness. Though the smell of bread graced the house, she had no appetite. The basket of herbs lay on the table; the task of putting them away would wait until the morning. Again, she felt alone.

Isolated.

She should have readied the home for the night with happiness in her heart, but the numbing cold prevented any happiness from growing there. The bedroom hearth crackled, and the door closed for the night to keep the bedroom warm.

She slipped the ring from her finger and placed it on the nightstand with deliberate care as though setting down the weight of the decision she couldn't carry. Her fingers quivered as they traced the carved surface, its simplicity reflecting the quiet life Hugo promised. It was beautiful in its own way, but the smooth wood felt cool against her skin. Her hand drifted to Rollant's shirt, neatly folded on the bed. She pulled it over her head, the worn fabric falling loose and familiar against her skin. The faint scent of old wood and candle smoke still lingered, a memory of him that refused to fade and instead clung to her twisting heart. She curled beneath the blankets, clutching the shirt as if it could bring him back.

Her tears slipped silently down her cheeks at first, but soon turned to heaving sobs that wracked her chest. Why had she called him a monster? Why had she told him to leave and never return?

Waves rippled down her back, shaking her body until exhaustion claimed her, and when sleep finally came, she dreamed of Rollant.

CHAPTER 37
The Silence of Mercy
THE TEMPLE, PARIS, JANUARY 1793

THE COMMUNE INSTITUTED the new National Convention, which stripped Louis of his title and renamed him Citizen Louis Capet. Madame and Monsieur were gone, replaced by Citizen and Citizeness. To the Convention, all were equal—except for the king, who had been reduced to a criminal awaiting his sentence.

Rollant stood silent among the guards at the Temple as they jeered at the former royal family, their laughter echoing through the cold stone halls. Graffiti marred the walls of Louis' chambers, depicting him hanging from the gallows—a sight his children should never have seen.

Rollant's stomach churned at their cruelty. He wanted to believe they would at least spare the children, but the Revolution left no room for innocence.

The Convention set up a trial with the judgment and sentence already written for Louis. Riots broke out in favor of the former king across the countryside; the rioters were disturbed by the trial and possible execution.

Rollant had watched Louis revise his last will on Christmas Day, bent over his desk with the soft scratch of the quill the only sound in the cold, still air. His hand moved steadily, unflinching, as he inked his final thoughts to his family. For a moment, Rollant's gaze fell on the king's shoulders, stooped under the weight of centuries of monarchy—and the burden of its end. It should have been just another moment in his centuries of servitude, but Élise's face rose in his mind. The tremble in her voice when she called him a monster flooded his memory. He had traded love for duty and sacrificed his chance for happiness on the altar of an eternal oath. But what was his service worth if it could not save the man doomed to die?

A new year began, and the Convention voted to execute Louis for his high crimes of treason. They had let him see his family one last time as they delivered the verdict. Rollant gritted his teeth. The family did not even have time to grieve together, except for a few hours the day before his execution. The unfairness of it all turned his stomach. The irony was sadistic: A government that would kill for alleged injustice yet commit the same injustice and consider it righteous.

The guards laughed as Marie-Thérèse and Louis Charles clung to their father's legs, their hands trembling with desperation. "Look at them," one guard sneered, "clutching to their precious king as if he could save them."

"Do not mock pain," Rollant barked, his voice sharp enough to cut through the laughter. "Especially the pain of children."

The guards fell silent, muttering curses as they shuffled into the hall. Rollant stood his ground, his fists clenched. He had made enemies with his outburst, but he didn't care. Let them hate him. Let them mock him. He would endure it all for the sake of the family. Night fell, and Louis retired to his cell.

Rollant let himself into Louis' room and closed the door. Tomorrow would be the day the new king took the proverbial crown, the young Louis Charles, a new master to serve. Rollant glanced through the bars in the door's top at the other guards, laughing at crude jokes.

Louis sat at his desk, dry-eyed with a vacant stare. His calm demeanor unsettled Rollant, who had witnessed the man's moments of indecision and weakness far too often in life. But tonight, the king seemed resolute, as though he had made peace with the inevitable.

"Hugh Capet," Louis whispered. "June 1, 987 AD. The day my ancestor was elected to the throne. Louis XVI. January 17, 1793. The day the last king was elected to die."

Rollant remained silent, unsure what to say, but Louis spoke again.

"I will miss my son's laughter," Louis murmured, his voice low. "And Marie-Thérèse's stubborn wit. I wanted more time to guide and prepare them for a life without me. But perhaps the Lord will grant me mercy and take me before I see them suffer further. Perhaps . . ."

He trailed off, his gaze distant.

"Perhaps my death will mean something. Perhaps it will bring peace. If not for France, then for them."

Rollant lowered his head. He wanted to reassure Louis and promise him everything would be fine. But lies had no place in this room. "Your children will remember you as a king and as a father," Rollant said softly. "That will be your legacy."

Louis nodded with a finger rubbing his lip. "You don't think a rescue would bring more bloodshed?"

Rollant thinned his lips. For all the qualities Louis was not, he had always wanted peace.

"They are closing the city walls in the morning to fend off any rescue attempt," Rollant whispered as he stood by the dim flicker of a candle, its feeble glow casting long shadows across the cold stone walls. "They have stationed me in the crowd to prevent revolt. My only regret is that I will not be by your side."

Louis nodded, controlling his hand's fall to the table. "At least I will have Father Edgeworth with me on the scaffold and my friend Chevalier Rollant de Montvieux in the crowd. I shall look at Father for the strength of my spirit, and I shall look at you to bring strength to my body."

"It was an honor to serve your crown," Rollant said in hushed tones to not draw the other guards' attention.

"My name and monarchy are blameless," Louis said with a reassuring nod. "Though few believe it."

"I would argue most of France believes it," Rollant said. "I can see the corrupted minds of those leading the Convention. Half of the deputies attempted to argue against a trial and execution. I wish I were able to save you from this."

"Oh, Rollant," Louis said as he cradled his forehead between his thumb and forefinger. He reached out and patted Rollant's forearm. "I never knew how much you cared for us. I only assumed you were this silent, stoic knight forced to live an oath."

Rollant hung his head. "I was for a long time. I feel I have failed you."

"You haven't failed anyone, my friend," Louis said softly.

Rollant lowered his gaze to the floor. It felt like a lie, even if Louis believed it. He had watched the monarchy falter under a weight he couldn't lift, seen centuries of kings and queens fall to their human frailties while he stood powerless to save them. He was no guardian. He straightened his shoulders, shoving the thought aside. "I only wish I had done more."

Louis removed his hand and rubbed his lip. "No, you have watched over me all of my life, Rollant, and I am sorry I did not listen to you for most of it. Perhaps it would have been different had I listened and leaned on you in the cabinet from early on." He shook his head. "Now, all I ask, my immortal guard, is that you watch over my family the best you can."

"If I could give my life for them, I would. You know this."

"I do, but the numbers are too great. Just as they subdued you in the Tuileries, they would do it again, and rather than take my children prisoner, they'd execute them on the spot if they saw you resurrect from the dead . . ." Louis chuckled with sorrow and a shake of his head. "Or they'd all burn for associating with sorcery."

Louis palmed his face. "I will own my fate, and I am again sorry yours is tied to the crown. Maybe with my death, you will finally be rid of your oath."

"It has been an honor to serve the crown faithfully for six hundred years. And, there will always be Frenchmen who regard your family as the true kings—I will serve your son, and once he passes, his son or your brother. Just as it were when the House of Bourbon took the throne, I'm sure other descendants of Hugh Capet will vie for it once the people realize your death will not be sufficient for them."

Rollant shook his head at the coming bloodshed. He'd seen it in the Hundred Years War, the Wars of Religion, and the War of the Henrys. More blood would be shed even in the new Republic.

"But I will miss you, Your Majesty, as I miss all your ancestors. I doubt I will ever see you again, but I know you will see Sophie and Louis Joseph and all your friends already passed in the Lord's fold. The Queen, Louis Charles, and Marie-Thérèse, they will all see you again one day in the far future."

Louis was silent for a moment before speaking again. "When the world ends, and the Lord comes in his might, I'm sure the sorceress' magic will also end, and then, my friend, I will see you again."

Rollant's lips pressed tight. Louis spoke of heaven with certainty, of peace and reunion. And yet, for six hundred years, Rollant had been denied such solace. Death offered no end, only a brief escape before the torment began again. He envied Louis—envied the finality of his fate. If the sorceress' magic ever did end, what would be left of him? A man without faith, without family, without purpose, and without the only two women he had ever truly loved.

"To death, then," Rollant lifted an imaginary toast.

Louis nodded and pursed his lips as he lifted his imaginary glass. "Or rather, to a new beginning."

Rollant smiled. "To a new beginning," he whispered.

The Captain of the Temple Guard approached, and Rollant pulled a prayer book from his pocket and loudly said as a cover, "As requested, here's your prayer book."

Rollant lobbed the small-bound leather book on the desk as the Captain opened the door. He glanced at Rollant and then at Louis before sneering.

"Lights out," he barked and shut the door after Rollant left Louis. "And you," the Captain addressed Rollant, "you're retiring for the night. The procession starts at eight in the morning. Be ready."

Rollant dipped his chin. "Yes, Captain."

The January cold seeped into the walls as Rollant settled into the barracks for the night. A fire crackled faintly at the far corner of the room, its warmth too distant to reach him. His breath fogged before he closed his eyes. He tugged his coat tighter around him, but the chill wasn't just from the stone walls.

Élise's tear-streaked face came unbidden to his mind, a memory that cut sharper than the draft. He'd told himself a thousand times she was better off without him and safer in Charonne with Hugo. He clung to it, though it never quieted the ache. He had traded love for duty and lost both.

Her name trembled on his lips like a ghost of hope. He closed his eyes and whispered a prayer, not for himself, but for her. For her safety, her happiness, and for the hope that one day, she might forgive him.

There would always be a crown, he mused. And it would always keep him from Élise, from knowing love, and he had done it to himself. He wondered if she was happy in Charonne. He hoped the violence in Paris had not seeped into the countryside. He hoped Élise had followed his advice and not spoken her mind, for he feared the radicals in the Convention would not stop with Louis. They would go after any supporter of the King, any who disagreed with their clown trial and vote of execution. Robespierre was not a man to be trifled with. He prayed to God that Robespierre would keep his hands off Louis Charles. But prayers meant little in this new world, where faith was scorned, and virtue twisted into terror.

Rollant's curse might have made him eternal, but it also made him helpless. Perhaps he could protect Louis Charles from assassins, but what shield could he offer against a mob baying for royal blood? Against the guillotine? The royalists and the Austro-Prussian forces would reinstate Louis Charles as King if they won the war, and if the child died, the crown would fall to Louis' brother, the Count of Provence, who had fled the country. What service could he offer an absent king?

CHAPTER 38

The Blood of Kings

PLACE DE LA RÉVOLUTION, PARIS, JANUARY 1793

THE PLACE DE la Révolution was a sea of faces, each more ravenous than the last. They surged toward the scaffold at the center of the square, their voices a discordant symphony of jeers, cheers, and cries for vengeance. Élise stood among them, her brown scarf pulled tight against the January cold, her breath clouding in the air as she stared at the looming guillotine. They had been standing in the cold for hours and barely made it in before the city gates were closed.

Hugo and the rest of the community had ventured into the city walls to witness the heresy. Though Hugo had begged them not to go, something stronger than her fear had pulled her back to Paris. The Revolution had taken so much—her friends, her city, her sense of safety—and now it would take the king.

She hated what Louis represented, but watching him die felt like watching the world end. This wasn't the future she had fought for. She wanted the king's abdication, but not for him to face execution built on bias and hate. She feared the foundation the new Republic was laying with such a decision. The guillotine's blade gleamed in the pale winter morning sun, like a false beacon of hope cutting through the fog.

The carriage rolled to the scaffold, which guardsmen surrounded. Louis Capet walked up the steps with a composure befitting a king. They bound his hands and shaved his head as his priest whispered words of comfort to him.

Drums rolled and drowned out the former king's last words; the poor man was not even allowed to be heard. They forced him onto the plank and dropped the blade. Élise closed her eyes as it fell. The crowd roared, surging forward as Louis' head thudded into the basket beneath. Élise's stomach turned, bile rising in her throat as she stumbled back, away from the wave of bodies pressing toward the scaffold. The crowd cheered, but she couldn't summon a sound. The executioner held up Louis Capet's dripping head, and the crowd cheered louder, deafening the drums. She doubted his son would survive, and when he was of age, he'd meet the same fate. They would make sure of that.

She surveyed the crowds, at what she helped to create. A man stared at her as he cheered. The corners of her mouth rose, fearing what he might think otherwise.

They gathered up the body and threw it in the dirt with nothing more. The crowds dispersed in a swell, forcing Hugo's hand from hers. They drifted apart, but his eyes darted toward Charonne, and she knew to return home as planned. She nodded before losing him in the crowd. They pushed against her and wouldn't let her turn around.

"Please," she whispered and nearly turned before she bumped into a man.

"Pardon me, Citizen," she said, flustered. She noticed his blue uniform—a National Guardsman. She stilled and forced her breath to calm. Her head down, she tried to step aside not to garner trouble, but his fingers graced her arm. She stiffened. Time halted as his familiar voice cut through the cacophony of the crowd.

"It is my pardon, Élise," he said. The chaos fell away, and her forehead lowered to his chest. Her knees went weak as she leaned into him, fearing that her mind had conjured him, but the scent of old wood and candle smoke lingered in his shirt, like a memory made real.

Her arms wrapped around his waist, as if she were meant to be there. For a moment, the world could crumble, but she would be whole.

He grasped the seam of her coat and pulled her close. Tension fled from her shoulders, and tears burned the back of her eyes. Fate had answered. The years apart compressed into moments as if time had stood still, affirming their love was never meant to fade. She had fought the town to marry in the summer rather than Christmas, and standing before Rollant, unmarried, fate validated her resistance. Hating Louis to die, she thought maybe it meant Rollant could come home with her. She lifted her face to his.

She had begged the stars for Rollant's return, and now that he was here, Hugo crept into her mind. Hugo, who had stood by her, steady as the earth beneath her feet, who had loved her when she could not love herself.

But she couldn't let go of the ache in her chest for Rollant, the place where he had taken root years ago. That part of her had never healed; it had only grown, biding its time. Standing before him, her heart's desire roared back to life.

"Oh, Élise," he whispered, stroking a loose piece of hair behind her ear.

"I am sorry, Rollant," she spurted. "You are not a monster, and I have hated myself every day for telling you to leave." Her lip quivered.

He sighed in relief. His back rounded, and his grip tightened on her coat as if he wanted to hold her.

"Come with me, Rollant," she whispered, feeling the aching love in his gaze. "The king is dead. The crown is gone. Your curse is lifted. We can be together."

His eyes darkened, and he looked down at his hand, where a bloody handkerchief sat against unbroken skin. "I thought perhaps," he said. "But there is still a king. And as long as there is a crown, I remain bound."

Her words were a raw mixture of anger and disbelief. "I thought—I thought the curse—"

"I know," he said gently, cutting her off. "I thought so, too." He lifted her chin, his thumb brushing her cheek. "But the crown still stands, and so do I. Why are you here? Did you come alone?"

"I was with Hugo," she said. "But we got separated in the crowd."

Rollant's jaw grew taut. "It's not safe. I'll take you home." He tucked her arm under his and pushed through the crowds.

They passed through the city gate with a few crude jokes about where Rollant was taking such a girl by the guardsmen on duty. But once the rolling hillside greeted them, they slowed their gait, talking and walking hand in hand, hidden in the folds of their coats as they once did.

"I dreamed of you, and I still wear your shirt," Élise said with a chuckle.

Rollant leaned down to whisper in her ear. "You have healed my heart with such secrets."

They came upon a large step in the walkway, and Élise jumped atop it to face him, eye-to-eye. "I have decided I want a life with you," she whispered. "I wish to grow old with you, though you may never change."

She slipped her hands to his shoulders.

"Élise, I—" He covered her hand, but the jewelry she wore took his words and attention. He pulled her left hand to view her carved wooden ring. "You are married already?"

"No," she whispered with a violent shake of her head. Her eyes tingled with guilt and shame. "Only promised to be."

"To Hugo?" he asked.

"I wish it were to you," she said.

But sorrow swept over his face as if he hadn't heard her. "Our former king sent me to plan the escape route where he was caught in Varennes. I took the long route to see you, and I saw you and Hugo in a passionate kiss. I have had that image burned in my mind ever since," Rollant whispered.

A man shouting Élise's name echoed from down the road. Hugo's—he was pounding at her door.

"You came back two years ago?" she asked, wishing she had seen him. "That kiss wasn't real—"

"Is he good to you?" Rollant changed the subject.

She smiled beneath a knitted brow, allowing his question. "I wish he weren't. I wish he gave me a reason to hate him, refuse him."

Rollant swallowed hard. "Do you love him?"

She peered over her shoulder with tear-blurred vision at his frantic search for her in the stable. "Not as much as I love you."

Rollant nodded, pulling her closer by grasping the side seam of her coat. "Then your love for me will fade if I stay away."

"No," she cried, grabbing his arms as Hugo's shouts echoed from the stable. "I don't want you to stay away, not now that I know you have loved me all these years. I have never stopped loving you. Even now, I know I am meant to be with you."

"What can I offer you, Élise?" Rollant said with a glistening in his eyes and a slight shake of his head. "A cold bed alone at night? I am tied to the king. I will stay at the Temple in the barracks. I cannot risk coming here any more than I have done, not for my sake, but for yours."

"What if France wins the war and the crown ends?" she asked. "Will you come back to me?"

Rollant pressed his forehead to hers. "I will, but what would I find? It could last a hundred years."

Tears ran down her cheeks. "Well, I refuse to let you go," she said, hovering her lips over his. "Not after I have you again."

He pressed against her. The familiar spark ignited in his kiss, but before it flamed, he pulled away and whispered with breath hot on her lips, "You'll always have me."

Hugo's shouts grew closer, cutting short their time together. Rollant's fingers slowly released her coat, letting them slide down the length until his hands swayed at his sides. If there was any doubt of his devotion, they were all but gone.

She cradled his face in her hands, her fingers slipping into his curly locks. "I fear if I am married, you will become mortal. I can't—"

Rollant smoothed his hand over hers and removed her touch as Hugo's shouts tipped time out of their favor. "I will likely never become mortal, Élise," he whispered. "Marry Hugo. He loves you. He is good to you, and in time, you will love him more than me."

But Élise knew her heart, and the intimacy of her pain over the last three years sealed her decision. "No, Rollant, if I marry Hugo, I will spend the rest of my life in love with another man."

"Not if you let me go," he whispered.

"Élise—" Hugo's shout stopped short of its full bellow. "Rollant?" he whispered, stepping forward as a new sense of urgency replaced the former.

Élise tore her gaze from Rollant's as she turned around. "Yes, he found me in the city and brought me home," she explained to Hugo, but tears choked her words and had already stained her face.

Hugo pulled her into an embrace. "I had packed a bag to come looking for you. I was so scared to lose you, Élise." He kissed her on the cheek, near the mouth, before addressing Rollant.

A raw, jealous insecurity lived in Hugo's gaze. "Thank you, Citizen Montvieux, for bringing her home." His words were brittle.

Rollant nodded, his stoic nature superseding the warmth he held in his gaze just moments prior.

The silence between them stretched with unspoken words, suffocating the space, until Hugo's hands dropped down her arms and slipped into her hands. "Why don't you go let Giselle and Gabrielle know you are home? They are worried. Mama made stew, and you are freezing. I will be there in a moment."

Élise nodded with her gaze down, unable to see the hurt in Hugo's eyes. As Hugo pulled her into his arms, she felt the weight of the wooden ring on her finger—simple, honest, and binding. She had tried to love him. She might have wanted a life with him, the stability and security he offered, if she had never met Rollant. But every beat of her heart thudded for Rollant over the years, no matter how much she tried to silence it.

She walked the cobblestone path and peered over her shoulder. Rollant's gaze briefly slipped to her while he conversed with Hugo.

It wasn't fair to Hugo. And it wasn't fair to herself. She knew now, with aching certainty, that there was only one man she could ever love—and when Rollant left again, she would wait for him to return, even if it meant waiting forever.

Hugo stood on the step higher than Rollant, widening his stance with his hands on his hips. "National Guardsmen, now?" he asked, gesturing to Rollant's blue coat.

Rollant smiled and nodded, remembering his navy man persona. "Yes, I realized the sea was not for me once the King could no longer fund my wage."

Hugo nodded with exaggeration. He crossed his arms and stepped closer. "Do you plan to arrest us for not agreeing with the king's execution?" Hugo asked, his tone half-joking but edged with tension.

Rollant shook his head, a faint, hollow smile tugging at his lips. "No, but don't tell anyone that. These days, silence is the only thing that keeps us alive. Don't enter the city again."

"Understood," Hugo gritted, his eyes searching for something else, his lip twitching as he debated what to say, what question to ask.

"About Élise," he finally said.

Rollant expected it to come. His gaze drifted to her, and they locked eyes in the faint fog before she stepped inside. "Yes, ask your question, state your statement."

Hugo shifted his weight. "I assume you saw her ring?"

"I did," Rollant said. The words fell like stones between them. Guilt gnawed at him; he hadn't respected Hugo or his ring. He had pulled her close and kissed her, knowing she wore it. But if she married Hugo, at least he would remember her not recoiling in fear, but offering love—a gift given once, and never taken back.

"Well," Hugo began. "She loves you more than she does me; she's made that plain enough. But if you will not marry her, and she marries me instead," his voice tightened, "you cannot keep coming back and haunting her."

Rollant thinned his lips, forcing himself to quiet the rebuttal rising in his throat and to speak the words that needed to be said. "I told her to marry you, Hugo."

Hugo's arms dropped. "You did what?" he stammered. His eyebrows lifted in surprise. "You told her to marry me?" His voice cracked. "Why? If you love her, why tell her that?"

Rollant's voice was steady, but the weight behind the words burned like ash in his throat. "I do love her more than life itself. But you're a good man, and you love her." He looked away, his gaze trailing to the mid-morning sun on the horizon. "I told her you could give her everything I can't—a future." His voice dropped lower. "But knowing it doesn't make it hurt any less."

Hugo shifted, as if unsure what to say.

Rollant's gaze drifted to where Élise disappeared into Hugo's family home. "Though I long to be with her, my circumstances might never allow it. I told her that her love for me would fade if she let me go, but I would always love her. That will never change." Rollant locked eyes with Hugo. "Therefore, the choice is hers—to wait for something that may never be or to nurture what she already has in you."

Hugo nodded, running a hand through his hair. "So if she chooses you, then I'll be the fool," he muttered.

"Give her time. Give her space," Rollant said, placing a heavy hand on Hugo's shoulder. "I envy you," he said quietly.

Hugo frowned. "Me? Why me?"

Rollant shook his shoulder once, a faint, sad smile touching his lips. "You're here with her. You heal people. You have the kind of life I'll never know."

Hugo studied him, his brow furrowing. "And if I were you?"

Rollant smiled faintly, though there was no humor in it. "You'd be trapped with no end in sight."

Hugo hesitated, searching Rollant's face. "Could you resign?"

"If I resigned, they would follow me here, assuming I opposed their policies, and they would likely imprison all of us."

His tone dipped.

"I am stationed at the Temple now. If the atrocities spill beyond its walls, I will come for you and take you to another of my estates."

He met Hugo's gaze, grim.

"The four families. Élise. All of you must be ready to leave at a moment's notice. The National Guard watches for any sign of dissent. If they suspect Charonne harbors sympathies for the crown, they will not hesitate."

Hugo's face paled. "And if they come?"

"All of you will be imprisoned or worse," Rollant said, his words like a blade. "So you must be prepared. Tell no one else. The wrong word to the wrong person could cost every life here."

Hugo's expression softened, though his grip tightened on his coat. "We'll be ready," he said.

Rollant nodded once. He turned to leave, but Hugo's voice stopped him. "And what of Élise?"

Rollant didn't look back.

"She'll make her choice," he said, praying she chose Hugo for her sake and future, though the thought wrenched his soul.

THE JEWELER'S workshop smelled of molten silver and oil, the air thick with the hum of industry. Rollant stood before the counter, turning a plain silver band between his fingers, his expression unreadable. The craftsman watched him carefully, waiting for approval.

"This will do," Rollant murmured, though his voice lacked conviction.

The ring was simple—unadorned, save for the small, circular insignia etched onto its surface: a mountain with three stars above it.

Faith. Honor. Duty.

The Montvieux crest.

Inside the band, barely visible, the engraving read: *À jamais*—forever.

It was not a promise nor a plea but a truth he had long accepted. The ring would ensure her survival and grant her safe passage on his haunted estate in the Chartreuse mountains. And there, if she ever crossed the threshold, she would find all the proof of his past, every secret he had ever dared to share with her.

But perhaps she would never need it. Perhaps she would heed his request, forget him, marry Hugo, and live a quiet life unburdened by his cursed existence.

The thought settled like lead in his chest.

The jeweler wrapped the ring in a soft cloth and handed it to his customer. Rollant hesitated before slipping it into his coat pocket. He would place it in her hand if the day came she needed it.

But if fate were kind, she would never wear it at all.

CHAPTER 39

A Truth to Keep

CHARONNE, PARIS, JUNE 1793

WINTER TURNED TO SPRING, and Élise tried to bury the memory of that January morning in Paris when Rollant had walked back into her life. But it refused to be buried. She had returned to Charonne, Hugo, and the comforting routines of village life, yet her thoughts drifted to Rollant in moments of stillness. His whispered words, his tortured gaze—it all lingered like a haunting refrain. And now, with her wedding only weeks away, she could no longer silence the question she had tried so desperately to ignore: Would her love for Rollant ever fade?

The scent of lavender drifted through the home's open windows as Élise sat at the table, her hands folded tightly in her lap. She could hear the sounds of the community preparing for the wedding—Giselle's voice carrying orders to the children gathering flowers, Gabrielle laughing with the neighbor women as they spoke of the celebration dinner. The village was aglow, celebrating a union that would bring joy and new life to Charonne.

But inside Élise's chest, her heart thudded with a hollow ache.

Hugo entered quietly, brushing dirt from his hands after tending to the herb garden at his family home. His hair was damp with sweat, his face as kind as ever. He smiled when he saw her, but the light in his eyes faltered when he caught her expression.

"What is it, Élise?" he asked softly, coming to sit across from her.

She opened her mouth, but the words caught in her throat. She had practiced what she would say, but now, under his calm gaze, her courage faltered. "Hugo," she began; her voice trembled. "I can't."

His brow furrowed. "Can't what?"

She lowered her gaze to her lap, unable to meet his eyes. "I can't marry you."

Silence fell between them. Hugo's jaw tightened, his hands clenching on the table. "Why?" he asked, though his voice betrayed that he already knew.

Her throat tightened. "After seeing Rollant—"

"Stop." His voice was sharp, cutting through her words. He stood abruptly, his chair scraping against the wooden floor. "I'll always be second place, won't I?" His voice cracked, anger and sorrow warring within him. "He'll show up once in ten years, and you'll throw my ring to the ground."

Tears spilled down her cheeks. It was true. She couldn't refute it. But something told her to hold on. To wait for Rollant. "Hugo, I don't want to feel this way. I've tried to love you the way you deserve, but I can't."

He shook his head, pacing to the window. His back was to her, his shoulders rigid with tension. "Yet he rejected you. And I'm here." His voice softened, thick with hurt. "I've been here every day, Élise. Through everything."

"I know, and that's why it's so absurd." Her voice broke, yet Hugo had not been through everything. Rollant had brought her out of Paris, equipped her with a weapon, and sacrificed his home, land, life, and love for her. She turned her face away, ashamed to look at her betrothed.

"You've done nothing wrong, Hugo. You're kind, loyal, and generous. I love you for all those things—but not in the way a wife should love her husband."

She hurried to wipe away her tears, but they kept falling.

Hugo blinked, pushing back tears. "He'll never stay, Élise. You know that. He'll leave you again, just like he always does."

She crumpled into herself, sobbing. Hugo crossed the room in three quick strides, wrapping her in a sweeping embrace. She collapsed against his chest, clutching his shirt as he rubbed soothing circles on her back. His touch was everything Rollant's could never be. And yet, it wasn't enough.

"I'm sorry, Hugo," she whispered, her voice muffled against his chest. "I'm so, so sorry."

He rested his chin on her head, speaking with a low and pained voice. "Can you . . . can you ever see yourself with me, Élise? Truly?"

She shook her head helplessly. "Every time I think of our future, it's not your face I see. It's his."

He let out a slow breath, his arms tightening briefly before he pulled back to look at her. "You've been honest with me from the beginning," he said, his voice thick. "But it doesn't make this hurt any less."

She nodded, fresh tears spilling down her cheeks. "I never wanted to hurt you."

Hugo studied her for a long moment, his bright blue eyes searching hers. Then, as if making a decision, he said, "What if we waited?"

Her brows knitted in confusion. "Waited?"

"What if I told the community that we decided to postpone our marriage because of everything happening in France this year—the war, the executions, the uncertainty of it all? We'll say it's not the right time to bring children into this world."

Élise's throat tightened. "Hugo, I—"

He held up a hand to stop her. "I'm not saying we'll get married next year or even the year after that. Just . . . give yourself time. If your heart tells you to wait for Rollant, even though he might never return, I'll end our promise to wed by telling the community that we've grown apart. But if, after that time, you decide you can see a life with me . . ." He trailed off, his voice cracking. "Then we'll marry, and I'll spend my life trying to make you happy."

Fresh tears streamed down her face as she nodded, her heart breaking for him. "I admire your patience, Hugo," she whispered.

He smiled faintly, though it didn't reach his eyes. "I will wait forever for the woman I love," he said.

Élise stood and draped her arms around his waist, burying her nose into his neck. Why couldn't she love him? Why did her heart still ache for a man who might never return?

And yet, if Rollant did return, she knew she wouldn't hesitate. She would also wait forever for the man she loved.

CHAPTER 40

Ashes of the Crown

THE TEMPLE, PARIS, NOVEMBER 1793

THE STREETS of Paris ran red, and the blood of priests, peasants, and political rivals oozed between the cobbled pathways. Rollant's boots splashed through puddles of crimson, leaving scarlet pinpricks on his white culottes. The stench of decay clawed down his throat and turned his stomach. He had seen cities crumble and kingdoms fall under the weight of war, but never had he witnessed a nation devour itself with such brutality.

The Convention had become a terror, but he had seen the fate of those who spoke out against it, even those who had fought to give it life. Robespierre was at the helm, directing the ferocious beast to devour any enemy of its contorted reason and logic.

King Louis had been but the first victim. Others had followed, including Queen Marie Antoinette. Priests, nuns, and the common man—all victims of the beast's appetite were convicted, sentenced, and executed on the same day. He hadn't seen any inmates at the Temple from beyond the city walls, but he knew it was only a matter of time.

The eight-year-old Louis Charles bore bruises on his arms and legs, and Rollant's heart twisted at not being able to prevent them. He could not be there morning and night or give away his true identity and purpose, ultimately preventing him from protecting the boy while he stood guard. He'd already pushed away Louis Charles' caretaker, the drunk Antoine Simon, with his coarse wife. Rollant didn't want to know what they were doing with little Louis at night, for his screams were heard throughout the Temple.

In the beginning, Rollant marched to Louis Charles' room, where screams radiated, and pounded on the door to break it down, but his commanding officer stopped him.

"He is a child!" Rollant had screamed in his face.

"Return to the barracks, soldier," was the cold reply.

Rollant protested but was met with, "He is not your concern. Now, be gone before you appear to be an enemy of the state."

The following day, Rollant entered Louis Charles' room and sat on the edge of the bed. Louis Charles was curled in the corner. "I am afraid of Citizen Simon," he whispered. "But he doesn't do anything to me when you are my guard."

His words nearly crushed Rollant's spirit. "As long as I am breathing," Rollant offered. "I will be here as much as I can."

The days turned into weeks, and winter neared. He often wondered if Élise had married Hugo or if she had waited in vain for his return. She occupied his thoughts as he stood guard and fell asleep, though the image of Hugo and her sharing a kiss in the meadow still burned in his mind.

One November evening, Rollant walked the prison corridor to turn in for the night when he passed by a cell with a nun inside. He'd seen priests in prison, led to the guillotine, never to return, but it was the first time he'd seen a nun at the Temple. He debated whether to stay or keep walking.

The notion of forsaking a nun knotted his belly, so he turned his head. Her familiar face still held kind eyes that sparkled upon meeting his gaze.

"Rollant de Montvieux," she whispered.

His head swiveled to ensure no one was listening before shrinking beside her. "It is Rollant Montvieux in here," he whispered.

"I remember you from Le Marais," she said and laid a finger alongside his lips. "You loved dear Élise. I still keep her in my prayers."

"You remember us?" He asked with a scrunched brow. "After all these years?"

"Yes, I remember all of my patients," she said.

"But I was never your patient." Her face came to him. "Sister Francine," he said.

"No, but you were a haunted man, one I pray for."

"Why do you say that?"

"Wanting to love but afraid to," she whispered.

His jaw fell agape. "How did—"

She shook her head as if it were not important.

"What are you doing here?" he asked instead.

"I pledged my allegiance to God, the true king. For my crime, I am due for execution in the morning at the order of the Revolutionary Tribunal."

Rollant sighed. His shoulders slumped as he leaned against the door and slid down.

"I will be in paradise soon. Do not be sad for me." Her voice soothed his angst.

"You may think me a fool, but I envy you," he said, hoping he could finally share his secret with someone who had least cared to remember him.

"You could have eternal life as well," Sister Francine said with a gentle smile.

"No, God has cast me out. I've made too many mistakes."

"Nothing separates you from God except your—"

"No, Sister," Rollant said and drew a deep breath. She was not a priest, but he hadn't been to confession in centuries. His head hung on his chest. "I accepted magic, and now I cannot die. I am immortal."

Her silence mocked him. She didn't believe him. He looked up at the stone wall across the way. He rolled forward to stand, but at her whisper, he paused.

"Magic is a serious offense, but nothing is too serious if you keep your focus on God," Sister Francine said, watching him.

He sat back. "I feel as if God has forsaken me. I spat in His face by becoming immortal, trading the natural for the supernatural as he is."

Sister Francine nodded, but hummed in debate. "You're immortal, you say, but were you born?"

"Yes, in 1122," Rollant whispered.

"If you were born, you have a beginning, and you will have an end," she said with absolute certainty. "Your body is not eternal."

"But when? When will it end?" he asked, feeling as if he were about to confess six hundred years of sins to her. The overwhelming sense of losing control made him shut his mouth.

Sister Francine reached through the bars and stroked Rollant's cheek. "Perhaps it is not when you die, but when you choose to live," Sister Francine said.

"Live?" He scoffed. "What is life?"

"Life is love," Sister Francine said.

"No, life is pain. I should never have fallen in love with Élise or let her fall in love with me."

"You say life is pain, but I say life is love," Sister Francine said softly. "Pain is a part of love, yes, but it is also the proof of it. Why would God let your heart ache for Élise if not to show you that it still beats?"

Rollant winced at the truth in her sentiment. His indifference had melted away when he fell in love. "But I told her to marry another, one she could have a future with."

"Why can she not have a future with you?" she asked.

"Because I am cursed. She would die, and yet I would live on without her."

"Maybe she is the balm to your curse, Rollant," Sister Francine said.

"It is too late; she was to be married this past summer in Charonne," he said.

"Well, was to be and is are two different states," Sister Francine patted Rollant's hand. "If you care about her, you must go to her, especially now, if you say she is in Charonne. I was in Saint-Denis, where I was arrested."

"That is outside the city walls," Rollant whispered.

"Yes," Sister Francine nodded. "They are expanding their reach."

Rollant sat in silence as Sister Francine's words faded into the dark abyss of his mind. His heart ached. Élise. Her name came as a whisper in his head, and with it came the memory of her tear-streaked face the day he left her in Charonne eleven months prior. He had told himself she was safer without him, but had he been wrong? The Revolution's shadow was growing, well beyond the city walls, if it had reached Saint-Denis. And if it reached her—if she fell victim to the chaos—could he live with himself?

"I need to warn her," he finally said. "But I can't leave Louis Charles to the tortures alone."

"I heard his screams," Sister Francine said with tears in her eyes. "He needs protection, but what more can you do? You are not there now. Élise needs protection as well. Two souls—equally important. Right now, you can only help Louis Charles so much. Warn Élise. You'll come back for the child."

Again, torn between duty and love, love and duty. But she was right. Both souls were equally important. They wouldn't kill Louis Charles, though they didn't mind bruising him; they needed him as leverage in the war. However, they did not need Élise.

He rose, indebted to Sister Francine. "Come with me," Rollant whispered. "I can help you escape."

Sister Francine shook her head. "My child, I'm exactly where I need to be, and by tomorrow's end, I will be with my Lord, which is where I wanted to be all along."

Rollant knelt and kissed her hand.

"Bless you, Rollant Montvieux," she whispered. "Now go and warn your love."

Rollant dipped his chin to her in gratitude before going to his commanding officer's quarters to ask for a few days of reprieve for an urgent personal emergency. He hoped that, with the little humanity left, they wouldn't hurt Louis Charles too much in his absence. Upon review, Rollant Montvieux had never requested a reprieve; it was granted, and Rollant left for Charonne by nightfall.

TRUE TO HIS WORD, Rollant went to Hugo's family home first rather than to Élise, in case she had gone through with the marriage. His heart wished she had not, but logic and reason desired her to be blissfully happy with Hugo. He pounded on the door.

Jacq, dressed in a long shirt and breeches, holding a small candle, opened the door. Rollant's heart sank, thinking Hugo had moved in with Élise as her husband.

"It is near midnight. Is all well, Citizen Montvieux?" Jacq asked.

Rollant shook his head. "We need to leave Charonne now."

Jacq nodded. "I'll have my family ready," he said and closed the door.

Rollant went to the other three families before he went to Élise. The path to her door felt longer than the journey from Paris itself. Rollant's boots crunched against the frost-coated earth, with each step weighed down by the dread of finding them together—her as Hugo's wife, the man who had taken his place. Jacq had opened the door to Hugo's family home, not Hugo as he expected, and with it, the flicker of hope he had dared to hold extinguished.

He braced himself as he stood before Élise's door. His fist rapped against the wood, louder than he'd intended. When the door opened, the sight of her clad in his shirt hanging loosely over her frame and a coat over her shoulders nearly undid him.

"Rollant?" Her whisper and the intensity of her gaze stole the air from his lungs. "You came back?" she asked with a quiver in her voice and a hopeful longing in her eyes.

For a moment, he couldn't speak. His name on her lips was everything he had imagined in his sleepless nights—soft, reverent, aching with unspoken feelings. The way she looked at him made his resolve falter. He wanted to close the distance between them, to pull her into his arms and place a parted mouth upon hers as he had dreamed of a thousand times.

She shivered from the night's winds, breaking his trance. "Why did Hugo let you come to the door in the middle of the night?" he asked, but he would deal with Hugo's carelessness later. He held up his hand to redirect. "We must leave now, Élise, pack your things—yours and Hugo's."

"Hugo does not live here," she said, her eyes locking with his, before his gaze dropped to her bare finger. "He suggested we wait to be wed," she whispered. "I always take off his ring at night and pull your shirt over my head and my heart." The action was implicit in her resolve.

His jaw fell agape. "You are not married?" he asked in disbelief, wondering why she had chosen to wait. Why was he deserving of such devotion?

She shook her head, a question in her eyes, but it never flowed off her tongue.

He shifted as he ran her words through his mind once more. "It has been nearly a year since I saw you, Élise," he said. "You still hold on to me so tightly?"

Her lips spread wide. "You told me I'd always have you, and you'll always have me too."

The community was gathering on the road. Eyes were on Rollant's back as he stood at Élise's door. She glanced over his shoulder. "I will pack my bag," she said, retreating inside, letting the door close with a soft click.

He stared at the door's wooden grains until a small smile took his lips and a soft sigh of relief. She wasn't married. But as soon as the smile came, it fell. He didn't deserve her. Didn't deserve to ruin her life. Maybe she didn't want Hugo and needed an excuse; perhaps that was her plight.

Rollant faced the gathered community until all were present, his breath fogging in the chill night air. Torches flickered, casting long shadows over faces etched with fear and uncertainty. Élise stood near the front with a scarf pulled tight around her neck. Hugo drew near her with a penetrating gaze, daring Rollant to take Élise.

"What do we do, Monsieur de Montvieux?" Camille asked, her voice pleading.

"It is Citizen, now. Do not use formal titles anymore. This is one of the reasons why we must leave," Rollant said. "I know your beliefs, and the community beyond my land also knows your beliefs. It is only a matter of time before the guillotine comes here."

His voice cut through the murmurs. "There are already reports of the cleansing all across France. You will be killed for not believing as they do."

"Where are you taking us? Hugo said you had an estate," Camille called out.

"To my estate in the Chartreuse Mountains," Rollant said. "We will travel by night and hide during the day. It should take us three days to reach."

"By night? It is freezing," a man called out.

"If we travel by day, we will be detained and questioned. We must travel by night and hide by day," Rollant answered.

A murmur rose as members shivered in their winter clothes.

Rollant continued, "The village is old and isolated. They have customs that have not been seen in centuries. Do your best to learn them and follow them," he said. "We need to leave now."

Reluctance lived on their faces, but Rollant warned them. "You risk your life if you don't come."

"We risk our lives if we do," Giselle spoke up.

Gasps rippled through the crowd, but Élise stepped forward, her voice firm. "I will go. Rollant has only ever taken me out of danger. I trust him completely."

Hugo's gaze dropped upon seeing Rollant and Élise lock eyes. His shoulders slumped as if resigned to fate. "That is true. I cannot argue." He glanced at Élise's hand, now wearing his ring. With renewed confidence, Hugo surveyed the hesitant community and spoke on their behalf, whether they were willing or not. "Lead us, Citizen Montvieux."

Rollant held a finger in the air to silence the murmurs.

"Hear my warning well—when we reach the village living on my estate, you must respect their customs. They believe my ancestor's home is haunted by a ghost knight. If you step onto the land and return alive, they'll accuse you of witchcraft and burn you at the stake."

Fear darted in their gazes, but they bravely followed Rollant to the south.

THEY FINALLY CAME upon the far outskirts of Lyon, the Chartreuse mountains. He led them off the main path into a grassy meadow, across an ages-old bridge, until a crumbling stone wall came into sight. Rollant warned them again, "Do not enter here, for the village will convict you of sorcery should you return alive."

Élise glanced at the overgrown land with its bent iron gate. Vines had captured a small collapsing house in the distance, and rock sections had been dismantled.

Hugo had stopped to help his sister with a ripped bag, but Élise made her way to Rollant's side. He hadn't said much to her in the three days' journey due to Hugo's proximity, but every glance told her what he wished to say. She took her chance and walked alongside him amid the chirping crickets and the owl's hoot. The community fell slightly behind as they picked up pace.

"Will you come back for us?" she whispered.

"Yes, when it is safe," he said. He peered down at her over his shoulder.

There was hesitation in his gaze.

"What do you wish to ask me?"

Rollant chewed his lip. "For the last three days, I have wondered about the meaning behind what you told me. Do you truly mean I will always have you, or do you not wish to marry Hugo, and I am your excuse?"

Her hand brushed his. "It means I want you, and only you. As far as Hugo goes, he doesn't want to let go. He thinks that in time, I will lose my love for you."

Rollant pulled his arm away. "It may not be safe for years; you may be older than I am when I return."

"Then I will wait," she said.

His brow furrowed as if her response was impossible.

"The village should have eligible suitors, should you want to see if one of them might give you the life you imagine."

She slipped her hand into his within the folds of her coat. The warmth instantly soothed the chill in her fingers. "I want to be with you."

Rollant's lip twitched like he was afraid to smile. "Then, promise me you will consider the possibility of growing old and dying while I remain as this. Consider the possibility of going years between seeing me and knowing I can never fulfill your physical needs as a wife."

"I've considered it," she said, hoping their eyes met, but his gaze was locked ahead.

Rollant shook his head. "I want you to experience life to the fullest, and it is not with me, but if you still choose me, then you can tell the village people you are my wife, and you will be allowed to go to my home where my first family is laid to rest. I have told you all the truths, but find the graves if you want to see how you will end under my curse. If you tell the village people you are my wife, you cannot consider any young man there. Of course, when you return to Charonne, I will not hold you to anything said here should you want to be free from me. But for a time, you will give up everything."

He patted his coat pocket and pulled out a small pouch. "If you choose to say you are my wife," he said. "You will need to wear this. It is a ring with my family's insignia—a mountain with three stars for faith, honor, and duty."

Élise studied the pouch. "Have you always carried this on you?"

Rollant shook his head. "No, I had it made after the king's execution for this very moment. I had to ensure your safety. I know you, Élise, you would have gone into my home and risked your life to see if I told you the truth."

She chuckled. "You do know me."

"How much farther?" Camille cried out in a huff.

Élise released his hand as Rollant turned to the community members. "Let's rest here until dawn. We don't want to scare the villagers. I will scout the village first and ensure it still stands before we enter," he said.

The community nestled into the woods opposite the crumbling estate, and Élise snuck off after Rollant. She had to make absolutely certain of her next action.

He turned around, letting Élise bump into his chest. The village torches and their community traveler's torches were specks of light in the distance on either side of their path.

"Why are you coming?" Rollant asked as the moonlight caused the shadows to dance across his face.

"Do you not want me? Is that why you push me away?" she asked.

"Of course, I want you. I want you more than death." His hand clenched, and her heart broke at his struggle. "I love you, Élise, but as I've said—"

She rolled to her toes and pressed her lips against his cheek like she'd done in Le Marais. His lips followed hers until they almost touched, but he stopped, longing in his eyes. "I won't drag you into my curse, Élise. Only step into it if there is no other way and your life depends on it."

"If I tell them I am your wife," she said. "Will you take me back with you to Charonne?"

Rollant shook his head. "Not until it is safe. I cannot protect you if you are arrested in the morning and executed by sundown. It is safer here being so isolated and unknown."

"But you will return for me?"

"Yes," he said.

"Then I will say I am your wife."

His eyes glistened with a pained gaze. "Consider it all first, please," he whispered, pushing her hair behind her ear.

The village still stood, and they returned to camp. Hugo saw them and shot Rollant a deadly stare.

Élise made her way to Hugo, and they walked to the edge of camp out of earshot.

"I can't do it, Hugo. I can't marry you. You're right, I will always choose Rollant," she whispered.

Hugo shook his head and rubbed the sides of her arms. "Let his presence wear off, Élise. I promise you'll forget him. I asked him to stop coming back, and once he does, you'll see."

She shook her head and attempted to return his ring, but he pushed it back into her hand. "I'm not ready to lose you," he said. "Please, wear it . . . for me."

"I'll wear it because you are my friend," she said. "But I cannot marry you."

Hugo licked his lip and nodded. "Rollant will leave tomorrow, and then we can talk about it some more," he said.

But she knew there wasn't anything left to say.

CHAPTER 41

The Town of Old

VALMONT, CHARTREUSE MOUNTAINS, NOVEMBER 1793

THE PRE-DAWN EDGED into the night as the community approached the village. The buildings were made of stone and cramped together, surrounding a square center with a well and a chapel on either end.

An old woman and a young man, maybe twelve, were before them, wearing clothes not of the century. The woman wore a long-sleeve brown dress that looked like a sack, with a rope tied around her waist as a belt. An earth-tone scarf wrapped around her head. The man wore a simple shirt, trousers, and a knee-length brown wool coat.

They stopped. "Who are you, and what do you want?" Their accent was hard to decipher.

But Rollant spoke it perfectly. "Odille, daughter of Eudes, do you not remember Rollant de Montvieux?"

He held his hands open wide.

"Rollant de Montvieux, Seigneur!" Her eyes opened wide, and she dipped her chin in his honor. Shooing the youth away, she said, "Piers, run, get the council elder, our landlord has returned."

Piers started to run.

"And the priest!" she called after him.

Odille approached the travelers with open arms. "Welcome to Valmont," she said and then kissed Rollant's cheek. "It has been at least twenty years." Her gaze slid to the strangers behind him. "Who are your companions?"

Rollant gestured to them, his eyes locking briefly with Élise while Hugo's gaze darted between them. "These good people come from Paris," Rollant announced. "I will explain more when the priest and elder are present."

"Of course, seigneur," Odille said. "Come, come. I shall get the girls to make the morning meal for you and your guests. We are most excited to welcome them if they are good to you."

She led them to a meeting place with long tables and benches. Élise made sure to sit by Rollant, and Hugo followed to sit on her left.

The buzz of the town was alight before the sun, and soon, the entire village was crammed into the meeting space. The priest and elder, noted by their long black and brown robes, entered and silenced the chatter.

"Ah, Seigneur Montvieux," the priest said. "We are so happy you have returned." He turned to address the Charonne residents. "I am Lorin Enguerran."

The elder piped in with a small bow. "Seigneur Montvieux, we hope you find the village satisfactory." Addressing the Charonne residents, "Clement Jourdain."

"Always is in your good hands," Rollant said. "Thank you for keeping it in my absence, though my duty requires me to leave at nightfall."

"Will your travelers be leaving with you?" Clement asked.

Rollant shook his head and stood up. "No. I come bearing ill news. There is a great evil sweeping through France, and these good people, like you, live on my land near Paris. Valmont will be a temporary sanctuary for them until the evil is subdued. They bring many skills: farming, gardening, milling, candle making, ranching, baking, and there is also an esteemed and learned herbalist."

The village broke out in a murmur at the mention of an herbalist. Hugo glanced up at Rollant with pressed lips of gratitude. Élise patted Hugo's hand beneath the table to emphasize there was no ill will between them.

Rollant continued speaking. "They will be good to Valmont, but your patience is needed. They come from a big city, and Valmont has been isolated from many changing customs. I have asked them to learn your ways and to follow them the best they can."

Gabrielle raised her hand. "Why can we not go on to Seigneur Montvieux's ancestral home?"

The village people chuckled and shook their heads. The priest, Lorin, lifted a finger, and the crowd hushed.

"No one enters there, young lady. As the legend goes, the knight who owned this land was a great protector, the ancestor of Seigneur Montvieux,"—Lorin gestured to Rollant as the descendant—"the first Seigneur Montvieux. His lands were as far as the eye could see and were granted to him by King Philip II Augustus. His gardens provided food for our ancestors. He and his company protected us. But he was killed in battle in the Levant, or so the storytellers say. His wife and child lived there on that estate, and he guards them fiercely from beyond the grave. He will kill you; he will. No one who ventures there returns alive."

Clement pointed to Rollant. "Our Seigneur Montvieux is the knight's descendant, and as seigneur of this land, he has allowed us to live here and cultivate it. He returns every now and then to check on the property or bury a family member."

Lorin began again with a lifted finger. "This reminds me. Graves are on the property—another reason we do not enter. Generations of the knight's family are not buried in the church grounds, so their spirits walk the land. To warn you before you go further, only those of blood or bond to Chevalier Rollant de Montvieux enter and leave alive."

Élise slipped Hugo's ring to the other hand and slipped Rollant's ring on the third finger of her left hand—a perfect fit. Fate had answered her again, and she knew her next action would be the right one, even though her community would alienate her for hurting Hugo.

She glanced at Hugo and mouthed, "I'm sorry."

"Sorry?" he whispered. "For what?"

Odille stepped forward and loomed over Gabrielle. "That means, young lady, you will not enter and live."

Lorin glanced at the solemn, scared faces. "Unless Seigneur Montvieux has taken a wife, only he can enter the estate," the priest said, calm but firm, his gaze sweeping over the crowd.

Rollant leaned back and crossed his arms. His expression was neutral, but Élise could feel the tension radiating from him. The room was silent, save for the faint crackle of the hearth.

But Élise raised her hand. "I am his wife," she said, her voice clear, though her heart hammered in her chest.

Gasps rippled through the room, and every pair of eyes turned toward her. Rollant stiffened, his head snapping toward her. Hugo froze beside her, his knuckles white as he gripped the edge of the bench.

Camille started laughing. "No, sweet Élise, you are to be wed to *my* son, the esteemed herbalist, Hugo. You can't be married to Rollant de Montvieux."

Hugo and Élise shared a glance. Hugo's jaw clenched, and for a moment, she thought he might contradict her, call her a liar in front of everyone. But his shoulders sagged as if the fight had drained out of him.

Hugo stood up slowly, his eyes locked on Élise before turning to answer his mother.

"It . . . It was so, Mother," he said, after a moment of hesitation. "But Élise and I grew apart, and we ended our promise to be wed."

"Ended it!" Camille stood up. Her face flushed with anger. "But you wear his ring. Show it!"

Élise held up her hand, first showing Hugo's simple wooden ring on her right hand, then the silver ring with the Montvieux crest on her left. The room fell silent.

Camille's mouth opened and closed, her indignation sputtering into silence. All eyes turned to Hugo, who stood with his head bowed and face turned away at the sight of Rollant's ring.

Élise closed her eyes at the hurt in Camille's gaze and the condescending stares of the community. Rollant's touch warmed her back, giving her strength to face them all.

"You should give it back, Élise," Camille said, hitting a fist on the table.

She opened her mouth to agree, but Hugo spoke first with a tightness in his voice.

"I made the ring for her, Mother." He was slow to sit, and his gaze never met Élise's again. "It was a gift, and she is still a friend to our family. I will let no harm come to her for wearing it as I asked her to."

The room erupted into whispers—murmurs of scandal, betrayal, and questions that would linger long after the meeting ended. Élise's cheeks burned with shame under Camille's glare, but she kept her head high.

Rollant stood up, silencing the room. "Please treat my wife with respect due to my family," he requested of the entire assembly, who had lived on his land, whether for decades or centuries.

Clement bowed his head. "It shall be as you say. Dame Montvieux will be our beloved, just as you are. We shall speak of the matter no more."

Rollant nodded with pressed lips. "You are wise in your counsel," he complimented the elder. "Now, I must return to Paris tonight, and I would like to leave my guests with the knowledge that they know their sleeping arrangements and that I can rely on your patience as they learn your customs."

"It shall be so," Lorin said as the morning sun tipped the horizon.

The villagers and Charonne refugees busied themselves, making introductions and assigning living quarters throughout the day.

As the sun dipped lower in the sky, the villagers dispersed, their curious and judgmental glances lingering as they returned to their homes with their assigned guests. The Charonne residents had avoided her all day, speaking only when necessary. She had hurt Hugo, and she hoped that, in time, he could forgive her. She had tried many times to tell him, but he wouldn't listen.

Élise stood by the meeting house, watching as Rollant instructed the elder and the priest. She approached them, overhearing the conversation and feeling at ease with his calm and commanding voice.

"To keep your village as safe as you possibly can, I would restrict all trade. Do not let anyone know you are here, for the zealots will come for you. They were already rampaging the countryside of Paris, and I heard reports of the same events happening all over France. They are even executing priests and nuns."

Lorin scoffed. "They wouldn't dare behead a man of God."

"This new regime does not believe in God. Priests are to take an oath to the state," Rollant said.

Lorin's jaw fell agape. "To the state? Our oath is to God."

"Yes, and that is why many priests and nuns are being arrested and sent to the guillotine," Rollant said.

Clement noticed Élise. "Dame Montvieux," he said with a tip of his head. "I am sorry if you heard us speaking about such atrocities. Please forgive us."

She smiled. "I heard nothing," she lied and threaded an arm through Rollant's. "I only wanted to say goodbye to Seigneur Montvieux before it was time for him to leave. Have you finished with your 'atrocities?'"

The three men nodded, and the priest and elder bid Rollant farewell. "Stay alive with the great evil. We have given you a horse packed with our best food. She is tied to the gate at your ancestral home, Seigneur Montvieux," Clement said. "Dame Montvieux, there are dangers in the mountain forest. Do not leave the city by yourself or in the dark."

"I will respect the rules of the village," she said with a nod.

Both men dipped their chins to Élise and left.

Rollant and Élise walked to the edge of town, but Rollant said nothing.

When he finally turned to her, his eyes softened. "I hope you don't regret your choice," he said quietly.

She stepped closer. "I will never regret choosing you."

"How can you be so sure?"

She tapped the ring on her finger. "It was a perfect fit."

He chuckled. "Superstitious?" He peered down at her. "You will fit right in with the villagers."

She stepped in front of him. "Don't leave me here forever, Rollant. You promised you would return."

"When it is safe," he said. "It may be years, as I told you."

She rolled to her toes and pulled him into a kiss. "Then I will wait," she whispered.

His fingers grasped the side seams of her coat. She realized that was how he would hold her for the rest of her life, and it was enough.

Her arms draped around his neck. "Please kiss your wife once more to last us until we see each other again."

Rollant pulled her against him, kissing her until she was breathless. His forehead rested against hers. "I want to stay," he whispered. "I have always wanted to stay with you."

"I know," she whispered, her hands against his cheeks, shielding them in a sense of privacy. "Dream of me as I dream of you."

The corners of his lips turned up. "Yes, my love." His hand slipped to her cheek and pressed his lips on hers until a twig snapped, breaking their moment of serenity.

"Oh," Hugo said and dropped his eyes. "I . . ." His voice trailed off. "I was just—" He turned to leave.

But Rollant released Élise and strode to Hugo with Élise trailing behind. "Please wait," Rollant said.

Hugo debated with shifting feet but finally stilled when Rollant reached him.

"Thank you, Hugo," Rollant said. "I know of no nobler man to protect the woman he loves from what could have befell her in this village for wedding one man while promised to be wed to another."

Hugo's eyes were still downcast, and a small quiver shook his body as if it could barely contain his grief.

Élise's chest heaved with unshed tears, but she stepped toward him, her hands trembling as she pulled him into an embrace, if only to comfort her friend.

"Why? Élise?" Hugo asked, burying his nose into her neck. His arms wrapped tightly around her. Rollant said nothing as Hugo's body convulsed against hers as he stammered, "He could die tomorrow, and you'd never know it. You'd never know, and you'd be alone. Why throw away a life with me? Why? Why would you do this?"

Élise wanted to soothe his pain, but some pain was inevitable. She cradled his face. His crystal blue eyes pleaded for an answer that she had already given many times before.

"Hugo, maybe it is time to stop asking why," she whispered. A single tear slipped down her cheek, falling to her lips. "And start seeing what is and what will never be."

His face contorted, pain written in every line, and he pressed his forehead to hers, his breath uneven against her skin. "I would have been good to you," he said, his voice thick. Hugo's arms encircled her, and for a fleeting moment, she allowed herself to lean into him. Rollant could never hold her like Hugo, but she had chosen the sacrifices that came with loving the cursed, immortal knight. She would endure because it meant staying true to her heart.

"I would have given you everything," Hugo whispered.

"I know you would have, but it's not fair to you. I would have been a fraud," she said with a hitch. "I gave my heart to Rollant. I never tried to hide it. I . . . " Her voice trailed off.

"I tried to steal it back," he whispered.

Élise whispered, "But there was nothing left to steal."

The words were as daggers. His lip quivered, and a small whimper escaped.

"I'm sorry," she whispered through her tears. "I'm so, so sorry you are hurting."

He didn't reply at first, his arms tightening around her in one final, protective gesture before he gently pulled back. "I can't win your heart," he said quietly, his eyes downcast. "Then I'll stop trying."

Élise closed her eyes, deciding on her next words. "You deserve someone who loves you how you deserve to be loved. Not a half-hearted version of what I can give." She mustered a small, sad smile, her hands falling to her sides, but Hugo caught her left hand.

"Is it because I could not afford a ring of silver?" he asked, glancing at Rollant's ring.

Élise shook her head. "No, Hugo. It was never about that, and you know it."

He kissed the back of her hand. "I do," he whispered. "I had to ask, though." He fought a smile through the pain.

Her heart tore at his hurt, so she offered an observation she had made earlier in the day. "The miller's daughter keeps looking at you, did you see?"

He laughed bitterly, shaking his head as he rubbed the back of his neck. "She's a child."

"She's a woman," Élise said gently. "And old enough to know how she feels."

He sighed and looked at her, his hand cradling her cheek one last time. "You'll be the one I compare her to, Élise," he said. "For the rest of my life."

But Élise overlaid her hand on his and whispered with a warm smile, "When you find a woman who loves you as much as you love her, there will be no comparison."

Hugo leaned forward but hesitated with a glance at Rollant. But at Rollant's silence, he pressed a lingering kiss to her forehead.

Her throat tightened, and she closed her eyes, letting the moment wash over her. When she opened them, Hugo was already stepping back and turning to address Rollant.

"Even though she chose you, I—I couldn't let the village know the truth . . . She told me her heart was yours since I asked her to be my wife. Even before then. Years before." Hugo shook his head. "I just—I never listened. I kept hoping. I kept thinking you were just an infatuation, one that would fade to nothing." His jaw grew taut, and his hands clenched by his sides. "I blinded myself."

Rollant stepped forward and put a heavy hand on his shoulder. "You are a good man, Hugo. One I was willing to leave Élise with; one I trusted and will continue to trust. You are the respected leader of your community. They look to you. You should walk with your head held high. Love will come to you just as it came to me. In the most random of chances, it will come. When you find a woman who loves you, she will wait for you, just as Élise waits for me, and I for her."

Hugo nodded with thinned lips. He drew a deep breath through his nostrils and blew it out. "I was honest, Monsieur de Montvieux; I will let no harm come to Élise while you are away. I will not infringe on your love any more than I have. I will respect her ring."

Rollant dipped his chin to Hugo. "You have my gratitude."

Hugo's quivers ceased, and a resigned grin washed over his face as his gaze darted between Rollant and Élise. "I wish you the best in life," he said before leaving them alone again.

Élise wrapped her arms around Rollant's waist. "You're a good man, too."

Rollant sighed. "I wish I were a better one."

She rested her chin on his chest. "You need to believe you are a good man and deserve love. You are not alone anymore, Rollant. I am here with you even when you are away. You'll always have me."

He smoothed her cheeks with his thumbs and kissed her lips.

"I . . . " He sighed with a bright smile. "I don't deserve you, Élise. That is true." His smile faded. "And one day, you will realize what you gave up here, and once we return to Charonne, whenever it may be, I will release you from this lie."

"It is not a lie," she said, her brow furrowing. "I don't understand why you can't believe I love you and will always love you."

"Because I am not natural, not living, not dead," he replied. "I exchanged death for service to the crown. One, I have failed time and time again. What makes you believe I will not fail you as well?"

"Because—"

But he interjected. "I love you, Élise, and will carry your love for centuries, but I refuse to believe you would give up your life for someone like me. I will cherish these days, months, years, however long I have with your belief in your love for me, but one day, I know it will end, just as all things do, just as Hugo hoped. One day, your love for me will fade to nothingness."

She shook her head. Her words jumbled, leaving her speechless.

He tenderly kissed her, fresh tears on his lips. "I will cherish the time I do have your heart," he repeated again in a whisper, his hot breath fluttering against her flesh. "I will never forget your love and hold it close to warm me on my darkest nights."

He said, "I will return when it is safe. Then, you will know what the rest of your life will be like and decide if you want to rescind your ring."

"I will never rescind," she said as he cradled her face.

"I hope it to be true," he murmured before placing a parted mouth over hers and kissing her with every passion she wanted.

"If I don't leave now, I won't leave," he said, tearing his lips from hers. "And who knows what other curse may befall me," he whispered.

He pulled away and walked off into the night without another word. The sunset was in the distance as she watched him walk away toward his ancestral home, his first home, his home with Amée, his first love. She would find his secrets there and find a way to show him his guilt, and his self-imposed penance would keep them apart if he let it.

Her fingers grazed her lips as she calmed her rapidly beating heart. "You're wrong, Rollant de Montvieux. You will always have me," she whispered to herself, bringing her hand to her side in a relaxed fist, feeling the warm silver ring between her fingers. Her back straightened, and her chin lifted. "And one day, you will finally believe it."

CHAPTER 42

The Twilight of Fate

VALMONT, CHARTREUSE MOUNTAINS, MAY 1794

THE WINTER HAD NOT BEEN KIND to the village. It had gnawed at the crops, at the livestock, at the bones of those unable to find warmth. But Hugo had healed many and, in doing so, gathered many hearts unto his own—until one, at last, had claimed him.

Élise had smiled at their betrothal, standing in the gathering dusk of the spring festival, hands clasped in quiet resolve. At the elder's request, she had even given them her blessing on behalf of Seigneur Montvieux as though Rollant had been there to bestow it himself. And when May arrived, she watched Hugo take the candlemaker's daughter as his wife.

Afterward, the community still shunned her, as if the stain of her broken betrothal had not yet faded. Hugo's mother had been the most unrelenting. But the villagers—those who had welcomed her from the start—had not turned her away. They called her one of their own. It was a new type of home, a place of possibility. But as soon as the last of the frost melted from the fields, Élise found herself saddling a borrowed mule and turning toward the hills. Toward the estate that had belonged to Rollant before time had stolen it away.

The early morning sun struggled to pierce through the heavy canopy of trees, casting the world around Élise in shades of green and gray. A damp stillness clung to the air as if the forest itself held its breath. She pulled her scarf tighter around her shoulders, her heart pounding with each step closer to Rollant's estate.

"Hello?" she called out, her voice breaking the unnatural silence.

A flurry of birds erupted from the branches above, scattering into the brightening sky. The rustle of leaves and the distant scampering of forest creatures reminded her she was not truly alone—but not truly safe, either.

Her thoughts turned back to the villagers' tales, the way their voices would drop to hushed whispers whenever they spoke of the ghostly knight who haunted the grounds. "He takes the souls of those who trespass without blood or bond to Montvieux," they had warned her, eyes wide with fearful reverence.

Her fingers curled tighter around the reins.

She had no true claim to Rollant—not by marriage, not by name. They had never spoken vows, never built a life in the way a husband and wife should. What if the villagers were right? What if the knight, whoever or whatever he was, saw her as an intruder?

She hesitated at the gate, staring at the iron bars laced with vines.

"His great-great-great-great—" she faltered, the legend catching in her throat. "Grandfather." She exhaled sharply. "He still stalks the place. An angry man clad in chainmail, with the fleur-de-lis on his chest . . ."

She shook her head at its absurdity. "You've already faced ghosts, Élise," she told herself. "One has been haunting your heart for four years."

Swallowing her unease, she tied the mule to a post and pushed open the gate. The rusted hinges screamed in protest, the sound tearing through the quiet woods like a warning.

The birds scattered again, and the underbrush rustled with unseen movement as if every living thing fled at her intrusion. Élise tightened her grip on the reins.

"I'll be back," she whispered to the mule, leaving it by the gate as she stepped through.

Grass had overtaken the cobblestone path, and roots clawed at the stones beneath her boots. She knelt to clear a patch of the pathway, revealing the once-proud road leading to the house, now a crumbling husk of its former glory.

The sight of the manor sent a pang through her chest. It wasn't just the decay—it was the weight of time, of loss. The roof had collapsed in on itself, and the walls leaned precariously, gaping where solid stone had once stood. Windows that might have gleamed with candlelight and life were now dark voids, staring blindly into the world.

"Chevalier Rollant de Montvieux?" she called, half-expecting a shadow to emerge, half-dreading what she might find.

No answer came.

She sighed in relief as she passed by what had once been a garden. The outlines of beds were faintly visible beneath the wild overgrowth, and she spotted the crumbling remains of a dilapidated well half-sunken into the earth. Beyond the house, a small creek bubbled quietly, its serenity at odds with the ruin surrounding it.

And then, beyond the creek, she saw it: a patch of vibrant grass and wildflowers that seemed untouched by the decay around it. The sight drew her in, a bright, living space in a world of shadows.

Her foot caught on something hard, and she stumbled forward. A sharp corner jutted out of the earth—a headstone, hidden beneath the tall grasses and flowers. Kneeling, Élise began clearing the overgrowth, her fingers brushing against the cold stone as she uncovered the engraved name:

"Cateline de Montvieux et de Conti | Beloved Daughter of Chevalier Rollant | Beloved Spouse of Chevalier Serge de Conti | Born to Noble Lineage | A Light of Love and Devotion | May Her Soul Rest in Peace | 1143 to 1203."

The words swam before her eyes. She glanced around, spotting another stone nearby. Clearing it with trembling hands, she revealed:

"Amée de Montvieux | Beloved Daughter of Chevalier Thibaud de Toussaint | Beloved Spouse of Chevalier Rollant | Daughter of Honor | Departed in the Service of God | Resting in the Lord's Peace, Awaiting the Return of Her Knight | 1126-1188."

She fell back on her heels, her heart hammering in her chest as she scanned the field. More graves dotted the space, each covered in a thick shroud of grass and time. She began uncovering them one by one, reading names, dates, and the legacies of Rollant's family etched into the stone.

The last headstone bore the date 1344: Ninette de Conti. After that, the field was empty.

Her gaze returned to Amée's grave, the flowers growing wild around it. "1188," she whispered. "Six hundred years." She stared at her name, the dates, and the unshakable proof of Rollant's tale written in stone.

The realization hit her like a blow. Every word Rollant had ever spoken about his past, his curse, and his family—it was all true.

She sank into the grass next to Amée's headstone, reclining beside her grave as the flowers towered above her. The petals brushed against her cheeks, framing her vision with their vibrant colors as she stared up at the sky.

"Is my Rollant also yours?" she whispered as she turned toward Amée's headstone. "Why did you choose to stay married to him? Were you happy with your choice?"

The silence that followed was both comforting and maddening. There was no answer, no voice from beyond the grave to soothe her doubts or confirm her hopes. Only the gentle rustling of the wind through the flowers echoed through the meadow.

She lay there for a long time, the weight of six hundred years pressing down on her as she envisioned the struggles, the obstacles, and the sacrifices that would come with being Élise de Montvieux.

Her arms wrapped around herself as though trying to hold the pieces of herself together. Her gaze drifted to the flower blocking the sunlight from reaching her eyes, and a sudden thought struck her.

Her hands stilled.

The memories came to her—Rollant, waking before her each morning in Le Marais and Charonne, carefully preparing her meals. It wasn't much, just bread and cheese or whatever provisions they had managed to secure, but it was his way of caring for her. She had thought nothing of it at the time, assuming it was practicality, nothing more. But now, as she lay by Amée's grave, she understood.

It was his love.

Rollant, the man who could never embrace her, who could never hold her without risking her life, had shown his love in the only ways he could. He had given her his knife and taught her to fight, ensuring she could protect herself. He had drawn her baths and brought her clean clothes, his hands trembling with restraint as he handed her the simple comforts she needed. He had kept her safe, over and over again, because he couldn't give her the one thing he wanted most—his embrace.

Tears welled in her eyes as her hands covered her face. He had loved her all along in ways she hadn't even noticed. His love had been in the quiet gestures, the unspoken actions, the things that had seemed so ordinary at the time.

And now, knowing that, she couldn't imagine a life without him. A quiet determination took root in her heart. The sacrifices would be worth it. Rollant was worth it. She would make him see.

She closed her eyes, letting the moment's peace wash over her.

For better or for worse, she had made her choice.

CHAPTER 43
A Love to Hold
VALMONT, CHARTREUSE MOUNTAINS, SEPTEMBER 1794

A NEW GROUP seized control of the National Convention and turned its blade inward, executing the democratic tyrant, Robespierre, by the same instrument he had so liberally used on others. He and his radical followers fell beneath the guillotine, and the Terror's reign of blood waned after July. France stumbled forward, weary and fractured but yearning for peace.

The war had not been kind to its soldiers. The National Guard, stretched thin and underfunded, sent the Temple guards home in shifts or forced them to volunteer without pay. With Antoine Simon executed, Louis Charles was in better hands—though not good ones. Rollant could do little for him. Marie-Thérèse was left forgotten in the Temple's tower. Rollant could do nothing for her.

For two days a week, Rollant was forced home, and for two more, he stayed without a wage. But his thoughts were elsewhere.

Élise.

The memory of her lingered with every breath, with every night spent in the barracks. He should have returned to her sooner—should have gone back the moment he knew Charonne was safe. But a selfish fear had held him back.

She would not choose to stay his wife.

She would not choose him.

Still, he had promised. He left the city behind in the middle of September and rode through the countryside, the familiar path stretching before him in golden fields and shadowed woods. It was a day and a half on horseback, and he pushed through most of the night.

By noon, he reached Valmont. The crisp mountain air refreshed his lungs, and he dreaded returning to the stench of the city.

As he entered the square, the town came alive around him. People rushed from their homes, pressing against his horse, hands reaching toward him, some clutching flowers. A murmur of anticipation rippled through the crowd.

He searched the sea of faces, his pulse quickening. He recognized them all but could not find the one he wanted to see.

Instead, he found Hugo.

The herbalist stood at the front, a woman at his side. Her hand was tucked firmly beneath his arm, and their fingers intertwined in a quiet declaration.

Rollant pulled his horse to a stop as Hugo stepped forward, flanked by the village elder.

"Seigneur Montvieux," Clement greeted, lifting his hands to calm the crowd. "We are glad you have returned."

A hush fell over the people.

Rollant glanced at Hugo before dismounting. "The land is safe again," he said slowly. "The residents of Charonne are free to return home."

A flicker of hesitation passed over Hugo's face. His grip on his wife's hand tightened as he glanced toward the people who had followed him. "I have decided to stay with my wife. And I believe the community has chosen to remain as well."

The words landed like a blow to his stomach.

Rollant kept his expression still, but the unspoken question rose in his chest like a tightening fist. "All of them?" His whisper was barely audible.

Hugo hesitated, rubbing his thumb along his wife's wrist. "Not all," he finally said, voice low. "One has not decided."

Rollant's stomach twisted. The words hung between them, and he almost didn't dare ask. But he had to.

"Élise?" His voice was barely more than a breath.

Hugo nodded.

Clement clapped his hands together with an air of forced joy. "Your wife will go with you, Seigneur Montvieux. She would not stay with us now that it is safe for her to return."

His gaze swept the crowd, searching. His heart pounded as he scanned the square, expecting her to step forward—to emerge from behind one of the villagers with those same fiery eyes that had haunted his dreams.

But she was not there.

His throat tightened. "But where is she?"

Hugo's expression darkened. His wife cast her gaze downward as Hugo spoke. "She has been living in your ancestral home since the early summer. She ventures into the village now and then, but—"

Clement interrupted, his voice carried a slight tremble. "We did everything we could to ensure she was respected as your wife. We begged her to stay."

Rollant's jaw clenched. He inhaled sharply, glancing between Hugo and the elder.

"I have no doubt you all tried," he said, though his voice was tight. He imagined the shunning she endured and how bad it must have been to drive her to solitude in a place with the dead.

Hugo stepped closer. "She left of her own accord," he insisted. "She went there once and then a few more times, a few days, then she stayed. We did not drive her away."

Rollant's throat burned. He dipped his chin to Hugo. "I believe you," he said, though a few doubts still lingered.

Hugo gestured toward the distant hills. "None of us dared follow her. The ghost of your ancestor, you see. But she never seemed afraid. We helped her cut wood and give her what she needed."

"Cut wood?" Rollant asked.

"She decided she wanted to make a home there again . . . for you," Hugo said with eyes full of sincerity.

For a month, he had let his fears hold him back, convincing himself that she would choose another life, that she was better off without him. But the idea of Élise waiting for him, alone in the ruins of his past, gnawed at something raw inside him. He had been a coward to stay away so long, wasting time convincing himself she would choose another life while she waited for him.

Rollant nodded slowly as his doubts about her treatment faded but did not vanish. "Then, I must go to her."

Clement smiled. "Very well, Seigneur Montvieux," he said, with the hesitation in his voice gone. "We shall not hold you any longer. Please, take our finest foods for your return journey and give our well wishes to Dame Montvieux."

"Thank you," Rollant said with a gentleman's nod to Hugo and the elder. Then, turning to the crowd, he spoke with quiet certainty, "Thank you, people of Valmont, for taking in the residents of Charonne. To the community I brought here, I see why you would wish to remain. The land is beautiful, and life is simple." His voice steadied. "I will not return for some time. But I will always see to my lands."

The villagers moved forward, pressing baskets of dried meats and fresh bread into his hands. Flowers were tucked into his saddle.

He took it all in, but his mind was already elsewhere.

As he mounted his horse, the elder stepped back. Hugo gave a final nod.

Then Rollant turned his horse toward the distant hills.

To the place where she waited. To the home she had rebuilt for him.

Rollant dismounted and tied his horse at the iron gate, still bent from time. Though stubborn weeds still crept between the cracks, the cobblestone path had been cleared of its wild overgrowth. The house, once a proud stone estate six hundred years prior, was a pile of rubble. Near the well, a small, simple wooden lean-to had been constructed. A few of the old garden beds had been recently harvested as a quiet testament to the life of solitude Élise had embraced there.

His gaze fell beyond the garden and the ruins, where the creek ran clear. There, bent over the water, filling her cup, was Élise. She had cleared headstones and placed fresh flowers on each one.

His throat tightened.

"Élise?" he called out.

She glanced over her shoulder and stood. The moment recognition set in, her expression transformed—weariness melting into a radiant smile.

"Rollant!"

She ran toward him with her skirt billowing behind her.

He barely had time to restrain himself as her arms wrapped around his waist, and her head slammed into his chest.

His hands clenched at his sides. He wanted to hold her. More than anything, he wanted to hold her. Instead, he stood rigid, willing to endure her touch.

"I've missed you," he whispered, his voice hoarse.

She lifted her face to his and, without hesitation, kissed him.

His resolve shattered.

He let himself feel her lips against his, the warmth, the desperate certainty in how she held him. But as quickly as he gave in, he pulled back, his hands gripping her arms to put space between them.

"Why?" His breath came unevenly. "Why would you live here?"

Élise cupped his face, her thumb brushing along his cheekbone. "You told me to see what my life would be like with you," she said softly. "So I did."

His brow furrowed.

"I thought—what better way to understand than to live as Amée did? To see, to feel, to know." Her fingers tightened against his jaw. "And I found clarity here, Rollant. I want to be your wife. Forever."

His chest tightened.

"I meant for you to see the graves," he said, his voice barely above a whisper. "That is where you will end up. A name carved in stone. An empty plot beside you." His throat burned. "Is that what you want?"

"Yes."

His stomach dropped.

"I will never be able to hold you, Élise. Never. I will never wrap my arms around you. I will stay as this, and you will age and die." He searched her face, willing her to see the life she was throwing away. "Is that truly what you want?"

Her gaze did not waver. "You have my heart, Rollant. That is all that matters."

A muscle in his jaw ticked.

"I ask only this," she continued, her voice filled with raw vulnerability. "When I die, lay me beside Amée with an inscription just as beautiful as hers. And when you have forgotten my face, I hope you find another love and do the same for her. And the next. And the next." She swallowed hard. "Because life is nothing without love, Rollant. Until I met you, I never truly believed that."

His fingers curled into fists.

"Life is nothing without death, too," he said, a tremor in his voice. "Do not be disillusioned with love."

"I am not disillusioned." She stepped closer. "You have always given me a choice. Since the day we met, you let me find my own fate and make my own decisions, and you supported each one. Why won't you support this one?"

"To make it easier for both of us," he bit out the lie to save her from a life with him. "You should find someone else."

"No!" Her voice rose, desperate, determined. "Let me choose, Rollant! And please, honor my choice." Her breath shuddered as she exhaled. "I choose a life with you—even if I never feel your embrace. Even though I will age and you will not." She lifted her chin. "I choose you. Just as Amée did."

His heart slammed against his ribs.

"She only chose me because she was already my wife," he argued, his voice raw. "She had taken vows when I was mortal. If she had known the truth before—"

"She still would have chosen you," Élise cut in.

She stepped away, walking to Amée's grave. With a quiet reverence, she pressed her palm against the cold stone.

"If you loved her as you love me," she whispered, "then she loved you as I do now. And she chose you for the same reason I am choosing you. As I stand over her grave, there is no doubt in my mind." Her gaze flicked up, her eyes blazing. "Because life without you is not a life I want."

Rollant's breath hitched.

He had laid it all bare—his curse, his pain, his unworthiness—and yet she still chose him. She still wanted him.

His head fell forward, his hands gripping his hips, as if trying to steady himself beneath the weight of her decision.

"I want you to know love, Rollant," she continued, her voice softer now. "Please, do not go back to your wretched existence, hiding yourself away, doomed to live forever alone." She stood and stepped closer. "Live forever, you will. But make your lifetimes good, Rollant. Fill them with joy. Fill them with love." Her voice caught. "And I will be honored to be part of one of them, as Amée was. Her heart was always yours, and so is mine."

She lifted a hand to his chest, and he grasped it before she could press her palm against his heart.

"I fear I will take your life, Élise," he admitted. His voice was rough, pleading. "With Amée, I could never enter my home, or I would kill them both—her and Cateline. We never slept beneath the same roof for forty years." His breathing was shallow. "If you stay with me, I want you in my arms. I want to hold you." His hand trembled against hers. "I fear waking to find you—"

"I want to be your wife, Rollant." She pressed her forehead to his chest. "I will take the risks our love demands. Stay with me in Charonne. Let us have whatever time we are given."

He exhaled a shuddering breath, his hands ghosting over the fabric of her dress.

"Élise, do you know how difficult it was for me to see you in my shirt? To see your bare legs, your hair long, to kiss you?" His voice broke. "I ached every day. Even now—"

"As did I," she whispered, meeting his eyes once more. "But isn't it worth the ache—to be with someone you love?"

Her hands slid up his belly to his chest. "Your presence gives me peace; that is all I want for you too. Live in our home. Lie beside me at night and build a life with me."

His fingers found the silver band on her hand. He turned it gently, watching the Montvieux crest catch the light—three stars over the mountain.

"Faith, duty, honor," he murmured.

"The Montvieux crest," she murmured in return.

"Only two other women have worn it." His voice was reverent. "My mother and Amée."

Élise brushed her fingers over his scarred hands, steadying their quiver. "Then, I am honored to be the third."

He kissed the palm of her hand before pressing it to his cheek. He had spent centuries denying himself love, warmth, and even the dream of a future that did not end in loss.

But she was asking him to choose it. To choose her.

There, in her arms, he found something greater than his fear: the unbearable joy of having her, even for a time.

His hand hovered at his side, fingers twitching. He could not hold her.

He loved her, though he should never have loved her. He wanted to choose a life with her, but knew he should not, for its end would be too much to bear as it was with Amée.

But as he searched her eyes, something broke inside him.

He exhaled, slow and trembling, and let his hands rise, grazing the soft linen of her dress.

A quiet shudder ran through him as he relinquished his restraint. His fingers, calloused from centuries of wielding a sword, trembled as they curled into her dress and pulled her close—the only way he knew to return her touch. He exhaled against her temple, his breath unsteady, as if her warmth alone could undo six hundred years of solitude.

He pulled back to gaze into her deep chocolate eyes.

"I promise to honor you in every word and deed," he whispered, his voice rough with emotion.

Élise relaxed into his chest with a bright smile.

"To cherish you every morning, noon, and night—" he hesitated, then let out a quiet laugh, shaking his head. "Even if my way of showing love is making breakfast."

Élise laughed with tears catching the golden light of the afternoon.

He pressed on through his vows, his forehead brushing hers.

"I promise to be a dutiful husband. To provide, to protect, to put your needs above my own—" His fingers curled at her waist. "Even when you refuse to let me."

Her lips parted as if inviting his kiss.

"I promise to be faithful to you in heart, body, and mind." His breath caught. "Until the end."

The wind stirred the wildflowers at their feet, rustling through the ruins of the past and carrying with it the faintest whisper of the lives that had come before.

Rollant pulled Élise closer, memorizing the pull of her, the weight of her hand in his, the fierce certainty in her eyes.

Once, he had feared time. Now, he feared not having enough of it with her.

He closed his eyes and whispered his choice—not to the stars, not to the past, not to fate, but to her.

"I choose you, Élise."

And for the first time in centuries, he did not hold love at arm's length. He held it close.

par [illegible] chere lettre du [illegible]

[illegible] Datrouve vous [illegible]

[illegible] 900 à 1000 livres [illegible]

[illegible] Canta [illegible] vous [illegible]

[illegible] Commande par [illegible]

[illegible] Graisse [illegible]

[illegible] 1200 livres de Graisse [illegible]

CHAPTER 44

The Solace of Night

CHARONNE, PARIS, APRIL 1795

WINTER'S icy fingers lingered into the early months of spring. The village of Charonne had been blanketed in silence as though the cold had seeped into its very soul, leaving everything still and untouched. The homes on Rollant's land remained vacant, save for the occasional cry of a bird or the rustle of wind through bare trees. The pale light of the early morning sun barely pierced the fog, casting a soft glow over the frost-dusted rooftops of the empty homes.

Élise liked the silence—it was comforting in a way. It was the kind of quiet that came with knowing nothing would change—nothing but the chores that needed to be done and the thought of Rollant coming home to her at the end of the week.

It meant more work for her, but she didn't mind it. There was peace in tending a garden and the sheep, knowing Rollant was hers and she was his. With him, she felt whole. At the thought, her lips turned into a smile. If she had chosen Hugo, she would have spent her entire life in a hollow paradise, wondering what could have been. There was no regret with Rollant, even if their life together had thus far been challenging, sometimes frustrating. But the challenge of his curse had only deepened their bond. She had never felt more alive. Even if their life together was unconventional, it reignited the spark and sense of purpose she had been missing with Hugo. Her years of pining had not been in vain, and Rollant's acceptance of her as his bride affirmed the desires of her heart. She had chosen the right man, and she was proud to be Élise de Montvieux.

She walked to the fence of Hugo's family home and gazed at the city walls. Rollant stayed six days at the Temple and one with her. It was over an hour's walk to the Temple, and he worked long days, earning only two livres a day, barely enough to live on, but she made it work, only venturing into Popincourt for items she could not make herself. She missed him. It was as if he was still accustomed to being alone, but she wanted more of him, more of his mind that he would not share, more of his body he could not share, and more of his presence that he did not share.

She pulled her shawl tighter around her shoulders and adjusted her coat. Rollant was coming home for the night, and she looked forward to it. Dinner was cooking on the hearth, and all the chores had been done.

She retreated to the house to read the book Rollant had given her as a wedding present. She had almost finished it, a book of fables. Her reading was not good, but the stories helped her skill.

The rich, hearty aroma of stew filled the air, mingling with the earthy scent of the crackling fire, wrapping the room in warmth and contentment.

She was deep with her nose in the book past nightfall when a knock came at the door.

"Rollant?"

"It is me, Élise," he said.

She jumped to her feet, her heart racing, and unbarred the door in a rush, barely keeping her balance as she flung herself into his chest. The cool spring air left her shoulders, replaced by the comforting heat of his body. He smelled faintly of the earth and the road—sweat and leather mingled with the sharp scent of old wood and candle smoke.

His rough hands were warm against her arms, and she sank into him with a soft, relieved sigh. She rolled to her toes and kissed him, draping her arms around his neck. At least without neighbors, she could kiss him however she wanted outside their home.

He stroked her arms before grasping her belt and pulling her so their bellies touched. His chest was firm and solid against her, as if grounding her after the long days spent alone.

The roughness of his coat under her fingers, the heat of his breath against her skin, and the softness of his lips sent a rush through her, making the world outside vanish.

Even after the months they had lived as husband and wife in Charonne, the fire still sparked with every kiss and every touch. But one of them had to ensure the fire did not flame. They had already failed twice before, and each time, it ended with Élise on the floor near death.

"May I come in, Dame Montvieux?" he asked with lips hovering over hers.

She gave him one more kiss before allowing him into their home.

"I just swept the floors," she said, pointing to his boots, and retreated to the main room to plate the meal.

"Yes, Madame." Rollant removed his muddy boots by the door and slowly removed his coat with a groan.

She paused at his groan, hoping he had not been hurt on the way home. She hadn't smelled or felt blood on him.

"You did not have to wait to eat with me," he said upon entering the main room.

"Oh," she said as she sliced the bread and cheese. "I didn't want you to eat by yourself. You do that all week long, and besides, I made your favorite stew," she said, glancing back at him. Her tone betrayed her hidden concern. The hearth light showcased his weary face and the dark circles under his eyes as he washed his hands and face in the basin. The soft splash of water from the basin was the only sound, punctuated by the low groan Rollant gave as he wiped his face, the weariness of his week evident in each movement.

"Thank you," he whispered with a soft smile beneath dull eyes. He pulled her chair out for her, and they sat down to eat.

"This is delicious. You have quite outdone yourself," Rollant said.

Élise beamed.

"After having gruel all week, this stew is everything my belly could hope for." Even his words dripped with exhaustion, though his eyes sparkled when he looked upon her. He reached across the table, and Élise slipped her hand into his.

"I'm worried about you," she said. "You look as if you carry the weight of the world."

Rollant chuckled with a shake of his head. "It's only been a long week."

But Élise knew the lie. Rollant carried what he would not tell her for much longer than the past week. His silence always spoke louder than his words. Her direct nature drove her to ask the question. She was tired of guessing. She was tired of him pulling away from her to protect her, shelter her, or for whatever reason.

"No, it's more than that," she said in a whisper.

Rollant scrubbed a hand over his face, his jaw tightening.

"Why do you look so worn, Rollant? Why do you never tell me what happens during your days at the Temple?"

His face paled. His thumb ran over her fingers as his gaze turned inward.

She was losing him to his past horrors. With a gentle but firm tone, she said, "You've carried this burden alone long enough. Let me carry it with you."

Rollant's fingers tightened around his spoon with knuckles white. His gaze dropped to his bowl, his usual confident demeanor giving way to something raw. The strain in his shoulders and the way his lips pressed together meant he was holding back words he didn't want to say. He sighed and ate his stew.

It was his way of telling her he would answer in a moment, so she finished her meal in silence to allow him time to gather his thoughts. He was always so careful, so reserved, and she threw all of that to the wind.

The scrape of his spoon against the bowl was the only sound for a long moment, the rhythm of its quiet punctuation to the silence between them.

When they were finished, Rollant took the dishes and washed them. With his back turned to her, he spoke with a shake of his head.

"If I tell you, Élise, it cannot be undone. You will carry it with you, as I do. Are you sure you want that?"

Élise rose and wrapped her arms around his waist, leaning her cheek between his shoulder blades. "I want all of you, Rollant," she said, her voice catching. The plea was evident in her tone. "Not just the parts you think are safe to share."

"Six hundred years is a long time to be alone," he whispered as he washed out a bowl. "Habits are hard to let go; I'm sorry if you feel I have kept my darkest moments from you. I only wish for your happiness."

"Are you happy with me, Rollant?" she asked.

He lowered the dish into the basin and dried his hands before turning in her arms. He cradled her face and placed a sweet, gentle kiss on her lips. "Beyond happy," he whispered. "You are my greatest strength."

She closed her eyes as he kissed her cheeks and forehead. "Then I want to help you carry your dark moments so they are not so dark. You are not alone anymore. I am your wife, let me help you. Let me be close to you in all ways we can be."

"Then I will tell you," he whispered and led her to the sofa. Rollant stared at their entwined hands for a long time before he began.

Her chest tightened as she listened, the words falling from his mouth like stones in the room's stillness, impossible to take back. Her throat tightened, her hand trembling slightly as she reached for his, the warmth of his skin grounding her amid his despair: Louis Charles—the screams, the bruises—even still, after Antoine Smith's execution.

"There is nothing but desperation in his eyes," Rollant said. "And I feel I have failed him just as I failed his father. I am immortal. I cannot die, and yet I cannot save anyone." His gaze dropped, and his shoulders released centuries of regret.

Élise's heart broke at his words, the weight of his pain pressing down on her chest. Her thumb brushed across the calloused skin on his hand, trying to offer a small comfort for the anguish he couldn't escape and had carried alone for so long.

"I am trapped in an endless cycle of seeing everyone suffer and try as I might, fate does not change anything. Everyone dies. There is no peace. I long for an end to the torment, Élise," he said, tears breaking free.

Élise's chest constricted at the pain in his voice and could feel him withdrawing even further into himself to pull out each confession. She took his hands in hers, holding him tightly as if she could stop the sorceress' deal and grant his desires.

"Yet my duty to the crown binds me to a future I never chose in full understanding."

He wiped his eyes in vain. "And knowing I will have to be alone again after knowing you, after loving you, losing you,"—he kissed the back of her hand—"It is more than I can bear. This home bringing me such joy with you alive will be nothing but pain."

Élise rubbed his back and shifted on the sofa to be as close to him as she could.

"You see," he started and wiped his tears. "I did not want to darken your day with such morbid thoughts."

She leaned her forehead to his. "You did not darken my day," she whispered. "You can't do everything, Rollant. Though immortal, you are still one man. You stayed with Louis Charles more than you had to because no other royalist would risk their life posing as a Temple Guard. You've told me he believes he is safe with you, and that matters, Rollant. You have not failed him."

His tears fell atop her hands, and she nuzzled his cheek, her whispers finding the crevices between their flesh. "Find peace, Rollant. Come home to me. Let this place be your refuge. Let me be your sanctuary as you are to me, and when I am in the grave, come here with a smile, not in pain. Remember our life together. Talk to me. Talk to my grave. I will still share your burdens. You will never have to be alone again."

Rollant looked at her, his eyes filled with both gratitude and sorrow. "Oh, Élise," he said, gingerly stroking her neck. "I must have done something right over the past centuries to be blessed with you by my side."

She wiped his tears with her thumbs and brushed his lips.

"I hate leaving the boy, but after my shift, there is nothing more I can do," he said. "I will come here every night and leave every morning."

"It is over an hour's walk each way," Élise said with eyebrows raised.

"I don't care. I don't want to spend another night away from you." His hand slid up to her cheek. "We've already spent so many apart."

She reached for his hand again, squeezing it tighter this time. The silence between them thickened as the fire crackled softly in the hearth. His thumb traced circles on her skin, and for a moment, the rest of the world felt distant.

Rollant's breath was shallow. His hands trembled as he cupped her face, his calloused fingers feather-light against her skin. The intensity in his eyes dove deep into his soul, raw and clear.

Élise swallowed, her heart pounding. She should pull away, seeing the flame of desire in his eyes. She should remind herself of the risk of what happens when his arms enclose her. But how could she, when every fiber of her being ached to ease his sorrow? To be the light that chased away his darkness? To fuel the flame neither wanted to extinguish?

She lifted her hands, threading her fingers through his hair.

His gaze searched hers, still holding back.

"Let go," she whispered, knowing his desires, his needs, her needs, her desires. "Just this once."

And so he kissed her—soft at first, tentative before the pressure of his lips deepened as if he was letting go of everything he'd been holding back: centuries of restraint and the fear of losing what he had finally found.

The fire crackled softly in the hearth. The weight of time, of fate, of curses—none of it mattered at that moment. There was only this. Only them.

As they moved, the kitchen hearth dimmed behind them, and the bedroom hearth light flickered.

The dark closed in as if it already knew what they were about to risk.

He made her forget he was cursed. But curses never forget.

HER LUNGS BURNED, clawing for air that wouldn't come. Darkness crowded the edges of her vision, and panic swelled in her chest. Death waited.

"Breathe! Élise, breathe!" Rollant's voice cracked with fear and carried her through the darkness. His hands trembled as he cradled her head, trying to pour life into her through sheer will.

Death receded. A haggard breath filled her lungs.

The next thing she knew, Rollant had her head up and a cup of cool mint tea at her lips.

The curse's weight on her chest pressed against her lungs in a dull ache. She rolled to her side and coughed it away. Rollant pressed his hand against her back, supporting her as she regained her breath.

The cool wood floor soothed her forehead until normalcy returned. She sat up, rubbed her chest, and then lifted her gaze to Rollant's. He sat back against the bed. He was pale. Shaken. His elbows rested on his knees, his face buried in his hands.

"Élise, I want to be with you as much as you want to be with me, but I was cursed for a reason." He shook his head with eyes full of fear. He slammed his fists on his knees and let out a shuddering breath with words barely composed. "I can't—I can't keep risking your life, Élise."

She reached for him, but he pulled away, his hands balling into fists on his thighs.

"I've spent centuries as a knight and a soldier. Fighting, killing, watching others die—this body has been my weapon, my curse. And now, with you, it's supposed to be something more, but all it does is hurt you." With a clenched jaw, he fidgeted with the hem of his linen breeches with angry fingers. "I'm afraid to love you as a husband should. I'm afraid I'll kill you."

A small groan escaped her lips as the last of the curse pricked her chest.

Rollant whispered, "Three times. It has happened three times. I will not risk a fourth." He stood up, offering her a hand, which she took. Instead of pulling her to her feet, he pulled her close, grabbing the sides of her chemise. His lips brushed against the curve of her neck—a kiss full of longing and restraint. "This," he whispered, his voice trembling, "is all I can give you."

Élise's hands caressed the scars on his chest as her gaze fell there. Rollant exhaled sharply as she traced the lines of his scars, her fingertips featherlight over skin that had long forgotten gentle touch. "I've seen your scars, but I've never asked. Where did you get these? I thought your body always healed?"

He let out a soft, bitter chuckle. "Scars from my first life never left."

"Were they painful?"

"Yes," he whispered. "But it was so long ago, I don't remember as vividly."

"Was your life at risk?"

"Yes, but . . ." His voice trailed off, and a flicker of understanding flashed in his eyes.

Élise lifted her gaze, meeting his. She had spent years aching for him, and living with the emptiness of not trying was unacceptable.

"I'm willing to bear unseen scars as we learn how to be husband and wife," she whispered.

He stepped back as though physically recoiling from her words. "But I'm not."

"You think this curse is punishment, Rollant, but what if it's a test? A test of how much we're willing to fight for each other."

His lips thinned as he shook his head.

"I don't care if it hurts," she said. "I don't care if it leaves marks. I want you. Whatever that looks like. Whatever it costs. It's worth it to me. Please don't shut me out."

Their life struggles together would not break them but strengthen them. Rollant's curse would be something they faced together rather than a barrier between them.

It was as if her words pierced him, straight into the part of him that still dared to hope. He swallowed hard, but tears pricked his eyes. "You deserve better than this, Élise." His voice was hoarse and pleading. "I cannot keep control of myself, and you end up—"

Rollant's jaw tightened, his hands flexing at his sides as though resisting the urge to reach for her. His shoulders sagged, and he looked away as if afraid his gaze alone might hurt her.

Élise stepped away from him, watching his body quiver with longing and fear. She stooped and hesitated before pulling a box from under the bed. Her fingers trembled slightly as she unboxed the last week's worth of labor. She ran the twine through her fingers, tracing each knot she had woven by hand. It was a simple thing—humble, rough, imperfect. Her heart pounded in her chest at the ridiculous insinuation behind it. He could laugh at her or hate it.

A flush crept up her neck. She met his gaze, feeling the longing in his eyes. She had to try, at least. Her hands unfurled the twine as she presented it to him. "I made this for you," she whispered.

"A rope?" Rollant's eyes searched hers.

Élise's gaze dropped. "Yes," she said, lowering it and unable to say anything more. Shame rose on her cheeks.

But Rollant's hands were warm against her skin as he cradled her neck, and she could feel the faint tremor of his fingers, the lingering notes of his desire and restraint.

She stepped closer to him, the twine between their chests. "If we could . . . " Her voice trailed off as they searched each other souls.

His thumb grazed the edge of her jaw, a touch so light it ached before his hands slid down to the rope between them. He ran his fingers over the fibers, their fingers brushing. "If I fail you?" he asked.

"Then I will lose breath, and you will let go, and then I will recover like before."

As he let her loop the twine over his shoulders, she realized it was a mirror of them—fragile in places, strong in others, something woven together with care. Her fingers trailed the strong curve of his arms, traveling to his wrists. She pulled it gently, testing its hold.

Rollant's lips curved into a faint smile, but his eyes softened with something far more tender.

For a moment, the world narrowed to just the two of them. The need to close the distance, to taste his kiss, burned through her like fire.

But his breath hitched. "I keep seeing you collapsed on the floor," he confessed with a voice thick with pain. "I hear how your breath stuttered and the look of fear in your eyes."

Her breath mingled with his, stirring the space between them. She traced her fingers along his forearm, feeling the quiet tension beneath his skin—the restraint, the wanting. The firelight flickered, throwing shadows across his face and deepening the fearful expression in his eyes.

"Trust me," she whispered, her voice steady. "We'll figure it out together."

She leaned to kiss him, but he remained still.

"What's wrong?" she asked. Her brow furrowed at his stillness. She opened her mouth to ask him again what was the matter, but he leaned forward, biting her lip in a sensual kiss. She cradled his face in her hands and pressed her body close to his until she felt a tear crash into her fingers.

"Rollant?" she whispered.

His hazy gaze was full of adoration, and a soft smile spread over his lips. "You've taught me eternity is empty without love," he whispered on her lips. "I would trade the thousand lifetimes I've lived for just one life with you."

Élise pulled back slightly, her heart tightening in her chest as she registered the depth and pain of his raw confession. His words etched into her soul.

Her eyes burned. She brushed away his tear that had fallen onto her fingers, tracing the hard line of his jaw, and memorizing the vulnerability in his eyes as if she could hold onto it forever.

Her gaze fell to the twine between them—the simple rope she had woven, imperfect but strong. A promise bound by her own hands. A thread linking past and future. A tether between them in the only lifetime that mattered.

She curled her fingers around it, gently pulling, drawing him closer, not to fate, not to eternity, but to her.

"Then let this be the life that matters," she whispered, kissing him softly. "Let this be the one where we choose each other. Where we choose love."

The muscles in his arms twitched as if still resisting, still afraid of taking what she had given him long ago. But as her lips brushed his again, he surrendered and leaned into her warmth, her love, and their fragile, fleeting miracle.

And in that moment, Élise knew—love was not measured in lifetimes but in moments. And she would make every moment of her life with Rollant count for the thousand lifetimes he would endure without her.

CHAPTER 45

Fate of the Bourbons

THE TEMPLE, PARIS, JUNE 1795

It had been centuries since Rollant first swore to protect the crown, yet he could not remember a time when the oath had felt so heavy—so utterly futile. Rollant had watched kings rise and fall, but never had he felt so powerless as he did now, kneeling at the bedside of the boy who would never grow into his crown.

The room was dim, and the flicker of a single candle cast trembling shadows across the damp stone walls of the Temple. Louis Charles lay still, save for the faint rise and fall of his tiny chest. Each breath was harder won than the last, rattling, a sound that echoed in Rollant's ears like the tolling of a bell for a life too short.

Rollant's immortal hands were useless against the cruel march of death.

"Monsieur," Louis Charles said, his eyes slits. His hand touched Rollant's face while the other clutched his father's small cross. "I remember you at the palace."

Rollant held a finger to his lips. "Don't tell anyone," he said.

The boy labored to breathe. "You are my father's friend," he whispered.

Rollant nodded. "And now yours."

Louis Charles' ashen skin paled. "I am glad you are here."

"Me too," he said, taking the boy's hand. Louis Charles squeezed it with what strength he had left, the fear palpable in his touch.

"Do you believe my father and mother will be waiting for me at the gate of Heaven?" he asked, sputtering with labored breath.

Rollant smiled. "Waiting with open arms."

"Will they recognize me?" Louis Charles whispered, his small hand clutching the cross. "I don't look like I did before."

Rollant blinked back tears. "They'll know you, Your Majesty. A parent always knows their child."

The corner of Louis Charles' mouth twitched. "I am trying to be brave," he whispered. "But I am afraid."

"There is nothing to fear, Your Majesty." Rollant leaned forward and stroked the boy's sweaty brow.

"I am afraid they won't love me for the bad things that mean man made me say about them," Louis Charles sputtered. "I am sorry I said them," he whispered through weak coughs. "I didn't mean them. I just wanted the man to stop hitting me."

Rollant's jaw grew taut. "None of that matters now," he said through clenched teeth, wishing he could do more for the child. "They know. They see," he whispered.

"I am so tired, but I'm afraid to die," Louis Charles rasped.

"Death is easy," he said, clenching his teeth as he watched Louis Charles struggle for breath. "The journey to it is hard, as you well know." Rollant kept his gaze locked with Louis Charles but took in the bruises on his arms and neck and the one on his cheek. "You are brave, my king, but let it come. Sleep, and it will find you in peace."

Louis Charles closed his eyes and whispered with a cough, "Will you stay with me?"

"Always," Rollant said. His thumb swiped the child's tear away. "You will be with them soon," he whispered.

He had seen children perish before, but Louis Charles was the only one he had seen beaten to the point of illness and death. It turned his stomach that an illness would give him a respite from the cruelty he incurred.

When the boy's small chest stilled, Rollant knew it wasn't just a child's life that had ended—it was the last fragile thread of an eight-centuries-old kingdom unraveling in his hands.

He stayed kneeling beside the boy's body long after the candle had burned low, staring at the fragile fingers loosely curled around the cross. The silence in the chamber suffocated any peace that was supposed to come with death.

"I have fought for kings for centuries, and yet, when it mattered most, I have been powerless," he muttered.

His fingers brushed over Louis Charles' cooling hand. His hoarse whisper cut through the silence, "I am sorry."

He sat back on his heels, his fists clenched at his sides. The weight of his oath had never felt so empty. The hot sear of anger burned through his heart.

"He was just a boy," Rollant muttered, his hands balling to fists. "And I failed him. The Revolution failed him, allowed him to suffer in this dank place."

He had lived through countless deaths, but none pierced him like Louis Charles. What was the point of his immortality if he couldn't save a boy—a child who had done no wrong except being born to a king?

The door opened. "Ah, Garde Rollant Montvieux," his commanding officer said. Footsteps echoed behind him as he peered over Rollant's shoulder. "What a pity." The commanding officer grunted. "Well, looks like you have the rest of the day seeing your prisoner no longer needs you, and we are short on funds, so take the week."

Rollant's chin dipped. "What will happen to his body?"

"Buried beneath the Temple with the others," the officer said.

Rollant stood up, taking one last look at the boy king. The family cross lay loose in his hand. "He loved the cross," Rollant said, ensuring his voice was devoid of any emotion. "If you can, please keep it in his hand."

The officer patted Rollant's shoulder. "I knew you took a liking to the boy. I am sorry."

Rollant nodded and began to walk out.

"One last thing, Garde Montvieux," the officer said, holding up a finger. "We have orders from the National Convention to tell no one that Louis Charles is dead. He lives and is well if anyone asks. Do you understand?"

"Yes, Captain," Rollant said and left with dismissal. He glanced up at the tower where Marie-Thérèse was held under lock and key. He had promised their father he would watch over them, but she was not the king, and no one remembered she was there.

As he made the long walk back to Charonne, he wondered what would become of him. The king's brother was now the rightful heir but had fled France and resided in Verona. He wondered if his oath extended to kings regarded as traitors to the country. But even then, the king's brother had no children and would likely never have children. He remembered the few breaks in royal lineage throughout the centuries when distant cousins claimed the throne and took it for themselves. But would there be even a crown to claim? If the war ended in France's favor, the royalists surrendered, and the constitutional monarchy remained abolished, what would become of Rollant? It was a lot of factors for the sorceress to consider. He hadn't felt fate guiding his steps to Verona as they usually always led back to the king.

As he walked the cobblestone path to his home, he saw his love hanging laundry to dry.

Her voice broke through the haze.

"Rollant?" She ran to him, her hair streaming behind her in the summer breeze. He wanted to close the gap, to let her warmth break through the chill in his chest—but his feet were heavy, rooted in the weight of his thoughts.

Her face came into view, crystal clear amid the blur. "Why are you back so soon in the day?" she asked and touched his arm. Her eyes scanned him, likely looking for blood or evidence of a wound. "Is everything—" She stopped and gazed into his eyes. "It's the boy, isn't it?"

Rollant nodded. "They told me to take the week since they are low on funds, and he no longer needs a guard." His voice was monotone.

"I'm so sorry, Rollant," she said, slipping her fingers through his and leading him home by the arm.

He knew he should open his heart to Élise, but he just wanted the quiet. He changed his clothes and began working in the garden while she finished the laundry. With both working, their chores ended early. They ate silently, and while Rollant washed the dishes, Élise wrapped her arms around him and lowered her forehead to his back.

"Leave the dishes," she whispered. "I'll wash them tomorrow."

He threw the dish back in the basin before leaning both hands on the counter. Élise tightened her embrace at the sudden clatter. His head hung with a furrowed brow. "They killed him," he said.

Élise's tears pressed against the soft cotton of his shirt. "I am sorry, Rollant. And I'm sorry for my role in it. The movement was never meant to be what it became. Those poor children were never supposed to be orphaned and beaten and killed. Louis Charles was a victim of the violence I once believed was necessary."

He didn't want Élise to feel responsible. She wasn't. She only wanted food for the starving. He turned around and cupped her face. "You did not kill Louis Charles," he whispered and kissed her forehead.

He took a deep breath and walked from her embrace to the sofa and sank into the worn cushion. His head drooped back on the wood railing, and a sigh released from his belly. He stared up at the ceiling, jaw tight.

"Everyone dies," he whispered, his voice thick. But would he too now that the king was dead and the heir a traitor and absent?

He pulled a knife from his belt and laid the blade on his hand while Élise watched, her eyes darting between him and the blade.

"I'm afraid, Élise, that when I become no longer immortal, I will fade to dust given my age." He swallowed hard. "Or I will relive every death and then die."

"But you have not done those things," she whispered.

"Because there is still a rightful heir to the throne, and the war is not decided."

"The Count of Provence," Élise said with a nod to Louis XVI's younger brother. "But he is not here. How do you serve a king who left his country?"

Rollant chuckled, stained with sorrow. "If I am immortal still,"—he slid the blade across his palm—"then I fear I have to leave France."

Élise retrieved a cloth and gingerly tended to the wound in his hand, holding her breath. Her shoulders slumped, and her gaze dropped when the gash healed. She wiped up the rest of his blood and sat down next to him. Her fingers caressed the healed gash in his hand as if to calm the cut's phantom burn.

"What do we need to do now?" she asked.

"It means I need to leave."

"No." She shook her head. "What do *we* need to do? If you leave, I leave with you."

"Élise, I can't protect you. I can't protect a ten-year-old boy, a king, a queen. And a sorceress tied me to them. How am I supposed to protect you across the country? Across all of Europe?" He threw his hands up, letting lifetimes of pent-up anguish escape. "It's all futile anyway. Centuries! Centuries of service—all for what? Nothing!" He jolted up.

"Everyone dies," he yelled, his voice hardening with every word. "But not me. No! I'm forced to watch while the world crumbles." His hands curled into fists, his knuckles white. "For what? What has any of this been for?"

He screamed at the ceiling and summoned the sorceress to answer. "Witch! You cursed me with this hollow life! Was it mercy—or punishment? Did you know what it would do to me?" His voice cracked as he threw a chair across the room, the splintering wood echoing his torment. "I have paid my price and my debt. Release me!" he yelled and kicked the table over.

The silence that followed was deafening. A splintered leg of the chair rolled to a stop at Élise's feet.

Rollant's breath heaved. His hands shook. He had faced battlefields and betrayals, but never had he felt this lost.

The sofa creaked as she stood and took a cautious step toward him. "Rollant," she whispered.

He looked at her then—the fear flickering behind her eyes.

And it broke him.

His knees hit the floor. He loosened the collar of his shirt and sat back on his heels with a shaky breath. He palmed his face to calm himself. "I am sorry, Élise." He couldn't bring himself to look upon her after his outburst. "I . . ." His voice trailed off.

She sniffled, and it crushed his heart. He had scared her and the guilt for doing such a thing was more than he could bear.

"I don't deserve you," he whispered, wiping his face, not realizing tears ran freely down his cheeks.

"Your curses don't define you, Rollant." Her voice was smooth and soft like the most decadent silk. She kneeled beside him. Her arm wrapped around his waist as her other hand gripped his and brought it to her lips.

"You call it pointless," she said softly. "But would Louis Charles have died afraid if you hadn't been there? Would he have died alone? Would I have survived the Revolution or Gabin if you hadn't found me at the bakery? Would Hugo and the others have all met their fate at the guillotine? Rollant, your life isn't meaningless. You've saved more than you know."

She pulled his head into her chest until he laid his ear to her lap and let the years' worth of suppressed guilt, anger, and loss run down his face as a stream of tears. She bent over and kissed his temple as she crooned, "The choices you've made because of your curses define you. And those choices show me who you are—a man worth fighting for, a man worth my love and my life."

He brought her fingers to his lips. "What would I do without you, Élise?" He brushed her off, not believing his worth.

"You're not hearing me," she said and turned his face to hers. "There is more to life than your duty to the crown; for once, consider what you want for yourself. Not for me, not for the king, not for France. For you."

They locked eyes, and he swallowed hard. His brow furrowed. "For me?"

She nodded.

He caressed her hand. "I just want a simple life with you right here in Charonne. I want children and grandchildren, and when we are old, I wish to die together."

"You are my home," she whispered.

"And you are mine."

It was then that Rollant realized loving and losing are part of what it means to be human and that he had shut himself off from both for far too long.

"Then maybe we stay here for a while and see what becomes of the new king," she said, threading her fingers through his hair and brushing away his tears. "And in the meantime, if you want to, an orphaned girl is still at the Temple."

"Marie-Thérèse," Rollant whispered the royal daughter's name.

Élise nodded. "She has lost everything, Rollant. She is a victim of circumstance, just as her brother was. You're the only one she has left."

Rollant closed his eyes, letting the memory of Élise's fingers through his hair imprint upon him.

"She deserves a chance," he said, his voice steadier now. "And I've spent too long letting this duty dictate my life. If I can't leave it behind, maybe I can reshape it. On my terms."

Élise kissed his brow.

"She is not in danger, and I believe most have forgotten she is there," he continued. "I can take fewer days at the Temple and be with you most of the week. And I promised the former king I would watch over his family," he said.

"And you are a man of your word," she said with a smile.

He grinned as he stared up at her. "The exiled king can wait," he said. He exhaled, a breath so deep it felt like centuries of sorrow peeled away.

For the first time since he began training as a knight, his duty did not feel like a chain around his neck or the weight of a servant's pierced ear. His new path had not been forced upon him. It was something he chose.

CHAPTER 46

The End of Oaths

RUE DE SAINT-ROCH, PARIS, OCTOBER 1795

THE CANNONS ROARED like the trumpets of judgment, shaking the cobblestones beneath Rollant's boots as he sprinted through the smoky streets, caught in the revolt on his commute to the Temple. Screams of the dying mixed with the thunder of grapeshots. He ducked behind an overturned cart as royalists rushed past him, their muskets raised and their faces grim with determination. They were emboldened by the aristocrats' return and their hope to rid France of the corrupt Convention, which had done nothing but make life worse. Rollant knew, deep in his soul, that this battle would mark the end of something far greater than the uprising itself.

Twenty-five thousand Parisians raised arms against the new French Republic and marched toward the Tuileries Palace, where the National Convention met, to overtake it. But their objective wouldn't be gained so easily.

The Republic Guardsmen had cannons and blasted grapeshots at the royalist insurrection, ripping men apart. Civilians lay dead, caught in the crossfire. The acrid smell of gunsmoke clawed at Rollant's throat.

He stayed crouched, watching the chaos ensue. The wood splintered just above his head, hit with an iron shard.

The royalists were the remnants of the monarchy he swore to protect, but their violence felt futile and dishonorable. Where were they when the king needed them? But the French Republic had only left blood and brutality in its wake. He'd seen people starved to death and frozen in the streets the prior winter, rotting because their families could not afford a burial. He no longer knew where he stood or where his loyalty lay. Duty compelled him to act for the royalists, but witnessing the civilians' plight tore at his heart. Families tried to run; some made it whole, while others were not so lucky.

A young boy tripped as he followed his parents; his father held a baby. A grapeshot blasted, tearing the side of the building and causing its stones to fall on the boy's foot. He called for his father, but the father did not hear amid the ruckus.

Rollant bolted for the boy, ripped the stone off his foot, and carried him. He took a bullet in the back but pushed through the pain, clutching the child as tightly as possible to prevent stray bullets from catching a limb. He wore the blue coat of the National Guardsmen, and it drew attention. He caught up to the family, handing them their boy, when a shot ripped past the side of his face.

"Republic Guardsman!" The royalist shouted as he reloaded. His shout summoned four more royalists.

"Run," he told the father, who took off with the child.

"I am Captain of the King's Bodyguard," Rollant shouted as he approached them, hoping not to spill blood that day.

But he was met with a volley of bullets. He dodged two, but one caught his arm and the other his hat, knocking it to the ground beside a civilian woman with lifeless eyes. Rollant's gaze ran down her bloodied dress.

For centuries, the crown had been his compass, his reason for enduring. But now, staring into the eyes of the rogue men who fought for a crown already lost, putting innocent lives in danger, the weight of his oath crumbled like ash in his hands. These men didn't fight for a king—they recklessly fought for vengeance. And vengeance had no honor.

"If that is your answer," he growled, drawing his sword to attack his supposed allies. They were not defenders of the monarchy but pawns of chaos.

The wounds stitched together as he approached them, his large frame cutting through the smoke. Their knees shook, and their hands fumbled the gunpowder.

The Royalist charged first, musket raised as a bludgeon. Rollant twisted his body, letting the wooden stock narrowly miss his shoulder, before slamming the pommel of his sword into the man's jaw, sending him into the cobblestone. Rollant stepped over him as the royalist writhed in pain.

Another musket shot rang out, echoing in Rollant's ears. He ducked instinctively, the lead ball grazing his shoulder and tearing through the fabric of his coat. The heat burned his skin, but he pivoted on his heels.

The Royalist, advancing with a sword, lunged, his blade aimed for Rollant's gut. Rollant sidestepped, parried with a sharp clang of steel, and twisted his wrist to rip the blade from his opponent's grasp. The Royalist's sword clattered to the ground, and Rollant drove his shoulder into the man's chest, sending him sprawling. He wasn't there to kill them if he could avoid it, but restraint was becoming more challenging to maintain with every musket ball fired his way.

"Lay down your arms!" Rollant bellowed, his voice cutting through the chaos. He advanced on the reloader, sword drawn, his footsteps deliberate and heavy against the cobblestones. "I do not wish to kill you!"

"Traitor!" the man spat, his voice trembling with fear. The snap of the musket and the click of the flint striking steel jolted Rollant to the street as the musket ball whizzed past his head.

Another shout rang out from the smoke. Three more Royalists emerged, charging with bayonets fixed. Rollant had no time to think. The first attacker thrust his bayonet toward Rollant's chest, but the immortal knight pivoted, grabbed the barrel of the musket, and drove his sword into the attacker's thigh. The man screamed, collapsing onto the blood-soaked street as Rollant wrenched his blade free to block a bayonet thrust aimed for his head.

The reloader had scrambled to his feet and was fumbling for his pistol. Rollant charged before the man could fire, closing the distance in a blur. His blade came down in a clean arc, removing the threat. He grabbed the man by the collar and slammed him against the stone wall.

The soldier gasped, his eyes wide with terror as Rollant's blade hovered at his throat. "Go home," Rollant growled, his voice low and menacing.

The man nodded and tore loose. Rollant surveyed the smoky scene; the royalists lay in pain but were alive. He turned to go, but a sharp, burning pain exploded on his side. Another royalist, whom he hadn't seen in the haze, had swung his sword, slicing Rollant on his side and across the chest. His blood soaked his coat, staining the blue. The blade came back down in the kill strike, but Rollant parried, gripping his wound from the vibration of steel hitting steel. He staggered backward, his knees nearly buckling, as his attacker advanced. Cannon blasts sounded near, and debris flew at them, knocking both men down.

Rollant groaned and forced himself to stand, still gripping his open wound. But the attacker was up first and growled as he pulled a pistol, "Die Republic scum."

But Rollant was not about to lose this fight, not from a royalist; he heaved his body with force conjured from a knight's battlefield and hit the attacker full-on in the chest. The pistol clattered on the cobblestone as Rollant fell atop the royalist. The others were standing again and started approaching to aid their fellow royalist.

Rollant sent a fierce uppercut to the man beneath him, knocking him unconscious before rolling to the pistol. The pain in his side was unrelenting. He should have felt the burn of healing, but it hadn't come.

There was only one shot and three royalists. His sword was more than an arm's reach away. He sat back against a building, gripping his side as his body screamed in agony. He glanced at his chest. The bloody gash was still open and unhealed.

"I don't want to kill you," he yelled out and lowered his pistol, but hate lived in their eyes.

Another grapeshot hurdled through the air following the thunder of a cannon blast. The shockwave sent debris and smoke in all directions, killing two of the royalists. The third disappeared into the chaos.

Rollant's chest heaved with shallow gasps as he pressed his hand to his side, expecting the familiar warmth of the wound stitching itself shut. But the pain remained—a searing, unrelenting agony that spread with each breath. There was no tingling rush, no fleeting burn, only pain. Real, raw, deep, human pain.

He gasped, his breath shaking. The blood didn't slow, didn't dry—it pooled beneath him, dark and thick. His vision blurred, his strength ebbed. For the first time in centuries, he was not a man suspended between life and death. He felt . . . fragile. Mortal.

The realization hit harder than all the deaths he had endured.

"I can die," he whispered.

He winced. "I am . . . dying."

What had bound him to this life had deserted him in his need.

He had prayed for this moment for centuries. But not now. Not when he had Élise.

He clawed at the cobblestone, desperate to return to her. He forced himself to rise, each step agonizing, each breath a battle.

He screamed in agony as he crawled out of the battle but collapsed on Rue de Faubourg Saint-Antoine. His hands trembled, and his body shook, but his mind fixated on his one objective: Élise. Return to Élise. He had to tell her goodbye.

He fought again to rise, but the world tilted. He took a halting step forward, then another, before his legs gave out beneath him. He collapsed to the cobblestones. His vision darkened as he gripped his wound tighter. A hand fell heavy on his shoulder.

"Where are you going?" a soft voice asked.

Rollant peered up to see what officer had caught him deserting, but instead, he recognized the father of the boy he'd saved.

"Charonne," he whispered, his voice hoarse.

The man pulled him up and helped him into a deserted cart with his children. He and his wife pulled them along. Rollant's boot heels dragged on the cobblestone as he looked up at the boy and the little girl. The boy held his wrapped foot, and the girl stared in a state of vacant numbness.

Rollant could feel his life slipping away, as it had on the battlefield six hundred years before. The world stopped, and the sounds of distant cannon fire faded to silence.

"Why?" he called out. Why then? When he was happy with Élise and finally found love again. Why had the sorceress forsook their deal at that moment? Though he had wished for mortality for centuries, he did not want it then. But it seemed, life again was unfair. Thus, he only wished, needed, to see Élise one last time.

As if fate had heard him, Élise's face came into view. Her hands caressed his face, and her lips brushed his. Tears fell onto his cheeks. He blinked, coming out of his haze. The man and his two children stood off to the side with their cart, watching them in somber silence. The mother pressed strips of her dress against Rollant's wounds.

"Rollant!" Élise's voice sounded far away as he lay on the path to his land with their home in the distance. She had dropped to her knees beside Rollant; her hands trembled as they brushed his blood-matted hair from his face.

But cutting through Élise's screams, an ethereal whisper revisited the dying.

"Do you wish to live, Rollant?" The same chill of night pressed in heavily above him as it had six hundred years prior.

Élise faded from sight as the celestial hair of the sorceress preceded her starlit face, hovering above his.

"Why now?" he croaked.

"You abandoned your duty to serve the crown and attacked royalist soldiers rather than fight alongside them. Because of your actions, Napoleon Bonaparte put down the royalist rebellion, and he will become emperor. Marie-Thérèse and Louis XVIII will never have children, thus ending the Capetian dynasty. For the first time, neither side of your deal is upheld."

"Then let me live my life with Élise," he said as death edged his vision.

"You would trade eternity for a few fleeting moments with a mortal woman?" she hissed. "You are nothing without me. A mere shadow of what I made you."

She circled him like a vulture. Her dark tendrils wrapped around his limbs. "But I offer you a new purpose," she said with an air of deliverance. "Serve Napoleon's empire that will last forever with your service, or reject me and turn to dust—"

"No," Rollant said with certainty.

"You would willingly fade into dust? After all I have given you? You beg for death like a fool? You are bleeding out on a filthy street like any other worthless man." Her voice dripped with venom.

"You could live forever with an empire that will never end. You could have riches unforetold. You have paid your penance for Arnoul's blood, and you may love again, and you say no?" the sorceress asked as if her vain promises were worth the pain of immortality.

"No," Rollant urged.

"What of Élise and the king's daughter? What will they do without you? The poor orphans will live a life they know nothing about. Who will take care of Élise and Marie-Thérèse?"

The sorceress had asked him the same question about Amée and Cateline to twist his reasoning and logic and to compel him to accept her offer.

Amée's beautiful face appeared in memory as clearly as if he had seen her that morning. With the clarity of her visage, clarity of reason came with it. She and Cateline would have been fine without him. Amée would have grieved him, but she would have been well-cared for; she could have found love again or chosen to live alone. She had everything she needed. And now Élise had his fortunes and gold. She was young and beautiful. Her whole life was ahead of her, just like Amée. Marie-Thérèse was well cared for in the Temple, bored but well. He couldn't do much to help her beyond that.

Could he spit in the face of God one more time? He knew the answer. He would not make the same mistake again. He had inflated the importance of his life, and it had cost him his humanity.

He prayed instead of answering the sorceress. "Forgive me, Lord. I only wish to say goodbye to Élise and hope for your forgiveness. Please allow me into your fold."

Rays of light broke through the celestial hair and starlight face, dispersing the image of the sorceress who curdled an agonizing scream.

A warm, golden light surrounded Rollant and lifted him off the ground, giving way to a blinding brightness that gradually faded, revealing the crisp October day.

Fresh air filled his lungs like a babe after birth. Every breath was sharp, raw, and alive. Élise's hands cupped his face, and her touch burned like fire—no longer muted by the dull ache of centuries. Tears blurred his vision, but for the first time, they weren't tears of regret. They were tears of life. The cobblestone pressed into his back. The sounds of the children crying were full force in his ears. Élise's fingers gripped his hair. Tears streamed down her cheeks.

"Rollant, you aren't supposed to die." The words tore from her lips in a frantic whisper. "You can't. You can't do this."

His body was warm beneath her touch, but it was the warmth of fever, not life.

Centuries of breathing false, foreign air faded to nothingness. He had forgotten how pure the air was, how fresh and rejuvenating. Élise's scent was of linen and lavender. He turned his face and breathed her in for the first time at the expense of agony ripping across his chest. His body ached. It hurt from centuries of abuse. But somehow, his newfound peace diminished the pain of his wounds.

"The bleeding stopped," the mother said as she worked, pulling needle and thread from her pocket. "I'll sew him as best I can." She shouted over her shoulder, "Jehan, alcohol." He produced a small flask.

Élise's gaze never unlocked with Rollant's. The questions flooded her eyes. "You're not supposed to die," she whispered in repeat, her voice cracking.

Rollant swallowed the lump in his throat as his eyelids fluttered. "Thank you . . . for showing me love again," he whispered in a stutter as pain ripped through his chest with each breath.

"No." She shook her head, her grip tightening. "No, no, you don't get to thank me. You don't get to say goodbye." Her voice cracked, thick with rage, grief, and terror.

"You will stay with me," she whispered, nodding—begging. "You will."

The afternoon sunlight dimmed, and the sounds and smells faded. Death closed in. His time was fleeting, and his soul met Élise's in their gaze.

"No—Rollant, please!" She clutched his coat as if sheer will alone could tether him to life.

His breath shuddered and slowed. "You'll always have me," he murmured, and the darkness took him.

But in the black abyss, a voice called to him. Soft, familiar, surreal.

"Rollant."

A golden glow bathed the abyss, chasing away the shadows. Rollant turned, and there she stood—Amée, radiant and untouched by time, draped in robes as white as morning mist.

Behind her, Cateline and Ninette stood in solemn reverence among the lost kings of France—Louis, Philip, Charles—all those he had served, with centuries of gratitude etched into their faces.

"You have carried your burdens long enough," Amée whispered in sorrow and pride. Her fingers brushed his cheek, warm and real—not the ghost of a memory, but a promise of something beyond. "Live, Rollant," Amée crooned. "Live for her as you once lived for me."

The kings raised their hands in solemn blessing, their voices joining hers in a chorus that echoed through the void:

"Live, Rollant. Live as we lived."

TWO DAYS PASSED, and Élise refused to let Rollant give up. She thought of the first time she'd met him—the quiet strength in his gaze, the fire that had never dimmed. Now, that fire was flickering, and the thought of it going out forever filled her with terror. He had always seemed larger than life, a man untouchable by time. But now, time was clawing at him, and she couldn't stop it.

She cleaned and dressed his wounds, but she didn't understand why he was no longer immortal. The family that helped Rollant moved into Hugo's old home, as they had lost everything in the city. Bertille, the mother, came over regularly to check on Rollant and to force Élise to sleep, though sleep never came easily. Each time she shut her eyes, she feared they might open to find Rollant never breathing again.

His pain was evident even in unconsciousness. Low, pained groans accompanied the hard rise and quick fall of his chest. She lifted the cloth on his side, cringing at the angry, jagged wound. The gash across his chest was healing well, but the one on his side looked worse with every passing hour. Élise poured more alcohol over it, the scent making her stomach churn.

"At least Bertille is a good seamstress," she muttered, trying to lighten the weight in the room, though her voice trembled. She caressed Rollant's face, her nails scratching the stubble on his jaw. Her hands ran down his neck and arms to soothe the tension in his muscles. His body felt so strong, so solid beneath her touch, but it terrified her how fragile his life had become.

"Don't you leave me," she stammered. Her voice cracked on every word. Her tears fell freely onto his chest, tracing unseen paths down his fevered skin.

"Not now. Not after everything. Not when we've fought so hard for us." Her fingers trembled as they curled into his.

The silence of the room mocked her. No whispered reassurances, no teasing quips—just the shallow, ragged rhythm of his breathing.

"You promised," she choked. "You told me once that I'd always have you. So don't you dare make yourself a liar, Rollant."

Still, he did not answer.

Her body shook with exhaustion, her head falling to his chest, listening —waiting—hoping.

"Please," she whispered into his skin, voice breaking. "I love you. That has to be enough."

Élise sat up, rubbing the exhaustion from her face. Her mind swam in the haze of sleepless nights. She pressed a warm cloth over his side, hoping to coax the wound to heal, and her tears blurred the sight of his ashen face. It wasn't fair—not after all they'd endured, all the years she'd waited. He was hers. Hers to love, hers to fight for. But what if that wasn't enough? What if she was too late?

The first rays of dawn crept into the room, bathing Rollant in a golden glow. Élise froze as his chest rose slower now, steadier, each breath pulling at the quiet stillness of the morning. Had she imagined it? The way his chest moved.

Her breath caught. She leaned in, hands trembling as she pressed her fingers to his wrist. The faintest flutter of a pulse met her touch.

His lips parted, a soft groan escaping, and his hand twitched beneath hers.

"Élise?"

She shattered.

His voice was faint and less than a whisper, but it was enough to send her weeping into his shoulder.

"Rollant," she sobbed. Her fingers clutched his hand, clinging as if she could anchor him there, pull him fully back into life. "You're awake. You're awake."

He moaned, his head rolling weakly on the pillow as if testing the limits of his body. He rasped in a voice, hoarse and broken, "Am I dead?"

Élise laughed through her tears. "No," she whispered, pushing his hair back from his forehead, "But you're stubborn enough to come close."

His voice rasped, hoarse and broken. "I have so much pain," he said. "But so much life." Her hands cupped his face as his eyes fluttered open, their dark brown meeting hers with a dazed focus.

His lips twitched into something like a smile, and it sent a flood of hope rushing through her. For two days, she had wondered if she'd ever see him smile again. Yet, he was here, and he was alive.

"Don't you ever scare me like that again," she said, tears brimming once more as she pressed her lips to his.

Rollant took Élise's hand and pressed it against his chest. Beneath her palm, his heartbeat was steady and strong. His eyes softened, and she swore she saw a glimmer of peace there that she'd never seen before.

He exhaled, a sound between a laugh and a sob. Tears filled his eyes, but they were not of pain.

"For the first time in six hundred years," he whispered, his voice breaking, "I'm finally alive."

Élise held his face in her hand, her own tears falling freely now. "And you're mine," she whispered fiercely as she touched her forehead to his. "All of you. For as long as you live."

THE DAYS STRETCHED into weeks and months, and Élise watched Rollant recover. The strong, stoic knight she had first met began to reappear, though there were moments when his pain lingered in his gait and the lines of his face when his breath caught from the wounds that had nearly killed him.

Élise worked tirelessly beside Bertille, tending to him, cooking meals, and keeping their small world in order. The weight of everything she'd endured—from her childhood, Gabin, Hugo, and the Revolution—settled over her, but it did not crush her. If anything, it strengthened her resolve. Once, she had lived in fear, always bracing for the next fight, the next loss. Now, she had something to hold onto—someone to hold her back.

Each moment with Rollant, each breath he took, reminded her that she had not only survived—she had built something worth living for.

One day, Élise glanced up at Rollant as they walked through the garden, arm in arm, her hand resting in the crook of his elbow. The golden light of evening bathed the garden in a quiet glow, painting the lavender and thyme in hues of amber and violet.

Rollant still carried himself like a knight—head high, shoulders strong, every movement deliberate—but his face had changed. The burdens of centuries had not disappeared, but they no longer consumed him. The weight was still there, but now, he carried it differently. He carried it with her.

Her fingers laced with his, and he squeezed gently as if grounding himself in this life they had built from the ashes of war.

She smiled. "What are you thinking?"

Rollant exhaled, his eyes scanning the garden—the place they had nearly lost each other and, against all odds, found their way back. His fingers curled tighter around hers. "I never thought I'd be this happy," he whispered as if the words themselves were fragile, too precious to speak aloud.

He turned to her then, and the achingly tender love in his gaze made her chest tighten around a fast-beating heart. There wasn't just love, but certainty. He had searched across centuries and found his answer in her. She hadn't just chosen him; she had chosen love. And every day, she would choose it again.

CHAPTER 47

A Legacy to Leave

CHARONNE, PARIS, JUNE 1807

ROLLANT BLINKED AWAKE. His vision blurred with the golden light of dawn spilling into the room, casting a warm glow over the familiar space. The air smelled of lavender and the lingering embers from last night's fire, and for a moment, he only breathed, relishing the sensation of waking up with the weight of another beside him.

Élise lay nestled against his chest, her breath a soft, steady rhythm against his ribs. Her hand clutched his as if she were anchoring him to this world. For centuries, he had awoken alone; he had felt nothing but the cold emptiness of immortality stretching endlessly before him. Now, her warmth and touch grounded him. He allowed himself to indulge her embrace as he had every morning since his second brush with mortal death.

He shifted slowly, sliding his arm around her shoulders and pulling her closer, pressing his lips to her hair, breathing in the faint scent of lavender and linen. He had imagined this moment for lifetimes—but nothing compared to the reality of holding her. Of feeling the weight of her in his arms, unburdened by fear. His hands, so used to wielding swords and shields, now held something infinitely more precious. He felt the gentle rise and fall of her breath against him, the soft flutter of her lashes as she stirred, and the silken weight of her hair against his skin.

For so long, love had been a painful memory buried beneath the endless march of time. But now he knew love was meant to be a presence, tangible and alive. He tightened his arms around her, marveling at the simple miracle of touch. It was no longer fatal; it was theirs. It soothed him and gave him a reason to keep fighting—not for kings or crowns, but for love. For her.

"Élise," he whispered, testing the shape of her name on his lips as if it were a prayer.

She curled closer to him, fitting against him like she belonged there. Her head tilted up, still with closed eyes, as she murmured an incoherent mumble. He cupped her face, his thumb smoothing over her cheek. "I had forgotten what this felt like," he murmured, his voice raw with wonder. "To hold someone. To hold you."

Her lips curved into a soft smile, and she leaned into his touch. "You held me yesterday and the day before that, and for the past few years, decade, really," she whispered and stretched.

A loud crash in the kitchen jolted her up with eyes open wide. "What are you doing?" she called through the closed door. Her voice was still thick with sleep.

Muffled giggles followed. "Playing, Mama." Their daughter's voice rang out—far too innocent to be believed.

Rollant let out a low groan and pressed his face into Élise's shoulder. "Those pesky children," he muttered with a smirk. He pulled her back into his arms, holding her as if the world itself might try to steal her away.

"You adore them," she teased, running her fingers through his hair.

He gazed at the sparkle in her eyes and kissed her long and slow. "I never thought I'd have this again," he whispered, his lips hovering over hers as if afraid she might disappear. "Not after so long. But I swear to you, Élise, as I do every morning—I will cherish every moment. Every day, every breath, every smile. I will waste none of them."

And as the morning's light bathed them both, Rollant held her, the ache in his chest a distant hum compared to the overwhelming joy of embracing love again.

"As will I," she whispered back, her breath hot on his lips, as he placed a parted mouth over hers.

The door swung open, and their four-year-old boy stood in the doorway. "I'm hungry, starving," he whined with both hands dropped near the ground, showcasing bent knees as if the poor child hadn't eaten in weeks.

Rollant sighed and kissed Élise again before dragging himself out of bed to tend to his son. He winced as his side protested. The scar on his side and chest still ached with every breath, and his muscles grew stiff after the days of recovery, but he was painfully, beautifully alive. It was humbling to be fragile, but with that fragility came purpose. He no longer had centuries stretching endlessly before him, only the finite years he and Élise could carve out together. The ache of time, which had once loomed over him like an endless shadow, now felt like a gift. Precious. Fleeting. The exhilarating wonder of what the day could hold.

THE SUN WAS SETTING, and the Montvieux family took their daily familial walk. The sun painted the sky in soft hues of gold and rose and cast the rolling fields of Charonne in all of its glory.

Rollant walked beside Élise, his hand wrapped firmly around hers, their steps slow but steady. Each step was a reminder of the life they had chosen to build together, the life he had once believed would never be his.

He could feel the stiffness in his side, the ache of a body that no longer healed with supernatural prowess. But with each passing day, he had come to love that ache. It reminded him that he had once belonged to kings, crowns, and wars that truly never ended, but in his mortality, he belonged to Élise, and his time was his own.

His fingers tightened around Élise's. The weight of the past seemed to melt away in her embrace. It paled in comparison to the fleeting moments of peace.

The rich scent of lavender and thyme wafted through the air, mingling with the earthy warmth of the evening, as they passed the garden. Their children's laughter rang out, clear and bright, as they darted through the tall grass. It was a sound that carried joy and an earned peace. Rollant's fortune had been used sparingly to ensure it lasted generations. In Charonne, there was no need to worry about what went on behind the city walls. No cares could come to them. The once vacant homes now brimmed with new families seeking sanctuary and peace.

Neighbors waved from across the path, their smiles warm and genuine, and Élise returned the gesture, her head leaning lightly against Rollant's shoulder.

Rollant's gaze swept over the fields and the cobblestone path leading to the rolling hills in the east.

For centuries, Rollant had been bound to a legacy that was not his own, a servant to the dreams of kings long gone. Yet in the simple beauty of Charonne, he had found a kingdom of his own—a kingdom not built on magic, war, or conquest, but of love, laughter, and life. Every stone, every blade of grass, every echo of their children's laughter carried the weight of what they had endured and the promise of what they would leave behind. This was not the legacy of a crown. It was the legacy of love. It was what he'd fought for, what he'd prayed for without daring to hope.

He pulled Élise into a strong embrace, and when her head leaned against his chest, he felt it—the profound peace of a man who had all he ever wanted. This was their land, their legacy, their life.

emme venons d'et à imme

successions Ducloux, p

e sa mère de Antoine p

es composa et encore pour

des les vendeurs qui l

frères et dépendant des

Bout Vernes sœurs et passé

nte-cinq. dans le courant

e ce jour partie des Ain mo

ble venou le sieur Dejoux

comme bon et il pourra

te année lui semblera

dites successions supportera

au onze mais aussi,

Epilogue: Threads of the Past

CHARTREUSE MOUNTAINS, FRANCE 1958

THE SIMCA ARONDE hummed along the mountain road, its modest engine a steady counterpoint to the soft rustle of the summer wind. Rollant de Montvieux VI gripped the wheel lightly, his dark curls brushing against the collar of his jacket. Beside him, his new bride, Cassandre, perched eagerly in the passenger seat, the crisp photo-copied deed and map spread across her lap. She traced her finger over the thermal-inked lines, her face alight with curiosity. The copy hadn't done the original justice, but the original was so old it almost crumbled in her hands.

"I still can't believe your parents had this deed tucked away in the attic," she said, her voice filled with wonder. "And that your family owned an estate in the Alps—in the middle of nowhere?"

"My father has always said it wasn't worth thinking about," Rollant said with the corner of his mouth twitching into a half-smile. His gaze stayed on the road ahead. "When our land in Charonne was annexed into Paris, they moved the family graves here and sold the rest. The estate was forgotten." He shrugged. "To him, it was just history."

"And the gold bars?" Cassandre teased, tilting her head with a playful smirk. "He just handed us one like it was loose change."

"Well," Rollant said with a laugh. "Apparently, one of my great-grandfathers hid his fortune during the Revolution. He probably never imagined how long it would last. But the family was set financially when they sold the land. Father says there's more gold stashed away somewhere, but he never cared much for treasure hunts. Thus, he's never cared to look."

Cassandre's eyes grew wide in disbelief. "Never cared to look?" She scoffed. "I'd be searching every day!"

Rollant chuckled, "I'm sure it's somewhere in that attic of theirs. Good luck."

Cassandre shook her head, clutching the deed. "A noble lineage. Hidden fortunes. A mysterious estate in the Alps. A story about an immortal knight. Your history! Your ancestors! How are you not more excited about this?"

Rollant chuckled, his eyes fixed on the winding road ahead with fingers tight on the steering wheel. "They lived, they died. Same as us. That's all there is to it." His tone was light, but Cassandre caught the faint shadow of dismissal behind his words.

Cassandre leaned back, crossing her arms with exaggerated frustration. "You're impossible," she said, rolling her eyes. "I married the least romantic man in France."

Rollant reached over and squeezed her hand, his smile tugging at his lips. "I'm here, aren't I?"

Cassandre huffed but couldn't keep from grinning. "Fair enough."

As the road signs pointed toward Saint-Pierre-d'Entremont, Cassandre straightened in her seat, her excitement bubbling. "That's it! We're getting close!"

Rollant turned the car onto a narrow dirt path, and the couple parked at the foothills of the communal forest after grabbing a bite to eat in the small mountain town.

With backpacks slung over their shoulders, they followed the map into the trees off the beaten path. Cassandre carried the map like it was the Holy Grail, her eyes darting from the paper to the path ahead. They crossed an ancient stone bridge that groaned beneath their steps and dribbled crumbled stone pieces into the creek below. The air smelled of pine and earth, heavy with the whispers of history.

"Do you think it's still here?" Cassandre asked, glancing around at the overgrown forest.

"If the map is right, it should be," Rollant replied. His tone was calm, but a faint quiet anticipation stirred in his chest.

They walked for what felt like hours before the trees thinned, revealing a stone wall clearly reconstructed. Ivy vines climbed its surface, clinging to the past like fingers unwilling to let go.

"This is it," Cassandre whispered, her voice reverent amid a hitching breath.

They followed the wall until they came to an archway, its keystone etched with faint markings: a mountain with three stars above it. Beyond it, the overgrown cobblestone path stretched to a pavilion with a memorial stone beneath its roof. Beyond it, the shadow of the mountains tucked a graveyard away, covered in wildflowers.

Cassandre folded the deed and map and secured it in its metal case as they stepped through the archway, the weight of history settling over them like a tangible presence. She approached the memorial.

"Memorial Erected in 1879," she read. "You are standing on the original estate of Chevalier Rollant de Montvieux, a gift from King Philip II Augustus (1180-1223). It was cared for by the village of Valmont two kilometers to the east (now abandoned) until well after the land was made public in 1827."

Rollant had moved to the graves and brushed away the dirt and moss from a few headstones to view the weathered engravings.

Cassandre came up behind him. Her gaze swept across the field of wildflowers. "Rollant, your whole family is here!" she exclaimed, her voice tinged with awe. She knelt beside Rollant and traced the weathered names etched into a stone:

"Rollant de Montvieux and Élise de Montvieux | Life is Love, and Love is Eternal | The Faithful Guardian and the Radiant Flame Together in Rest | Died 1842."

Cassandre leaned her head against Rollant's shoulder. "Faithful guardian . . . like an immortal knight," she mused. "And a radiant flame. Oh, they must have been extraordinarily in love, just as your grandfather told us."

Rollant ran his thumb over his ancestor's engraved name, stirring a strange connection twisting in his chest. "It's just a story," he said more to himself than to her. "A fairytale passed down through the generations that ends the same for everyone, as I said."

Cassandre turned his face to him with a soft grasp of his chin. She placed a kiss on his lips. "You are such a cynic," she said with a smile, but the adjacent headstone caught her eye. She gestured to it. "But isn't it interesting: see here on Amée de Montvieux, Beloved Spouse of Chevalier Rollant, the same Rollant de Montvieux who owned the estate in 1180, and there is no other Rollant except here, in 1842. And then, he happens to have six generations of Rollant's?" Her eyebrows lifted in positive suspicion, letting him draw the conclusion.

"And," she said, holding a finger in the air, "Amée's grave is next to Rollant and Élise's."

Rollant opened his mouth to speak, but Cassandre cut him off.

"And," she said with a gleam in her eye, "there are no dates of birth for Rollant de Montvieux in 1842. What if the first Rollant really did live through it all—what if he really was immortal for a time, just as your grandfather said at Christmas?"

Rollant laughed, shaking his head. "No one lives six hundred years, Cassandre."

Her eyes sparkled with curiosity. "But what if *he* did? What if he survived wars and revolutions only to choose to die in love's embrace at the end?"

Rollant stared at the gravestone, his fingers brushing over the words *Life is Love, and Love is Eternal.* For a moment, the idea didn't seem so far-fetched. He thought of the stories his grandfather had told him as a child—the faithful knight, the fiery revolutionary, a love that endured beyond time.

"Well, I'll give you one: it's an interesting thought," he admitted, his voice softer.

Cassandre patted his cheek. "I knew you had a romantic side."

He stood and pulled her to her feet with a chuckle. "I wouldn't go that far," he said, though his lips curved into a smile. "But if it's true, I'd say he made the right choice."

His fingers curled into hers as he slipped his hand behind her back to pull her close.

"Then I rest my case," she whispered before he kissed her with gentle lips.

"Good, I'm glad. Let's get back to the path while there is daylight left," he said, but they lingered for a moment longer.

The mountain air was cool against their skin. The graves stood silent, bathed in the golden light of the setting sun. The wind rustled through the wildflowers, carrying the faintest echo of laughter.

"It's strange," he said quietly as they walked back toward the archway. "It feels like they're still here somehow."

Cassandre smiled, threading her fingers through his brown waves. "Maybe love like that never really leaves. Maybe it's in your blood."

Rollant looked down at her, his heart swelling. "Maybe it is."

"Well, whoever they were, one and the same, or not, you can tell their bonds were strong by their inscriptions, not just by your grandfather's stories."

Rollant pushed a stray piece of hair behind Cassandre's ear before wrapping his arms around her. "Our bond will be extraordinary, too," he whispered.

Cassandre kissed him before walking away with Rollant's hand in hers, but Rollant looked back one last time.

The breeze whipped through the wildflowers as his gaze lingered on the stone etched with their names. A sense of pride stirred in him—pride in their love, their resilience. For the first time, a connection to the name he shared ignited in his heart. It was strange, he thought, how love endured. Long after the hearts that held it had stopped beating, it lingered—written in the land, whispered through time, and carried in the stories and generations who came after. He would tell his future children the stories his grandfather had passed down, and he would bring them here when they were older.

They stepped back onto the path, leaving the past behind them but weaving its fingerprints into the promise of their legacy ahead.

Also by Lauren Lee Merewether

For all of Lauren's books, visit:

www.LLMBooks.com

The Curse of Beauty

The myth remembers a monster. The Muse remembers a woman. And the story they carried burns through time.

Winner of the 2022 Readers' Favorite Gold Medal for Mythology and shortlisted for Historical Fiction Company's Book of the Year, The Curse of Beauty is a gripping saga readers call "unstoppable," "incredible," and "a masterful work of fiction."

1650 BC. Tiryns is fracturing.

The gods are silent. The sea brings strangers cloaked in bronze. And Thais, daughter of the chieftain and priestess of Lady Atana, stands at the crossroads of war and sacrifice.

To protect her people, she must become the voice the goddess still whispers to and the one who remembers what others will forget—even if it means falling for the one she must never love.

But love has a cost. And the choices Thais makes will echo through generations—until her song becomes myth.

Salvation in the Sun

(The Lost Pharaoh Chronicles, Book I)

This future she knows for certain—the great sun city will be her undoing.

Amidst a power struggle between Pharaoh and the priesthood of Amun, Queen Nefertiti helps the ill-prepared new Pharaoh Amenhotep enact his father's plan to regain power for the throne. But what seemed a difficult task only becomes more grueling when Amenhotep loses himself in his radical obsessions.

Standing alone to bear the burden of a failing country and stem the tide of a growing rebellion, Nefertiti must choose between her love for Pharaoh and her duty to Egypt in this dramatic retelling of a story forgotten by time.

Scourge of the Shores

(The Shadow Sails, Prequel)

Legends rule the seas. Power conquers kingdoms. But the sea always takes its due.

He's the pirate king who takes what he wants.

She's the captain who refuses to kneel.

Together, they'll either conquer the seas or destroy each other.

With alliances built on blood and betrayals lurking beneath the waves, Danna Chadwick must decide if her destiny lies anchored to the island she swore to protect or with the pirate who threatens to steal her heart. And Robert "The Ruthless" Jaymes must choose between the crown he's fought for and the woman who could cost him everything.

The Shadow Sails is a **slow-burn, fade-to-black pirate romantasy set in a dark world** with high-stakes romance, political intrigue, morally gray characters, and a world where love might be the most dangerous treasure of all.

Warrior King

(Egypt's Golden Age Chronicles, Book I)

Expelling the foreign kings of Egypt is proving costly.

1575 BC. Surrounded by her enemies, the future of the rebellion is in the hands of Queen Ahhotep as her husband's body is laid at her feet.

To unite the divided kingdom, Ahhotep must be the commanding leader to those still loyal to her family, a guiding voice her children require, and meet the impossible expectations of her mother, the Great Wife Tetisheri. Feeling alone and finding no consolation in the palace, Ahhotep seeks counsel with a man she loves but cannot have, inviting conflict into her family and her heart.

With obsolete weaponry, inferior resources, and the royal family's divided front, their supporters dissent and leave. To keep their borders secure, Ahhotep must find a way to consolidate power, raise a capable army, and mold her son into a Warrior King before death comes for her and her people.

Warrior King is a beautiful ode to the powerful women behind the crown and how their love, determination, leadership, and sacrifice propelled the once-called Kemet into a golden era of ancient Egyptian history.

"total immersion into the complex world of ancient Egypt"

- *K.C. Finn for Readers' Favorite*

Acknowledgments

First and foremost, I want to thank God for blessing me with the people who support me and the opportunities he gave me to do what I love: telling stories.

Many thanks to my dear husband, who supported my late nights of writing this book.

I want to give a special thank you to my volunteer book production and launch team members. Without both teams, I would not have been able to make the story the best it could be and successfully get it to market.

Thank you to the Self-Publishing School Fundamentals of Fiction course, which taught me invaluable lessons on the writing process and how to effectively self-publish, and its students, who gave me friendship and encouragement in supporting my goals.

Finally, but certainly not least, thank you to my readers. Without your support, I would not be able to write. I truly hope this story engages you, inspires you, and gives you a peek into the past.

I hope that when you finish reading this story, your love of history and romance will have deepened a little more—and, of course, that you can't wait to find out what happens in the next story!

In Memory of Chuck

Though you couldn't read this book, your generosity, keen eye, and quiet encouragement shaped the stories I wrote—stories that made it into readers' hands.

You offered your time generously, your feedback with care, and your encouragement in quiet ways I will always remember.

You helped build the foundation that led to this story, even if you never turned its pages.

I'm sorry I didn't get to say thank you one more time.

May your legacy live on in the words you helped strengthen, and the writers you quietly championed.

About the Author

LAUREN LEE MEREWETHER writes multi-genre romantic family sagas inspired by ancient places, legends, and myths. She loves to delve into the shadows of the past, spinning slow-burn, fade-to-black romantic narratives that merge the timeless passions of history with the mysteries of ancient mythologies. Her award-winning novels invite readers to explore the thrilling depths of legends, emotions, and humanity, spanning high-seas adventures to the splendors of ancient empires.

Lauren loves to daydream about times long past while sipping green tea and watching the experts on Discovery unearth our ancestors' civilizations.

Go behind the scenes, say hello, and stay current with Lauren's latest releases at www.LaurenLeeMerewether.com.

facebook.com/llmbooks

x.com/llmbooks

instagram.com/llmbooks

bookbub.com/authors/lauren-lee-merewether

goodreads.com/laurenleemerewether

amazon.com/author/laurenleemerewether

youtube.com/LaurenLeeMerewether

tiktok.com/@llmbooks

What Did You Think?

DID YOU ENJOY THE DARKEST OATH?

Thank you for reading *The Darkest Oath*. I hope you enjoyed immersing yourself in another culture and reading about Rollant and Élise's fictional love story.

If you enjoyed *The Darkest Oath*, I would like to ask a big favor: Please share with your friends and family on social media sites like **Facebook**, **Instagram**, or **TikTok** and/or leave a review with book retailers, **BookBub** and **Goodreads**.

I am an independent author; as such, reviews and word of mouth are the best ways readers like you can help books like *The Darkest Oath* reach other readers.

Your feedback and support are of the utmost importance to me. If you want to reach out to me and give feedback on this book, ideas to improve my future writings, get updates about future books, or to just say howdy, please visit me on the web.

www.LaurenLeeMerewether.com
Or email me at
mail@LaurenLeeMerewether.com
Happy Reading!

www.ingramcontent.com/pod-product-compliance
Lightning Source LLC
Chambersburg PA
CBHW030628310726
48979CB00003B/927

* 9 7 8 1 9 6 1 7 5 9 2 8 2 *